RANDOM
HOUSE
LARGE
PRINT

The Last Night in London

Also by Karen White
Available from Random House Large Print

Dreams of Falling
The Night the Lights Went Out

THE
Last Night
IN
London

KAREN WHITE

RANDOM HOUSE
LARGE PRINT

This is a work of fiction. Names, characters, places, and incidents either are the product of the author's imagination or are used fictitiously, and any resemblance to actual persons, living or dead, business establishments, events, or locales is entirely coincidental.

Published in the United States of America by Random House Large Print in association with Berkley, an imprint of Penguin Random House LLC.

Cover design by Rita Frangie
Cover photographs of women: (left) © RetroAtelier / Getty Images, (center and right) © Elisabeth Ansley / Trevillion Images, (with umbrella) © Drunaa / Trevillion Images

The Library of Congress has established a Cataloging-in-Publication record for this title.

ISBN: 978-0-593-39577-6

www.penguinrandomhouse.com/large-print-format-books

FIRST LARGE PRINT EDITION

Printed in the United States of America

10 9 8 7 6 5 4 3 2 1

This Large Print edition published in accord with the standards of the N.A.V.H.

To Tim, for everything.

And to the 32,000 citizens of London
who were killed during the Blitz.
You are not forgotten.

Feelings . . . of unremembered pleasure:
such, perhaps,
As have no slight or trivial influence
On that best portion of a good man's life,
His little, nameless, unremembered, acts
Of kindness and of love.

WILLIAM WORDSWORTH

The Last Night in London

PROLOGUE

LONDON
APRIL 1941

The cool, clear night shuddered, then moaned as the fluctuating drone of hundreds of engines eclipsed the silence. A wave of planes like angry hornets slipped through the darkened sky over a city already wearing black in preparation for the inevitable mourning.

She tasted dust and burnt embers in the back of her throat as she hurried through a crowd of stragglers running toward a shelter. A man grabbed her arm, as if to correct her movement, but an explosion nearby made him release his hold and hurry after the crowd. She shifted the valise she cradled in her arms, the pressure on her chest making it difficult to breathe. Fatigue and pain battered her body, both eagerly welcomed, as they disguised the bruise of overwhelming grief. She staggered forward, the blood dripping unchecked from her leg and forehead, the acrid stench of explosives mixed with the sharp smell of death.

Gingerly, she moved through the darkened high street so familiar in the daylight but foreign to her now. The night sky blossomed with fire and scarlet light as the loud bark of the antiaircraft guns answered the banshee wails of the warning sirens. Pressing herself against a wall, as if she could hide from the noise and the terror, she closed her eyes. **Moonlight Sonata.** Someone—she couldn't remember who, in an underground club, perhaps—had whispered that that was what he called the music of the nightly bombings. She'd thought then it had been a beautiful sentiment, that it was a wonderful way to make something good out of something so terrible. But she'd been younger then. More willing to accept that the world still held on to its beauty when everything lay charred and smoldering, with roofless structures like starving baby birds, mouths open to a useless sky.

Another incendiary bomb fell nearby. Another fireball lurched upward. Another building, another home, another life destroyed as the haphazard finger of fortune pointed with random carelessness. The sidewalk rumbled beneath her, causing her to stumble into the street, almost losing hold of her precious bundle. The shrill whistle of an air raid warden rang out, the sound padded into near oblivion by the thunder of the engines above them. The baby lay still as she ran, the partially closed top of the valise protecting him from the ashes that drifted from burning buildings.

She ducked into a doorway to catch her breath, oddly grateful to the fires for lighting her way. Fairly certain she was on Mac Farren Place, she flattened herself against a recessed door, imagining she could hear approaching footsteps coming for her. She needed to keep running until she reached her destination. She wasn't sure what she'd do after that, but she'd think about it then.

Another wave of planes slithered overhead, the rumble of their engines echoing in her bones. She was tempted to collapse on the doorstep and remain there until dawn or death, whichever came first. But she couldn't. She felt the heft of the valise in her arms again, a small movement within it reminding her of why she couldn't give up.

She stood, planting her feet wide for balance and for the false sense of strength it gave her. As the world vibrated beneath her, she clung to that tenuous spark of will that wouldn't allow her to stop. It pushed her out onto the street again to begin moving as the roar of the next approaching wave of planes swelled behind her.

She hid in another doorway as the planes flew overhead, letting go of their bombs as they neared Oxford Street. Her shoulders and arms ached from carrying the valise. How could such a small thing seem to weigh so much? But she couldn't stop. Not now. Not after everything that had happened. One more loss would be insurmountable, the largest and final hole in her cup of luck.

Her ears rang from the cacophony of destruction raining down around her, the coppery tang of blood filling her mouth from biting her lip to keep it from trembling. A stray bomb could explode on top of her and her precious cargo regardless of its intended target, the erratic hands of fate never quite sure where to land.

Avoiding wardens and anyone else who would veer her off course, she continued to hurry forward until she reached Davies Street and the square of beautiful Georgian terrace houses now sheathed in black, the windows darkened like sleeping eyes. She knew the house, had been inside it even. Knew that the basement was being used as a private bomb shelter, one complete with electricity and stocked with food and soft mattresses and blankets. But that was not why she was there. She wouldn't be staying.

The flashing white undersides of an air warden's gloves beckoned two women dressed as if they'd just been dragged from a party; they stumbled toward him as he guided them to a public shelter. Holding the valise closer, she pressed herself against the wrought iron fence of the house, ducking her face to hide its paleness. When the three disappeared, she moved cautiously along the fence, then unlatched the gate. She carefully took the steps down to the lower level, then turned the doorknob, not thinking until she did so of what she'd do if it was locked.

The door opened to an unoccupied room, filled only with mattresses and cushions piled against the windows and walls, the flickering firelight from outside showing her a closed door across the room. Memorizing her path, she shut the door behind her, enveloping herself in complete darkness. Soft, murmuring voices came from behind the door opposite as she approached. She stopped in front of it and raised her hand to knock, then paused to mouth an old prayer she remembered from childhood to a God she no longer thought listened. "Amen," she whispered to the dark when she was finished, then brought her knuckles down sharply against the wood.

The voices stopped, and she held her breath as footsteps approached.

"Hello?" A woman's voice, clear and refined. English.

Her knees almost buckled with relief. "It's me. Please open the door."

The door was jerked open, allowing her to see inside the small room with the tidy cots around the perimeter, a small crystal lamp sparkling from the polished surface of a round table with cabriole legs. If she hadn't been so exhausted, she might have laughed at the absurdity of crystal and fine furniture in such a place, at such a time, when the world above was being smothered with ashes and blood.

The person she'd been might have been amused. But she wasn't that person anymore.

The woman looked into the darkened room as if expecting to see two other people seeking refuge.

"I'm alone. There's no one else."

A look of understanding and grief crossed the woman's face before she nodded briefly and straightened her shoulders. "You're hurt," the woman said, her fine skin glowing like alabaster in the lamplight. Reaching out manicured hands with scarlet nails, she said, "Come in. Quickly. We have a doctor."

She shook her head. "I can't. I have to go." For the first time, she relaxed her hold on the valise. She set it down and picked up the baby, his soft body stirring sleepily in her arms. Pressing her lips against the smooth forehead, she smelled deeply, the stench of the torn night erased by the sweet scent of new life. She lifted her head, then handed him over before she could change her mind and be the ruin of them all.

The woman's pale eyes widened with surprise, then showed understanding, as she accepted the child, pressing him against her chest, an unasked question dancing in the air between them.

"I've got to go back. He . . ." Her arm gestured aimlessly. "It might not be too late. . . ." Despair escaped from her chest and filled her mouth.

"But you can't leave. Not now. There's a raid. . . ."

"I have to. There's no one else." A sob caught in

her throat. "I have to try." Her eyes moved to the squirming bundle, but she dragged them away.

The woman hadn't reacted to the news except for a quick intake of breath. With studied composure, she said, "But you're hurt. Surely you can wait five more minutes."

"No." She shook her head. "I've already stayed too long." She took a step back to emphasize her words. "I think they might be looking for me."

"All the more reason you should stay here. We can keep you safe. We can help you get the proper papers. . . ."

As if the woman hadn't spoken, she said, "You'll take care of the baby?"

"Of course. But—"

"Good."

The woman looked so lovely standing there with the light prisms sparkling against the wall behind her as she held the baby. She'd done the right thing, coming here. "Be safe," the woman said. "But this won't be good-bye. We'll see each other again, when this is all over."

"I hope so," she said, allowing her eyes to rest on the pale moon of the baby's cheek for just a flicker. She took another step backward. "When this is all over." She turned and let herself out of the second door and back into the wounded night.

She passed through the gate and hurried toward the street corner and paused, getting her bearings, knowing only that she had to keep running. Just for a moment, she allowed herself to close her eyes, to see the baby's face one last time.

A high, keening shriek split the air around her, jerking open her eyes. Her chest heaved from the percussion of the bomb hitting the building across the street, bricks and glass and plaster being thrown into the air like the discarded toys of a petulant child. Something hard struck her in the back between her shoulder blades, throwing her against the pavement, knocking her to her hands and knees. The stray thought of how she'd never be able to repair the damage to her clothing trickled across her brain as she watched the debris falling in slow motion around her, a lit piece of floral wallpaper drifting down and extinguishing itself on the sidewalk.

She struggled to stand, pain radiating like fever, the bleeding scrapes on her palms and forehead merely an afterthought. Her right leg buckled under her, her knee bending in a way it wasn't intended to. **No, no, no. Not now. Not like this.** Sucking in her breath, she began to crawl back to the shelter, a fading glimmer of self-preservation driving her forward, defeat nipping at her heels.

Darkness danced behind her eyes, seductively calling to her. She fought it as she pulled herself up on the gate, reaching for the latch, forcing herself to stay conscious as she felt for the release. Propelling herself forward with her elbows, she tumbled down the steps, her body landing against the door with a thump, her face turned toward the sky in silent supplication. For a brief moment she imagined she was walking in sand, the sound of a distant ocean teasing the air. **Home.** It was there, as it always had been, just beyond her reach.

Please. The word echoed inside her head, but she remained mute as the darkness overcame her and the sky above screamed with a thousand unanswered prayers.

CHAPTER 1

LONDON
MAY 2019

The plane jolted and bumped down the runway at Heathrow, the usual rain of a gray London morning spitting on the windows, a timid sun doing its best to push aside the clouds. The plane finally rocked to a stop and its travel-weary passengers stood in the aisles and began pulling cases from the overhead bins, the sound of zippers and latches filling the rows like a choreographed routine to signal the end of a journey. I remained in my seat, my recent dream still lingering, recalling the images of the old magnolia tree and the large white columns of my aunt Cassie's house and the red flowers she planted along the front steps each year in memory of my mother.

A polite throat clearing brought my attention to the aisle, where the line of passengers waited for me to exit. I nodded my thanks, grabbed my backpack from beneath the seat in front of me, and headed for the exit, my thoughts still clinging to the place I'd called home for the first eighteen years of my life and where, if pressed, I'd still tell people I was from. Which was stupid, really. I'd been living in New York for seven years and hadn't been back to Georgia for the last three, with no plans to return anytime soon.

I turned on my cell phone as I made my way toward the baggage claim. My phone dinged with five texts: one from my father; one from my stepmother, Suzanne; one from my sister Sarah Frances; one from Aunt Cassie; and the most recent from Arabella, my friend from my junior year abroad at Oxford and the reason I was in London now.

I opened my phone to read Arabella's first, smiling to myself as I saw that she'd been following my flight on her phone app and knew I'd landed and that she was waiting in the short-stay car park. I was to text her when I'd passed through passport control so that she could meet me outside Terminal 2. It was typical Arabella, the kind of person whose organizational skills were simultaneously helpful and annoying. Despite her thriving career as a fashion editor at British **Vogue**, her main job seemed to be organizing the social calendars and lives of her large circle of friends.

I tossed my phone into my backpack, deciding the other texts could wait, and joined the throngs of people walking through passport control and customs, then began texting Arabella as I made it outside. I had barely typed my first word when I heard the rapid beeps of a car horn. I looked up to see my friend in a red BMW convertible—a hand-me-down from her mother that she'd driven while in college. The top was lowered despite the threatening skies, so I could see her curly hair creating a blond halo around her pixielike face. She looked like a Barbie doll, an image she liked to cultivate if only because it hid her sharp wit and killer intellect.

I did a quick double take at the large animal sitting in the driver's seat, my mind processing the image before I could remember that the British drove on the wrong side of the car and the wrong side of the road and realize that the dog wasn't actually driving.

"Maddie!" my friend shouted as the car screeched to a stop, her door opening at the same time. She ran toward me with very un-British-like enthusiasm and threw her arms around me.

"It's been ages!" She hugged me for a long moment, then smiled brightly as she held me at arm's length. "Still gorgeous, Maddie. And still wearing your same uniform of jeans and button-down shirt."

I pulled back, grinning. "You're just jealous because it only takes me five minutes to get dressed in the morning."

"Oh, Maddie," she said in the prim-and-proper accent that I loved mimicking almost as much as she enjoyed imitating my Southern accent. "What am I to do with you?" She looked behind me and frowned at the small suitcase sitting by itself. "Where's the rest of your luggage?"

I took in her leopard-print jumpsuit and stilettoes with grudging admiration. I loved trendy clothes—as long as someone else was wearing them. My toes ached in sympathy as I estimated the height of her heels. "My laptop and camera are in my backpack, and my clothing is in the suitcase. Don't worry. All the jeans are clean, and I brought one dress. You said it shouldn't take more than a couple of weeks, but I brought enough underwear for three just in case."

"Yes, well, Jeanne Dubose modeled for Coco Chanel in Paris. She might be an easier subject if you dressed as if you cared."

"I do care—about the story and writing it to the best of my ability. Not about what I'm wearing when I'm interviewing a subject. Besides, Jeanne Dubose is ninety-nine years old. I doubt she'll even notice."

Arabella opened the trunk of her car, still frowning. "Whatever you do, don't call her old. It doesn't suit her. I've known her all of my life, and even as a child, I never thought of her as old. But she's your relation, so you probably already know that."

"A very distant relation, and I've never met her, remember? Her side of the family moved to Tennessee from Georgia right after the American

Civil War, so I can't say our families are close. In fact, I wouldn't even know we were related if my sister hadn't done one of those ancestry searches and found them. Miss Dubose is my fourth cousin twice removed or something like that, which means I'm already forgiven for referring to her as old because we're not just family but Southern. She'll say, 'Bless your heart,' and move on." I lifted my suitcase and placed it in the tiny trunk, keeping my backpack with me.

"Yes, well, I've never heard her say, 'Bless your heart.' I **have** heard her say, 'Are you sure you want to wear that?' more times than I'd like to admit." Arabella shut the trunk. "You must be exhausted. Let's get you to Miss Dubose's flat so you can have a quick lie-down. I wanted you to stay with me, but Miss Dubose was insistent. She's got a large flat, and she rarely leaves her suite. She has full-time nursing care, so there's nothing you have to do except to interview her about her modeling days and the gorgeous vintage clothes we've pulled together from storage. And there's a lovely desk in the front room you can use to write. The museum exhibition isn't until July, and I'd like to run the article concurrently with its opening. It's not exactly crunch time, but I'd rather not wait." She paused. "Maddie, Miss Dubose isn't in the best of health, so I thought the sooner the better. I already have a title for the exhibition and the article, but you're the writer, so you can change it if you don't like it." She cleared her throat.

"'Furs, Gowns, and Uniforms: The Changing Role of Fashion in a World at War.'"

"It's a little clunky, but it has a certain ring to it," I said, moving to the side of the car. "I won't know until I interview Miss Dubose and start writing. But it sounds like I'll have lots of peace and quiet without interruptions while I'm there, so I should be able to get it done in no time. I've cleared my calendar and turned in a few other projects early so I won't feel rushed."

"Splendid. Although there is one thing . . ." She stopped, smiled.

"One thing?" I prompted.

"Yes, well . . ." She moved to the driver's side and slid in while I was left staring at the large animal in the passenger seat—either a horse or a dog; I couldn't tell—whose lolling tongue kept me at a respectful distance.

"Should I sit in the back?" I asked around the dark brown head.

"Oh, gosh, sorry." She turned toward the beast. "Come on, George." She reached around and patted the leather of the rear seat.

The dog gave what sounded like a sigh before forcing its girth over the console and between the seat backs to perch itself on the ridiculously small backseat.

"George?" I asked, crawling inside with my backpack and putting on my seat belt.

"After Prince George—they're the same age apparently. Colin thought that the little prince and the dog had similar expressions."

"Colin?" I asked, unprepared for the jolt of surprise his name registered. "Your cousin Colin, our schoolmate? Colin who avoided me?"

"Technically, I think he's my second cousin. His grandfather David—his paternal grandmother, Sophia's, husband—and my grandmother Violet were siblings." She avoided looking at me, focusing instead on the gear shift. "And don't be daft, Maddie. Colin only avoided you because you made it clear you wanted nothing to do with him. You two just . . . Well, you were a bit like chalk and cheese, but I think that was just a matter of two people being separated by the same language."

"Ha. As if **I** were the one with the accent."

Arabella sent me a sidelong glance. "Admittedly, he was a bit miffed that you didn't say good-bye to him when you left Oxford. He thought you owed him the courtesy of a farewell."

I sucked in my breath. "I don't say good-bye to anyone—it had nothing to do with him. I only said good-bye to you because you drove me to the airport. I doubt he remembers that now—or me. It's been seven years."

"Yes, well, he's been in Devon—Salcombe, actually, a nice little resort on the coast—on holiday with friends for the week, and he asked me to watch

George. And since . . ." She stopped as if suddenly aware of what she was about to say.

"Since what?"

Arabella made a good show of focused concentration as she pulled out into traffic, nearly sideswiping a taxi. For our survival, I allowed her to wind her way out of the airport traffic, waiting until she was on the A4 before repeating, "And since what?"

She was silent for a beat and then allowed the words to rush out, as if speaking quickly would hinder my interpretation of them. "Since Colin lives with Miss Dubose, I thought I'd kill two birds with a single stone and deliver both you and George at the same time."

A cold sweat erupted over my scalp. "Excuse me? Colin lives there? In the flat I'm going to be staying in?"

"Yes. They're very close—Miss Dubose has always been like a grandmother to him. She just dotes on him—he even calls her Nana."

I couldn't imagine stony-faced Colin calling anyone by such an endearment. I, for one, had always been Madison to him, a solid brick wall I wasn't ever likely to scale.

Arabella continued. "Sophia, Colin's grandmother, owned the flat. When she died, Colin's parents inherited it. But even when she was alive, Sophia allowed Miss Dubose to live there. They were great friends since before the war. Miss Dubose never married, you see, or had children, so she more or less adopted her best friend's family as her own. When she went into hospital last month and her doctors told us to prepare for the worst, she asked that Colin move in so that they could spend more time together and he could help get her finances all settled. That's his specialty, so it made sense."

"You said she wasn't in the best of health. So she's ill?"

"No specific illness, but she's ninety-nine. Her heart is weak, and her doctors say her body is beginning to shut down. She looks rather good, however. One would have to examine her very closely to agree with them."

"So Miss Dubose, the nurse, Colin, and I will all be living in the same flat. Together."

"Precisely. And George, too, don't forget. It's a very large flat, and Colin works extraordinary hours, so you'll probably never run into each other." She stopped talking as if there wasn't anything else she needed to explain.

"And you didn't think to mention this to me before—like when I agreed to come here in the first place? What did Colin say when you told him?"

Arabella kept her eyes on the road in front of her and remained silent.

"Seriously? You didn't tell him it was me?"

"I told him that a freelance journalist I'd hired to interview Miss Dubose would be staying in one of the spare bedrooms for a fortnight or so. He didn't have a problem with that."

"But you didn't tell him it was me."

She shook her head. "It didn't come up."

"Imagine him not jumping to the conclusion that it would be someone he knew during his university days." I rolled my eyes even though she couldn't see me.

Her shoulders sagged slightly under the leopard-skin print. "It's just that Miss Dubose was so insistent that you stay with her, and it would have been too complicated asking Colin to leave. It's only a couple of weeks—maybe more if you'd like to stay longer. Surely you two can be cordial for that long."

I pressed my head against the back of the seat and briefly closed my eyes. "Hopefully, he won't remember me. I haven't even thought about him in the last seven years." That wasn't completely true, but I would never tell that to Arabella. She had one of those overactive imaginations that created stories where none existed. I always told her that she was unsuited to her role as an editor and should have been writing cozy mysteries instead.

"So Colin has no idea that I'm about to show up on his doorstep."

"It will be such a surprise, won't it?" she said.

I shook my head with emphasis. "No, it will be a disaster. I think he dislikes Americans. Or maybe it's Southern Americans."

Arabella laughed. "Don't be daft. Miss Dubose is a Southerner, too, remember—and Colin adores her."

I didn't want to admit that I was intrigued by this

Southern centenarian and the fact that we were distantly related and would be meeting for the first time in London. I didn't want to know that Colin adored her and called her Nana. I wanted to turn back to the airport and return to the stable, uneventful life I'd made for myself in New York City, following in the footsteps of my aunt Cassie. Although she was in advertising and I was a freelance journalist, we'd both wiped the red clay of small-town Georgia off the bottoms of our shoes to start new lives in the big city. She'd lasted ten years, and I had every intention of breaking her record.

Arabella turned toward me with a wide grin. "This will be fun."

"Or not," I suggested, my words swallowed by the sudden rush of wind as the little car gathered speed and hurtled us down the highway as Arabella pressed the accelerator.

I closed my eyes and smelled dog breath and fur as the wind whipped at my face. No matter how terrifying this drive into London with my friend behind the wheel might be, it would pale in comparison with Colin Eliot's reaction to seeing me at his front door.

CHAPTER 2

When we'd made it inside the city limits and the increasing traffic slowed our progress, I released my tight grip on the door handle. Arabella's windblown hair was approaching steel wool status, and George looked as if he'd been electrified.

Arabella reached into a large purse on the floor by my feet and pulled out an Hermès scarf. As she tied it attractively around her head, she said, "Colin's mother, Aunt Penelope, is eager to meet you. I think she's a bit worried about you living with Miss Dubose, but I assured her that I knew you well and that you're trustworthy and kind. That did make her feel better, but at some point, we'll have to arrange a visit."

"Sure," I said. Though I'd seen them only from

afar, I vaguely remembered Colin's parents as seeming elderly to me seven years ago—at least ten to fifteen years older than the parents of the group of friends I hung out with at home and in college. Colin was an only child, and his mother sent frequent care packages of vitamins and scarves and thick socks, as if he'd forgotten how to take care of himself in his parents' absence. I recalled laughing the first time I'd seen one of the large boxes, telling Colin that I was one of six children, and it had always been survival of the fittest at my family's dining table. I might have embellished the story, told him sometimes blood was spilled and half of us were missing teeth due to the altercations.

It wasn't at all true—not with the amounts of food my great-aunt Lucinda insisted on heaping on the table—but I rarely got care packages. Not that I blamed my dad or Suzanne; they had five other kids to worry about. But looking at Colin's socks and knitted scarves, I'd felt a resurgence of the old grief I'd folded up and packed away, suffocated by thick layers of denial and years of absence. And I'd felt angry, too, that he could be so dismissive of his mother's care and love.

Arabella slowed the car and turned without signaling into a paved drive between an iron gate and an impressive Edwardian sandstone mansion block with multiple front entrances. Attractive cornices edged the roofline like cake frosting. Arabella was muttering to herself as she looked for a place to park. "Colin usually uses his nana's parking space since she doesn't have a car. But he said he'd let me have it today." She tapped her long red fingernails against the steering wheel. "I just need to remember which one it is."

I gathered my backpack and looked outside. "Nice building."

Arabella nodded. "It's called Harley House," she said, turning too sharply and hitting the curb. "It was built in nineteen-oh-three to house the Irish servants who worked in the large houses nearby." She maneuvered the car away from the curb. A man with a dog stood on the sidewalk, keeping clear. "Funny, isn't it? Decades later, it became home to a lot of VIP types—movie people, authors, that sort of thing. Cliff Richard and Mick Jagger lived here at some point. And Joan Collins, the actress." She hit the brake hard as a black Jaguar pulled out of a parking spot in front of us, causing me to bite my lip.

"Now it's mostly filled with American expatriates and the stray Russian oligarch." She began to back up into a parallel space against the curb, barely squeezing between two other cars. I sucked in my breath, as if that might help. "I sure hope it's this one, because I'm not certain I can do this twice." Satisfied with her parking job, she switched off the ignition and turned to give George a scratch behind the ears.

"Aunt Precious first lived in this flat in the late thirties, before the war—I'm sure she'll tell you all about that. Marylebone wasn't quite as fashionable then, but it's always been a perfect location—close to shopping and restaurants. And Regent's Park, of course." Arabella unbuckled her seat belt.

"Precious?" I asked. "According to my sister's ancestry chart, her name is Jeanne Dubose."

"Oh, sorry—thought I mentioned that. Precious is Miss Dubose's nickname. Her real name is Jeanne. The story goes that when she was born, the nurse took one look at her little face and said she was precious. From then on, that's what everyone called her. I think it's rather adorable."

"For a baby, but I can't imagine calling an old woman Precious."

"Just don't . . ."

"Call her old," I finished. "I remember. It's just going to be hard using her nickname. Although, come to think of it, I grew up with a Sweet Pea and a Stinky, so maybe it won't be as challenging as I first thought."

Arabella sent me a sidelong glance as I grabbed my suitcase from her trunk. I followed her and George toward the second block of flats and up a set of wide steps leading to two glossy and dark wooden French doors. They sat recessed behind a broad archway between two mottled marble Ionic columns. A tall man emerged from the outside set of doors as we approached.

George let out a loud yelp and leapt forward, pulling the leash from Arabella's hand and nearly toppling the man over. His paws held on to the man's shoulders, and the giant tongue bathed the man's face.

Blinking, I recognized the sandy blond hair that threatened to erupt in waves if allowed to grow just a little longer. And the intense blue eyes that were scrutinizing me as if he couldn't quite believe what he was seeing. A brief flash of surprise was quickly replaced by remembered wariness.

"Hello, Colin," I said stiffly. "It's been a while."

When he didn't respond right away, Arabella interjected, "You remember Maddie Warner, don't you? From our Oxford days."

The wariness remained as we continued to regard each other. His eyes seemed bluer against his vacation tan, and he still had a slim and muscled body. I recalled that he'd rowed during his years at Oxford; apparently, he still did. I remembered, too, how he loved dogs and **Star Wars**. And that he was a stickler for safety and always made sure everyone wore their seat belts when he was driving. Not that I'd ever let him know that I'd noticed any of it.

"Madison," he said curtly. "I do remember you. Vaguely. You liked your beer ice-cold, and you had quite a portfolio of unusual phrases that no one ever understood. You'd drop them like little bombs into conversations. You enjoyed childish pranks like substituting salt in the sugar bowl. And apparently you are loath to say good-bye, so you don't." He bent to scratch George behind the ears, his gaze sliding to

Arabella. "Am I to assume she's the journalist writing the article about Nana?" His tone was between forced politeness and white-hot annoyance.

"Isn't it lovely? A sort of mini school-chum reunion. I wanted to keep it a secret so you'd be surprised."

He stood, taking George's lead in his hand. "I'm surprised all right. Although I'm left to wonder why you didn't have her come while I was on holiday. The flat will be rather crowded, don't you think?"

"Don't be silly, Colin. There's plenty of room. And when I mentioned the journalist staying here, you didn't have any objections."

His eyes touched on me briefly. "Yes, well, that's because I wasn't fully informed. I'm glad I decided to work from home this morning, so I'm spared the shock of returning home in the evening after a long day and seeing Madison in my flat." He held his hand out toward me as if he wanted me to shake it, then said, "May I?"

I looked at him with confusion until Arabella tugged my suitcase from my grasp and handed it to Colin. "He'd never hear the end of it if his mother or Aunt Precious ever heard that he allowed you to carry your own suitcase," she said.

Before I could protest, Colin had opened one of the outer doors and was waiting for us to walk past him into the lobby.

Tall ceilings, a large brass chandelier, and a nonfunctioning dark wood-framed fireplace greeted us in the foyer. An old-fashioned elevator—or "lift," I corrected myself; when in Rome and all that—faced us, a small rectangular window in the outer door showing the empty shaft behind.

Colin pressed the "call" button, and we waited for several minutes, listening to the moans and groans of the ancient equipment. When the lift finally arrived, he opened the door, then slid open a black metal accordion gate and motioned for Arabella and me to step inside the wood-paneled space. A leather bench was attached to the back wall. As the elevator shuddered to life, I hoped the bench wasn't there for napping to pass the time while we were laboriously lifted to the higher floors. We were moving like snails slugging through molasses in winter.

"Why didn't we take the steps?" I asked, recalling the carpeted stairs in the lobby, one flight on the left of the elevator heading up, the one on the right heading down.

Colin shoved his hands into his pockets. "I didn't think Americans liked to physically exert themselves, so I assumed you'd rather take the lift."

"You know what happens when people assume, right?"

"Stop it, you two," Arabella said, stepping between us. "I do not enjoy playing nanny, so I'd appreciate it if you would both behave like adults."

The lift dinged, although we could see between the gate slats that we weren't quite there. We were all silent as we listened to the ancient lift squeak and gasp like an old man. Somehow it managed to grind to a halt on the third floor.

"Lovely," Arabella said, waiting as Colin opened the door into the middle of a short hallway with a black-and-white-checkered floor. Two massive dark wood doors with leaded glass transom windows dominated each end of the hallway, and Arabella proceeded left to the door with the number sixty-four marked in gold in the center. "Remember," she said, turning to look at Colin and me. "Behave." She pressed the buzzer. "To give them fair warning," she said as she dropped her hand.

The sound of a dog barking from inside was quickly followed by footsteps approaching. Then the door was pulled open, and we were greeted by an attractive middle-aged brunette with tortoise-shell glasses and a bright white-toothed smile.

A small, fluffy gray-and-white dog with antennae-like ears and of questionable parentage darted from around her legs and began sniffing our feet in earnest as George pulled on his lead with happy yips.

"Oscar," the woman chided, "they didn't bring you food."

With an almost audible sigh, the little dog slumped and sat at the woman's feet.

"Laura," Colin said affably. "And Oscar, of course." He squatted down and grinned with a warmth I hadn't yet seen directed at me. The little dog jumped into his arms as if they were old friends. They looked at each other with mutual admiration, and I had to admit that witnessing it improved my opinion of Colin by a frog's hair.

"Laura, I'd like to introduce you to Madison Warner, the journalist I told you about," Arabella said, moving forward with familiarity to greet Laura. "She's here to interview Precious."

Laura nodded. "It's a pleasure to meet you. I've got the guest room all ready. Precious is in a bit of a grumpy mood today, but I know she's looking forward to meeting you."

Arabella waved her hand. "Oh, no worries. Maddie will get her feeling better in no time. Everyone loves Maddie."

I chose that moment to pet Oscar, who was gazing lovingly up at Colin and licking his chin. The dog jerked his head in my direction and growled.

"Don't take it personally," Laura said. "Oscar loves Colin. He probably thinks you're trying to separate them." She held out her hand to me. "I'm Laura Allen, Miss Dubose's nurse, although she prefers to call me her companion, since the word 'nurse' makes her feel old."

She smiled warmly and I imagined if I had a need for friends, I'd like her to be one. I shook her outstretched hand. "Maddie Warner," I said. "You're an American?"

"I'm afraid so. We seem to be everywhere. I came over for what I thought would be a short-term assignment taking care of Colin's grandmother Sophia during her last few years. When she passed, Penelope asked if I'd stay on to look after Miss Dubose. Although, as I'm sure you'll discover, she doesn't need or want a lot of looking after, even with her recent hospital stay and declining health. So don't ask her how she's feeling."

"Got it." I stifled a yawn with the back of my hand.

"You must be exhausted," Laura said, taking my elbow and leading me inside. "I was just about to bring Miss Dubose her tea. Let me get something for you, too."

We moved inside to a large foyer dominated by a mahogany fireplace that no longer appeared to be functional. The towering ceilings and ornate moldings made me think of the Greek Revival house where my mother and my aunt Cassie had been raised. The highly polished parquet floor reflected the light from the brass chandelier, which hung from an elaborate ceiling medallion. My gaze was drawn to a curved wall of leaded glass casement windows that sheltered a lone chair and a small table holding a rotary-dial telephone.

It was definitely grand, and what I'd imagined an Edwardian flat in London would look like. No dust clung to any surface, and I could probably see the reflection of my tired face and dark circles if I got close enough to the high shine of the brass fittings on the doors and light fixtures. Yet . . . I paused my thoughts, wondering what it was that made me think of those odd days after my mother's death, when daylight and nighttime melded together in a gray fog that grounded us all.

Yes, there it was. An air of suspended breath, the anticipation like the moment before flipping on a light when you enter a darkened room. The antique furniture and phone all seemed to be waiting for something to happen, to welcome a visitor. To ring. For someone to walk through the front door after a long absence.

A dull pressure formed behind my eyes. It felt strangely like tears—until I remembered how exhausted I was and how my mother used to tell me how when I was small she'd have to lie down with me until I fell asleep; when I was tired, my imagination ran like wild horses.

"Are you all right?" Colin asked, surprising me with what sounded like genuine concern.

"Just jet-lagged. I could really use some caffeine. Or a lie-down, as Arabella suggested."

"It's best to stay up and live your day in the new time zone," Laura said. "Precious is so eager to see you—I'm sure you'll perk up as soon as we get some caffeine in you." She pointed to a corner of the foyer. "You can leave your suitcase right there—Colin can put it in your room later—and follow me."

Laura led us and the dogs into a bright kitchen with tall windows, a black-and-white-tiled floor, and a pretty oak trestle table in the middle of the room.

A refrigerator, barely larger than a dorm fridge, sat next to the sink, and two blue dog beds—one large, one small—were tucked neatly into the corner.

"Tea for everyone?" Laura asked, filling a kettle. She must have seen the disappointment in my eyes. "I've got iced tea for Miss Dubose if you'd prefer that, Maddie."

I felt as if I'd just been given a hug. "I would love that. Is it sweet tea?"

"Oh, yes," Laura said, nodding her head with conviction. "I always add two teaspoons of sugar to Miss Duboses's glass to make it sweet enough, but I'll let you add your own."

"I . . ." I stopped, not wanting to appear rude. But no Southern-born person would ever make sweet tea by dropping a teaspoon or two of sugar into a glass of cold tea. It had to be brewed with the sugar to be authentic. I knew a person's sense of taste diminished with age, which had to be the only reason why Precious hadn't revolted and demanded the real thing. Or her Southern roots made her too polite to say anything that might hurt Laura's feelings. That was the same reason why I smiled and said, "That's fine—thanks."

Laura chatted with Arabella and Colin as she added tea leaves to a rose-spotted pot and poured boiled water from the kettle over it. Both Colin and Arabella nodded when she held up a small pitcher, then poured a generous amount of milk into two empty teacups. While waiting for the tea to steep, she pulled out a glass pitcher of iced tea from the refrigerator. "Lemon?" she asked.

"Sure," I said, wondering how I was going to drink an entire glass of regular tea with undissolved sugar clumps floating in it.

"Shall we?" Laura asked as she placed a plate of McVitie's Digestives onto the tray along with our various cups and glasses. "It's good you're here, Colin. Seeing you always brightens Precious's day. You work so much that she considers it a treat to see you during the daytime."

Colin picked up the tray. "Is she in her sitting room?"

"Yes. I'll get the door."

Laura gave treats to the dogs and left them in the kitchen. We followed her through a swinging door that led from the foyer to a long hallway with doors on each side. Framed photographs covered the walls. I lingered at one of them that was larger than the others: a black-and-white picture of what looked like a car from the nineteen thirties or forties, with the steering wheel on the right-hand side. An elegant, slender man with slicked-back dark hair and wearing a tuxedo stood beside the back door of the car where a woman in an evening gown appeared in the opening. His head was turned from the photographer, obscuring his face, his attention focused on the woman. His hand was held out toward her; her long, slender arms were bare of jewelry. One delicate foot in a high-heeled stiletto had emerged from the car, only one slim ankle and her white face visible above a heavy fur collar. But what a face. It wasn't simply the beauty of it that I found so compelling. My stepmother, Suzanne, was a professional photographer. She had taught me that was the easy part of photography—taking pictures of things that most people want to look at, things that didn't challenge them too much. To the professional, the secret was finding what lay behind the obvious beauty and figuring out whatever it was that made the viewer want to keep looking.

The woman's bright hair and light eyes shone with vibrancy; the thrust of her shoulders and chest showed a level of confidence I usually didn't see in women that young. But it was her expression that made me pause, step closer. Her mouth was partially open, as if she'd just spoken, and I found myself leaning forward as if to hear what she was saying. Looking closely at her eyes, I imagined I could: **Help.**

"Maddie? Aren't you coming?" Arabella looked back at me.

"Sorry. I was just admiring the photographs." Before I turned away, I spotted an elegant box-shaped purse clutched in the woman's right hand, the paleness of her fingers stark against the dark fabric.

"You'll have time to look at them later. Did you see the one of Colin's grandparents on their wedding day? It was right before the war, and his grandfather is wearing his army uniform, although I believe he never saw active duty. But he looks quite dashing. Remember how we used to play dress up, Colin, and you paraded around in that same uniform?"

"That's enough, Bella." Colin glanced over his shoulder to glare at his cousin.

I followed them down the hallway, passing a large gold oval-framed photograph of a bride in white and a groom in uniform. They were perfect in their beauty and innocence, and appeared so very young and hopeful that it almost hurt to look at them. The groom held his hat, showing off a thick head of dark hair. He leaned into his bride as if he couldn't bear to be apart from her. Her small hand rested in the crook of his arm, pulled close to her side.

I hurried after Arabella. "Did he survive the war?" I wished I hadn't asked, not wanting to hear the answer if he hadn't.

"David? Oh, yes. Thankfully. He and Sophia only had one child, James—Colin's father—but by all accounts they lived long, happy lives."

"That's a relief." I was gladder than I probably should have been, considering they were strangers to me. Yet one of the reasons I loved old photographs was because of the stories they told, usually by omission.

Arabella followed Colin, then held open the door at the end of the hall. I stood blinking, trying to acclimate my eyes to the dimness, as she latched it behind me. Everything seemed swathed in dusky peach, from the silk wallpaper to the heavy drapes on the tall windows. Even the thick carpet was the same soft hue, all of it reminding me of my little sister's Barbie mansion.

"Precious says the light is more flattering to her complexion," Arabella whispered.

"I can hear you, you know" came a soft Southern voice from an upholstered chaise beneath a large bay window. Her words dripped like melted butter, the familiar accent an unexpected tug on my heart, making me homesick.

Laura pulled open the drapes, exposing a small balcony railing outside the French doors and illuminating an open doorway into an adjacent bedroom behind the chaise. Colin placed the tray down on a small table, and Laura excused herself.

I tried not to stare at the woman on the chaise, but then I imagined she was used to being the focal point of any room. She wore a long peach silk robe with floating feathers around the neck and peach satin kitten-heeled slippers on her slender feet, her ankles currently crossed. Thick blond hair in perfect waves rested on her shoulders, making me wonder if she wore a wig like my aunt Lucinda, who placed hers on a plastic head on her dresser each night.

She had the same high cheekbones as the woman in the photograph in the hallway, the same patrician nose and jaw, the angles of her face still sharp. Yet she was slighter, too, all extra skin and tissue jettisoned, as if she'd paid a balance due each year, leaving behind a woman who at first glance appeared diminished.

Or not. Maybe if I'd seen her first with her eyes closed, I would have believed that. But her eyes weren't the eyes of an old woman nearing the end of her life. Her pale blue eyes were like those of a cat perched on a ledge, deciding between the approaching stranger and a leap into oblivion.

"Good morning, Aunt Precious," Arabella said as she leaned down to kiss the old woman's lifted cheek.

This was definitely the woman in the photograph stepping out of the car. Even at her age, her bone structure and poise, the long limbs and elegant neck, the near-perfect alabaster skin still made her a beautiful woman. I recalled a book I'd read in high school lit class about a man who'd sold his soul to the devil so that he would have eternal youth. I'd never believed such a thing was possible. But now, looking into those eyes, I almost believed it was.

"Hello, Nana." Colin bent to kiss the offered cheek, and when he went to straighten up, Precious took his hand and held tight.

"Sit next to me," she said. "So I can get a good look at you."

"Of course," he said. "But allow me to introduce you to the journalist who will be interviewing you for the **Vogue** article."

"I'm Madison Warner," I said. "My friends call me Maddie." I reached out my hand, and she dropped

Colin's so she could place soft fingertips in mine, much like I imagined the queen did when meeting her subjects.

Precious peered at me closely. I wondered if she didn't wear glasses out of vanity, or if she didn't need them. "It's such a **pleasure**," she drawled, her voice lingering over syllables the short word wasn't meant to have. I wanted to let go of her hand, but she kept looking at me.

"Arabella tells me we're kin."

She hadn't indicated that I should sit, and Colin wouldn't sit until Arabella and I did, so we remained standing awkwardly. "We are. Arabella and I found out by accident when we were at Oxford. My sister had sent me a copy of our ancestry chart, and Arabella saw it and recognized your name. That's how I learned that you'd been a model before and after the war."

She continued to examine me closely, and I had to resist the impulse to squirm. Standing this close, I could see the ashen pallor beneath the makeup on her face, could feel the brittle, birdlike bones of her hand. It reminded me too much of my mother, and I wanted to jerk away. But she continued to hold on tightly, her eyes studying my face.

She let go of my hand. "I'm a very good observer of people, and if I had to guess, I'd say you have your own story to tell. I see it in your eyes." Precious didn't wait for me to respond. "I've changed my mind. Maddie, please sit next to me. Colin, why don't you and Arabella take your tea in the drawing room while I get to know Maddie better." She didn't bother with an inflection at the end of her sentence; it hadn't been a question.

"Of course," Arabella said brightly. "I need to get back to work anyway. My phone has been blowing up with texts." She leaned over and gave Precious a peck on the cheek. Colin moved the iced tea glasses to the table, then removed the tray. With a quick glance in my direction, he followed Arabella from the room.

I suddenly felt as if I'd been thrown from the side of a boat without a life preserver. I bumped into the small table as I maneuvered my legs beneath it, feeling like Alice in Wonderland as I overshadowed not only the table but the chaise, too. I wondered how Colin would have managed it.

"I'm glad you're here to write about the clothes and not about me. I don't like to talk about my past," Precious said without preamble. She reached for her iced tea glass, her hand shaking slightly. I somehow knew better than to offer assistance. "Although I suppose it's about time. Everybody tells me I'm dying, so I figure I'd better pay attention and tell my story to someone before it's too late. Maybe I've just been waiting for the right person to tell it to."

She leaned close, studying me intently. "I do believe I see the family resemblance." Her voice was more breath than words, the effect almost wistful. As if she wished that her words were true. Precious sat back. "Perhaps that's why Arabella thought we might get along like biscuits and gravy."

I watched as she brought the glass to her lips and took a small sip. I picked up my own iced tea and did the same, trying not to shudder at the blandness and avoiding a small clump of undissolved sugar. Our eyes met with silent understanding. Precious stared into her glass at the sugar clumps floating at the top like little icebergs. "Poor Laura—she's so kind to make sweet tea, and I don't have the heart to tell her that she's doing it wrong." She grimaced as she replaced the glass on the table, looking relieved either because she'd managed a sip or because she hadn't dropped the glass.

"One thing you should know about me is that I'm very good at noticing details about people. Why does Colin call you Madison if your friends call you Maddie?"

I considered evading the truth, but knew that her sharp gaze missed nothing. If I wanted her to be frank and open with me, I needed to do the same. "Because we aren't really friends."

She raised an elegant eyebrow. "And why is that?"

I felt her discerning gaze upon me again, seeing the truth behind my smile. I took a deep breath. "Because I dated some of his friends."

She frowned. "Did Colin never ask you for a date?"

"Actually, he did. We even went out once."

She didn't say anything but continued to look at

me as if waiting for me to say more. I sighed, deciding to be candid. "We had a great time. That's when I realized that Colin is the kind of guy a girl could really fall for. In a permanent way. So I never went out with him again even though he asked. More than once. With his buddies, there was no danger of anything permanent."

She was quiet for a moment—digesting my answer, I supposed. "And now?" she asked. "Do you still only date temporary men?"

I met her gaze. "Yes."

"In my day, they had a word for girls like you."

I swallowed. "Yes, well, if that makes you uncomfortable, I'm sure Arabella can find another journalist." I began to slide off of the small chaise, my legs bumping the table so the liquid in the glasses sloshed over the sides.

"Wait," she said, the force of the word surprising us both. "Don't go. I'm the last person in the world to judge."

I stopped and looked at her, trying to decipher the emotions crossing her face.

"Did you lose someone you loved?" Precious asked, and I knew she wasn't speaking of misplacing someone or leaving someone behind. And I wondered if that was one of the details she was in the habit of noticing.

"Yes," I said. "A long time ago."

She nodded. "Whoever said time heals all wounds

is a liar. Grief is like a ghost, isn't it? Haunting our reflections."

My eyes prickled. "I'm sorry," I said, standing, my hands on the table to keep it from moving. "I'll leave now. It was a pleasure meeting you."

"Good-bye, Maddie. Please take the tea and tell everyone that I'm going to rest for a bit. We'll speak again tomorrow after lunch. We can talk about the clothes then. And how they transformed my world."

"But . . ." I stopped. She'd closed her eyes, and although she couldn't possibly already have been sleeping, it was clear she was done speaking.

Knowing I'd been dismissed, I walked to the door, then turned to look at her again, admiring the beautiful lines of her face and wondering at the stories I knew lay hidden behind her closed eyes. **Grief is like a ghost.**

Yes, there were stories there. I just hoped there would be time to hear them all.

"I'll see you tomorrow, Miss Dubose," I said to her still form, then shut the door quietly behind me.

CHAPTER 3

LONDON
FEBRUARY 1939

Ethel Maltby dropped a teaspoon of Bovril into two cups just as the kettle began to whistle. Balancing both cups, she practiced walking gracefully without spilling, putting one foot directly in front of the other, moving in time with the rhythmic precision of the BBC news announcer on the wireless. She paid little attention to what the man was saying, listening instead to the way he enunciated his words.

Perfecting her accent was the reason why she and her fellow model and roommate, Precious Dubose, had splurged on the matinee they'd seen the Sunday before, **The Lady Vanishes**. Margaret Lockwood's intonation was exactly what Ethel had been aspiring to and practicing since she'd first realized at age twelve that her own Yorkshire accent would always put her back into her mother's world of doing someone else's laundry and mending.

Ethel carefully brought both cups over to the small table by the stove, which was used for eating, stockpiling mail, and applying makeup. Precious sneezed loudly, and Ethel gave her friend a worried look. "That's it. I'm putting you to bed with a hot flannel on your chest and making some chicken soup. But first, I'm going to run to the chemist for some Cephos powders. That will clear you up in a jiffy—that's what the adverts say."

Precious sniffled, staring into her Bovril. "If only this were sweet iced tea, I'd feel a whole lot better. But nobody in this entire country seems to know how to make it correctly. As soon as I'm better, I'm going to teach you so at least one person will know."

"I'll look forward to it," Ethel said. "For now please drink your Bovril, and you'll be right as rain in no time."

After retrieving the flannel and getting Precious settled in bed, Ethel pinned her hat to her hair. She was buttoning the large buttons on her serviceable wool coat when her gaze landed on a small box handbag hanging from the coatrack. Gold embroidered leaves sprouted against dark green velvet, a matching gold rope handle draped across the top and attached on each side. Her fingers itched to touch it, and she found herself picking it up and stroking the soft fabric. She felt beautiful fabrics all the time at House of Lushtak, where she and Precious had just started modeling, but she'd never seen a purse made of velvet, or one in the shape of a box. And she'd certainly never seen anything this fine in their flat.

"Where did this come from?" Ethel asked, turning around and holding out the handbag, unable to keep the note of accusation from her voice or her fingers from stroking the soft velvet.

"Isn't it just darling? Madame Lushtak copied an Elsa Schiaparelli bag design for last season's show. I couldn't resist. I paid five shillings for it, but if we both use it, it's like getting it half price." Precious looked hopefully at Ethel.

Five shillings! Ethel almost shouted out loud. She'd even opened her mouth, but her fingers couldn't stop stroking the soft velvet or imagining how smart she'd look on the street, running to the chemist with the beautiful bag hanging from her arm.

"Well, I suppose if you look at it like that . . ." She smiled at Precious, propped up on pillows in bed, her tissue clutched in her hands. Even with a red nose and glazed eyes, she was beautiful. Her long gold hair—just a shade lighter than Ethel's own—lay against her shoulders and reflected the light from the bedside lamp; her eyes, although moist and red rimmed, were an incredible pale blue that would have looked cherubic if they hadn't been placed in the sharply drawn and chiseled face of Precious Dubose.

"I'll be off, then." Ethel ran down the three flights of stairs, smelling boiled cabbage and sausages mixed with an assortment of other cooking scents that lingered like a putrid fog in the hallways and stairwells of their block of flats. She had begun the habit of holding her breath as she ran toward the ground floor so that she wouldn't absorb the smells of the working class. She understood that being a clothes peg—as Madame Lushtak referred to her models—was far from being respectable in most people's estimations, but to her it was much more refined than washing someone else's underpinnings. And if she continued to practice speaking and deportment, it could always lead to better things.

She hurried out the door and breathed deeply. Despite cooler than normal temperatures, the sun shone valiantly through indecisive gray clouds, a brisk breeze keeping the dirty fog at bay. Ethel walked four blocks, stopping to wait for a red bus and two black taxis to pass before crossing to the high street. She realized she was holding her arm at an angle, her elbow bent, so that the beautiful handbag could sway on her wrist as she walked, the gold embroidered leaves reflecting the meager sunlight. She wanted to believe that everyone must be looking, and kept her head held high and her shoulders straight, walking with determined poise, pretending that the rest of her outfit matched the extravagance of the purse. Even with her worn but polished shoes and unfashionable coat, she imagined she could be Bette Davis in **Dangerous.**

Ethel selected her items, then carefully placed the handbag on the counter and counted out the coins. As she took the proffered bag, the chemist, an older man with a bald head as round as his belly, said, "You'd better hurry, miss. It's about to rain cats and dogs."

Ethel sent a glance out the front shopwindow, surprised to see a dark rain cloud cocooning the sun. She'd forgotten to bring her brolly, and although her hat and coat could withstand a soaking, she was worried for the handbag.

"Thank you," she said, grabbing her purchases before dashing out onto the sidewalk without looking, eager to beat the rain. With her head bent against the first sprinkles, she was only vaguely aware of another door being thrust open.

She collided with something solid and warm, something smelling of new wool and sandalwood. Two firm hands grasped her arms. "I beg your pardon, miss. Are you all right?"

The deep voice was decidedly masculine and the words definitely spoken with the accent of what Lucille, one of Lushtak's workroom seamstresses from East London, would have called a toff. Ethel recalled overhearing a conversation between two of the other models about a person's social station being evident in the first words spoken. It was already obvious that whoever this man was, his station was far above hers.

Ethel shook her head. "It's my fault—I should have been looking where I was going, but I was afraid of getting my bag wet. . . ." Her voice trailed off as she looked up to see the man she'd run into. His intense green eyes were set in a deeply tanned face beneath straight sandy-colored brows. The smattering of freckles decorating the bridge of his nose and his high cheekbones was charming instead of boyish. His was the sort of face a girl would remember, the kind that made one believe in love at first sight.

Ethel looked at his eyes again, the light in them snapping as if with humor, giving her the distinct impression that he was amused by her. Was it her accent? Could he tell that she was still practicing the right pronunciation and had muddled a word? Humiliated, she tried to pull back but instead felt him tightening his hold on her arms and pulling them both into a building's arched entranceway, out of the sudden deluge.

"Your bag?" he asked, his generous mouth lifting in a smile as he looked at her wrist. Only the handle of Precious's new handbag dangled from her coat sleeve.

"Oh, no—I've lost it! I must have dropped it at the chemist." She made to run out into the rain, but he pulled her back.

"Stay here," he said. "I'll go fetch it if it's at the chemist and keep a look out if it's on the pavement."

Before she could protest, he'd slid his fedora lower on his head and dashed out into the deluge. Ethel pulled back, the splash of the rain on the pavement splattering her stockings and shoes. She imagined her hair curling tightly in the damp and almost dreaded the stranger's return to see her.

Then he was back, his arms wrapped protectively around something white held against his chest. When he joined her under the arch, he held out the object, and she recognized the square shape of the box bag, draped now in a white linen handkerchief.

She sighed with relief. "Thank you, sir. May I offer . . . ?" She stopped, feeling foolish. She could see the quality tailoring of his coat, the expensive shoes. He didn't need a shilling from her.

His lips twitched as if he wanted to smile. "I'm honored to have helped a beautiful lady in distress. But if you'd like to offer payment for my services, could I ask your help?"

Wary of what he might suggest, Ethel only nodded.

"I'm looking for St. Marylebone Parish Church—the old one, not the larger structure on Marylebone Road. I believe it was once used as the parish chapel after the new building was consecrated."

"You're a clergyman, then?" The words flew from her mouth before she could call them back, or at least check them for any signs of commonness. She pressed her fingers hard against her lips, as if to punish them. It was as if she'd never spent all of those hours watching movies and listening to the BBC.

The man's eyes sparkled as he grinned, his teeth a brilliant white in his tanned face. "No, actually, I'm not, although I do not doubt that my mother would desire such a vocation for her son instead of the one I've chosen. Alas, I merely admire the architecture of old churches. While I happened to be in this corner of London, I thought I might go have a look."

Her face reddened, and Ethel found she couldn't look at him. Of course he wasn't clergy. She'd known that merely from looking at his shoes. "It's that way," she said hurriedly, averting her eyes and pointing in the right direction. "You'll see the back of the new church, and you'll know you're there."

Tucking the handbag under her coat, she stepped out into the rain and began to run, impervious to the wet, wanting only to put the man and her humiliation behind her. To escape from the certainty that her mother had been right about the impossibility of her ever amounting to anything outside the life into which she'd been born.

"I don't know your name to thank you properly," he called out after her.

Ethel hesitated, then stopped. He wanted to know her name. She couldn't tell him, of course. Not the name that belonged in a washerwoman's cottage. She would never see him again, but she wanted to leave him with the memory of someone with a name that would be at home in the circles he undoubtedly moved in.

She turned. "It's Eva."

"Eva," he said, the single word a thing of beauty on his lips. "Where can I find you again, Eva?" He took a step toward her.

She pretended she hadn't heard and resumed running, not stopping until she was inside the flat, dripping water all over the parquet floor their landlady took so much pride in. She glanced in the corner to see Precious sleeping, turned on her side with her back to the door. It was only then that Ethel realized she had the man's handkerchief still wrapped around the handbag. Peeling back the corner, she saw an embroidered **GBS** stitched in dark blue.

"Ethel? Is that you?" Precious mumbled without turning around.

"No." She bit her lip, feeling foolish and excited all at once.

Precious turned slightly to get a better look at her and blinked, confused.

"It's me—but I want to be called Eva now. It's much more high-class sounding than Ethel, don't you think?"

Sitting up, Precious smiled, her eyes brightening. "It is. I picture a whole different person when I hear 'Eva.' Like a Hollywood star. Eva can be your nickname—like Precious is for me. It can be something else we share. Except Eva is more special since you're giving it to yourself."

"You think so?"

Precious nodded enthusiastically. "Absolutely. You're reinventing yourself, so you might as well have a new name." She sniffled into her tissue, her eyes turning serious. "But won't your parents mind? Ethel is the name they gave you."

Ethel had told her friend very little about her background, only that she'd lived in northern England with her mother, who supported them both by taking in laundry from the big houses and working as a seamstress for the well-to-do. She'd confided in Precious that she sent her mother money from every paycheck, but she hadn't admitted that she never included a letter, because her mother couldn't read or write.

Nor had she mentioned her father or his meaty fists, or how he'd been sent to jail for beating a man almost to death in a bar brawl after the man had accused him of cheating at cards. She'd never told Precious about her mother's smashed face and broken fingers, or how they had moved several times just in case her father ever got out of jail and took it upon himself to find them.

Ethel knew that Precious would understand, would probably hug her to show that she did. Ethel didn't tell her friend because the shame she felt was a hot, living thing that smoldered in her core. In her new life as a model in London, she'd gotten in the habit of ignoring it, the equivalent of placing a small lid over a raging stove fire. It was still there, but as long as she didn't look at it, she could live her life as if Ethel Maltby had never existed at all.

"No. I don't think they'll mind," she said, unpinning her soaking hat. "I'll go put the kettle on and then see about making you chicken soup." She took off her coat, almost dropping the purse tucked inside. Ethel lifted the man's handkerchief to her nose, the faint scent of sandalwood making her think of freckles and a deep chin cleft. Of eyes that laughed and were the color of the dales surrounding her home.

"I met a gentleman on the high street." When her friend didn't respond, Ethel turned toward the bed, not surprised to discover Precious had fallen asleep again, her face pressed into the pillow.

Ethel folded the handkerchief carefully and placed it inside her dresser, making sure it was tucked on top, where she'd see it each time she opened her drawer. It would be her talisman to remember the day Ethel Maltby had reinvented herself as an enigmatic woman named Eva. And the man who'd asked for her name and made her believe that her mother might have been wrong, that her world was full of possibilities that she hadn't yet begun to imagine.

CHAPTER 4

LONDON
MAY 2019

I stood by the phone in the small alcove in the front foyer, glittering gems of sunlight filtering through the leaded glass casement windows and dotting the walls and floor, making me think of ghosts. **Grief is like a ghost.** I imagined years of ghosts trapped in each dust mote and shard of light in the old flat, waiting to be set free. I stared at a gray leaf frozen in the glass of the window, my thoughts making me pause, giving me a new perspective on my assignment.

I was supposed to interview a ninety-nine-year-old former model and write an article about how contemporary fashion had been influenced by the Second World War. The idea had seemed very accessible, and I'd had the time available, so I'd agreed.

Arabella planned to run my piece in the magazine in conjunction with an exhibition of 1940s fashion at the Design Museum, many of the clothes provided by Precious. It had all seemed very standard.

Then I'd met Precious Dubose, and I'd realized that the assignment wasn't as clear-cut as I'd assumed.

Grief is like a ghost. Maybe Precious Dubose had been waiting all these years to set some of hers free.

I yawned, feeling completely exhausted. I hadn't been able to sleep past five o'clock—midnight New York time—and not just because of the time difference. My phone had been binging since five with incoming texts from my sister Knoxie asking me to call her. I had a feeling it was about the small-rodent taxidermy-of-the-month club I'd enrolled her in for her birthday, so I was in no hurry to call her back, even if she just wanted to chat. My family and Walton, Georgia, seemed so very far away, like a movie I'd watched and loved a long time ago that was no longer relevant. It was how I wanted it, and the main reason I now lived in New York.

I bent my head over my phone as I walked toward the kitchen, in desperate need of coffee.

My progress was stopped by a solid chest in a starched white shirt that smelled faintly of soap and dog.

I stepped back quickly and looked up into blue eyes that could have been amused or annoyed—it was hard to tell this early in the morning and without coffee. "Excuse me," I said. "Could you please point me in the direction of a coffeemaker?"

"And good morning to you, too, Madison. Follow me." Colin led the way into the kitchen, and I dutifully followed, my phone vibrating with another text. The door to the small bedroom off of the kitchen—the former maid's room, I'd been told, but now occupied by Laura and Oscar—was slightly open, revealing an empty room and a made bed, making me assume the nurse was already with Precious.

"I have a **cafetière**. I hope that's all right." Colin motioned for me to sit at the table while he poured coffee beans into a grinder and turned on the kettle. At my blank expression, he said, "A French press."

I glanced behind him to the counter to make sure there wasn't a regular drip machine or a Keurig. "As long as it has caffeine, I'm good."

He shook his head slightly as he scooped in the coarsely ground coffee and poured in hot water, then pressed down the lid.

"Seems like a lot of trouble," I said.

"Some things are worth it. I suppose that's why fast food was invented in America. It's not so much the taste and experience, but the haste in which it can be prepared and consumed." He pulled out two mugs and a pint of milk and set them on the counter.

I wanted to argue with him, but I was useless before my first cup of coffee. And he was probably right.

Leaning against the counter, he said, "I already spoke with Arabella. She didn't want to disturb you if you were still sleeping."

Another text vibrated my phone, and I resisted the urge to roll my eyes.

"She'll be here shortly to go over some of the outfits she's selected for the exhibit, although she's sure Nana will have her own opinions and will most likely request more or different ones. There are quite a few boxes down in the storage room that I will be happy to bring up after work, but there are plenty already in the spare room down the hall to get you started. Arabella thought you might use Nana's memories of when she wore each outfit and what was going on in London at the time as a framework for your article—her words, not mine."

Colin turned around and poured milk into the largest mug, then poured in the coffee before handing it to me. I accepted it gratefully and took a sip before looking up with surprise. "How did you know how I like my coffee?"

He looked at me over the rim of his cup. "I suppose I have a good memory."

There was something in his voice that made me look away, feeling as if I'd just been scolded.

"Why did you decide to become a freelance journalist? At university, you and your camera were never apart. I thought you wanted to be a famous photographer."

"I did. Once. And I still love taking pictures—I actually brought my Hasselblad with me, and I'll take photographs of Precious and the clothes for inspiration. I know Arabella will use the magazine's professionals for anything that will go in the actual issue. But I still love photography—can't really imagine ever stopping." I took another sip of my coffee, feeling the steam brush my nose. "I guess at some point I realized that the written word is sometimes needed to complete the story that a photograph has begun."

I allowed a smile to creep across my face. "I'm surprised you remembered that about me." I'd almost used the word "embarrassed." Not because he had remembered so much, but because I hadn't remembered very much about him. That had been intentional. Because there was a lot about Colin Eliot that I'd wanted to remember and hold on to. Or would have if life was different and I was meant to have long-lasting relationships.

"Like I said, I have a good memory." As if to change the subject, he said, "I forgot to mention—there are several boxes containing miscellaneous items that belonged to my grandmother Sophia stored at my parents' town house in Cadogan Gardens. Papers and letters, maybe a few photographs—that sort of thing. Arabella thought they might be helpful for your article."

I nodded eagerly. “Definitely. They could provide some background for the era. When can I go collect them?”

“It would be easier if I brought them here—I still have my ancient Land Rover.”

I smiled in surprise. “I remember that—your parents gave it to you when you went to university. And it was practically prehistoric back then, right?” An old memory hit me. “I remember being driven back to my room more than once from the local pub. You were always the designated driver, I think.” I stared at him, recalling something else. “Did you drink?”

He reached for my empty mug and turned his back to refill it so I couldn’t see his expression. “Someone had to be sober. You couldn’t even manage a pint before your knees went soft. You’re also rather talkative when you’ve been drinking.”

“I am?”

“Quite,” he said, facing me again and returning my now-full mug. “You once accused me of being a misogynist for carrying you up to your room when your feet didn’t seem to be working properly.”

“I don’t remember any of that. What else did I say?”

He was silent for a moment, thinking. “You talked a lot about someone named Rob. You’d been engaged, I believe.”

The light seemed to dim in the kitchen, but I knew it had nothing to do with the ceiling fixture or the clouds outside. The gloom came from inside of me, from the dark place that I liked to keep hidden. Until someone said something and dimmed the light.

"I told you that?" I asked, my voice sounding thick and unnatural.

"Yes, you did."

I turned away, spotting a small fishbowl on the counter by the sink, two fat goldfish swimming around inside, happily oblivious that they were headed right back to the place they'd started. "We broke it off."

"I gathered."

"He's married now with a baby girl. He has my dad's old job teaching English at the high school and coaching the football team."

"And that's not the sort of life you wanted."

I slid my chair back and stood before rinsing my empty mug in the sink. "No," I said softly.

Colin didn't ask why, as if he knew I wouldn't say any more. He joined me at the sink and placed his mug next to mine. "Well, then. I need to get to work. George is with Laura and Oscar, and Arabella will be here soon. I'll see you later this evening."

I nodded, not ready to meet his eyes, waiting for the light to return to my own.

He paused in the doorway. "Look. Madison." He cleared his throat. "I'm about as thrilled at this situation as you are. Should we just make a truce to be on our best behavior so you can do your job and be done?"

"Sure. Of course." I nodded like a bobblehead, unable to stop. The tension between us hummed like unseen radar, bouncing against our invisible walls. I needed to make it stop, or I'd never be able to focus.

"So . . . ," he began.

"I'm sorry," I interrupted, feeling the need to clear the air so that the little ball of guilt didn't clog my throat every time I looked at him.

He raised an eyebrow.

"For not saying good-bye. I don't like good-byes, so I avoid them. It wasn't personal. And to be honest, I didn't really think you'd notice."

"Duly noted," he said. "And apology accepted." He didn't smile, but at least he wasn't frowning at me anymore.

We both turned at the sound of the front door opening, and then Arabella appeared in the kitchen doorway next to Colin, looking nervously between us. "Is everything all right?"

"No blood's been spilled, if that's what you mean," I said.

She smiled. "Splendid. Come, then, Maddie—let's take a look at the clothes. I only have thirty minutes, but you're a self-starter. I won't need to hover. My assistant, Mia, will be contacting you later today with a schedule of appointments I took the liberty of setting up for you with the museum people as well as with a historian whom I think you will love getting to know and chatting with. You are welcome to talk with as many people as you like, but I thought they would be a good start. I will happily step back now and let you take up the reins."

"Sounds good. I look forward to speaking with them." I met Colin's eyes and could tell he was trying not to smirk. We were all too familiar with Arabella's penchant for organizing and moving friends and others in her sphere of influence into position like a master chess player.

Colin said good-bye and left as Arabella led me toward the long hallway of bedrooms. My room was at the end, next to Precious's, past all the framed photographs on the wall. Several other doors lined the hallway, and Arabella took me to the first one on the right.

Like all the other bedroom doors in the flat, this one had a leaded glass transom window over it, allowing light from the large plain window on the far side of the room to spill into the hallway even when the bedroom door was closed. The small, sparsely furnished space contained only an iron double bed, a 1920s-style armoire, and a dressing table with a stool and an attached trifold mirror that looked as if it had come from the same era. Smoky clouds bloomed behind the glass like age spots on elderly hands, distorting my reflection.

"Wow." Metal rolling racks had been piled into the room, leaving just enough space to maneuver between them and the furniture. It was a little girl's dress-up fantasy: long gowns with sparkling stones;

an entire rack devoted to furs—the old-fashioned kind found in the black-and-white movies that Aunt Lucinda had allowed me to stay up late to watch with her. Silky chiffons in various hues floated from another rack, Ginger Rogers–type dresses that seemed to be begging to be twirled in. "Wow," I said again.

"Back when Aunt Precious was a fashion model before and after the war—here in London and then in Paris—the models were allowed to keep some of the clothes they modeled or to buy them at an enormous discount. This is her collection. The pieces are quite valuable, but they were choking on mothballs in the storage room until Aunt Penelope—Colin's mum is very active as a supporter of the Design Museum—rang me up with the idea of an exhibition. I thought it was brilliant, and I immediately thought of you—not just because of the personal angle, but also because you are an amazing writer. I knew you would do it all justice."

Arabella followed me into the room. "All these gowns and beautiful materials," she said. "I sometimes wish we still dressed like that—but can't imagine what my cleaning bill might be like."

"And no children to leave them to."

"Sadly, no," Arabella said, shaking her head. "I've always wondered why Precious never married. From what I've gathered she had plenty of suitors. Aunt Penelope has lots of fascinating stories from before and during the war—Miss Dubose was quite the heroine in the French Resistance, not that you'd ever hear her say it. All of those stories were told to Aunt Penelope by Colin's grandmother Sophia, since she and Precious were such great friends. Aunt Precious has never been keen to talk about her past. Until now, of course. I suppose when one is at the end of one's life, it becomes imperative to pass along our stories so they won't be lost to posterity."

She moved past me to a row of evening dresses, the clusters of pearls and rhinestones shimmering like sea glass on the beach. "Just look at these! Imagine everything they've seen." She carefully lifted a long silky sleeve crusted with jet-black beads. "I thought that once we've decided which pieces will go in the exhibit, you could write the description cards they'll use at the museum."

I nodded, then stepped closer, a faint mothball scent wafting across my face. "What happens to them after the exhibition?" An odd sense of nostalgia hit me, the same feeling I got while looking at the scrapbook album of the first eighteen years of my life, the one my mother had started and Suzanne had finished. Like the old photos, these dresses were merely pale shadows of the vibrant life they had once been a part of, static reminders of something irretrievably gone.

I turned my back on them, waiting for Arabella to answer.

"I'm not sure. Aunt Penelope is trying to work it out. She thinks one of the old country manor houses that are now open to the public might be interested in hosting them as a permanent exhibit." She offered me a bright smile. "I've got to run. You go take a look—just try not to drool. The fabrics are rather delicate. They really are quite beautiful."

Arabella left, and I retrieved my camera from my backpack, the Hasselblad that Suzanne had given me when I'd gone to college. It was old and lacked the technology of the newer cameras, but it was still my favorite.

I touched the sleeve of a tweed jacket with a deep shawl collar that seemed more silk than wool, rubbing it carefully between my fingers, enjoying the feel of the lush fabric. I let the sleeve drop as I lifted the camera and snapped photos of the clothes hanging listlessly from the racks like dancers waiting backstage.

Finally satisfied, I stooped to stash my camera in my backpack. As I stood, a reflection of light from one of the racks caught my attention. I moved aside several hanging garments and spotted a dark green velvet purse in the shape of a box poking out from the silk lining of a woman's coat, a gold cord chain dangling from the same hanger.

Unlike my sisters Sarah Frances and Knoxie, I wasn't into purses, but this one was different. Gold embroidered leaves seemed to grow out of the velvet; the fabric was a bit crushed but still soft. A rhinestone clasp—the source of the reflection I'd seen—latched the lid at the front. I lifted the bag. Something about the texture and pattern of the embroidered leaves begged to be touched. It was heavier than it looked, surprising me. I put my fingers on the clasp, then paused, the sense of invading a stranger's privacy stopping me. My mama had taught me better.

I let go of the bag, watching it dangle as it caught the light again, almost as if it were winking at me. A door opened and shut at the end of the hall, followed by the jangle of dog tags announcing the approach of Laura and the two dogs. I left the room, feeling the need to close the door behind me, as if to guard all the stories lingering like moths within the old fabrics and inside a green velvet purse.

CHAPTER 5

LONDON
FEBRUARY 1939

Eva sat on a padded bench amid the chaos of silk stockings, shoes, and underpinnings that covered the floor. The exhaustion of a full day of showings and being jabbed mercilessly during fittings for the spring show had caught up with her, and she could barely keep her eyes open as she waited for Precious so they could take the bus home together. Two of the models, Odette and Freya, sat on the floor in their dressing gowns with their bare feet straight out in front of them, wriggling their toes.

"Ês-tu fatigué?" Eva asked Odette.

Odette smiled brightly. "**Oui. Très bien**, Eva! Your accent is almost as good as mine."

"Merci beaucoup," Eva said, pleased. Because she had a good ear for accents, she'd decided to see if her talents might extend to learning another language. She'd chosen French not just because of her access to a native speaker, but because French was the sort of thing well-brought-up girls were taught in school. It was all part of the background she was constructing for the newly created Eva, a history that had to be more than just a name. She wasn't going to be a model forever, but while she was, she was determined to learn everything she could about deportment and poise. It would take her as far away from Yorkshire as she could get.

Alice pranced in, wearing a sunflower yellow frock that was all ruffles and lace, followed by Precious already in her street clothes. Alice was the youngest model and looked so waiflike that Eva was always surprised she managed to get to work on windy days. She had a way of speaking that made her seem either extremely bored or half-asleep—something Eva had noticed in many of the well-bred young ladies who shopped at Lushtak's. She enjoyed imitating it, which usually resulted in Precious and the other models—except for Alice—being reduced to peals of laughter.

"Mrs. Ratcliffe is on her way," Alice announced in her usual desultory tone. "And she doesn't appear to be very happy. Lucille left before she'd been fitted for a late showing, and Mrs. St. John and her daughter are already on their way, expecting to be shown an entire wardrobe. I daresay pins are going to fly."

Odette and Freya had both pulled themselves up by the time the dressing room door flew open to reveal their supervisor, Mrs. Ratcliffe, her jowls and bosom quivering in unison. She grasped the doorframe with one hand; the other arm cradled a patterned crepe evening gown. Mrs. Ratcliffe's officious voice was another one that Eva enjoyed mimicking, when she was sure she wouldn't be overheard.

Mrs. Ratcliffe lifted the glasses that dangled on a chain on her voluminous chest like an anchor thrown over the prow of a ship, and placed them on the end of her nose.

As she drew in two deep breaths, her gaze scanned the room, pausing on Precious for a moment and then on Eva before moving on to the other models, all in various stages of disrobing. "I need a model to fill in for Lucille, someone tall and slim so no new alterations will be needed." Her gaze fell back to Eva. "You, then. You'll do. Put this on and come down to the fitting room as quickly as possible. You need to see Mr. Danek. He'll make you presentable before you head out into the showroom. The client is very particular, and we can't be having you look tired and deathly pale."

Eva stood, making sure her spine was straight, her shoulders back. "I'd be happy to." She slid her dressing gown off of her shoulders, glad she'd been too tired to remove her stockings, step-in, and backless brassiere.

Mrs. Ratcliffe tightened her lips as she eyed Eva

again. "Very well. You have five minutes. Not a minute more. We are already far behind, and we simply cannot be delayed further."

"No, Mrs. Ratcliffe," Eva said, reaching for the gown.

As soon as Mrs. Ratcliffe left, Precious rushed to Eva and took the dress from her. "Freya, Odette—could you please help Eva into the dress? I'll get her shoes."

"Close your eyes and raise your arms," Odette instructed, and Eva did as she was told. The two models slipped the dress over her head, being careful not to scratch her skin with the pins.

Precious placed Eva's good shoes—the strappy high heels she'd bought with her first paycheck—on the floor in front of her and guided one foot, then the other, into them as Odette and Freya adjusted the dress on Eva's body.

Quickly, Precious brushed Eva's hair and pinned it up into a loose chignon. "Pretty as a peach," she said. "Now, hurry—just don't trip. I'll stay and help you change."

"You don't have to. Besides, aren't you supposed to see a film tonight with that young solicitor you met last week?"

"He can wait. I hear Mrs. St. John is a bit of a bear, so you'll need a friendly face and helping hands each time you return from the showroom."

Eva smiled, more relieved than she cared to admit. "Thank you. I owe you."

"I'll remember that. Now, go. I'll meet you in the fitting room."

Eva nodded once, then ran through the door. "Just don't pull out any of the pins," Precious called after her, but she didn't slow down until she reached the fitting room. She was glad to see it was empty except for the makeup man.

"Mr. Danek!" she said eagerly as she approached his cosmetics-strewn table, happy to see her friend.

"Ah, the beautiful Ethel," he said, returning her smile.

"It's Eva now, remember? I'm still working on a surname that fits better than Maltby."

"Of course. I will try harder. I have a few lipsticks for you that I think you will like."

A small, wiry man of around sixty with a vague European air and salt-and-pepper hair, Mr. Danek was generally assumed to be mute: He never spoke when getting the girls ready for a show. Eva suspected it was because no one ever spoke to him. Her suspicions had been confirmed when she'd spotted Mr. Danek struggling up the back steps of Lushtak's prior to a rehearsal, overburdened with cases and bags. She'd offered her assistance. He'd gratefully accepted and even smiled, showing surprisingly even white teeth.

A friendship had been formed, then cemented with regular visits to Horvath's Café near Lushtak's, run by either friends or family of Mr. Danek. At least Eva assumed this, since they greeted him by name in a foreign language. She wasn't sure which one, and she hadn't wanted to appear foolish or uneducated by admitting her ignorance. It had taken a week before she'd found the courage to ask and discovered that Mr. Danek was from Czechoslovakia, a small town called Lidice outside of Prague. It sounded very foreign to Eva, and the names on his tongue made it much more glamorous in her mind than Yorkshire.

In exchange for help with his English, he would give her broken lipsticks and half-used loose face powder tins, as well as crumbling rouges and bent mascara brushes, along with tips on the best ways to use them. Now he held out his palm with two lipstick tubes as she sat down at his table and pulled the chair closer.

"Thank you!" she said. "I don't even have to look—I know I'll love them. You always choose just the right shades."

His dark eyes shone. "It is always a pleasure to work on such a flawless canvas. You and Miss Dubose both. No flaws to cover. It's a good thing not everyone is like that, or I'd have no work!"

He smiled at his own joke as he rifled through a drawer of rouge pots. "How is your French coming along?"

"Très bien!" Eva said, careful not to move her face too much.

"Maybe one day you will allow me to teach you my language." He placed a finger on her chin to move her closer, then dipped a mascara brush into a dark pot.

"Maybe," she said doubtfully. "Although I think French and English should be enough, don't you?"

His eyes met hers briefly before he leaned in to put mascara on her eyelashes. "The world is a very large place, although some right now in Germany are trying to make it smaller by gobbling up countries like hungry lions."

He sat back to admire his handiwork, then met her confused expression. "You would do well to read the newspapers, Eva, and keep informed. Most educated women do, although they won't admit it at the dining table, of course. But I know how much you like to appear educated."

His words weren't condemning or reproachful. Simply informative. Eva had told him very little about her background, except that she was from Yorkshire and her mother did laundry and sewing. He had seemed to know without asking that her past was something she was trying to excise, like a cancer.

"All right," she said, sitting back in her chair. "Then I also need to come up with where I was educated, someplace where a woman named Eva would have lived a sheltered, genteel existence."

He placed his forearms on the table and said quietly, "If you ever want to rise above your station, you must have a good reason why you model. The circles you wish to move in look down on your profession, you know. Like they do actresses and opera singers. But if you have a respectable background, then moving up is possible, yes?" He turned his head slightly, as if to ensure they were still alone. "You are very good at reinvention, Eva. The best, I think. You will go far with a skill like that." Leaning back, he laughed. "You remind me of the girl in that Leslie Howard film—**Pygmalion.**"

"Do you mean Eliza?" She shook her head, feeling a spark of anger. "I've never been that low-class."

"No, you haven't. And it was a play first. You should know those things, Eva. Read more, go to plays and concerts. Remember—**reinvention**."

Mrs. Williams, the head seamstress, bustled into the room, a tape measure around her neck and a pincushion attached to her wrist. She took hold of Eva's hand and helped her onto the fitting platform. "Hurry, hurry—I've got to tack up those seams before Madame Lushtak sees you."

Eva looked back at Mr. Danek, who smiled with approval as Eva straightened her spine and regarded herself in the mirror. Mrs. Williams set to work, her white and flabby arms quivering like netted fish as she made her way around the platform on her knees, measuring and pulling pins from the cushion bracelet on her wrist. When Mr. Danek said his goodbyes and left, the room went quiet but for Mrs. Williams's labored breathing as she moved around Eva, tugging and pinning and occasionally inserting small stitches.

Eva's cramped toes became numb, and her back began to ache, but she remained still, moving only as directed. A door slammed down the corridor, followed by the sound of two sets of hurrying footsteps. Mrs. Williams paused and turned her head, but Eva stared straight ahead, afraid to move and disrupt the intricate draping knot that cinched in her waist.

"Mrs. Williams, are you almost finished?"

At the sound of Madame Lushtak's voice, Mrs. Williams stood, loosening her grasp on the fabric, but not letting it go completely. She'd spent the last ten minutes gathering and pinning the drape so that it lay just so. "Not quite, Madame. I'm finishing with this rosette and pleats, and then I'll be as good as done."

Eva could see Madame's pinched face in the mirror, her expression matched by Mrs. Ratcliffe's behind her. Madame Lushtak's dark eyes raked over the dress, closely studying every line and angle, her gaze stopping short of Eva's neck. Eva froze, afraid to move. Madame walked closer, examining the seams, the flutter sleeves, the exquisite folds of the long skirt.

"It will have to do." She turned to Mrs. Ratcliffe. "I will be waiting in the showroom." Then Madame looked up at Eva for the first time. "This is an important customer—do you understand? Mrs. St. John has brought her daughter up from the country. She's newly engaged and needs new clothes for all the events she will be attending."

Eva nodded. "Yes, Madame."

"Good. Remember, modeling isn't just walking about, wearing beautiful clothes. It is about showing the joy and confidence my clothes will impart. I trust you will not disappoint me."

The room was silent as they listened to Madame's footsteps fade down the corridor. Mrs. Ratcliffe regarded Eva and frowned. "Mrs. St. John is hoping to find a few new outfits her daughter will wear when she appears in the society pages. Madame thought this gown would be perfect, and there are several other outfits she has already had pulled from the showroom. You will be expected to show them all, so you can expect a late night."

It wasn't a request, not that it had crossed Eva's mind to refuse. "Yes, of course."

Mrs. Williams quickly threaded a needle and began sewing Eva into the dress. "Don't you worry, lamb. Mrs. St. John is a bit of a battle-ax, but her daughter is a kind soul. I've fitted her before, and she won't allow her mother to bully you. Besides, you look lovely."

Precious, with a compact and a tube of lipstick in her hands, joined Mrs. Ratcliffe as she waited behind Mrs. Williams to finish her last stitch. After Precious quickly refreshed Eva's powder and lipstick, Mrs. Ratcliffe instructed Precious to put a dab of pancake makeup on the small birthmark on Eva's neck.

"There," Precious said, standing back. "Absolute perfection. It's invisible."

Eva tilted her head and regarded her reflection. The small mark had become so much a part of her that she didn't even notice it anymore. "You're right. Thank you."

Mrs. Ratcliffe nodded her approval. "Are you ready, then?" She didn't wait for a response, but turned and led the way down the hall, not checking to see if Eva followed.

All of the lights in the spacious showroom had been turned on, illuminating the racks of ready-to-wear lining the perimeter of the large space, the bright colors of the clothes against the white walls like rouge on pale cheeks. Eva smiled her best Myrna Loy smile, the one she thought inspired confidence while also reflecting beauty and approachability.

With a slow and steady saunter, she walked down the center aisle of the showroom toward the back, where the comfortable sofas and chairs were set along with glass and brass tables filled with glasses of champagne and tea cakes. Two women sat on a small sofa, each holding a glass, their conversation stopping as Eva approached. The elder of the two, presumably Mrs. St. John, was fair and very slender, her long legs elegantly crossed at the ankles. She was encased completely in a houndstooth tweed suit, a fur stole perched on her shoulders as if she didn't intend to stay long. She was a handsome woman, and in her youth, she might have been considered beautiful. Perhaps if her expression weren't so dour. She didn't smile as she took in the gown, nor did she look up at Eva.

"Oh, Mother, it's lovely, isn't it? Look at the way it flatters the figure. The drapes are almost Grecian, aren't they?"

Eva turned her smile toward the other woman, a younger, slightly rounder version of her mother, with darker blond hair in a fashionable cut covered by a smart hat, a smattering of freckles on the bridge of her nose, and hazel eyes fringed with black eyelashes. But it was her smile and elfin chin that animated her face and made Eva wish they could be friends.

Eva took a step backward and swiveled so they could admire the low back. Mrs. St. John took a sip from her glass and said, "I daresay it looks best on someone tall and slender."

Madame Lushtak appeared from where she'd been standing to the side, nearly hidden by a mannequin wearing one of the previous season's suits. "It has been designed to flatter the female form, emphasizing the waist or creating one where none exists. And of course, the length can be shortened if necessary. It is the perfect transitional fabric. It wears well in cooler or warmer temperatures."

"Perhaps," Mrs. St. John said dubiously. She waved her hand. "Walk some more so we can see how it moves. Those sleeves are quite interesting."

Eva faced the women again, moving her shoulders to emphasize the fluttering sleeves; then she turned completely to walk away and give them a better view of the dress. That was when she noticed the man sitting in one of the cushioned chairs, his legs crossed nonchalantly. He held a cigarette in one hand and a champagne glass in the other. "I rather like it." He smiled, and her cheeks flushed at the familiarity. She'd seen that smile only once, but it had been the subject of her daydreams ever since. And she'd even taken to sleeping with his handkerchief under her pillow every night in the hopes that his smile would invade her nighttime dreams as well.

He lifted his glass in her direction. With an even broader grin, he said, "But is it waterproof?"

Eva stumbled but quickly recovered, disguising it as a twirl, the skirts floating prettily around her ankles and earning her an admiring nod from Madame Lushtak.

"Really, Graham," Mrs. St. John said. "Don't be ridiculous. It's not meant to be worn traipsing through the fields."

Eva stood still and placed her hands on her hips, seemingly showing off the trim waistline and the delicate sleeves but actually trying to stop her legs from acting like rubber. She had to walk out of the room without making a fool of herself. She dared not glance at the man again, but kept smiling at the two women as she pivoted her hips from side to side.

"Naturally," the man said.

Graham. Finally, Eva had a name to go with her fantasy. She stole a glance at him over her shoulder and flushed again when she realized he hadn't dropped his gaze.

"Still," he continued, looking directly at Eva, "I think it's absolutely stunning."

It seemed as if he wasn't speaking about the gown at all. Eva felt as if she were standing completely naked, open for all scrutiny. Without waiting for the nod from Madame Lushtak, she turned away from the small group and, taking deliberate, slow steps, made her way to the showroom door without stumbling. She closed the door and leaned against it, panting as if she'd just run a great distance.

Graham. His name was **Graham**. She felt giddy and weak and worried all at the same time—three emotions she couldn't explain. Was he the fiancé? The thought nearly made her sick.

"You were magnificent," Precious said. "Just magnificent. And did you see that man? He couldn't keep his eyes off of you!"

Eva nodded. "But I think he might be the fiancé."

Precious tucked her chin. "I sure hope not, because that man had eyes for nobody but you. No other girl would stand a chance—if I were a betting girl, I'd bet on you for sure."

Her friend's appearance and reassuring words quieted the fluttering in her stomach. Mrs. Ratcliffe appeared and took Eva's arm. "Hurry, girl. There's no time for dallying. Mrs. St. John doesn't like to be kept waiting."

Eva nodded, and she and Precious followed her back to the fitting room. Mrs. Williams was pressing the pleated skirt of a cream silk and linen street frock with a tucked bolero section at the front and a scalloped border and collar.

"Hurry, hurry," Mrs. Ratcliffe shrilled, unpinning the dress while Eva was still walking.

"There's a man in the showroom," Eva began.

"There are usually men in the showroom," Mrs. Ratcliffe said brusquely. "Many of our ladies require the opinions of gentlemen before they make a purchase."

"Is he Miss St. John's fiancé, then?" Eva didn't really want to hear the answer, but she needed to know. She held her arms out so one outfit could be removed and the other put over her head. It fit almost perfectly; after one small stitch to the waist, she was ready to return to the showroom, where **Graham** was waiting.

Mrs. Ratcliffe huffed as she roughly adjusted the shoulders. "That is none of your concern. Come now. They're waiting."

Precious touched up Eva's makeup, and Mrs. Williams gave her a sympathetic smile as

Mrs. Ratcliffe whisked Eva back to the showroom. But Eva felt different this time. When she'd seen herself in the full-length mirror, she hadn't recognized herself. The woman staring back at her had been poised. Sophisticated. Beautiful. A world apart from the Ethel Maltby who'd boarded a train in Yorkshire with only three shillings and a suitcase full of hope.

"You look finer than a frog's hair split four ways, so act like you own the place," Precious whispered loudly, giving Eva confidence and making her smile.

When the showroom door opened this time, she was ready. She was Myrna Loy, Bette Davis, and Jean Harlow all at once. Ethel Maltby had begun to fade, replaced by an exquisite creature named Eva who'd always remember this day as the day she'd truly been born.

She strutted across the room, smiling at Madame Lushtak, her pace slowing when she reached the sofas and chairs. Mrs. St. John still sat with her back ramrod straight, her daughter smiling from the seat next to her. But the chair where Graham had sat was empty, the cigarette stub smoldering in the ashtray.

Eva pushed her disappointment aside, feeling foolish for having imagined he'd exhibited any interest in her at all. She threw all of her energy into modeling the remaining outfits, making sure to highlight the silk linings of the coats, the functional pockets on the skirts.

When she returned to the fitting room for the final time, her feet screaming and her back aching, Mrs. Ratcliffe actually smiled at her. Mrs. St. John and her daughter had ordered all five outfits that Eva had modeled for them, she said.

After Mrs. Ratcliffe left, Precious descended on Eva in a flurry. "Did you get his name? Did you find out where he's going?"

Eva shook her head. "Maybe he'll come back." Her smile slipped.

Precious hugged her. "He will. Trust me. I've got to go now—Ronald is waiting. I'll see you back at the flat."

"Thanks for all your help. You're a good friend. I'd have been too nervous to walk straight without you."

Precious hugged her again. "I don't believe that for a second." She winked, then left.

Mrs. Williams helped Eva dress, pursing her lips as she slipped Eva's simple frock over her head. She tutted when Eva retrieved her wool coat, and said, "Is that all you have to wear? You'll catch your death."

"I'll be fine—I'm on the bus most of the way."

But Mrs. Williams was already hunting through one of the racks of clothes. She pulled a long red cashmere cape off a hanger and handed it to Eva.

"Wear this instead. It's from last year; it has a moth hole, but you can barely see it. It was brought here for repair, so no harm if you wear it tonight. And it will look right smart with those shoes."

Eva wanted to say no, that her wool coat was fine. But when she touched the soft fabric and saw the tightly gauged weave and quality of the cashmere, she couldn't refuse. "Thank you," she said, allowing Mrs. Williams to place it over her shoulders, then fasten the large silk-wrapped button at the neck. She showed Eva the slits in the front to stick her hands through, then stepped back to admire her work as Eva pulled on a pair of kid leather gloves. They were mismatched, which was why Eva could afford them, but similar enough that no one would notice unless they examined the pair very closely. Eva had meant to change her shoes, as her feet hurt and she didn't want to risk damaging them, but Mrs. Williams was right. They looked perfect with the cape.

"Beautiful," Mrs. Williams said.

And when Eva looked at her reflection in the long mirror, she had to agree.

She let herself out the back door, looking up at the darkened sky, her path lit by streetlights. The earlier fog had lifted, lending a crispness to the air, reminding Eva of the freshly laundered linens she'd folded with her mother. They'd smelled of soap and sunshine, the two forever linked in her mind. It was one of her few good memories of home.

Her step was light, her feet nearly forgetting their fatigue as she imagined what she must look like in the stylish cape. It seemed the sprinkling of stars and the slender crescent of the moon had been set there just for her. **God's smile.** That was what Precious had called the sliver of moon, and Eva was inclined on this night to believe it was.

She walked in the direction of her bus stop, skirting Hanover Square, her steps slower than usual as she embraced the night and her buoyant mood. She was thinking of picking up fish and chips from the corner shop, and was looking inside her purse to see if she had enough coins when she nearly collided with another pedestrian.

"Pardon me . . . ," she began, then stopped as she raised her gaze to meet familiar green eyes. "Oh." She stepped back in surprise, attempting to quell the fluttering in her stomach. "It's you."

"I thought you'd never be allowed to leave. Park benches can be dreadfully uncomfortable if one sits on them long enough. How my nanny must have suffered." He grinned boyishly, and Eva felt the flutter again. "I trust my mother and sister made it worth your while."

Sister. Eva focused on the word as she stared at him foolishly. If only Precious were there. Her friend always knew the right things to say.

When she didn't speak, he took off his hat. "Where are my manners? I'm afraid we haven't been formally introduced." He gave her a mock bow. "Mr. Graham St. John. At your service."

He grinned again, and Eva was so charmed that she laughed.

"Ah, so the lady has a voice after all."

Eva pictured herself in the red cape and smart shoes, and the girl who'd been Ethel Maltby vanished forever. Mimicking Katharine Hepburn's character in **Stage Door**, she held out the tips of her gloved hand. "Miss Eva Harlow."

She felt the warmth of his fingers through her gloves. "Miss Eva Harlow," he repeated, the name like music on his lips, filled with meaning. "And where are you from, Miss Harlow?"

Mr. Danek's voice seemed to whisper in her ear. **Reinvention.** "I'm from Devon. It's a pleasure to meet you."

"Likewise." He replaced his hat on his head. "I've been hoping to see you again. I wanted to thank you for giving me directions to St. Marylebone. It was all that I'd hoped it would be, and I owe it all to you."

"Actually, I believe you owe it all to the architect who designed it."

He grinned broadly, and her heart flipped in her chest. "Yes, you would be right. But I never would have found it without your help. Would you allow me to thank you properly with a drink or—dare I hope—a meal?"

Eva stared up at this beautiful man, wondering if finally her luck had changed. Or if she blinked, would he and the cape and the shoes all disappear?

Misreading her silence, Graham said, "You've already met my mother and sister, so you can be assured that I am completely respectable."

"In that case . . . ," Eva began.

He held out his arm, and she slid her hand into the crook of his elbow, allowing him to lead her down the sidewalk while the stars and the moon shone above them with infinite possibilities.

CHAPTER 6

LONDON
MAY 2019

My phone buzzed, and when I peeled my eyes open, I realized I was slumped over on the elegant sofa in one of the two front reception rooms of Precious Dubose's flat, George snoring at my feet. Oscar sat on the floor in front of me, staring. Not an unfriendly stare, but definitely one of wariness.

The last thing I remembered was turning on the television to watch the morning news. That had been—according to the carriage clock on the fireplace mantel—four hours earlier. I sat up and grabbed my phone, staring at it as I tried to remember how to answer it. The television was now turned off, presumably by Laura, the same person I assumed had placed a knitted blanket over me.

The phone stopped ringing. I was considering

going back to sleep when a text popped up on my screen. I'm downstairs. Have boxes. Tell Nana yes to lunch. I also saw that, despite my sending Knoxie a text telling her to just call me if it was an emergency or, if it wasn't, to text me her question and I'd respond when I could, there were three texts from her, all with the same message: CALL ME.

My foggy brain took a moment to realize the most recent phone call and text were from Colin. Before I could register what he meant, I noticed how he'd used punctuation but no shorthand in his text. Not that I would ever tell him, but I appreciated it. I'd thought I was the only person in my age group to do so.

The lift bell dinged in the outside foyer, jerking me out of my stupor. I stumbled to the front door and opened it to find Colin moving corrugated boxes from the lift to the hallway. "I think I've got all of the ones from the town house," he said. "But there are still quite a few left in the storage room. I was afraid to bring up more—we won't have room. I thought after Arabella and Precious have chosen what they don't want, we can switch them up with a fresh box."

"Sounds like a plan. Let me help," I said, lifting one of the boxes and finding it surprisingly light. "Where should I put this?"

"Wherever there's room. The dining room can be used for overflow. There are about a dozen hatboxes in the storage room, too, that I can bring up. They take up a lot of space, so I thought you'd want to go through these first." He straightened as the door to the flat opened wider. Oscar and George bounded right past me into the hallway and attacked Colin with exuberant affection.

"I hope you had a good nap," Laura said to me from the doorway. "I was afraid the dogs would wake you, but you were down for the count. Lunch is almost ready, and Precious is expecting you both." She looked past my shoulder at Colin, who was being licked to death by the two dogs. "Glad you got my message—she really wanted to see you. I'm happy you could make it."

Hoisting a larger box and carrying it toward the door, he said, "I can't stay long—I've got a meeting at two."

"I know she'll understand. I've added more hangers to the racks in the bedroom so you have a place for some of the additional clothes. I have no idea how one person could have so many."

I placed the box on the dining room table and returned to the hallway. Oscar was busy sniffing one of the boxes, and when I bent down to scratch him behind his ear, he snarled at me.

Laura picked up the little dog. "It takes him a while to warm up to strangers. Just give him some time, and I'm sure he'll be flopping over for belly rubs in no time." She gave me a reassuring smile.

"I'll make sure Precious is ready to see you. Lunch will be ready in about ten minutes."

I watched Oscar's sweet face over Laura's shoulder as she walked down the hallway. I was unable to decipher his stare, but decided to like him anyway. I picked up another box and brought it into the bedroom, managing to find room for it on top of the dressing table. Then I moved toward the window to allow room for Colin, who dropped a box on the bed. I pushed aside the partially open drapes, tying them back with heavy cords attached to the frame.

Light streamed in. I could see into the windows at the backs of the flats in the next block, which explained the heavy curtains. But opening the curtains afforded a view of Regent's Park if I pressed my forehead to the glass and looked over the roofs of the terrace buildings behind Harley House. Since it was still morning, most of the windows were dark, and I noticed that bay windows with patterned leaded glass were dotted along the facades of both buildings like a checkerboard, the design apparently having no rhyme or reason.

"Why are some of the leaded glass windows missing?" I asked.

Colin looked up from another box he'd just dropped on the floor. "The Blitz." When I didn't say anything, he added, "The Germans. During the war. They dropped a lot of bombs on London."

I gave him the look I remembered using with my

younger siblings when they were making excuses or trying to avoid punishment. It meant many things, but it was generally intended to imply that I wasn't stupid and that to proceed further would mean repercussions.

"I know what the Blitz was. I remember learning about it in school. I just . . ." I shrugged. "I knew a lot of civilians were killed. But I guess I always assumed the bombs were dropped by the river or somewhere strategic like that. Not . . . here. Not where people were living. I probably forgot that part because it's so horrible."

Colin moved to stand next to me in the window, pointing toward the backs of the terraces I'd seen before. My gaze followed his finger, and I watched a woman on one of the back patios gently pushing a small child on a rocking horse. "One dropped right there on York Terrace East—demolished the whole building and damaged this one quite a bit. At least one bomb landed in front of Harley House on Marylebone Road. Shrapnel and debris would have flown a good distance and broken some of the windows. The damage to homes and civilians was intentional. Hitler assumed it would make Britain surrender within weeks. Instead, they endured nearly nine months of almost nightly attacks. The bombings stopped then only because the Germans needed their planes to fight the Russians."

The child on the horse kicked her feet wildly,

and I imagined I could hear her squeals of laughter. "Would the people have had any warning so they could go somewhere safe?"

"Yes—there were sirens and wardens to show people where the nearest shelter was."

"What about Precious? Did she live here during the Blitz?"

"For part of it, I believe. Nana has never offered much information about the war."

I turned my head to say something and found myself standing so close to him that our noses were almost touching. The armoire was behind me, so I couldn't step away. Colin remained where he was, and I was forced to stare into his eyes and notice how they were a solid blue without a fleck of any other color. "Well, then, it's a good thing I'm here, so I can ask her."

My phone rang: Rick James's "Super Freak." "It's my aunt Cassie . . . ," I started to explain, but Colin was already leaving the room. I'd wanted to tell him how during my last visit home, my then-eleven-year-old brother, Harry, had innocently asked to borrow my phone to play games. Then he'd assigned all family members on my contact list a unique ringtone—without my knowledge or approval. I had a strong suspicion that he'd had help from my uncle Sam and that he was retaliating for me sending him off to school with baby food packed in his lunch bag. It had been almost three years, yet I still hadn't changed them back.

I hit the "answer" button. "Hello?"

"Hey, sweet Maddie. It's Aunt Cassie. Have you got a minute?"

I glanced at the unopened boxes on the bed and floor. "Sure—let me put you on speaker." I hit the "speaker" button and set the phone on the dressing table. "What's up?" Turning my attention to the large box on the bed, I stuck my finger under the tape and began peeling it off.

"Oh, the usual—runnin' around like a chicken with its head cut off. The ad agency is doing well, and I've hired some more people, so I don't have to do as much traveling and can work from home most days. By the way, your uncle Sam and little cousins Suzy and Sam Junior say hey."

"Hey back," I said, the sound of her voice warming my insides. Although I hadn't met my mother's sister until I was fourteen, in the years since, Aunt Cassie had more than made up for lost time.

I pulled open the box flaps to reveal neatly folded clothing. Reaching inside, I felt soft silk shantung beneath my fingertips and pulled out a dress the color of midnight, the nap changing from deep blue to black as I moved it in the light. I reached for a hanger dangling from one of the racks.

"And since you won't bother picking up the phone to call your sister, I'm actually calling for Knoxie." I could hear the smile in her voice. "She's engaged!"

I dropped the dress. "But she's only nineteen! That's way too young!"

Cassie's voice was soft and reassuring, something she'd had to relearn since she'd moved back home from New York City nearly fifteen years before. "She and Tyler have been dating since freshman year in high school. They've both got solid heads on their shoulders, and they're committed to getting their degrees. They're making good grades at UGA and planning on law school, if that makes you feel any better. And as Knoxie keeps reminding everybody, your mama was that young when she married your daddy. Not to mention that you and Rob Campbell were engaged at nineteen."

I picked the dress off of the floor and rehung it. "That was a million years ago, when I was young and stupid." The familiar sting pricked at my eyes. I swallowed the bitter lump that had settled in my throat to pretend that I'd forgotten all about my ill-fated engagement. "So, why isn't she calling me instead of you? I told her to call me if it was important."

Colin reappeared with another box and placed it next to the first before leaving the room again. I reached inside the box for another dress, and heard Cassie exhale into the phone.

"Knoxie said she's been texting you for the better part of two days and figured you were avoiding her, so she asked me to call. She has a request, and she thought I'd have a better chance of getting you to say yes. Something about me being bossy."

I tried to smile and make a joke about how my

sister was right, but a fist of dread had collided with my stomach, and I couldn't find the air to speak.

"She wants a Christmas wedding. It was your mama's favorite time of the year, and since Knoxie is the first one to get married, she thought it would be fitting."

"Oh. Right. Sure." I waited for the feeling of dread to pass, but it kept jangling inside my head like a nightmare.

"Well, good, I'm glad you're on board. 'Cause there's one more thing."

"Is this about the taxidermy thing? Tell Knoxie it's only for a year."

I heard the smile in her voice. "No, it's not. I thought that was pretty funny, by the way, although Knoxie's afraid to open her mail now. This is about something else."

I closed my eyes tightly, waiting for the blow.

"She wants you to be her maid of honor, which means you'll have to come home. She says you don't have to stay more than two days—for the rehearsal and the ceremony and reception—but she'd like for you to stay longer. We all would, Maddie. You haven't been home in three years."

I wanted to argue that it hadn't been that long, but I knew it had. Just like I knew how each December my family placed Christmas ornaments and poinsettias on my mother's grave. And how they waited until the following January to celebrate Harry's birthday, a month late. It had been Cassie's idea to separate the two events so the youngest Warner's birthday wouldn't be overshadowed.

A thump on the floor by the bed announced Colin's return. "I'm not sure if I can," I said into the speaker as I hung up a shawl-collared jacket with large round buttons on the front. "My work schedule is so unpredictable. . . ."

"Madison Warner." My aunt's tone and the use of my full name reminded me of why we called her bossy and why Knoxie had asked her to call me in the first place. "We are talking about your family here. Your little sister, who has always looked up to you and who loves you, is asking you to be here for her wedding. It's not a lot to ask, and it should take priority."

I closed my eyes, then snapped them open to block out the images of the kitchen table we'd all sat around, the magnolia tree in the front yard of the old house where our mother had been born and raised. Of chasing lightning bugs in the backyard at night, clutching peanut butter jars labeled with our names. "Can I think about it and let you know?"

Aunt Cassie sighed. "Fine. I'll call you tomorrow. But as your uncle says, there's not a lick of a chance that there can be more than one answer, and I'm not going to accept an alternative."

I opened my mouth to tell her that meant it wasn't really a choice, but she spoke again. "How are your menstrual cycles?"

The sound of tape being ripped off of cardboard jerked my attention to Colin standing next to me. "Aunt Cassie! You're on speaker, and I'm not alone here. Can we talk about this another time?"

"Maddie, there is nothing to be ashamed of. You're a girl, and all girls menstruate. It's a fact of life. And you of all people should know why it's important to pay attention to your body."

Colin was busy removing clothing from the box and wasn't looking in my direction, but he had two ears, and they'd turned an interesting shade of pink.

"That's enough for now, Aunt Cassie. We'll talk about this later, all right? When you call me tomorrow."

"Sure. There's one more thing. Sam was in Atlanta for a medical conference and ran into Dr. Grey. She mentioned you'd had some test results forwarded to her office from your doctor in New York, but the follow-up requests to make an appointment have gone unanswered, so she was concerned. What's going on?"

I was painfully aware of Colin in the room. "It was no big deal—just some blood tests. I simply wanted Dr. Grey to see them. It's not an emergency, all right?"

I could almost hear Cassie's brain working in the pause before she spoke. "Fine. Then you can make an appointment to see her when you're here for Knoxie's wedding. Assuming you haven't already seen your doctor in New York by then. Although I understand why you might want to see Dr. Grey. She's been with us through a lot, hasn't she?"

A loud shriek emitted from my phone, followed by my fifteen-year-old niece shouting at her eleven-year-old brother, "Give it back, Sam Junior! That's mine!" A door slammed and then, at an even higher volume, Suzy screamed, "You're like a booger you can't thump off!"

I made the mistake of looking up and meeting Colin's gaze as his eyebrows shot up.

"Well," Cassie said calmly, "I'd better get off the phone before World War Three starts and go see what those two hellions I gave birth to are up to. I'll call you tomorrow. Love you."

"Love you, too," I said, but she'd already hung up. I kept staring at my phone, listening as Colin pulled clothing from the boxes, trying to think of something to say to explain the conversation.

"Excuse me, you two."

I looked up with relief as Laura appeared in the doorway. "Lunch is ready."

"Great," I said, "because I could eat the north end of a southbound polecat." I saw that they were both eyeing me strangely. "Sorry. Something my uncle Sam says and that my aunt Cassie tells me I shouldn't."

Laura smiled. "I'll go let Miss Dubose know you're coming."

I blushed and was just wondering how much of

the conversation Colin had actually heard when he said, "I'm wondering if I need to Google the word 'booger' for alternate meanings or if your cousin's intent needs no explanation."

I stuck my head deep into the box, but I wasn't fast enough to hide the bubble of laughter that escaped from my mouth. As I tossed another pile of clothes onto the bed, I caught sight of something blinking in the light. The box purse I'd seen partially hidden the previous day. I slid it off its hanger and held it up. "Look what I found. Should I bring it, start a conversation?"

"Sure," Colin said. "My mother packed a boxful of purses, actually. I left them at the town house, not thinking we'd need them. If Arabella wants more, we'll know where they are."

I nodded and slipped the handle over my wrist, noticing a small repair, the rope strands held together with nearly invisible stitches. I held it up for Colin to see. "This was damaged—they might not want it at the exhibit, which is a shame. It's so beautiful and unusual."

"Maybe the story behind how it broke will make it interesting enough to display."

"Very true," I said, impressed with his ability to think like a writer.

We made our way down the hallway toward Precious's rooms, stopping quickly to retrieve my pencil and notebook. I was old-school with my notetaking, loving the scratch of a pencil against paper.

Oscar met us at the door with a snarl until he saw Colin, who scooped him up, presumably to save my ankles from attack.

"Hello, Nana," Colin called out. "We're here."

Laura came to greet us and took the little dog. "Miss Dubose is out on the balcony."

Precious held court at a round wrought iron table, wearing peach silk lounge pants and a matching long-sleeved tunic. Even though the table was in the shade, she had on a straw hat with an enormous brim and a matching peach ribbon. Large sunglasses hid her eyes. She resembled a movie star from the glamorous days of old Hollywood. I waited for Colin to kiss her on each cheek before I greeted her with an outstretched hand.

"Nonsense," she said, holding out her cheek for me to kiss. "We're kin, remember?"

"Of course." I leaned down to kiss her, seeing again the ashen pallor of her skin beneath the makeup.

"We're having pimiento cheese sandwiches on white bread with the crusts cut off." She leaned forward conspiratorially. "Laura found the recipe in **Southern Living**. It's not bad, but it's never quite as good as my mama used to make."

I accepted the chair Colin had pulled out for me before he sat down on the other side of Precious, and I placed my notepad in my lap. Not knowing where to put the purse, I set it gently on the table.

Precious's smile faded. Her peach-colored lips

opened, but no sound emerged, her beringed hand finding her chest.

"Are you all right?" I asked with alarm.

Colin half stood until she waved him back. "I'm fine. It's just a bit of a surprise, is all. It brings back a lot of memories." She stroked the velvet, delicately picked at one of the embroidered leaves, then smoothed it with her finger. "Don't you wish sometimes that objects could speak?"

"Yes, I do." I thought of my mother's clothes, which had hung in her closet for years before Aunt Cassie convinced my daddy to let her take them away.

"I thought so," Precious said quietly. Lifting the purse, she gave it a gentle shake. "I'm wondering if I might have left my powder compact inside." She slid it closer and fumbled with the rhinestone latch.

"May I help you with that?" I asked.

She stared at the reluctant latch with pursed lips, as if to force it open just by willing it. Eventually, she nodded her head in defeat. I played with the clasp, twisting and turning it until it clicked and popped open. The lid hinged backward, and after waiting for a nod of approval from Precious, I reached in and pulled out a slim, rectangular box, the silver tarnished to a dull bronze.

"I think it's a cigarette case." I pressed a narrow button on the edge, and it sprang open, the faintest scent of tobacco vanishing almost as soon as I became aware of it. A single cigarette, shriveled and yellowed, lay diagonally across the bottom. I turned the case to the side, but the cigarette didn't roll, stuck to its prison.

"You smoked, Nana?" Colin watched as I rotated the case in my hand, allowing us to see the intricate curlicue pattern in the silver.

"No." The single word sounded as if it had been forced through sandpaper. "It's not mine. It belonged to a friend." She swallowed.

"A friend?" I prompted.

"Yes. Another model. We lost touch. It was during the war, you see. So easy to lose touch with friends." Her hand reached out for the case, and I placed it on her palm. Carefully, she snapped it shut. With deliberation, her fingers brushed against the tarnish on the lid, partially revealing a raised emblem in the center. It looked like some kind of insect. The case slid from her hands and fell onto the table with a clatter. I met Colin's gaze before turning back to Precious and reaching to get the case.

"May I?" I asked.

She hesitated only a moment before nodding. I picked up the case and then, using my thumbs, rubbed at the marks, feeling like an archaeologist as the figure of a bee emerged. I could see now the careful marks on the translucent wings and striped body, the furred sections of the legs, the two stubby antennae. I studied the insect before flipping the case over, looking for an explanation. There was something so intentional, so precise, about the engraving that I wanted it to be more than just a decoration.

Again I rubbed the tarnish with my thumbs, revealing a British sterling hallmark in one corner, and a line of tiny words along the bottom edge. NIL CREDAM ET OMNIA CAVEBO. I knew it was Latin. But having not taken Latin at Walton High School (I somehow doubted it had even been available) or in college, I had no idea what it meant.

I held it up so that Colin and Precious could see. "Do either of you know what this means?"

Colin nodded. "Give me a minute." He read the words silently, his eyes moving from left to right, and then back again. "It's an old Latin proverb I remember reading somewhere back in my school days. Loosely translated, I think it means, 'I will trust to nothing, and be on my guard against everything.'"

Precious reached over, and her hands enveloped the slim case, pulling it into her grasp. "Betray before you are betrayed."

"And this belonged to your friend?" I asked.

Precious slid off her sunglasses, her pale fingers trembling, her light blue eyes bright against the whiteness of her skin. Slowly, she nodded. "Her name was Eva. She's the one who told me what it meant." A small smile teased her lips before failing completely. "We were like sisters." She dropped her gaze, studying the bee on the case.

Betray before you are betrayed. The words lingered in my head. I wondered at their meaning. And why this Eva had had them engraved on her cigarette case. An idea occurred to me. "Precious, Eva might still be alive, you know. Since you were both models, I'd love to interview you both for the article. She might even have her own collection of clothes! Would you like me to try to find her?"

Precious's eyes clouded, but not with tears. It was as if some deep memory had tried to reappear, and she'd slammed down the shutters to avoid seeing it. "Just because a person is lost doesn't mean they want to be found."

Colin leaned forward. "You were like sisters, though. Wouldn't you like to see her again?"

"It could be very interesting," I added. "Two friends in conversation about the fashion through wartime and over the decades."

Precious's eyes met mine, shadows running behind hers like elusive ghosts. "Yes, Maddie. You're right." She took a deep breath. "And I think you're just the person. To find Eva. To tell our stories. For our families. You understand, don't you?"

I nodded because I did understand. Stories passed from one generation to the next were the cornerstone of Southern family tradition. It was fitting that I, as a blood relation—albeit a distant one—would be the person to tell hers. "And even if I can't find Eva, you can include her in your stories so she's not forgotten."

"So she's not forgotten," Precious repeated. A smile touched her peach-tinted lips. "I like that. I like that very much."

Despite the confidence of her words, I could still see the shadows in her eyes. **Grief is like a ghost.** "All right," I said. "I'll get started today."

Colin leaned forward. "What was her surname?"

"I'll think of it. It's been so long." Precious pressed her hands against the edge of the table. "I'm feeling poorly. If you will excuse me, I'm going to go for a lie-down." Colin pulled out her chair and helped her stand. She gave me a wobbly smile. "I'll have Laura pack up the pimiento cheese sandwiches so you can have a picnic in Regent's Park. Queen Mary's Gardens are lovely this time of year. It would be a shame to let this beautiful day go to waste. And I'll let you know when I'm up for another chat. Maybe this evening or tomorrow morning. But you have all those lovely clothes to look at for inspiration. Choose the ones you find most interesting, and we'll start with those."

I stood, too, meeting Colin's gaze, but he just gave me a quick shake of his head as he escorted Precious inside. I picked up the cigarette case to put it back inside the purse, noticing as I did a label sewn into the satin interior. It was hard to read, but the stitches had been done in gold thread, and the sunlight picked out the letters.

HOUSE OF LUSHTAK, LONDON

I closed the clasp, hearing Precious's words echoing in my head. **Just because a person is lost doesn't mean they want to be found.**

My gaze drifted past the roofs of the terraces, toward the park, and I tried to imagine bombs dropping from the sky, fire and debris filling the air. I couldn't. The dual images were too opposed, like sand and sea.

I carried the purse inside, closing the balcony doors behind me, wondering why Eva, wherever she might be, might have chosen to remain lost.

CHAPTER 7

LONDON
MARCH 1939

Eva paused to catch her breath outside the door of Horvath's Café, her gaze moving from the painted letters on the glass window, advertising Builders Breakfasts, Horlicks, and Bovril, to her own reflection. She was late meeting Mr. Danek but eager to show off her new look and to get his approval for the smart outfit on which she'd spent almost an entire paycheck. It had been foolish, she knew. But it was an investment in her future. If she wanted to rise above her station in life, she needed to dress for her new role.

Closing the door, she paused to take off her coat, aware suddenly of the change in the air, of the conversation spoken in rapid Czech that was halted and absorbed into the clouds of cigarette smoke that hung over the small tables like secrets.

Then someone shouted an order in English from behind the Vitrolite bar, and things seemed normal again. Almost. Eva shook off the sense that she'd interrupted something, too excited about sharing the details of the last two weeks with Mr. Danek.

"Eva."

She turned at the sound of her name. With her shoulders back, she walked toward the table in the back, taking careful steps in her new suede pumps, feeling everyone's gaze on her. She'd felt people's attention on her walk to and from the bus stop and on the bus. Men and women alike watched her as if she were some prize to win. Or a dream to attain.

And she was both. She was Lady Blakeney in **The Scarlet Pimpernel**, an object of envy. A clever and beautiful woman admired by all, capable of holding the attention of an intelligent and handsome man of means.

Mr. Danek stood as she approached, his gaze one of open admiration. Too high on her cloud of elation to check herself at the subdued tone of the voices in the café, or at the crumpled newspaper on the table, Eva twirled, showing off her smart pale blue two-piece, beautifully cut so that it fit her to perfection, the solid color lightened by an enchanting red bow on the pocket and an identical one on her left breast. The hat, a fur felt Breton sailor, and the matching coat, thrown casually over her arm, made Eva feel as though she were dressed to meet the king and queen for tea at the palace. Her kid gloves and Precious's box purse were, as Precious had said, the exclamation point at the end of a sentence. As she twirled for the second time, Eva knew exactly what Precious had meant.

"You look stunning," Mr. Danek said, pulling out a chair for her. "But I hope you saved some money for food."

Eva laughed, but Mr. Danek didn't join her. It was then that she noticed the other man at the table, nearly hidden behind a cloud of cigarette smoke. Two dark eyes stared out at her from a round face, the skin ruddy with pockmarks. The man's tailored jacket fit his large shoulders and thick, muscled arms expertly. He hadn't stood as she'd approached, and he regarded her with only mild interest, as one might eye a bug crawling within range to crush.

"Eva, meet a countryman of mine, Jiri Zeman."

He looked at her, his gaze neither menacing nor friendly. He didn't offer his hand.

"Eva Harlow," Eva said, forcing a smile.

"It's a pleasure to meet you," Jiri said, his voice lighter than she'd expected. He moved his chair to make room. "Anton here has been telling me all about you."

Eva smiled again without commenting, focusing on arranging her skirts on her chair, not wanting to admit that Mr. Danek had never mentioned him to her at all.

Mr. Danek shouted something in Czech to the man behind the counter, and a steaming cup of coffee was set on the table in front of her. "I'd compliment you on your makeup," he said, "but there is something else that is making your face glow, I think."

"I'm in love," Eva said a little too loudly. She certainly hadn't planned on announcing her news in front of a stranger. But she didn't care. For the first time in her life, she understood what all the fuss was about in the movies she'd watched at the cinema.

Jiri said nothing, only continued to watch her, an odd smile playing on his face. Mr. Danek sat back in his chair and put his cigarette to his lips. He had beautiful hands, Eva thought. She'd first noticed them as he'd applied makeup to one of the models. They were the hands of a pianist or a painter. She'd said that to him once, and he'd looked at her with such sad eyes that she'd wished she hadn't said anything. It was only later, when they were packing up his makeup cases, that he'd told her he had trained as a pianist at Charles University in Prague but had had to leave his piano and his ambitions behind when his wife had died. Alone, he'd come to England. When she'd asked him why, he'd told her only that he'd left while he'd still had the chance to choose.

"Ah," Mr. Danek said. "That explains why your cheeks are flushed so prettily." His face darkened. "It is satisfying to know that love can still exist today when such horrible things are happening in the world."

Now Eva noticed the crumpled copy of the **Daily Mirror** on the table. She turned it around and read the bold black headline: HITLER ARRIVES IN PRAGUE. She looked back at Mr. Danek, wishing that she had paid attention to the BBC announcers for more than just to imitate their accents. It wasn't that she didn't care about world events; she did. It was just that it all seemed so far away and separate from the happiness she was feeling for the first time in her life. Eva pointed to a line in the lead paragraph. "It says here it was a bloodless invasion."

A short, dark man at a nearby table stood abruptly. "Bloodless?" He blew out a puff of air from his lips. With a heavy accent like Mr. Danek's, he said, "You mark my words: This is just the beginning." He pointed a stubby finger at Eva. "Your Chamberlain and his Munich Agreement, saying it meant 'peace in our time' to give the Sudetenland to Hitler." He shook his head in disgust. "All it did was feed a tyrant a little piece of my country, and that made him hungry for more. Now he's taken the rest of Czechoslovakia, and he's still hungry. What's next, hmm? Look what he's done to Austria, how the Jews have been thrown out of all professions, and their synagogues and homes burned. He means to take over all of Europe until there are no more Jews."

He leaned closer to Eva. She could smell coffee and cigarettes on his breath. "Hitler won't stop until he's moved into your Buckingham Palace. And **that** won't be bloodless. I tell you that."

The man threw money on his table and stalked out of the café, the door slamming shut behind him. Stunned by the odd noise next to her, Eva turned her head, realizing it was Jiri. He appeared to be laughing. Except it wasn't the sort of laugh she was used to, the sound of joy. This was a brittle, choking sound, as if he had just swallowed something bitter.

Leaning over to crush his cigarette in the ashtray, Jiri said, "There will always be some who are uneducated and ignorant. They will not see two sides of a story."

Eva found she couldn't look at him. Her eyes focused instead on the coffeepots—an eclectic collection of all sizes, shapes, and colors—displayed on a long shelf over the counter. The man who'd stormed out had seemed not ignorant but passionate about his beliefs and more knowledgeable about a situation she hadn't considered very important because it hadn't affected her. Her eyes stung with embarrassment, and she waited until her vision had cleared enough to read the stick-on-letter wall menus before turning back to Mr. Danek.

"Is it true? Is everything as dire as that man said?"

"Jiri and I were discussing just that thing. Weren't we?"

Jiri lit another cigarette, his movements blunt and decisive. "Is that what you call doing all the talking?" He blew out a mouthful of smoke. "Interrupting someone who is attempting to make a point does not get a point across, no?"

Mr. Danek gave Eva a wan smile. "The situation in our country has a lot of people concerned. Some see it as a good thing. Others see it as a foreign invasion. Jiri is rather set in his opinion. He hopes to sway me and others." He smiled, and Eva tried to pretend that she didn't notice how it lacked the brightness she'd grown used to. "I prefer to wait and see, to form my own opinion."

Jiri stood, slamming his chair against the table as he prepared to leave. "I prefer to speak with someone whose head is less like a brick." He gave Eva a slight bow. "Miss Harlow," he said, and walked away. He was surprisingly light on his feet, giving the impression of a dancing gorilla.

"Jiri used to be in charge of a large stable at an estate near Karlovy Vary in the Sudetenland owned by the uncle of a mutual friend. His specialty was breaking horses." Mr. Danek blew out a puff of smoke to punctuate his words.

"Did he leave Czechoslovakia for the same reasons you did?"

"Something like that. But enough talk of unpleasant things."

Trying to hide her relief, Eva reached into Precious's box purse for a cigarette, a Matinée brand. She purchased them only because an advert in the paper said that smart women smoked Matinée cigarettes.

Her fingers shook, and she was surprised to feel Mr. Danek's hand on her arm. Their eyes met, and he smiled.

"Don't feel embarrassed that you have other things on your mind, Eva. Your job is making the world a beautiful place. Beauty is always welcome, even in difficult times. Love and beauty—those are the things worth holding on to. They are what shine light in a dark world."

"Thank you for saying that." Eva frowned down at her cigarette case. She'd found it at a charity shop; it was engraved with someone else's initials, and she'd bargained down the price. Now one of the hinges had broken, so loose cigarettes spilled into her purse. She sighed and held the case up for Mr. Danek to see. "I'll have to wait for the next paycheck and get a new one."

"Or maybe someone will give you one as a gift. Like your young man. Tell me—who is he?"

Eva felt her cheeks heat at the mere thought of Graham. They'd gone to dinner twice, danced at the Café de Paris, and attended an outdoor concert in Regent's Park. They'd also attempted to go boating in the park but had discovered the lake was closed until the end of March. It had started to rain; by the time they'd found shelter on a bench beneath a large ash tree, they'd both been soaked. He'd kissed her then, his lips warm and soft, and it was everything Eva had always imagined it would be. He'd tasted of rain and heat and old winter and new spring and she'd wanted to melt into him and disappear in their new world beneath the sheltering leaves of the ash.

"He's lovely," Eva said, thinking not just about Graham's green eyes and broad shoulders, but the sound of his voice when he said her name, and his crooked smile, and the cleft in his chin. She loved the small scar on his left brow. He'd been eight and had fallen out of a tree, trying to save his sister's kitten. It was all of that. It was the way her chest burned when she was near him, how her skin ached when he looked at her. It was how her whole world now seemed full of light, her past only a dim shadow behind her.

She cleared her throat and said, "He's Mr. Graham St. John. He's been with the Diplomatic Service in Rangoon, Burma, for the past two years and has just returned to London. He works in Whitehall at the Home Office. I'm not sure what he does, exactly—something to do with fire services. He says he doesn't want to bore me with the mundane details. He's staying with his sister, Sophia, in their parents' town house in Berkeley Square until he can find rooms of his own. Sophia is getting married in July, and her parents are giving her and her fiancé, David, the house as a wedding gift."

The waiter placed another cup of coffee in front of Mr. Danek, who sat staring at the steam for a moment before looking up again. "You will let me do your makeup for your wedding, no?"

Eva took a sip from her coffee cup to hide her

face, not wanting to reveal the hope there. It was too soon to hope for anything. "If and when I do get married, Mr. Danek, I promise you that I wouldn't trust anyone else to do my makeup."

She looked at him with a sudden thought. "Sophia is having a dinner party next week and has invited me—we haven't yet formally met. Would you consider doing my makeup for that? I want to look my best."

"Absolutely," Mr. Danek said, leaning forward to stub out his cigarette in the ashtray. Sitting back again, he crossed his legs. "I must ask. Does this mean your Mr. St. John knows about Ethel Maltby? Are he and his lovely sister, Sophia, accepting of your past?"

Eva's fingers froze on her cup, gripping it so hard she put it down so it wouldn't break. "No," she said quietly. Looking up at Mr. Danek, she said with more force, "At least, not yet. I didn't want to ruin things. I think he feels the same way about me, but I wanted more time to be sure." She bit her lip. "I told Graham that I was the only child of a doctor and his wife from Devon. I said my parents were killed in an automobile accident, that I had no other family or means of support, so I came to London to make a respectable living as a model."

"And what did Graham say to that? Daughters of country doctors don't usually move in the same lofty circles as the St. Johns."

Eva sat taller and straightened her shoulders. "Graham said he loved my resourcefulness, and he admired my courage. He also said that since he believes me to be wonderful and worthy of spending time with, Sophia would, too. They're very close."

Mr. Danek's eyes were kind, softening the harshness of his words. "But you will tell him the truth, yes? Because lies are not a good foundation for any relationship. They will unravel everything built on top of them."

"I will tell him. I will. I just want more time so I can be sure of his feelings for me."

Mr. Danek's eyes narrowed. "You are a very clever girl, Eva. And very ambitious. Both are to be admired." He uncrossed his legs. "Just remember not to forget your good judgment."

She bristled. "I always have good judgment. I do. I couldn't have come all this way without it, could I?" With horror, she realized that her Yorkshire accent had slipped in. It happened sometimes when she was tired or agitated. She had to be more careful. Especially with Sophia's dinner party approaching.

Mr. Danek pulled out another cigarette for himself and lit it. "What else can you tell me about your Graham? Humor me, Eva. I feel as if it's my place to play the father."

Eva smiled, appreciating the new lightness in his tone. She picked up her coffee cup and took a sip, considering her response. "He has a great interest in architecture, and his mother would like him to be an architect instead of in government. She thinks it's more seemly."

Mr. Danek blew out smoke rings, and Eva watched them rise to the ceiling before vanishing. She rushed on, eager to steer the conversation. "Graham's promised to take me to the Eton and Harrow match at Lord's Cricket Ground in July. He attended Eton and is quite proud that Eton has been the victor for thirty-one years. It should be a smashing time."

"And you are a fan of cricket?" This time Mr. Danek's smile was genuine.

"I don't know the first thing, but Freya has promised to teach me enough so that I don't seem ignorant. She has three brothers, and they all play. She's been to more matches than she cares to recall."

"And Freya, she's doing this for free?"

Eva shook her head. "No. In return I'm letting her borrow my new cape with the fox fur collar for two nights of her choosing. I thought that was a fair deal."

Mr. Danek appeared thoughtful, pulling on his cigarette while regarding her with slightly narrowed eyes. It made Eva nervous, as if she'd given the incorrect answer in an exam.

"Was that your idea or hers, to offer payment?"

"Mine, of course," Eva said proudly. "Nobody should get something for free. It's just not the way it's done."

"So you always expect payment for kindness?" He almost appeared to be laughing at her.

Eva found herself coloring. "I've offered to pay for the makeup. . . ."

Mr. Danek waved his hand in the air. "I would not accept. It is a gift, given freely. That is how it should be between friends, no?"

"Yes, of course."

"So may I give you free advice, as a friend?"

Eva, painfully aware that she hadn't fooled Mr. Danek at all, considered standing up and leaving the café but instead remained where she was and nodded.

"There is an old saying in my country. **Čeho nelze předělati, darmo na to žehrati.** Loosely translated, it means, take the world as you find it."

Eva frowned, not understanding. She was always much better with black and white, with numbers and exact prices for goods exchanged. Proverbs were like the fairy tales her mother had told her as a child, stories about make-believe people in pretend worlds that had nothing to do with putting food in her stomach.

Mr. Danek took one of her hands in his. "It means that you cannot control everything, Eva. Let things happen as they are meant to happen, or you will go mad."

Her anger boiled to the surface, and she spoke before she could think better of it. "Like your country? Why fight Hitler if he's going to win anyway?"

Mr. Danek kept smiling. "Maybe it is more about choosing what is most important to us. And choosing the time to fight for what we believe to be right. You, Eva, are too young and beautiful to be doing anything but enjoying life right now." His face darkened. "Life is short and unpredictable. Enjoy it while you can."

She looked down at her hands. "I love Graham. I don't want anything to change."

"Things always change, Eva. You cannot control change. You can only be prepared for it."

She wasn't sure what he meant but was eager to leave before his words intruded into her conscience too deeply. "I must go. Good-bye, Mr. Danek. We'll talk again soon." She stood and began to walk quickly toward the door.

Mr. Danek called after her, "I have another lipstick for you. Brand-new, from Max Factor, only available in Hollywood. I hear it is a favorite of Carole Lombard."

Eva wanted to leave, to show him that she didn't care, that she couldn't be tempted by a lipstick. But he'd taken off the lid to show her the deep cherry red shade, the perfect color for the gown she was planning to wear to Sophia's dinner party. Against her will, she walked back, her hand reaching to accept the lipstick before she could tell it to stop.

"It's beautiful," she said. "Thank you." She turned toward the door again but paused. "Mr. Danek, it's not my way to let the world unfold as it wants. If it were, I'd be doing laundry in Yorkshire with my mother."

"Very admirable. That sort of courage will steer you well. And your Mr. St. John would agree, yes? If he knew, of course."

Eva wanted to be angry with him for judging her. But his eyes held such despair and sadness that she held back. Her mother's eyes had been the same, seeming to darken every year, until Eva was sure if she didn't leave, she'd drown in their reflected misery.

"Good-bye, Mr. Danek. Thank you again for the lipstick," she said instead, and left the café. She walked down the sidewalk, the swish of her new skirt and the tapping of her suede shoes buoying her mood again until she'd almost forgotten the sadness in Mr. Danek's eyes and everything that he had told her. Almost.

CHAPTER 8

LONDON
MAY 2019

Once again, I found myself flying down the highway with Arabella in the red BMW, this time headed toward Colin's parents' home in Guildford, Surrey. My phone buzzed, and I didn't need to look at it to know it was Cassie calling me again for my answer about coming home for Christmas and Knoxie's wedding. If there was one thing I knew about my aunt, it was that she was more persistent than a termite in an old barn.

The day was warm and sunny—or warm and sunny for England in the spring—and Arabella had the top down. As we passed yet another car on the motorway, I recognized familiar looks of shock as the passengers stared in our direction.

"There are speed limits in the UK, right?" I asked, shouting over the wind.

Arabella actually appeared to be thinking. "I believe so." Her phone, resting in the cupholder, rang. "Could you please answer that and tell whoever it is to call my assistant, Mia? She's been instructed to hold all of my calls today while I'm working away from the office. Unless that **is** Mia."

I sent her a sidelong glance as I looked at the screen. We were on a mission to find Precious's lost friend, Eva, and discover anything else we could about Precious's past. Arabella was seeing her idea for the article growing into something much larger than either of us had originally imagined, from what was an article simply about fashion before and during the war years into a personal look at the lives, loves, and friendships of the people who'd experienced it all firsthand. This was why we were headed to Surrey and why she could consider this drive "working away from the office."

"It's someone named Wil. There's no picture."

Her cheeks pinkened. "Oh. Well, then. Could you please respond with a message telling him that I'll ring him back later?"

"Sure," I said, tapping at the screen. I didn't ask her who Wil was. It wasn't that I wasn't interested—I was. It was just that I didn't like to reciprocate with information about myself. Besides, I knew she'd tell me eventually.

"What's in the extra bag?" Arabella asked, indicating the backseat.

"Yesterday's picnic lunch. Laura packed it up for Colin and me, but Colin had to go back to the office. So I brought it for us. You like pimiento cheese, right?"

She made a face, which I silently cheered; that meant more for me. "Yes, well, I don't think we'll need it. It's only a little over an hour's drive, and Aunt Penelope is planning on lunch for us." She glanced over at me. "I'm still not sure why Colin didn't come. He mentioned that he's interested in helping with the research and seemed quite excited by it."

I didn't say anything, just kept my gaze focused on the rapidly disappearing asphalt in front of us. I heard her groan over the rushing wind. "Does he not know?"

I looked away so she couldn't see my guilty expression. "When I suggested asking his mother for help finding Eva, Colin said it was a good idea but probably would have to wait until the weekend because of work. I didn't want to wait, so I called you."

Which was all completely true. I didn't bother mentioning that I didn't want to spend any more time with Colin than I had to. There was something unresolved between us, an obscuring fog that kept threatening to clear. I needed it there, because there had always been something about Colin Eliot that strained to shift my resolve regarding relationships.

"So I'm the bad guy. Very clever of you, Maddie. If not Machiavellian."

"I'm trying to do my job and make an old lady very happy by finding her long-lost friend. How is that Machiavellian?"

Arabella grimaced. "You and I both know this has more to do with you and those feelings you won't talk about. Just know that Colin won't like it when he finds out you've gone behind his back."

"Me?" I asked innocently. "You were the one who called his mother."

She glared at me before returning her focus to the road.

Eager to change the topic, I said, "I've never been to his parents' country house. Is it old?"

"A bit. Originally, there was a medieval manor on the property, but a St. John ancestor built the current house sometime in the fifteen hundreds. It's been in the family ever since."

"Wow. And I thought my grandfather's house was old. But that was built in the middle of the eighteen hundreds."

"Still quite old by American standards," Arabella said graciously. "But I bet Hovenden Park has had more distinguished guests."

"Hovenden Park? Colin's house has a name?"

"Oh, yes. And a dairy farm. Actually, the house

is called Hovenden Hall, but the entire estate is Hovenden Park. We can go pet some of the cows if we have time. You've heard of Hovenden Ice Cream, right?"

She pulled off the motorway, giving me a few moments to think. "How have I never heard any of this before?"

"You never asked, did you? And you're not very forthright about yourself, either. If it weren't for your accent and my amazing powers of deduction, we wouldn't even know you were from America. As for Colin, well, he has his reasons, too. It's a good thing you both have me, or you'd never meet anyone."

I was silent as she maneuvered the car down a narrow lane with thick hedgerows that threatened to remove her side mirrors. "You mentioned distinguished guests?"

"Well, Queen Elizabeth the First came once, and her successor, King James the First, visited twice, I believe."

"You win," I said. "General Sherman and his troops stomped past my grandfather's house during his march to the sea during the Civil War, but he didn't stay there. Not that I know of, anyway. And he didn't torch the house, which was nice. Legend has it that my great-whatever-grandmother met him with a broom on the front porch, and he was so charmed by her gumption and beauty that he ordered no harm to come to the house or the people inside."

"Well, that's something, then, isn't it?" Arabella smiled brightly.

"Yes, I suppose so," I said, the thought of home tugging at my heart just as my phone began buzzing again.

"Aren't you going to get that?" Arabella asked.

I silenced the call and slid the phone into my purse. "Not right now. I'll call her back later."

"Her?"

"My aunt Cassie."

"Your aunt Cassie? So you have an aunt."

"My mother's sister. I'm sure I've mentioned her. She lives in my grandfather's house now." I leaned forward, looking out the windshield. "How much farther? I'm starving."

"No, actually, I don't believe you've mentioned her. It must be urgent if she keeps calling. We're almost there, but I can slow down so you have time to call her back."

I sighed. "It's not urgent. She just wants to know if I'm coming home for Christmas. My sister is getting married."

"Sounds like a simple answer to me," Arabella said, stopping the car in front of a gate with a cattle grate beneath it.

"I'll get it," I said, eager to end the conversation. Arabella was too good at dissecting the inner psyche. And I'd had enough professional therapy to know that what was wrong with me couldn't be fixed. I stepped out of the car, smelling the familiar scent of sun-soaked grass and another smell I recognized as cow related. Not entirely unpleasant but definitely earthier than I was used to. I unlatched the gate and returned to the car, avoiding Arabella's eyes, sure she was still waiting for me to explain why I didn't want to go home.

Neither of us spoke as she continued along the dirt-and-gravel drive, our pace slowed by the threat of loose rocks dinging the BMW's red paint. Then Arabella navigated the little car around a bend, and the house came into view, and for one of the rare times in my life, I found myself speechless. It wasn't a house really but more like an abbey, as in Downton, constructed of white stone with multiple wings on both sides of the main entrance, six chimneys, and too many steeply pitched roof gables to count. There were more tiny-paned windows than stone, and I found myself wondering what the heating bill must be like in the winter.

Arabella pulled into the wide circular drive and parked in front of the main door, which was set beneath a massive broken pediment and a wavy fan window. Fluted stone columns set flush against the house framed the door and did nothing to take away the warmth offered by the pots overflowing with brilliantly colored flowers on either side. Two worn marble steps led the way up, and before I could suggest we enter through the back, the door was opened and a tall, slender woman in her late sixties stepped out. She wore riding pants and a white button-down blouse, and her face creased with a wide, welcoming smile. I recalled that Colin's parents were older, although this woman had a youthfulness about her that belied her age. Her riding pants were splashed with mud above the knees, but the riding boots had been replaced with clogs.

"Fantastic timing! I've just taken the quiche out of the AGA and was deciding on whether or not it was warm enough to sit outside in the back garden." She and Arabella gave each other a kiss on each cheek before she turned to me.

"Aunt Penelope, this is Maddie Warner, a school friend of mine and Colin's from our Oxford days."

I wanted to correct her, to explain that I wasn't really a friend of Colin's, but before I could speak, she grasped both of my hands in hers and smiled at me warmly. "You're the one who took all those beautiful portraits of Arabella and Colin at university, aren't you? You have a real gift."

I'd forgotten those initial forays into portraiture, most likely because I hadn't kept any of them. "Thank you," I said, trying to keep the surprise out of my voice. "It's a pleasure to meet you, Mrs. Eliot."

"Oh, please, call me Penelope. May I call you Madison? I feel as if I know you, although we've never actually met, have we?"

"No, I don't believe we have. And do call me Maddie. All my friends do."

A small "v" appeared between her brows. "Just not Colin?" Without waiting for a response, she ushered us inside to what could have been a cathedral, but was actually an incredibly grand and bright entrance hall. "Please excuse my attire—Frieda, my mare, slipped a shoe on our ride this morning, so I walked her back. Sadly, that didn't leave me enough time to change. I hope my famous quiche will make up for it." She laughed a deep, chuckling laugh that seemed completely alien to anyone who claimed to be Colin's mother.

Her laugh and smile were infectious, and I couldn't help but smile back. Penelope had the pretty, fresh-scrubbed face of a woman who loved being outdoors in a climate that allowed exposure without visible sun damage. Only a thin map of wrinkles lined her forehead and the corners of her eyes. I imagined the latter was because she smiled a lot. She wore only mascara, which made her blue eyes stand out, and her cheeks were naturally rosy. Aunt Lucinda would have had a field day plying her with cosmetics, but I had to admit that Colin's mother fit in so well as the lady of the country manor that I wouldn't have changed a thing.

"Let's go out to the back garden, shall we?" Penelope said, slipping her arm through Arabella's. "I'm very intrigued by your quest to find Precious's friend, but first we must eat. I am absolutely famished."

They began walking past the giant staircase, but I stopped, too awestruck to do anything but stare.

Light poured in from a wide bay window that ran the entire height of the tall wall. An ancient grandfather clock stood near the heavy wood balustrade of the wide staircase; it would have been dwarfed by the space but for the dark carved paneling that encircled the large room and climbed up the walls, lending the space an almost cozy appeal. An enormous brass chandelier hung down from the coffered ceiling, illuminating the oil paintings of people in old-fashioned clothing hung above the paneling.

The staircase in my grandfather's house had a lot of old paintings of long-dead Madisons who'd lived there way before I was born. I'd always thought it was strange having dead people watching me, and I used to run up and down the stairs to escape their scary gazes. I tried to imagine a younger Colin racing up these stairs for the same reason, and couldn't. He didn't seem the type to give in to childish fantasies.

I stepped closer to one of the largest paintings: a family group consisting of a mother, a father, three children, and a large dog posed in the exact same room I stood in, on the very same carpet and in the identical spot. Footsteps approached behind me.

"It's like gazing in a mirror and looking back in time, isn't it?" Penelope said, her words reflecting my thoughts.

"Exactly. How old is that painting?"

"Mid-seventeen hundreds, I believe. But the

painted canvas panels on the other side of the room are much older. They are said to have come from King Henry's banqueting tent."

"King Henry?" I asked, spinning around to examine the colorful panels depicting hunting scenes that covered most of the wall.

"The Eighth. The one with six wives and a proclivity for removing their heads."

The weight of what I was looking at hit me, and I had to remember to close my mouth as I stared. All this hung in Colin's boyhood home.

"Well, butter my butt and call me a biscuit," I said.

A choking sound made me turn to see Arabella stifling a giggle. Penelope wore a look of surprise. I was about to apologize for using the word "butt" in polite company, but then Penelope belted out one of her laughs, and I knew I'd been forgiven.

Still chuckling, she looped her arm through mine and led us through a vaulted doorway. "Come on, then—let's eat. And then we can talk about our dear Precious and her friend. It's absolutely fascinating that you're related, even distantly. It's a very small world, isn't it?"

A young woman, introduced as Anna and dressed in jeans and sneakers, brought out the food and placed it on an iron table set in the shade of the house. A riot of flowers filled every container on the back terrace, and in the near distance, I saw a more formal garden with precisely trimmed hedges and more flowers.

The table had been set with bone china, probably English and also covered with flowers, and the entire lunch of delicious quiche and salad looked like something from one of Lucinda's celebrity gossip magazines. Or maybe this would have been **Martha Stewart Living**. As we sat eating a dessert of fresh strawberries and clotted cream, I wondered how Colin had ever managed to leave home.

Anna returned with a teapot, and I resigned myself to yet another cup of hot tea. Although I still missed my sweet tea, I had to admit that I was getting used to the English version, along with a generous dollop of milk and sugar to make it drinkable.

As we sipped, Penelope excused herself. She returned with two large canvas Sainsbury's shopping bags and set them on the ground by my chair. "All of this belonged to my mother-in-law, Sophia. It is through her that we know Precious, and how Precious became Nana to Colin. Sadly, my mother passed when I was a newlywed, but dear Precious filled in as second grandmother very nicely. Sophia died five years ago, so Precious is our last connection to that generation."

She pointed to one of the bags. "These are most of Sophia's photo albums, letters, and trinket boxes that I found in her room after she died. I don't think she'd mind you rummaging through them, as long as they are returned eventually. If Colin ever has any children, they might like to have them. And I'm quite sure if this Eva person was a good friend of Precious's, then my mother-in-law would have known her, too. Something in these bags might be your best chance of finding her."

"This is wonderful—thank you," I said. "I'm curious, though. How did your mother-in-law know Precious?"

"They met because of fashion, of all things. Before the war. Precious was a model, and my mother-in-law was a customer who became friendly with a few of the models who showed the clothes. Sophia was one of those rare individuals who got on with everyone, regardless of class or nationality. She was certainly always aware of her status and could sometimes be quite the snob, but that was because of the world in which she'd been raised, I think. I always knew her to be a kind and giving woman."

Penelope picked up her teacup and sipped from it thoughtfully. "Sophia was quite the grand hostess, even during the war. Her bomb shelter was always well stocked with gin and champagne—don't ask me how she managed that with the shortages and rationing. The party could simply move from her drawing room to the shelter until the shelling stopped. She held grand weeklong parties here at Hovenden Park for entire flying squadrons. I think there are a few newspaper clippings in there," she said, indicating one of the bags.

Anna arrived to clear the table, and we stood to leave. As we walked through the house again, I tried to focus on what Penelope was saying and stop gawking at the architectural elements and artwork we passed.

"Arabella mentioned you're from Atlanta," Penelope said. "Do you get home often?"

"I'm actually from Walton—about an hour away from Atlanta, but no one's ever heard of it, so Atlanta works." I smiled. "And I don't get home often. My job keeps me pretty busy."

"But it's nice to have a hometown to go back to, I'm sure. Atlanta is lovely."

I looked at her with surprise. "You've been there?"

Penelope shared a quick look with Arabella. "Yes. I spent quite a bit of time in Atlanta. But that was years ago." She smiled tightly, making it clear that she wasn't going to say any more on the subject.

We had reached the front door. "It was a pleasure to finally meet you, Maddie. I've heard so much about you over the years. It's nice to put a face to all the stories." She leaned in conspiratorially. "I particularly loved the one about the goat herd in the dining hall. Quite ingenious, but don't tell anyone I said so." She winked. "And I owe you a belated thanks, too, for getting Colin to break out of his shell a bit back at university. I'm afraid that's our fault—we are prone to hovering. So thank you."

I wanted to tell her that Colin had enjoyed being in his shell, that he didn't seem to appreciate my "childish pranks," as he called them. Instead I said, "I think Arabella has been embellishing some stories."

"Arabella?" she said, shaking her head. "It was Colin who shared your exploits. His father and I enjoyed the laughs, as they made us feel a part of his life at university. Although I'm quite sure we weren't privy to **all** of them, thank goodness."

She laughed again, and despite my confusion, I found myself smiling. "Thank you, Penelope. For lunch and for these." I held up one of the bags. "Even if we don't find Eva in any of it, there might be photographs and letters I can use for the article and exhibit."

"Do keep me posted. I love a bit of mystery. I remember Sophia loved to share her stories of life during the war. But not Precious. What little I know, I gleaned from Sophia—and she never told her stories in Precious's hearing, or Precious would ask her to stop. But I know Precious had quite the glamorous life as a model in London before the war and then again in Paris afterward."

"She's considered to be one of the first 'supermodels,'" Arabella interjected, "before people knew what that was. She was in demand and traveled in social circles that were quite out of her league when she started modeling in the thirties. It's amazing how times have changed, isn't it?"

"It certainly is," Penelope said. "Precious lived in Paris—at the Ritz, just like Coco Chanel—until the seventies, when she returned to London."

"Arabella mentioned something about Precious being a hero in the French Resistance," I said. "Did Sophia ever mention anything about that?"

Penelope shook her head. "Very little, I'm afraid. Sophia remained in England for the duration of the war. I do believe there might be a few letters from Precious in those bags—not many, of course, since it was wartime. But hopefully something will prove useful."

She pulled open the heavy front door with both hands, and a memory from my childhood, sticky as a cobweb, plucked at me. It was of my own mother, laughing as she tugged on the stubborn front door of the house she'd grown up in, and once again I was reminded of home and the history of a family contained inside an old house.

Penelope's voice drew me back into the present. "Thank you so much for coming—both of you. Please come back soon—and bring Colin. Maybe when my husband is home. James has a brilliant sense of humor that I think you might appreciate, Maddie."

"I'd enjoy that. Thanks again."

We said our good-byes, and Arabella and I climbed back into her BMW, putting the top up this time, as raindrops had begun to fall. We rode in silence while I mulled over our conversation with Penelope.

Finally, I turned to Arabella. "How did Penelope know about those pictures I took back at Oxford?

That was nearly eight years ago. Did you give her the ones I took of you and Colin?"

"To be honest, I'd forgotten all about them. Colin must have mentioned them. Maybe he showed her that gorgeous one you snuck of him on the Bridge of Sighs."

I was silent for a moment, thinking. I'd given away all my portraits to the subjects, although I was sure I had the negatives stored somewhere, most likely in my bedroom dresser back in Walton. "I can't imagine why. He never seemed very interested in my photographs. Or anything else that had anything to do with me."

"I remember him being very interested in you, and I remember the interest was reciprocated. But after one date—despite you telling me that you had a wonderful time—you and Colin never went out again. After that date, I recall you being very committed to going out with everyone except Colin. That's a whole conversation you and I haven't had, isn't it?"

When I didn't answer, Arabella sighed and returned her focus to driving. My phone buzzed again, and Aunt Cassie's face appeared on the screen. I canceled the call, noticing that she'd already called eight times.

"You should answer that, Mads. And you should tell her that you'll be there for your sister's wedding. It's the right thing to do."

The phone buzzed again, but I didn't move to

answer it. Arabella continued. "I know you love your family. I just wish you'd share with me why you keep them at arm's length." She exhaled loudly. "You do the same to me. It makes it very difficult to get to know you. It's very un-American of you, you know. Most Americans will tell a stranger their life story within fifteen minutes of sitting next to them on the tube."

She smiled to take the sting out of her words. "I've known you for a long time, Maddie, and it's taken me nearly this long just to get the names of your siblings. I'm the one who always calls, who asks all the questions. I'd have given up on you a long time ago, except that I think you need me in your life. And because I rather like you. You're quite funny and personable when you're not being evasive and remote."

It was difficult to argue with someone who was so completely right. And because I wasn't sure I could explain any of it even to myself, I kept silent, feeling the buzz of my phone in my hand as it rang again. This time I slid my thumb across the screen and answered it.

Turning my face away from Arabella, I said quietly into the phone, "I can't really talk now. Can I call you later? And if this is about the wedding, I haven't really thought about it. . . ."

"This isn't about the wedding, Maddie, although we're waiting for that answer, too. I'm calling about those tests results. Dr. Grey didn't say anything, but

I know enough to be concerned if she's requested you make an appointment to discuss them. I'd sleep a whole heck of a lot better knowing you'd made an appointment already. Sam told me not to worry, but you're like a daughter to me. It's like telling a bullfrog not to croak."

"I will, Aunt Cassie—eventually. I'm just in the middle of something, and I'll think about it when I get back to the States."

"But you shouldn't wait, sweetheart. . . ."

"I've got to go," I said, cutting her off. "I'll call you tomorrow." I pressed the red "disconnect" button and ended the call, knowing as I did so that my aunt wouldn't give up that easily.

After a moment of silence, Arabella said, "I know I'm a bit chatty, but I'm a good listener, too. If there's anything you need to talk about, I'm here. I'm a good secret keeper, as well. Just ask Colin."

I looked at her in surprise. "Colin has secrets?"

She gave me a sideways glance. "Everyone has secrets, Maddie."

I turned away and watched the road flash by, my eyes focusing on the rivulets of water on my window. My thoughts drifted back to the elusive Eva's cigarette case found inside Precious's purse, and the Latin engraving. **Betray before you are betrayed.**

"What do you think that Latin phrase on the cigarette case is all about?" I asked.

"I've been wondering the same thing. There are so many ways a person can be betrayed, aren't there?

Betrayals of the heart, or within families, or by employers or employees. Political betrayals. It's a wonder we can sleep at night with all those possibilities."

I turned back to the window, thinking of another kind of betrayal, one Arabella hadn't mentioned. The kind a person was born with, the kind that sat like a ticking time bomb in the middle of their life, waiting to explode.

"It's a wonder," I said quietly before flipping on the radio to drown out my thoughts and the buzzing of my phone, which wouldn't stop no matter how hard I wished that it would.

CHAPTER 9

LONDON
MARCH 1939

Eva sat at the dressing table in the models' room at Lushtak's with her back to the mirror and her eyes closed. Gently, Mr. Danek applied a shimmery eye color to her lids from a small jar. When she felt him lean back, she opened her eyes and smiled. "Well?"

"Perfection. You hardly need anything—your skin is like porcelain. Just a little rouge, hmm?"

She nodded as he reached for another small jar. Mrs. Williams bustled in, holding a peach satin gown draped carefully over her arm. She studied Eva with pursed lips. "I think more mascara, Mr. Danek. She has such lovely eyes." Her mouth broadened into a smile. "Your gown is pressed, and I found a fur stole from last year's show that you can borrow. Just promise me you won't damage any of it." She closed her eyes and pressed a hand to her chest. "Promise me that. The show is next week, and I won't have any time to resew seams or clean any stains."

"I promise you, I will be more than careful."

Mr. Danek swiped a small brush against the black mascara compact. Looking up so he could apply it to her upper lashes, Eva said, "And I can't thank you both enough. I wish you'd allow me to pay you for your time."

"Nonsense," Mrs. Williams said with a wave. "I'm here into the wee hours anyway, sewing for the show. This was a nice diversion. And I do appreciate the steak and kidney pie for my supper. That was very kind of you."

"Likewise," said Mr. Danek with a small smile.

Eva smiled back but avoided his gaze. She'd confessed to him that she didn't want Graham to see where she lived, to smell the cooking grease and other odors from her neighbors as he climbed the steps to her flat. Soon she and Precious would find a more acceptable flat with the kind of address she wasn't embarrassed about giving to taxi drivers. Or to Graham.

When Mr. Danek was finished, Eva sat back. "May I look now?"

At his nod, Eva spun around on the stool and stared at the woman in the glass. It was like staring into the future, like seeing the woman she'd always wanted to become, a woman of elegance and beauty. Of substance. A lady. She leaned forward, trying to find the laundress's daughter, surprised by the thread of sadness that wrapped around her joy and squeezed. For one bright and fleeting moment, she found herself wishing that her mother was there to see her. To share this happiness.

"Your hair is lovely," the seamstress said from behind her.

"Thank you, Mrs. Williams. I did it myself." Eva reached up to touch the soft curls that framed her face and swept up at the back of her head in a tight chignon. She'd learned the style by poring over fashion magazines and studying the hairstyles of the actresses in the movies. She'd been shooed out of more than one newsstand for reading the magazines instead of purchasing them, but she'd needed the money for the new strappy gold high-heeled sandals she'd seen at Selfridges and set her heart on.

"Well, it looks like you went to one of those fancy salons, to be sure. Now," the older woman said, her wide face splitting with a smile, "are you ready for the gown? I've altered it, so it should fit you like a glove."

Eva let the peach-colored satin be slipped over her head, the fabric soft and liquid. "It's . . ." She paused, unable to voice what it was like to have a dream come true. She had the sudden memory of her mother bent over a washboard, her once-beautiful hair dull and lifeless. Eva had been telling her about the movie she'd just seen, **Libeled Lady** with Myrna Loy, about a beautiful heiress who wore beautiful clothes. Her mother had stopped her mid-sentence. "You'll never be more than what you are. You'd best remember that."

And Eva had. If only to prove her mother wrong.

"It's perfect," Mr. Danek said, finishing Eva's sentence.

Eva nodded. "Do you think I need a paste necklace or earrings? Something to brighten the front of the dress?"

Mr. Danek shook his head. "No. Showy jewelry is not in style right now, my dear. Believe me, this dress, your face, and your figure are all you will need. People will assume you are a princess. With all these exiled governments now in London, if only you could speak with a foreign accent, everyone would be easily fooled."

Eva laughed. "Oh, but I can. I am quite the expert at accents, Mr. Danek." She imitated his own with such precision that he threw his head back and laughed.

"Yes, my dear. You are quite good. You must be a very good listener."

Eva nodded earnestly. "Oh, yes. I'm always listening—on the bus and at the theater, and to the other girls at Madame Lushtak's. Odette says my French accent is better than hers!"

Mr. Danek laughed again and began packing up his makeup. "If you will excuse me, I will place you in the capable hands of Mrs. Williams. I have a bottle of champagne chilling for when your gentleman arrives. A small glass will help calm your nerves."

Eva wanted to say that she wasn't nervous to meet Graham's sister formally or pretend that she was comfortable mixing in high society, and that she was confident no one would suspect her true origins. But that would have been a lie. She hadn't been able to eat a thing all day, and even the thought of champagne made her queasy. "Thank you, Mr. Danek."

He bowed his head briefly in acknowledgment, then left.

"I think I'm ready," Eva said, her voice surprisingly steady.

"Except for this." Mrs. Williams handed her the fur stole.

"And my purse," Eva added, picking up Precious's box bag.

Mrs. Williams followed her to the door. "I'll be here early tomorrow before Madame Lushtak. Please, don't be late returning your dress and stole."

"Don't worry—I'll be here."

Very carefully, Eva walked down the hallway to the showroom door and opened it. Only a few lights were on, and it appeared she was alone. She tamped down her disappointment as she closed the door behind her; then she stepped into the room.

"'She walks in beauty, like the night of cloudless climes and starry skies.'"

Eva turned toward the sound of Graham's voice,

her thrill at his presence dimmed by the thought that she should know the poem he'd just quoted. A doctor's educated daughter from Devon would. And he'd paused, as if expecting her to finish the line.

"Graham," she said instead. She walked quickly toward him, and kissed him deeply.

"Darling," he said against her lips. "What a lovely greeting."

"I've missed you." Eva leaned in to kiss him again. "It's been a whole day."

His hands slid to her back, his fingers warm against her bare skin. He sucked in his breath, then pulled away slightly. "Perhaps a glass of champagne? Otherwise I have doubts we will make it to the party, and Sophia will be most disappointed."

"What have you told her about me?" Eva asked.

He seemed surprised by her question. "Why, the truth, of course."

"The truth?" she asked, her mouth gone suddenly dry.

"Yes, darling. You have nothing to be ashamed of. She remembers you, by the way. From the day you modeled clothes for her and our mother. She thought you very lovely. And she also finds it admirable that you have made a life for yourself after such tragedy. Being a clotheshorse for a reputable fashion house is quite respectable." He took her hands in his. "Our mother isn't as forward-thinking, but she'll come around, I'm sure. I can be quite persuasive."

He grinned, and Eva's own smile wobbled as she attempted to grin back. She almost told him the real truth then. But she didn't want to ruin the moment. And she knew with certainty that if Mrs. St. John would find a doctor's daughter forced to model of objectionable character, then her reaction to the truth would be unimaginable.

Graham reached for the opened bottle on the small table and poured champagne into the two waiting glasses. He handed one to Eva, his eyes never leaving hers.

"You look absolutely stunning, Eva. I daresay the other ladies could be wearing sackcloth tonight, and I don't think any of the gentlemen would notice."

She took a sip from her glass and smiled. "There's only one gentleman whose notice I care about. And he's looking quite divine himself." She allowed her gaze to slowly take in Graham's bespoke black dinner jacket, which fit his lean frame and accented his broad shoulders; the black bow tie and white piqué shirt with a turned-down collar highlighted his suntan. "And he's looking quite exotic, too—like Errol Flynn in **Captain Blood**."

He leaned down and kissed her, his lips tasting like champagne and lingering on hers while he breathed in deeply. "What is that perfume you're wearing? It's quite intoxicating."

"Vol de Nuit." Her husky voice sounded as if it belonged to someone else. When she'd been in Selfridges to buy the shoes, she'd passed the counter where a salesgirl was offering a sample dab. Eva knew she had to have it but couldn't afford it. Which was why she'd stopped by Selfridges on her way to Lushtak's tonight to tap on the perfume from the sample bottle.

"It means 'Night Flight,'" she said, having already asked Odette for the translation and practiced the pronunciation—which Odette said was flawless. "From a book written by Antoine de Saint-Exupéry, about a man's lust for adventure and success in adversity." The salesgirl had told her that much before it became clear that Eva wasn't a paying customer, at which point she had abruptly left to help a mink-clad woman.

Graham kissed Eva behind the ear where she'd put a dollop of the perfume, and her pulse jumped under her skin. "So you have a lust for adventure and a desire for success in adversity?"

She smiled against his lips, which had returned to her mouth. "Of course."

"Then I'd say we were well matched." He grinned, but his eyes were serious as he stepped back. "We should be going. Sophia wanted us there before the other guests so she can have time to get to know you."

He took her empty glass from her fingers and put it next to his on the table before adjusting the fur stole around her shoulders. "Ah," he said as she picked up her bag and slid it onto her arm. "We owe a lot to that purse, don't we? If you hadn't dropped it in front of the chemist, we might never have met."

"It was fate, wasn't it? Like Romeo and Juliet," Eva said proudly, happy to show off her newfound knowledge. At Mr. Danek's suggestion, she'd begun frequenting the library and checking out books she thought would improve her mind. She'd even read **Pygmalion**.

"I should hope not. I'd like to think we aren't fated for such a tragic ending." He winked at her to take the severity from his words, put on his hat and overcoat, then led her outside to the front of the building, where a long dark car awaited them.

A uniformed driver held open the back door. Graham must have felt Eva's hesitation, because he placed his hand on hers where it rested in the crook of his arm. "Sadly, it isn't mine—I'm a mere second son, and a humble public servant at that. The car is borrowed from my future brother-in-law, David Eliot. He has much deeper pockets than I do. I suppose the only thing we have to worry about is whether or not it will turn into a pumpkin at midnight."

She laughed, and he kissed her again, then held her hand as he helped her into the backseat. He broke contact only to move to the other side of the car to get in, then kept his hand solidly over hers as they made their way down Saint George Street.

The car slowed as they turned into Berkeley Square, with its flat-fronted brick buildings, each with four or five floors with regularly spaced sash windows and brass fittings on the front doors. The elegant town houses surrounding the private garden in the center of the square lent the whole neighborhood the illusion of being a perfect oasis despite how close it was to the bustle of the shopping district.

The driver stopped at the curb in front of an imposing entrance beneath an iron canopy with a hanging carriage light. A single stone step led up to a large black door. Beneath an elaborate fan window with wavy glass, a brass lion's-head knocker held court in the middle of the door, its mouth open in midgrowl. For a brief moment, Eva felt as if it were telling her that she should go to the rear, where she belonged.

The driver stepped out and opened Eva's door. Graham turned to her and asked softly, "Are you ready?" He squeezed her hand, and she loved him for that, for knowing without asking that she was nervous.

"Graham," she said, suddenly afraid, wanting to turn back. But the look he gave her was open and honest, his eyes full of light and longing.

"Yes?" he prompted.

"I . . ." She stopped. "I'm glad you're with me tonight. I feel at a loss when you're not."

His eyes widened. "Good," he said, a grin forming. And then he kissed her slowly, his lips lingering on hers.

The front door of the town house opened.

Anything else he'd been about to say was lost as he climbed from the car and escorted Eva to the door, where a butler waited.

Eva had a brief flash of a lofty entrance hall with a black-and-white marble-tiled floor and elaborate moldings, the bottom step of a grand staircase visible from the arched opening on the opposite end of the foyer. A handsome young couple waited in front of a tall gilded mirror. Eva recognized Sophia from the showing at Lushtak's, noticing that she wore one of the frocks Eva had shown her. The pale blue silk was more conservatively cut than Eva's gown, but flattered Sophia's fuller figure and rounded bosom. A double strand of pearls and matching earrings were her only extra adornments, besides the large emerald engagement ring on her left hand.

Graham kissed his sister on each cheek and shook hands with the tall, dark-haired man beside her. Graham turned to Eva, but before he could introduce her, Sophia took both of Eva's hands in hers.

"Graham has spoken of you so much that I feel as if I already know you. I remember you from Lushtak's. You looked so beautiful in all of the clothes that I had to have every single outfit in the hopes that I would look like you." She smiled and a dimple deepened on her cheek. "Of course, that's an impossibility, but one can hope."

Sophia let go of Eva's hands and turned to the man beside her. "This is my fiancé, David Eliot. If he weren't so besotted with me, I wouldn't have invited such a gorgeous creature as you to my home."

She beamed up at David, and the look of adoration he returned made it clear that she was absolutely right.

As Eva greeted them both, she felt the skin on the back of her neck prickle. She turned her head slightly and met the gaze of two gray eyes so pale they appeared silver. They were set beneath thick brows in a masculine face that was spared perfection by its angularity—and a nose that appeared to have been broken at least once. Sharp cheekbones and a wide forehead split by a dark widow's peak kept the man from appearing unapproachable. As did the grin he directed at Eva as he drew a cigarette to his mouth.

David followed her gaze. "Ah, Alexander. Come meet our guests."

The man put out his cigarette in an ashtray before walking over to the group in the foyer. His gait was casual as he crossed the marble floor. He was powerfully built, even though he wasn't tall; his silver eyes appeared to take in everything yet somehow find it all wanting.

"Alexander Grof," he said, extending his hand to Graham. "David and I are old friends from our Harrow days." They shook, and Graham introduced himself before placing his hand on the small of Eva's back to bring her closer.

"This is Miss Eva Harlow."

The man's unusual eyes met hers again, and what seemed like a jolt of electricity pulsed through her. The feeling wasn't the same as when Graham looked at her. More the sense of surprise caused by an intruder crashing through a locked door. Alexander took her hand and kissed it, making her wish that evening gloves were still in fashion. She didn't look down at her hand, sure his lips had left some kind of a mark.

"It's a pleasure to meet you, Mr. Grof," Eva said, although it wasn't, not really. He was an attractive, magnetic man, but he was like the luscious red apple hanging from the tree, beautiful to look at, possibly poisonous if eaten. Perhaps she'd seen too many films, but she couldn't avoid the unsettled feeling he gave her, the sense of having stepped into quicksand.

"Likewise," he said, and gave her such an engaging smile that she almost doubted her initial negative impression of him. "I'm afraid that I've quite upset our charming hostess by appearing unannounced and creating an uneven number at dinner. I tried to leave, but Sophia and David insisted I stay. I'm only saying this so that you won't think ill of Miss St. John's hostess abilities, which are beyond compare. I say that with all honesty, having been a guest at her dining table on several occasions."

"Oh, Alex, don't be absurd," Sophia said, blushing prettily. "And am I truly Miss St. John to you? I do believe we should all be on a first-name basis.

Those of us who know one another are such good friends, and those who don't soon will be." She linked her arm with Eva's and gave a small squeeze, then led her through the arched doorway toward the staircase. "Please, call me Sophia. And may I call you Eva?"

"I'd like that," Eva said, warming to the young woman.

As they reached the stairs, Eva gave a quick glance into the room opposite and saw shelves of books and a heavy wood desk—likely the library. Sophia led her on, bringing her upstairs to an elegantly appointed drawing room. A fire crackled in the fireplace, making the large room appear cozy but doing nothing to erase the chill Eva felt from the open back of her dress, or from the sense that something was askew.

She sought out Graham's gaze, and he smiled at her. Her uneasiness fled. Sophia noticed her shiver and led her to a small sofa, upholstered in a deep blue velvet, next to the fireplace. "I gave instructions for the room to be warmed, and here you are about to catch your death." She sent a glowering look toward the butler, who immediately pushed a call button, presumably to summon a maid to stoke the fire.

Eva sank down onto the sofa, grateful to relieve her feet.

Sophia continued. "I should get rid of the lot of them—they've grown too soft living in London.

Staff from the country are far better, I'm told. Not terribly intelligent, but hard workers. I imagine they're so eager to get out of their hovels and live in a London town house that they'd work twice as hard for half the money." She smiled at her own wit, apparently unaware of Eva's frozen expression. It had nothing to do with the temperature in the room and everything to do with what Sophia had just said, especially the word "hovels."

After Sophia excused herself to see to her other guests, Eva looked for Graham again, wanting him to sit next to her. He was facing away; she started to call out to him, but Alexander moved in front of her, blocking her view. After a brief bow and a perfunctory "May I?" he took the empty seat beside her without waiting for her to answer.

David came toward them before she could react. "I'm your official drinks man for the evening. Sophia says I'm quite good at it, says it's the main reason she's marrying me."

"Makes perfect sense to me," Eva said, glad for his interruption. "I'd like a French Seventy-five, please." Precious had assured her that this was the champagne drink all the smart women liked.

"Make that two," Alexander added, giving Eva another charming smile. He kept a respectful distance from her, allowing for a wide gap between them on the small sofa, and this made her relax somewhat.

After they chatted a few moments about the weather, a uniformed maid brought their drinks on a tray. Alexander took them both and handed one to Eva.

"Cheers," he said, lifting his glass. Eva did the same, then took a small, ladylike sip.

"Are you Czech?" she asked, belatedly recognizing the accent that hid behind his impeccable English.

He looked at her with surprise. "Very good, Eva. My mother is English, but my father is half-Czech and half-German, raised in Prague. As was I, until I attended Harrow at the tender age of thirteen. I find that my loyalties are split between three countries." He took a sip of his drink and eyed her appreciatively. "You have an excellent ear."

His silver gaze held such intensity that Eva was forced to look away. She focused on the bubbles rising to the surface of her glass and took another sip.

"Where have you heard my accent?" he asked.

"My friend Anton Danek. He does the makeup for the models at the House of Lushtak."

"Ah," he said, nodding slowly. "I suspected that you were a model. You have a rare sort of beauty. The sort that deserves to be shown off in jewels and beautiful clothes."

"Thank you," Eva said, nervous again. Something in the way he spoke hinted at indecent things; it made her skin heat. She put her glass down on the side table and fumbled for her cigarette case inside her purse. Her fingers moved clumsily as she attempted to open the case, and she dropped it on the floor. The hinge Precious had glued together with fingernail polish popped open, spilling cigarettes over the Persian rug.

The maid rushed over and retrieved the pieces of the case along with the three cigarettes that had been inside. "Thank you," Eva said, returning all but one cigarette to her bag. The maid, younger even than Eva, looked worried, as if embarrassed at being noticed.

"Allow me," Alexander said, leaning forward with a match.

Her hand shook as she held the cigarette to her mouth. He lit it, then his own, his eyes never straying from her face. "Where did you say you were from?"

"Devon," she said.

He sat back, studying her carefully. "No, you're not."

Her hand trembled as she brought her cigarette to her mouth, trying to disguise the white-hot fear that flashed through her.

"Your accent is very proper, but every once in a while, I can hear you use an inflection that isn't quite right—and it isn't quite Devon, either. You see, Eva, you're not the only one with a good ear."

She took her time blowing smoke from her mouth, trying to think of a response. Mr. Danek had told her that to make a lie believable, one had to mix in some truth. "I was born in Yorkshire, in a small town called Muker. We moved to Devon when I was a little girl, but I suppose that's where I learned to speak."

"Ah, yes. That would make sense." He took a puff from his cigarette, a knowing smile touching his lips as he continued to study her.

Sophia appeared beside Eva. "I do believe you're monopolizing our new friend, Alex. Would you please excuse us? We've lots to talk about." She held her hand out to Eva, and Eva tried not to seem too eager as she took it and stood. She met Graham's gaze from across the room, feeling her nerves settle at its warmth. Her pulse danced in her veins. She wished they were back in the showroom again, just the two of them.

Alexander stood and bowed formally. "It has been my pleasure."

Eva smiled noncommittally, then allowed Sophia to lead her away.

The rest of the evening passed in a blur. Later, Eva couldn't recall anybody's names or what they had had to eat, what the conversation had been about or what she had said. All she could remember was the nearness of Graham, his leg pressed against hers beneath the table, and the unnerving silver eyes of the man whose stares she did her best to avoid for the duration of the party.

CHAPTER 10

LONDON
MAY 2019

The doorbell rang, and I looked up from my laptop, where I'd been jotting down descriptions and anecdotes to attach to the outfits Precious, Arabella, and I had so far decided upon for the exhibition. Dresses, skirts, jackets, and gowns lay scattered around me on the bed, and as I stood to answer the door, a peach satin gown slid off onto the floor.

As I bent to pick it up, I let my fingers stroke the fabric, still soft and supple eighty years since it had been last worn. I placed it next to a one-shouldered black tulle confection and was tempted to touch that, too. I'd learned a new appreciation for fashion just by talking with Precious and taking notes, which was surprising, considering my usual attire of jeans and button-downs. I'd even come up with a new title for the exhibition and the article that Arabella loved: **War & Beauty: The World of Fashion in a World at War**.

I loved everything about this assignment. I loved talking with Precious and learning about the fashion industry of the late nineteen thirties and nineteen forties, and I loved the beautiful clothes that surrounded me. I loved everything except the presence of Colin Eliot.

As Arabella had promised, he worked long hours. Though it had been only three nights so far, I'd figured out that if I ate early, I could be in my room before he came home. But even after the first night, I'd found myself waiting for the sound of his key in the door. I resented him for that, which, I could admit to myself, was ridiculous. It might even have been unfair.

The doorbell rang again, and I moved to answer it, a little skip to my walk. It was Saturday, and Colin had mentioned the night before that he usually went into the office for at least part of the day. I was expecting Arabella, who'd also had to go into the office but was planning to deliver the Sainsbury's bags, which we'd forgotten in the boot of her car after visiting Penelope.

As I opened the door, I heard a familiar growling coming from the kitchen. I turned to see Oscar pulling on a red plaid leash and Laura on the other end of it. Arabella closed the door, then bent down to scratch him behind the ears, the little dog keeping a watchful eye on me.

"I am sorry," Laura said, shortening the leash so she could walk around us. "He loves Colin and therefore loves Arabella—he must be able to smell that they're related or something. Maybe he's jealous of you and the attention Colin is redirecting."

"Oh, no." I shook my head fervently. "There's no attention there, trust me. Oscar can clear his mind of that idea. Maybe he just needs time to adjust."

Oscar was now sitting quietly at Arabella's feet, looking up at me with a sweet expression. "Oh, so we're going to be friends now?" I bent down to let him sniff my hand, and he growled in the back of his throat. I immediately jerked back.

"We'll keep trying," Laura said. "We're off for walkies now. George is with Colin, and Miss Dubose has already had her breakfast and is resting. I'll see you later."

We said our good-byes; then Arabella turned to me with a grin. "At least George likes you. Of course, he likes everyone, but it's a start, isn't it?"

Before I could think of a response, a door at the rear of the flat opened, and George bounded down the long hallway and greeted me with paws on my shoulders and long tongue laps on my face. Colin approached from behind him, wearing what could be described only as a hostile expression, and pulled the dog gently back by his collar.

"That's enough, George." With a far less friendly tone, he said, "How was your visit to Surrey, ladies?" It was more of an accusation than a question.

Arabella brushed away a blond curl that had slipped in front of her eyes. "It was lovely. Thanks. Aunt Penelope was charming as always and made us a delicious quiche." She handed him one of the Sainsbury's bags and indicated the second, which she'd placed by the door. "Be a dear and bring these into the dining room. If you've got a few minutes, you can help us sort."

"I don't think that will be necessary, Arabella," I said. "It's what I'm here for, remember?"

For a moment it appeared as if Colin wanted to say something. Then he reached over and picked up the bags before following Arabella into the dining room. I hadn't spent much time in this room yet. The highly polished mahogany table could easily have sat twelve people in comfort.

"Now, this is a table," I said. "It would have been perfect for my five siblings and me—that's for sure. Easier to clean up, anyway. All of the thrown food would have missed its target, except anything thrown by Joey—he's a baseball player."

Almost against its will, Colin's mouth twitched. "Five siblings sounds like a lot of commotion."

"Imagine sharing one bathroom with five people and fighting to ride in the front seat of the minivan. Made me wish I was an only child many times."

"Your poor mother. She must be a saint."

I felt Arabella's eyes on me, but I didn't look at her. The familiar bruise ached, unused to being touched. I was usually more prepared for unexpected blows. "Yes. She is indeed a saint." I bent over one of the bags and pulled out what appeared to be a stationery box wrapped in a ribbon that might have once been bright red. Keeping my eyes down, I said, "She died when I was fourteen."

The room was silent except for the soft padding of George's paws as he walked into the room and lay down at my feet.

"I'm sorry," Colin said. He didn't say any more, as if he knew that no further words would excuse, explain, or diminish the loss of my mother. And I was left wondering what had happened in his own life to make him understand that.

"Thank you." Eager to talk about anything else, I pulled out a stack of photographs from the bag and placed them on the table next to the stationery box.

Colin cleared his throat, then moved closer to get a better look. "I'm assuming Mother gave you all this?"

Arabella pulled at the faded ribbon encircling the stationery box, removing her hand as the knot disintegrated and the remains of the fabric scattered like dust. "Yes. It all belonged to your grandmother. Your mother suggested that since Sophia knew Precious during the war, she probably knew Eva as well. I thought it wouldn't hurt to have a go at her letters and photos. Aunt Penelope mentioned on the phone that she'd already gone through everything after your grandmother died, and there's nothing scandalous whatsoever, if that's what you're worried about."

"Hardly. I'm just curious as to why I wasn't invited."

Arabella briefly met my gaze. "I had a small window of time away from the office and decided to use it wisely. No ulterior motive, I assure you."

Colin looked at me as if expecting me to say something, but I was distracted by my phone vibrating. I didn't bother looking at it. I knew who it was. The night before, I'd texted Knoxie and Aunt Cassie that I needed more time. But apparently unless my answer was yes, they'd keep on trying.

Colin reached inside the second bag and pulled out a small hatbox, the strap holding the lid frayed and broken. "Before we start digging, I'd like to suggest organizing everything by type. Once we've done that, we can sort through all of it and try to put everything in date order as best we can." He reached for the pile of newspaper clippings I'd pulled from an ancient manila folder.

"That's so very Colin of you," Arabella said. "All that organizing and analyzing of numbers and such."

He raised an eyebrow. "I'm an analyst, Arabella. It is what I do for a living."

I suddenly remembered that about him, how careful and methodical he'd been about everything, from deciding what to order from a menu to planning a route home from the pub. He'd always been the driver, too. It made me wonder now if it had less to do with him being the only teetotaler in our group and more with him wanting to be in control.

"I didn't forget, Colin," Arabella said. "It's how you can afford those fancy holidays with your mates."

He shot her a frown before examining the small stack of yellowed clippings. I watched as he carefully arranged them on the table in straight rows, faceup.

"Now that we've got that settled, I may as well get started with this," Arabella said, pulling out a chair and settling into it. She slid the stationery box toward herself and carefully lifted the lid.

"I guess that leaves this for me." I picked up the hatbox. A small stack of envelopes rested inside, and I scooped them up with the full intention of sorting them as best I could.

Most were addressed to **Miss Sophia St. John**, and a few to **Mrs. David Eliot**. A good number had a bold, masculine scrawl on the front, with the name **D. Eliot** in the top left corner. With the assumption they were from her husband, I put those in their own pile.

Quite a few of the envelopes, in an expensive heavy linen stationery, were postmarked from Surrey. The penmanship reminded me of the old letters from my grandmother, saved in my grandfather's desk, each character perfect in its even slant.

It was the kind of handwriting that was part of an older generation, now relegated to museums and attics, replaced with deletable texts and e-mails. I'd been lucky to be born before the advent of smartphones, and I had my own stash of notes and letters written by my mother, a solid reminder that she'd once been a part of my life.

I wondered if these letters might have been written by Sophia's mother, and I put them in their own pile, too. Finding an assortment from different sources, I placed them together in a single pile and flipped through them, noticing an envelope with odd handwriting. The characters were small and precise, as if the writer—most likely a woman, I guessed—had spent time crafting each character. It made me think of how a child learned cursive, but this was the handwriting of an adult. An adult being very careful to demonstrate that she had beautiful penmanship.

There was no return address, but the postmark was dated 12 March 1939. The dark red stamp in the top right corner showed the profile of the king—although I couldn't remember who was king in 1939. I'd seen **Wallis & Edward**, so I knew it wasn't Edward, but I couldn't think of his brother's name. My curiosity quickly overrode Colin's directions and I slid the paper from the envelope, then hesitated at the sound of a throat being cleared.

I looked up to find Colin's serious blue eyes trained on me. Before he could ask what I was doing,

I said the first thing I could think of to distract him. "How is it that Sophia's son, your father, inherited Hovenden Park? Was she an only child?"

"No. She had two older brothers." He paused, considering his words. "Twins, actually. I never knew them. The elder—by just a few minutes, I believe—William, was killed during the war. Not sure what happened to the other brother. He wasn't really mentioned. My parents probably know more. Neither one of the twins had children, so Sophia ended up inheriting everything." He looked pointedly at the opened envelope. "How is the letter sorting going?"

I smiled innocently. "Can we read just one for now? I'm intrigued by the handwriting."

His mouth started to form the word "no," but Arabella interjected, "Absolutely! What's it say?"

If Colin weren't British, he would have rolled his eyes. "Go on. It's not like I can stop you."

I unfolded the letter and, after clearing my throat, read out loud.

Dear Miss St. John,

Thank you for the lovely dinner party last evening. It was a pleasure to properly meet you, and I also enjoyed meeting your fiancé, Mr. Eliot, and your friends. They were a delight, as were the delicious food and

wine, and I appreciate your extending the invitation to join you.

There was such a flurry of good-byes when we left that I neglected to remember my purse. It's a small green box-shaped bag with gold embroidered leaves on it. I'd placed it under my chair in the dining room, and with all the wonderful conversation, I completely forgot all about it.

I would like to call on Thursday around noon to collect it, if that is convenient. I don't want to intrude, so if you'd like to tell your maid that I will come for it, I will stop by the back door.

Thank you again for your kind hospitality.

Most sincerely,
Miss Eva Harlow

I looked up and grinned in triumph. "We have a last name! I'm sure Precious would have come up with it eventually, but it's good to have corroboration."

"That's amazing," Arabella said, and clapped. "It'll make finding her a lot easier—that's for certain."

Colin actually smiled. "Good job, Madison."

"Did you just compliment me?"

"Don't let it go to your head."

I didn't bother to hide my smile as I refolded the letter and put it back into the envelope. I was reaching for another letter when Arabella slapped the table with her palm. I looked up to find her holding a photograph in her other hand.

"Oh, golly!" She seemed at a loss for words. Finally, she said, "Colin, was your grandfather in the RAF?"

"No—army. Why?"

She flipped the photograph over to see the back, then shook her head. "I don't know. It doesn't give a name. But someone wrote, 'Sweet dreams, darling' on the back."

I moved to stand behind her chair and looked at the head shot of a young man wearing an RAF uniform, a sense of déjà vu settling over me. The portrait wasn't static like most military photographs of the era. Not with that crooked smile and those laughing eyes. The faint shadow of freckles across the bridge of his nose and high cheekbones. The tilt of the head that made it appear as if he were in conversation with the viewer.

"He's . . ."

"Pretty hot," Arabella said, turning to look at me. "Is that what you were about to say?"

"I was attempting to think of something more refined." I smiled, thinking of what Sarah Frances had said about a boy she'd admired from afar in high school. "I wouldn't kick him out of bed for eating crackers, that's for sure."

Arabella gave a delicate snort. "Ah, yes. Much more refined." She turned her attention back to the photograph. "He certainly is a stunner." She leaned a little closer. "Except . . ."

Our eyes met in mutual realization. Before I could slap a hand over her mouth, she blurted, "He looks just like Colin! Or rather, Colin looks like him, as this gentleman obviously came first. But it's uncanny, isn't it? Even down to the freckles across the nose and the chin cleft." She had a familiar gleam in her eyes, and I tried to telepathically warn her not to say what she was about to say next. It didn't work. "Which means you think Colin's quite hot!"

"I didn't say that, Arabella," I warned, looking everywhere except at her cousin. It wasn't that I didn't find Colin attractive. I would have had to be blind not to. I just preferred to remain in neutral territory, where I never burned hot or cold for anyone. I didn't want to be tempted into a relationship, because the outcome would never change, no matter how much I'd wish it could.

"It could be my grandfather, David," Colin said. "Sophia's husband. Nana has always said I favor him. I never met him and only have pictures of him as an older man, so I have no idea." He came to stand behind me, and I was suddenly very conscious of how tall he was, and how much heat seemed to radiate from his body. He reached for the photograph. "I'll snap a photo and text it to my parents, although I'm not convinced there's a resemblance."

My gaze met Arabella's, and I rolled my eyes.

Our phones buzzed at the same time. I ignored mine, but she looked at her screen. "It's my assistant, Mia. A bit of an emergency, so I must dash."

"No worries," I said. "I'll finish sorting through all of this and let you know if I find anything."

"And don't forget the editorial meeting at three o'clock. I'd like to go over some of the ideas you discussed with Adam, the museum director. He's very excited about this collaboration, and I want to make sure we're all on the same page."

"I've got to run, too," Colin said, pushing back from the table. "I'll take George for a walk first and then be off." The large dog lifted his head at the sound of his name and seemed to smile. I realized with a start that he did, actually, resemble his namesake, Prince George, what with the big eyes and expressive eyebrows.

"You should go with them, Maddie. Clear your head." Arabella smiled innocently.

"I have so much work. . . ."

"You're welcome to come with us, Madison. It's a nice day. George and I can show you Regent's Park." I couldn't tell if he was asking out of politeness or if he simply wanted to show Arabella that he could be cordial.

I should have said no. But it really was a beautiful

day, and I'd been inside working all morning. I told myself that I would have gone by myself, anyway. Colin being with me didn't mean anything.

We said our good-byes to Arabella, then left, George eagerly leading the way. My phone buzzed once as we went down the stairs, then again five minutes later as we entered the park.

"Aren't you going to get that?"

I looked down at my phone, remembering telling Colin about my mother. How I'd known he somehow understood more than most. "It's my aunt Cassie—my mother's sister. She wants me to come home at Christmas for my sister's wedding."

"And you don't want to go?"

I started to say no but stopped, my hesitation surprising me. It wasn't that I didn't want to go. But there were some things in life too painful to contemplate and therefore easier to avoid.

Instead I said, "I don't like the winter. It might snow."

"It snows a lot in Georgia in the winter?" An almost-smile appeared on Colin's lips as he glanced at me. George spotted a squirrel and barked, pulling Colin forward in an attempt to reach it.

I shook my head. "No. Not really." I watched the squirrel scamper toward a playground. A lone child sat on a swing, spinning it, twisting the chains tightly before lifting his feet so that it spun wildly as he threw his head back in joy. I remembered that feeling from my own childhood, the time before I'd had to grow up. Maybe that was why I opened my mouth and said, "Mama loved the snow but had never seen more than a few snowflakes. She died the night of one of the rare big snowstorms in Georgia. It was like she waited to check that off her bucket list so she could die."

I wasn't sure why I'd told Colin that. I never shared details about my mother. But there'd been something freeing about it, the way telling someone about a nightmare made it suddenly less scary. And because he'd said he was sorry when I'd told him she'd died when I was fourteen. Because he hadn't tried to make it better. Because he'd **known**; he'd understood that nothing could ever do that.

"You should go," he said.

I looked at him in surprise. "Why do you say that?"

He kept his eyes on the path ahead when he spoke. "Because life is short."

For the second time that day, I felt the old bruise throb, pressing on my heart, stealing my breath. "Yes," I said. "It is." Surprised to find my palms damp, I rubbed them against my thighs. "I miss my family. But there are other things waiting at home that are hard to face."

"You should go," he said again.

"You don't understand. . . ." My words drifted away. I didn't know how to complete the sentence. Or maybe I wanted Colin to finish it for me.

"Did you have the chance to say good-bye to your mother?"

I swallowed, remembering. "Yes. I would never want anyone I love to go through that. It's too hard."

He looked at me sharply. "Are you dying?"

I shook my head. "No." **Not yet.** I glanced away toward a grassy area, not seeing anything except flashes of life. Just like we'd been led to believe our last moments on earth would be. Without looking at him, I said, "We're all dying, aren't we?"

He was silent for a moment. "Yes, presumably. But today you're living, and you have a family who loves you, inexplicably perhaps. Nevertheless they wish you to spend Christmas and attend a wedding with them. It's a week or so out of your life, and then you can return to your work or what have you and resume living each day as if you were dying if that's what makes you happy."

"I didn't say it makes me happy."

"Then why do you do it?" His voice was quiet, his question not meant to be antagonistic or even answered. Yet it made me angry.

"You know nothing about me."

"Correct. You make a point of not sharing very much about yourself."

I shook with anger at his audacity and presumption: that he could calmly interpret what would make me happy. I turned on him, my hands clenched into fists, the need to lash out too strong to hold back.

"My grandmother and my mother died of breast cancer. They passed on the gene to me, which pretty much guarantees I'll get it, too, eventually. When I'm home, all I see is the pity in the eyes of my sisters, who were lucky enough to bypass that genetic lottery. And I remember what my mother's death did to all of us. I don't want to witness them going through it again."

He silently regarded me for a moment, his blue eyes showing no shock or pity. Only understanding. I wondered again about his own past, how he knew the way to react in the face of grief. "I think it's rather simple, really. Your family loves you, Madison. And you love them. As an ignorant outsider, I can say that it seems you should go home."

The word conjured up the smells of frying bacon and Aunt Lucinda's biscuits baking in the oven, loud voices talking over one another interlaced with shouts and laughter. My anger dissipated, leaving behind a glowing river of memories and faces. Of running barefoot through warm summer grass. Of the buoyant feeling of being loved.

My phone buzzed again, and I stared down at the screen. "You make it seem so easy."

"Perhaps because it is."

My phone stopped buzzing for a brief period before it started again. **Perhaps because it is.** Before I could change my mind, I texted my answer and hit "send." "I'll call her later, so you don't have to hear the whole conversation."

"Are you afraid she's going to start talking about menstrual cycles again?"

The unexpectedness of his words made me bark with laughter, and I turned to him, surprised. "I don't remember you ever having a sense of humor."

Colin gave me a lopsided grin before returning his focus to the path ahead. "And I didn't think you'd noticed anything about me at all."

I sobered quickly. "I know that you expect people to say good-bye when they leave."

"Just some people."

I turned away, watching George's bushy tail sway to and fro as we walked in silence, and considered all the reasons I never said good-bye, ignoring the niggling thought knocking at my conscience, telling me maybe I'd been wrong.

CHAPTER 11

LONDON
MARCH 1939

As Eva stepped off the bus on Marylebone Road and hurried along the sidewalk, she smelled spring, a ripe green scent of new grass that reminded her of home. Except here in London, it was mixed with the acrid tinge of wet pavement and burning petrol from the ever-present motorcars and red buses lining the roads and carriageways. She wondered if she'd miss the scent of London when she returned to Yorkshire, and if she'd become homesick for the city. But of course she wouldn't. Because she would never go home. Not now, when she'd managed to shed Ethel Maltby like an old coat, one she would never wear again.

Eva ran up the stairs and paused outside the door to catch her breath, eager to finish packing up the kitchen area. They were moving to the new flat right after the big fashion show. And she wanted Precious to see the gorgeous yellow frock she'd paid five shillings for from the back room at Lushtak's. It was from last season's show and had a huge hole in the front, which Mrs. Williams had cleverly disguised by adding pockets. She and Precious would get a lot of wear out of it, Eva thought, which justified her paying so much for it. Her mother would have been appalled at her spendthrift ways, but she did her best not to think about her mother, except when she sent her money from every paycheck.

She put the key into the lock, then paused, hearing voices—one decidedly male—on the other side of the door. Pushing it open, she stopped and stared with surprise at Graham, sitting on the tattered sofa, his elegant form a contrast to his surroundings but still managing to look at ease as he smoked a cigarette. Precious sat on the armchair next to him, thankfully hiding the large hole in the middle of the seat cushion, which belched goose feathers when one sat on it too heavily.

"Graham," Eva said, the excitement at seeing him at odds with her disquiet at seeing him inside her flat. He'd been out of town for his work—something he'd explained only in vague terms—and she hadn't seen him since the dinner at Sophia's three nights before.

But why was he **here**? She pulled off her gloves, then hung up the dress she'd been carrying. Putting her hat on the rack by the door, her hands unsteady, she was acutely aware of their shabby surroundings and horribly embarrassed that he'd been given a glimpse beyond the carefully curated world she'd allowed him to see.

"Darling." Graham stubbed out his cigarette in the ashtray on the battered side table next to a half-empty teacup and stood to greet her. "I've missed you," he said, and kissed her gently on the cheek. Her lips burned with wanting, and she turned her face to his. Always the gentleman, and aware of the presence of another person, he pulled back, but the bright light in his eyes let her know that he wanted more, too.

"I've missed you, too," she said, glancing over his shoulder at Precious, who'd stood but remained by her chair. Precious grinned and nodded her head rapidly to show her approval. She hadn't met Graham yet, mostly due to his traveling but also because of Eva's insistence that she meet Graham outside the flat.

"I'm very happy to have finally met the wonderful Miss Dubose you've been telling me about," Graham said. "May I say that she's every bit as charming and lovely as you made her out to be?" Graham turned to Precious and gave her a mock bow.

"Likewise," Precious said, blushing prettily. "And please, call me Precious. All my friends do."

"Precious it is, then," Graham said, his eyes

wrinkling at the corners. He returned his attention to Eva. "I have something for you."

"You do?" He'd brought flowers to her at Lushtak's and taken her to dinner dozens of times, but he'd never given her a gift.

He helped her out of her coat and hung it beneath her hat. Then he moved gracefully back to the sofa, where he'd been sitting, and lifted something from the floor. The gold embroidered leaves shone against the dark green velvet background of Precious's purse, the one Eva had left behind at Sophia's party. The careful stitching she'd done to repair it was hardly noticeable, but she felt mortified at the thought that Sophia or Graham might have noticed the mending.

"I was at my club yesterday and ran into that fellow Alexander Grof, David's friend from Harrow. He said you'd left behind your purse and he'd taken it, hoping to run into you again." His brow furrowed. "I must say, he seemed reluctant to part with it, saying he'd be happy to give it to you in person. He even asked for your address. I insisted, however, and since we were so close to his hotel, I waited in the lobby while he fetched it for me." He smiled thinly, making Eva wonder what "insisting" might have involved.

"It's the reason we met," he said. "So I knew it was special to you, and I didn't want a delay in getting it back to you."

Precious rose and moved to stand next to her. "Wasn't he sweet to do that, Eva?" She smiled, and Eva sent her a grateful look for not letting on that the purse was hers.

"Yes, he is," Eva said. She turned to Graham. "Thank you for bringing this to me." Slowly she slipped the strap from his fingers, making sure her bare hand brushed his, reveling in the spark that moved between them. Sliding the purse over her wrist, she said, "That was very kind of you both. Please thank Alexander for me if you see him at your club again."

"I expect I will—he's apparently a new member. I'm not sure of his credentials, but David said he'd vouch for him. He's living at the Savoy because of all this German business going on in his home country. Apparently he's waiting to see what else happens before he returns." Graham's eyes moved to Precious. "He said he'd already met you—quite by happenstance, I believe."

"He has?" She looked genuinely surprised.

"He accidentally bumped into you on the sidewalk in front of Lushtak's last week. He said he thought it was Eva, until you started to speak and he heard your charming accent. When he mentioned it, I assumed it had to be Eva's American friend and roommate. Eva's always telling me how the two of you are known as the tall blond models and are often mistaken for each other because of it.

And of course, you were in front of Lushtak's, where Alexander knows Eva works."

Precious's eyes widened. "Oh, yes, I do recall. He apologized and walked on without an introduction. How funny that he'd remember that."

"He's suggested an outing for the four of us—to go to Kew and see the cherry blossoms. I said it would have to be after the fashion show, since that's occupying so much of your spare time now, and he was most agreeable."

"I would love to," Precious said. "I love getting to know people. Don't I, Eva? My daddy always said I've never met a stranger."

"I will pass on the good news to Mr. Grof. I know that he and I will be the envy of every gentleman at Kew." Turning back to Eva, Graham said, "I also have more news for you—good news, I hope. And since this involves both of you, this is a good opportunity to tell you together."

Eva held her breath while Precious clapped her hands like a little girl. "I love surprises," Precious said. "What is it?"

"Well, the other night while we were dining with my sister, Sophia overheard you mention, Eva, that you were planning on moving from this flat to a bigger one. It just so happens that David owns a flat not far from here, near the park. It's quite large and very nice and in a good location. He hadn't quite decided what to do with it after he and Sophia marry in July and move into the town house on Berkeley Square, so Sophia suggested they should allow you two to lease it for a nominal rate. He'll leave all the furnishings, and he's already found bachelor accommodations for before the wedding—I told him you were planning to move right after the show and wouldn't want to wait. It seems like the perfect solution, don't you think?"

Eva stared at him, waiting for him to tell her he was joking. The news was too good to be true, and her mother had always told her to take good news with a grain of salt; it was never as good as it sounded. She and Precious had found another flat, but certainly not as nice as the one David owned and definitely not anywhere near Regent's Park.

"Are you quite sure he was serious?" she asked.

Graham laughed and placed his hands on her arms. "Of course, darling. Why wouldn't I be? David has met you and believes you to be quite respectable and a good prospective tenant. I couldn't agree more."

Precious was nearly jumping with excitement, and Eva allowed some of it to roll onto her. "That would be lovely. Really lovely. I'll write them a note of thanks this evening." She smiled up at him, looking into his eyes, trying to be sure he wasn't holding anything back.

"Now, ladies, my errand is done, and I must go. I look forward to seeing you both at the show."

"I'll walk you to the door," Eva said.

Precious, understanding her meaning, said, "And I'll do the washing up. Good-bye, Graham. It was so nice to meet you." Her accent hadn't softened in all her months in England, and Graham seemed charmed by it.

He held the door open for Eva, and they stepped out into the small hallway, where the smell of liver and onions assaulted her nose. "I'm so sorry . . . ," she began.

Graham interrupted her. "Don't ever apologize to me. Do you think I care that the death of your parents has left you in reduced circumstances? It doesn't matter to me. I love your— What did you say it was? Your 'lust for adventure and success in adversity.' I find that more attractive than all of Croesus's gold." He stepped closer, his lips brushing hers. "You, Eva Harlow, are the most captivating and enigmatic woman I've ever known. And your circumstances now do not reflect who you are. Or where you're headed."

She felt light-headed, her breath coming in shallow gasps. "What do you mean?"

"I mean that this"—he indicated the dreary white paint and bare bulb above them—"is temporary. Your station in life will change because you want it to. You have ambition and drive, two attributes I find alarmingly attractive."

His hands slid from her waist to her hips as he drew her toward him. "Alarmingly?" she asked, the word hard to find. "Shall I go fetch the fire brigade?"

He grinned against her mouth. "No, because then you wouldn't be here for me to kiss."

And he proceeded to do just that until a door slammed on a floor above and heavy footsteps began to descend the steps. "I'll speak with Alex," Graham said, reluctantly drawing away. "We'll make plans for our trip to Kew. I'll borrow David's motorcar again, and we can pick you both up here."

Eva thought of Alexander Grof seeing this place and cringed, even more appalled to imagine him here than she had been at actually seeing Graham on her sofa. "We should be in our new place by then."

"I'll ask Sophia and David, too, shall I?"

A loud belch accompanied the heavy footsteps from the landing directly above them, making Graham laugh silently.

Better than being horrified, Eva thought.

"Yes, that would be—" Her last word was cut off, as he was kissing her again. Abruptly, he pulled away and headed down the stairs, pausing to look up at her. "I'll see you Saturday. I'll be in the front row."

"Won't I see you before then?" She felt oddly bereft.

"Sadly, I have work obligations. I promise to make up for lost time, though."

He smiled and was gone before she could question him about where he'd be and what he'd be doing. All she knew was that he was working in Whitehall for the Home Office, doing a job he said was too boring to talk about.

"Good-bye," she said, but he was already gone.

A large bearded man carrying a lunch pail lumbered past her in the hallway, lifting his cap before heading down the stairs.

Eva turned to go back inside, but when the purse swung on her wrist, she felt something slide from one side to the other with a solid **clunk**. The purse was heavier than she remembered it being, definitely heavier than her lipstick and pressed powder compact should have been. Curious, she opened the lid and peered inside. A rectangular silver box reflected the overhead lightbulb. Eva smiled, imagining it must have been a gift from Graham and appreciating the unexpected and unassuming nature of the way he'd given it to her. Securing the strap around her wrist, she lifted the silver box from the purse.

A delicate filigree design covered the entire case, with the exclusion of an oval space on the front, in which the etched body of a bee had been placed. Eva swallowed back her initial reaction of revulsion; having been forced to live with insects and rodents throughout her childhood, she'd learned to hate them. But then she remembered the case had been a gift from Graham and made herself examine it more closely, studying the almost transparent wings and striped body, the furred sections of the legs, the two stubby antennae.

Frowning as she struggled to determine the bee's meaning, she flipped the case over. A sterling hallmark had been etched into one corner, and tiny words sat on the bottom edge like a line of ants: NIL CREDAM ET OMNIA CAVEBO.

The meaning was foreign to her, the words something other than English. Eva had a panicked moment, wondering if this might be a test from Graham of her education. She quickly dismissed the thought. It just wasn't something he would do. She was convinced of that.

She turned the case over to look at the bee again, at how real it appeared, and a shudder flowed through her like a wave. What could it possibly mean? Why would Graham have given her such a thing? With her painted thumbnail, she carefully pried open the top. A cream-colored note sat inside, folded crisply in half. Eva opened it, her eyes scanning the words first without reading, and she realized with a start that she'd never seen Graham's handwriting before. The letters were thick and bold, all sharp angles and lines. Not at all what she imagined his handwriting would look like. Her gaze drifted to the signature, and her mouth went dry. **Alex.** Not Alexander, or Alexander Grof, but **Alex**. As if he were assuming a familiarity with her that didn't exist.

Her eyes drifted back to the top of the note, and she began to read.

Dearest Eva,

I can't tell you what a pleasure it was to meet you earlier this week. I must admit

that I'm quite besotted—embarrassingly so. We'd barely finished the soup course before I was plotting to see you again. Imagine my delight when you left your purse behind and afforded me the perfect opportunity. I thought my plans thwarted when St. John insisted on returning the purse personally, but then I realized it was an excellent chance to send you a note since I do not have your address.

Please accept this gift as a token of my esteem. I couldn't help but notice that you were in need of a cigarette case. I saw this in a shop and found it exquisite and unique. So of course I immediately thought of you.

Until we meet again,
Alex

Eva crumpled the note in her fist, interest and offense warring in her head. She examined the beautiful cigarette case again, felt the heft of the silver, calculated its value. Mr. Grof—Alex—had bought it for her because he found her exquisite and unique. She flipped the case over again and studied the words on the back, wondering how she could find out what they meant. The only thing of which she was certain was that she could ask neither Graham nor Alex. She'd rather remain ignorant.

She immediately thought of Mr. Danek, who'd

been educated at Charles University in Prague. Surely that meant he was worldlier than she, and he might at least tell her what language the writing was in. The one thing she knew for sure was that she wasn't going to return the cigarette case. It was much too beautiful to give back.

When Eva reentered the flat, Precious stood by the front window, looking down on the street. "Your beau is like a tall glass of sweet tea."

At Eva's look of admonishment, Precious said, "I know, I know. I couldn't help myself. There is no better way to express my opinion of your Graham. Not that my opinion counts, of course."

"It does," Eva said. She smiled. "It does a lot. I'm very happy you approve, because I imagine we'll be seeing a lot of Graham in future. And I'm glad you finally met although I wish it hadn't been here. I didn't want him to see where I live until we move into our new flat. These halls smell like a workhouse."

She felt Precious's gaze but turned away. She wished she hadn't spoken, hadn't reminded herself of the six months she had lived in a workhouse, a time when her mother was ill and unable to take care of her. Eva had wanted to die. Even their tiny cottage had been preferable to that.

She felt the weight of the silver cigarette case in her pocket. Her mother would have told her to give it back, that a gentleman didn't give expensive gifts to a woman unless he wanted something in return.

But wouldn't that mean she'd have to be willing? And Eva wasn't.

"Do you think we should go see the new flat before we agree?" Precious asked, her expression showing that she already knew the answer.

"No. If it's good enough for Graham's future brother-in-law, I'm going to believe it's good enough for us." Eva allowed herself a small smile. Maybe she was due a windfall. Windfalls never happened to her—she had to make them all by herself. But maybe, finally, her luck had changed.

"Graham's sure sweet on you, Eva. I hope his intentions are pure."

"What do you mean?"

Precious arched an eyebrow. "He's not from our world, is he?" Her smile took the sting from her words. "Men like him rarely marry girls like us."

Eva managed to hide the sharp blade of anger that sliced through her, because she couldn't be angry at Precious. Not when her friend had voiced the same thoughts that had been circling her head ever since she'd met Graham St. John and seen his smile. She felt the hard ball of the crumpled note in her fist. "I suppose I'll think about that when I have to."

Precious laughed. "You sound like Scarlett O'Hara."

"From **Gone With the Wind**? I haven't read it, but I know there's a film coming."

"Well, you should read it. Scarlett always waits until tomorrow to figure out her problems."

"And does that work?"

"Not really." Precious smiled. "But I suppose it's always worth a try."

Eva turned away to tidy the cushion on the sofa. She sat down to remove the pins from her hair as a stray thought buzzed inside her head, refusing to land. It wasn't until later, when she was applying cold cream to her face before bedtime, that she realized what it was: The encounter between Precious and Alex on the sidewalk in front of Lushtak's hadn't been accidental at all. It almost seemed like an attempt by Alex to see Eva again. The thought unsettled her, enough so that she thought she should mention it to Graham.

She finished taking off her makeup, chatting and gossiping idly with Precious, pushing aside all worries for another day, just like that Scarlett character. But when she fell asleep later, she dreamed of a bee buzzing about inside her head, and in the dream, when she looked at the top of her new silver cigarette case, the bee was gone.

CHAPTER 12

LONDON
MAY 2019

I was dreaming of bees. I was back in Walton, in the gazebo behind Aunt Cassie's house, the sun hot on my skin. The buzzing circled my head where I lay on one of the benches, smelling the summer grass. I couldn't move, and I lay still, anticipating the inevitable sting, the uncertain wait worse than the eventual pain.

"Madison?"

Confused, I opened my eyes and stared up at the porcelain ceiling fixture, trying to remember who called me by my full name. Something rough stuck to my face. When I turned my head, I realized it was the tulle underskirt of the yellow sundress I'd been writing about.

"Madison?"

I couldn't tell if the voice was annoyed or amused, but it was definitely Colin's. My eyes popped open to see Colin standing at the foot of the bed, his arms crossed as he watched me. I sat up, realizing I'd fallen asleep on top of a pile of Precious's clothes, my laptop still on but with its top sprawled open like a mouth, my screen saver scrolling through my album of family photos.

"Yes—I'm awake." I quickly slammed my laptop shut. "Sorry—the jet lag is killing me." I looked at him. "Weren't you going into the office?"

"I did. But that was five hours ago. Precious is waiting for us to have tea with her and chat."

"Right," I said, scrambling to get off the bed, hoping I hadn't caused any permanent damage to any of the dresses. I held up the sundress. "I love this one—I need to ask her about it and see if we can include it in the exhibition." I stood, swaying a bit from rising too quickly, and Colin grabbed my arm. "I'm fine. I'm fine. Just a little light-headed." I waved my hand at him. "Go on—I'll be right there."

I took a few minutes to brush my hair and teeth and grabbed my notepad and Precious's sundress. I found Colin looking at one of the framed photos along the corridor, his hands clasped behind his back as if he were in a museum. I stopped next to him and recognized the old wedding photo, the young soldier and his bride.

"Those are my father's parents," he said without looking at me. "David and Sophia."

"They're very much in love," I said.

He turned to me. "It's their wedding day. I would assume that would be the norm."

"Not necessarily. But these two—you can tell it's legit." I pointed to the groom's head. "Look how he's leaning into her." I tapped on the glass, where her hand rested in the crook of his arm. "And see how she's pulling him toward her. Definitely true love."

I leaned in to get a better look at the groom and frowned. "Didn't Arabella say that Precious thinks you look like your grandfather?"

"Yes," Colin said slowly, considering the picture. "Although I must say, I've never seen it."

"I don't, either," I agreed. "Not like that man in the photo we found in Sophia's papers."

"The one you think is hot."

I avoided his gaze. "I was just saying that to be nice." I slung the dress over my forearm and lifted the frame from the wall. "It looks like this is part of a larger photo—there is definitely a woman standing next to the bride."

I tapped on the side of a turned head, glossy light-colored hair twisted up in an elegant style under a small hat. After flipping the photo over, I began to remove the backing.

"What are you doing?"

"Don't worry. I'll fix it. But we know Sophia and Eva were friends. If this is a larger photo of the wedding party, maybe Eva is in it."

"But how will that help us find her?" Colin held

out his hands for the discarded frame and backing as I carefully separated the glass from the photograph, excited to see part of the picture that had been folded under, inside the frame.

"It won't, but how awesome would it be if we find Eva and we're able to document the two friends before and after?"

"Ah," Colin said. "So there's a method to your madness."

"Always." I held up the photograph, trying to decipher what I was seeing. "Hmm."

Colin looked over my shoulder. "I've seen many photos of Nana from her younger years, and that's definitely her." He indicated the woman whose face was half-turned from the viewer, smiling at the person standing next to her—a person who, judging by the jagged edge, had been torn from the photo. Even though Precious's full face wasn't visible, it was still a beautiful photograph of her, showing off her long neck and perfect profile, the porcelain skin.

As if reading my mind, Colin said, "That's probably why she didn't tear it off completely. She can be a bit vain. Don't tell her I said that." He ran his finger along the jagged edge. "But why tear it at all?"

"I was thinking the same thing." A satin-clad woman's shoe and slender ankle were all that was visible of the unknown person.

"Let's ask her," I said, bringing the frame and photo with me as I walked slowly, checking to see if any of the other framed photographs appeared to have been folded over. The photographs were mostly of Precious posing on catwalks or on fashion magazine covers, including several from **Vogue Paris**. Other than the one of her exiting the car, there weren't photographs of any man except for Colin's grandfather David in his wedding photo, and of Colin at varying ages.

"You have cute knees," I said, stopping in front of a young Colin wearing a schoolboy uniform of knee socks, shorts, navy blue jacket, and plaid tie.

"I'm glad you approve."

"Don't you find it strange that there aren't any photos of her with friends? No photos of her family in the States. None of Eva, yet she says they were like sisters. And none from before the war, except for the wedding photo and that one of her in the car."

"It's not inconceivable that they were destroyed during the war."

I paused at the photo of Precious as a glamorous young woman stepping out of the car, her expression, that cry for help, at odds with the rest of her. "It's still a part of her story. I've discovered in my years as a journalist that what people leave out is as important as what they include."

"Very true," he said. "And I'm not even a journalist."

I met his gaze, uncomfortable with its intensity. He hadn't mentioned my outburst in the park, as if he knew I'd already said everything I was ready to say. "Come on," I said, moving away. "Let's not keep her waiting."

Precious was holding court in the large front reception room, standing before a bay window overlooking Marylebone Road, the constant moan and huff of muted afternoon traffic part of the ambience. She wore her signature peach, this time in another lounge set but with a feather boa thrown around her neck, the only evident acknowledgment of her age a bejeweled hand leaning on the edge of the kidney-shaped writing desk I'd been using. The tea tray had been placed on top of the desk, but Laura and Oscar had already disappeared from the room.

Precious didn't turn around, and I thought she might not have heard us. I was about to say her name when she spoke. "I'm always surprised, despite the years that have passed since I first looked out this window in nineteen thirty-nine, how the view has hardly changed at all."

A brass carriage clock on the mantel chimed, and she faced us, a crease between her brows. "Why do you look so surprised to see me standing? I'm not quite one hundred, you know. Even before Jane Fonda, I believed in exercise. Lots of walking every day. Walking is the best way to learn a city and its citizens, I've found."

"Is it?" Colin asked.

"Oh, yes. And I have quite the knack for noticing details about people. It's one of my talents."

She smiled at me. "Come closer and let me see that dress."

I stood next to her and held up the yellow sundress. Precious nodded. "I remember that dress. We both wore it. We were the same size, you see."

"You and Eva?"

She nodded, her eyes focusing on the dress. "I remember when I wore it the first time. It was on a beautiful spring day in Kew Gardens. We'd gone to see the cherry blossoms. Have you been yet?"

"No, not yet. I'm not sure I'll have time for it on this trip. . . ."

"Don't be silly. Colin will be happy to take you." Ignoring my protests, she turned to Colin. "Would you please bring me my tea and fix my plate, dear?"

As he did, I said, "I'd like to add this one to the exhibition, if that's all right with you. It's so different from the other outfits, and I like the story about Kew. I think people will respond to it, since that's something people still do today." I placed the dress gently over the back of the sofa and held up my notebook. "So, you wore it for an outing at Kew. Was Eva with you?"

She smiled, then nodded. "We were always together, it seemed."

Colin set down her iced tea and plate on the table by the sofa and sat down next to her.

"I've already told Arabella, but I also need you to promise, Maddie, that any photographs taken of me for the article will only be taken from my best side." Precious smiled as she said it, but her eyes were serious.

I recalled the magazine cover photos and other pictures framed along the back hallway, her face always shown from the right or slightly tilted to the left. "Not that you have a bad side, but I understand. You're the professional model, and I will bow to your expertise."

With careful hands, she picked up her glass of iced tea. "Aren't you having any today, Maddie?" She winked. I wondered how much longer she could stand it before she confessed to Laura.

"Um, no, thank you. Just water for me."

Colin and I helped ourselves to the refreshments, then returned to the two armchairs in front of the sofa. As Precious and Colin ate and drank their tea, I excused myself and retrieved my Hasselblad. Arabella would be using a professional photographer for the article, but portraiture had always fascinated me, and Precious Dubose was a fascinating subject. I snapped the shutter, my eye looking for light and shadow, for the gray areas in between. It was those gray areas of a person, the places most people didn't notice, that always caught my attention. The part that gave away some secret the subject might not even be aware they were hiding.

Colin picked up the wedding photograph I'd taken from the frame and showed it to Precious. "These are my grandparents, right?"

She blinked, surprised. "Did you take that off my wall? Go right now and put it back. . . ."

Her voice faded as Colin unfolded the other half of the photo and pointed to the blond woman, her face partially turned away from the camera. "Is that you?"

"It's too hard to tell. My eyes aren't as good as they used to be."

"I'll be happy to go get your glasses, Precious," I offered.

She tucked her chin as if she'd been grievously offended. "I don't wear glasses."

"Yes, you do, Nana," Colin said. "I think that's the chain around your neck."

Her hand went to her chest, her fingers digging beneath the feather boa. She pulled out a pair of glasses dangling from a rhinestone chain and pretended to be surprised to find them there. Then she looked at the photograph and was silent for a long moment.

"Yes," she said at last. "That's David and Sophia on their wedding day. It was a beautiful sunny day. Funny the things a person remembers."

"It was July nineteen thirty-nine," Colin offered. "And you were a bridesmaid?"

She studied the photo again, then slowly nodded. "Yes, I was." She put a gentle finger over her image. "I remember that we were all in high spirits. Britain wasn't in the war yet, you see, and there were a lot of us who liked to pretend it would avoid us entirely, that life would always be like it was." She frowned. "I keep it on my wall to remember that day. So I can pretend we are all still young and happy. It's like we're all frozen in time."

Her gaze lifted, and I released the shutter. Her gaze moved to me, and she said, "That's the point of photographs, isn't it, Maddie? To choose which parts of our lives we want to remember?"

"Sometimes," I conceded. I pointed at the photograph. "There's a woman standing on the other side of you, but that part of the picture's been torn off. I remember you saying that you and Eva were like sisters and that Eva knew Sophia. We discovered that Eva's last name was Harlow—we found it in a letter addressed to Sophia—so we know they were at least acquaintances. But I was curious if she was in the wedding party, too, and what happened to the rest of the photograph."

Again, Precious's gaze met mine, her eyes a deep blue behind her glasses. Where there should have been a reflection, I saw only the gritty depth of despair, the debris left behind like coffee grounds at the bottom of a lifetime of sorrowful moments. I'd seen it many times in photographs of people following a calamity or natural disaster. Those people wore their suffering on their faces. But Precious was an actress wearing a mask of normalcy. I recognized it; it was the same mask I saw each time I looked at my own reflection. It was how I could recognize her regret and her emptiness. And why I wanted to snatch the photograph away, to forget I'd ever shown it to her. To beg her forgiveness.

"Yes," she said, her voice thready. "I remember both of us being bridesmaids. There was a third, too. Violet. David's sister. She went to Africa as a nurse during the war, I think." She cleared her throat. Her lips wobbled into a semblance of a smile. "Our dresses were pink silk shantung, and we wore beehive-netted veils that matched the bride's. Sophia's was white, of course. It was a small wedding, held at her parents' parish church. And then a party afterward at Hovenden Hall."

Her smile fell. Breath raced through her voice, deadening it. I handed her the glass of iced tea, and she swallowed a deep gulp.

When I leaned over to replace it, the small heart-shaped charm that I wore on a gold chain around my neck slipped out from the collar of my shirt. With surprising quickness, Precious grabbed my hand as I reached to tuck it back inside.

"What's that?" she asked, her eyes shuttering, the depths no longer accessible.

I could have said anything, because I was sure her only interest was in changing the topic of conversation, but I chose the truth. "My stepmother gave it to me when I graduated from high school." My hand clasped the heart-shaped charm made to resemble the chain full of heart-shaped charms that had once belonged to my mother, now worn by Aunt Cassie, the designated "keeper of the hearts" in our family.

"Is there something engraved on it?" Her glasses were once again hidden beneath the feather boa, a nod to vanity.

I nodded. "'A life without rain is like the sun without shade.'"

Her eyes met mine, and I was reminded of the first time we'd met, when she had told me that grief was like a ghost. And how I'd been sure she knew exactly what that meant.

Colin's phone began to vibrate. "Excuse me," he said, standing. "It's my mother. I'll be right back."

I nodded as he exited, leaving Precious and me alone; then I snapped a few more pictures of the room and of Precious holding the photograph. I sat down again and picked up the discarded wedding photo from the table. "I was hoping to find a picture of Eva. If we can't find her, I can at least use it with the article since so many of your stories include her."

Precious shook her head slowly. "I don't have any. This flat was severely damaged during the Blitz, you know. Thankfully it was mostly just two rooms, but one of them was mine, and all of my photographs were lost. The ones in the hallway are copies I received from Sophia so I'd have something to frame and hang on the wall when I returned to London."

"So you don't have any from when you were a little girl? My sister Knoxie would love to add some photos to the family tree."

"No, Maddie. My people were poor. We could barely rub two cents together. I can't remember a photograph of me taken before I moved to London." Her fingers grasped at the boa around her neck. "It's almost as if I didn't exist before the age of nineteen."

I tried to imagine not having a record of the first nineteen years of my life. Of my family and childhood. Of all the people and places I'd known that had brought me to this point. "Does that make you feel sad?"

She turned toward the bay window, looking out at the leaden sky. "Most people would love the chance to start all over again. They never consider the price, though. Of all you lose." Her head dipped, her chin tucked into the boa. "You can't reinvent yourself by dragging along anything from your old life. You have to get rid of it all—even the good parts. And you can't look back. Not ever. Living with regret is like having a permanent stone inside your shoe." She managed a half smile. "I think you're walking around with your own stone."

Her words stung. "Does it make you sad?" I asked again.

"Aren't all emotions relative? My sadness might be unrelatable to yours." Precious sat back, her slender fingers stroking the feathers of her boa, her eyes soft as she regarded me. "You tell me, Maddie. Does it?"

My eyes prickled. It had been years since I'd been confronted with my choices and forced to examine them.

"Sweetheart." Her voice was soft, her accent reminding me again of home and making my throat thicken. "One of the things I've learned in my ninety-nine years is that sometimes you get the answers you need by doing a little simple observation. People will just think you're shy and underestimate you." She leaned forward a little, her feather boa dangling. "And that will make you the smartest person in the room."

I looked down at my notes, in part to search for my next question, but also to hide my face from her scrutiny. I swallowed, then tried again. "I'd like to talk about your time in France during the war. I'm fascinated, because at the time France was occupied by the Germans, yet you left your life here and ended up modeling and living at the Ritz. I'm going to dig through the archives and try to find photographs of you from then, but I'd really like to know the details about that period in your life—about Paris's German-run fashion industry, about the clothes. About life in a city full of Nazis." I smiled, realizing I'd asked too many questions at once. "For starters, could you tell me why you went?"

She studied me for a long moment, and it was almost as if we were in a challenge to see who would speak first. "Oh, Maddie," she said, sighing. "For the same reason you left Georgia, I expect."

I sat up straight. "Excuse me?"

"Don't you know? To escape our ghosts."

We regarded each other in the dimming light, barely aware of the rain beginning to lash at the windows.

"Is everything all right?" Colin stood on the threshold, his gaze moving around the room as if he sensed the thick tension like a heat wave.

"Everything's fine," I said quickly.

"What did dear Penelope want?" Precious asked sweetly. "I hope she's not canceling our tea at Claridge's this Tuesday. I was so looking forward to it."

"No, actually. We found a photo of a man with Grandmother's papers. My parents believe they know who it is, but they said you would most likely be sure. May I show you?"

"Of course." Precious lifted her glasses to her nose and folded her hands delicately on her lap as Colin sat down next to her and showed her the screen of his phone. Her glasses reflected the light from the phone, obliterating her eyes. "Well, now," she said, her accent thicker, her voice controlled. "You are the spitting image of him, aren't you?"

Colin shot a glance in my direction. "Bella and Madison seem to think so, but I'm not convinced.

Father isn't sure, but Mother seems to think it's one of Grandmother Sophia's brothers. Did you know them?"

She looked away from the screen and took off her glasses. "I knew one of them. The younger one. They were twins, you know. But not identical. William was older, by only a few minutes."

"So this is William?"

"No. That's Graham." A soft smile lit her face. "He and Eva were lovers."

Fat pelts of rain hit the bay window, the sky outside ashen, matching the pallor of Precious's face.

"Do you know what happened to him, Nana? There's nothing we can find in the family records. My father says that when he was growing up, his uncle Graham was never mentioned—only William, since he was the hero who died in the war. Graham's uniform in the photograph says he was with the RAF, so I'm sure I can find something in the official record, but I was hoping you could give us a start."

"No, I'm afraid not." Her voice was so quiet I could barely hear her.

"Do you know what happened to him?"

She shook her head. "I lost touch with him at about the same time I lost touch with Eva." She looked past me toward the window. Softly, she said, "I always liked to think that they ended up together."

"Maybe they did," Colin said, his voice nearly lost in the violent thrash of rain against glass.

"Where do you think they might have gone?" I asked.

She gave a delicate shrug. "When I think of them, I imagine them living in a house high on a cliff, overlooking the sea. Eva always talked about the house she and Graham wanted to build." Her eyes met mine, and I saw that the darkness had returned, dulling their blueness. "Or maybe they simply went to a place where people go who want to stay lost."

I lifted my camera, eager to capture her face at that moment so I could study it later. A good photographer could find images that did the speaking for the subject, illuminating the emotions he or she kept under guard. And there was so much Precious Dubose had to say. It was as if she had two stories to tell: the one she wanted you to hear, and the truth.

I lowered my camera. "What about you, Precious? You were young and beautiful; you must have had lots of admirers. Was there anyone in particular?"

"Are you asking if I had a lover, too?"

Her candor took me by surprise, but I tried not to show it. "Yes. Did you?"

"You should go to Kew today." Precious was focused now on the photograph she held. "The cherry blossoms are so beautiful. Colin would love to take you, I'm sure."

"It's raining, Nana," Colin said. "I'll go get Laura. I think you need to rest."

I put the lens cover on my camera and stood, leaning over to kiss her soft cheek. "Thank you,

Precious. I'll keep looking for Eva. I'm sure if we find her, we'll find Graham, too."

Colin returned with Laura, and we said our good-byes as Laura escorted Precious back to her bedroom.

"What did you think of that?" Colin asked, pulling on his raincoat.

"I'm not sure. But there's definitely a story there. The good news is that now we can start looking for Graham, which might be easier, given his military record, and that might lead us to Eva." I looked pointedly at his raincoat. "I assume this means you're not taking me to Kew Gardens?"

His smile was as unexpected as it was charming, reminding me of the man in the photograph. "Not today, at any rate." He seemed to consider his next words, before saying, "I was going to head back to the office for a couple of hours, but we could do an early supper, if you like. We can make a plan of action on the best ways to find Eva Harlow and my great-uncle Graham. Unless you have other plans, of course."

I should have said no. It was too hard spending time with him and pretending to be indifferent. It had always been that way, but in college there had been other guys with whom I could deflect my interest. And his.

Besides, I had plans to go over my notes and browse the Internet for wartime photographs of the Paris fashion scene. But he looked so earnest, and I'd been so occupied taking notes that I'd hardly eaten anything at tea. "Sure. But can we go somewhere that serves normal food? I'm dying for a hamburger. Or barbecue. Either one of those is fine."

He quirked an eyebrow at the word "normal" but didn't say anything. "All right. I believe there are a few options on the high street."

"Let me run and get my jacket."

I found it buried under a mound of Precious's clothes on my bed, where I'd placed it before digging through one of the boxes that hadn't fit in the guest room. As I was fastening the large button at the neck, I thought I could smell the faint scent of old perfume clinging to the fabric. It was gone quickly, making me wonder if I'd imagined it. But it had somehow tugged loose a memory from an earlier conversation with Precious, when we'd first asked her if she'd like us to find Eva. **Just because a person is lost doesn't mean they want to be found.** And I wondered for the first time if she hadn't been talking about Eva at all.

CHAPTER 13

LONDON
MARCH 1939

Eva patted her hair to smooth any stray strands, catching sight of herself and Precious in the reflection of the hotel lobby door before a uniformed bellman opened it for them. She smiled without looking at him, the way she'd noticed many of the clients at Lushtak's did when encountering anyone in a service capacity. It was their way of showing appreciation while not lowering themselves.

She felt the appreciative stares as she and Precious crossed the black-and-white marble-tiled floor, their heels making gratifying clicks. She walked as if she were modeling, using a slow, steady pace to hide her nervousness. To act as if she belonged at Claridge's. Precious, her näiveté always misconstrued as confidence, simply moved forward as if tea at Claridge's were her due.

Sophia was already seated beneath the fluted arch when they arrived, making Eva falter, wondering if she'd gotten the time wrong. But Sophia smiled, stood to share air-kisses on each cheek, and fluttered her hands, as if to fling away Eva's apologies.

"I'm always dreadfully early, so I should be the one apologizing. Even Mother complains, saying I was an entire week early when I was born." She turned to Precious, her smile growing wider. "And this must be the lovely Miss Dubose whom Eva and Graham have told me so much about."

"I hope it was all good." Precious returned the smile. "And please, call me Precious. All of my friends do."

"Splendid," Sophia said, indicating the two seats on either side of her. "Only if you call me Sophia. I daresay I've heard so much about you that I feel as if we're already friends."

Eva relaxed, calmly sitting in the chair being held by a discreet maître d'. She even remembered not to look at him.

After they'd placed their orders, Sophia regarded Eva and Precious with open admiration, which was a relief—Eva had taken nearly two hours to dress. Her room was strewn with discarded outfits she'd considered before finding the knee-length pale blue suit with the formfitting belted jacket and adorable white pointed collar. It was the perfect mix of new and modern, elegance and poise.

Precious had known precisely what she would wear, a tea dress in lemon-colored silk chiffon, and had been dressed and waiting a good half hour before Eva was ready.

"You both look absolutely stunning," Sophia said. "I suppose I should never agree to be seen in public with either one of you because I dread the comparisons, but my guess would be that we'll be seeing quite a lot of one another. I daresay that Graham is quite smitten with you, Eva."

"Really?" was all Eva could think to say.

"Surely you know. And I can't tell you how many people have asked me about the gorgeous creature that Graham's been sporting on his arm of late. They think you're a foreign princess or some such nonsense. Not that I disabuse them of the notion, of course. It's much too fun to leave them guessing."

"I'm not surprised at all," Precious said. "She's pretty as a peach and smart as a tree full of owls. The best thing I ever did was bump into her at the train station and ask if she needed a roommate, which I guess makes me pretty smart, too."

Eva looked at Sophia for her reaction. Sophia laughed out loud. "And I would have to agree."

Eva sighed silently with relief.

Their sandwiches and cakes arrived, and while the tea was poured, they were silent, waiting to speak again until the servers had quietly removed themselves.

"What do you tell them?" Eva asked, hiding her interest as she sipped from her green-and-white-striped teacup.

"Catty girls I let believe what they will. But good friends I tell the truth."

Eva's hand shook as she replaced her cup in its saucer, spilling a drop of tea. "The truth?"

"Yes—about your parents being killed in a tragic accident and leaving you without any family. It does you credit, you know. That you reinvented yourself and forged a new life. You're very brave."

"Thank you for saying that." Eva looked into her teacup so she wouldn't have to meet Sophia's gaze.

"You both are," Sophia said. "Precious came all the way across an ocean, leaving her family behind. That would have been very difficult. You must miss them."

Precious nodded. "I do. I'm lucky to have found Eva. She's become my family here. It helps me not miss my family back in Tennessee so much."

She smiled across the table at Eva, and Eva smiled back, her eyes smarting.

Sophia cut off a bite of a custard-filled pastry, held it aloft with her fork, then replaced it on her plate. "I shouldn't eat that. Mother says I'll never be able to fit into my wedding dress if I'm not careful." She looked wistfully at Eva and Precious. "Both of you can probably eat anything you want, can't you? I'll attempt not to be green with envy."

Eva took a careful bite from her cucumber wedge sandwich and tried not to choke on it. She'd always been slender because she'd never had enough food as a child; she had gone to bed hungry more times than she cared to remember. She forced a smile. "I'm sure it will catch up with me one day, although I do think being so tall helps."

Precious nodded. "That's the thing with fashion, Sophia. Every woman can wear beautiful clothes, as long as they're cut to flatter her figure. You're built differently than we are, so different clothes will suit us best. You can still be the most gorgeous woman in the room."

"Do you really think so?" Sophia said.

"Of course," Eva said. "More important than what you're wearing is your smile and character. I'm sure that's what David loves most about you."

Sophia's cheeks flushed prettily. "Thank you for saying that. You are both such dears." After a brief hesitation, she picked up her fork and placed the sweet pastry into her mouth.

After another sip of tea, Sophia said to Eva, "I trust you were reunited with your purse?"

"Yes, thank you. I'd been planning to send an invitation to tea to thank you for its return, and for the flat, but I received your invitation first. But I do want to thank you so much for your kindnesses. I'd like to think we'd be friends even if we hadn't met through Graham."

"Of course we would be. All three of us. And don't be silly. The two of you are doing us a favor, accepting the offer to live in the flat. David's quite fond of it—good memories of his bachelor days, I suppose. Besides, I was hoping the offer would sweeten you both up before I asked a favor."

"A favor?" Eva said, surprised. She couldn't imagine Sophia needing anything from them.

"Yes. You're both models and have such wonderful taste in all matters to do with fashion, and I would like your help in selecting dresses for my two bridesmaids. I'm afraid my friends aren't quite up to the task."

"Of course. We'd love to help," Precious said. "Right, Eva?"

Eva nodded. "Will we get to meet them so we can determine a flattering style?"

"Sadly, no," Sophia said. "They've both recently married—breaking their mothers' hearts by having quick weddings because their husbands have signed up for the Territorial Army."

"Really? We're hardly at war. Isn't that a bit premature?" Eva looked down at her plate, where she'd just placed a large dollop of clotted cream on a scone, her appetite suddenly gone.

"Mother and Father don't like to talk about such things in my hearing, but thankfully David doesn't keep anything from me. He's convinced that we are headed toward war. He works in Whitehall, so I trust his opinion. He's actually talked about signing up himself."

"Oh, no," Eva said, her thoughts on Graham.

"I hope your David's wrong," Precious said. "For all of us." And because she was Precious, she reached across the table and squeezed Sophia's arm.

Sophia sent her a grateful smile, then turned to Eva. "Has Graham mentioned anything to you about signing up?"

Eva shook her head, her stomach turned sour. "No, he hasn't. Perhaps he gets enough talk of politics and such at work and leaves it there. Should I ask him?"

"It's all right," Sophia said. "Maybe we shouldn't know. I do rather resent David for telling me and spoiling some of the fun of planning our wedding." Sophia drew her shoulders back. "But I'm prepared to reinvent myself and be brave for the first time in my life. Right now I need to ensure that my wedding goes as planned so that I have a son or daughter to keep me company if David is right and our men have to fight."

Eva tried to offer a reassuring smile, but her lips wouldn't obey. "They won't, Sophia. I'm sure of it."

"Yes, well, it's all rather inconvenient, isn't it?" Sophia used her fork and knife to cut into a chocolate-covered eclair, then returned her silverware to her plate without taking a bite. "David and

I are looking forward to the fashion show this Saturday. We'll be in the front row with Graham."

"Will your mother be joining you again?" Precious asked, and Eva sent her a quick look of thanks for putting into words the question she'd been trying to ask.

"No. Not this time." Sophia stopped speaking as the waiter appeared with a pot of fresh tea.

Precious used the opportunity to excuse herself. "I need to go powder my nose," she said with a wink.

After the waiter had left, Sophia leaned toward Eva. "About Mother. It's best that she isn't at the show. Graham and I need time to get her used to the idea of you." Sophia sat back in her chair and looked across the table. Candidly, she said, "I like you, Eva. You're not like those vacuous debs Mother always throws at Graham. I say, a model isn't what most people would call suitable, but I think you're perfect."

Eva busied herself by putting another teaspoon of sugar into her already-too-sweet tea, unsure how to respond to a comment that was neither insult nor compliment.

Sophia continued. "Besides, you weren't born working-class, were you? A doctor's daughter is quite respectable. You're obviously educated and—What did Precious say? 'Smart as a tree full of owls.'" Sophia laughed lightly. "You're also very beautiful. A catch, in my opinion." She took a sip from her teacup, then replaced it on the saucer as she had undoubtedly been trained to do in the schoolroom, without making a sound of china against china. "I'm not saying this because Graham and I enjoy ruffling Mother's carefully coiffed feathers, either." She grinned devilishly. "Personally, I think new blood is a good thing."

Eva returned the smile, her spoon moving back and forth in the teacup, the sugar clumping on top in the lukewarm tea. Precious rejoined them, unaware of all the heads turning as she crossed the room.

"To reinvention," Sophia said, lifting her cup.

"To reinvention," Precious agreed, doing the same.

"To reinvention," Eva repeated before bringing her cup to her lips and taking a long sip. She didn't taste a thing.

"No, thank you," Freya said with a dismissive snort at Precious. "I'll stick with the Bromo-Seltzer. It's what we've always used before a show, and I don't see a need to change now."

Despite the other models' refusal to try her pre-show concoction, Precious remained cheerful. "You don't know what you're missing. But that's fine. More for us. Right, Eva?"

Eva looked suspiciously at the bottles of Coca-Cola and the bowl of shelled monkey-nuts Precious had set on the dressing table. Precious referred to them as peanuts, but Eva had known them only as the food fed to elephants at the circus. She'd been to one once when she was a little girl, sneaking in through an opening in the tent.

"Maybe I should take the Bromo-Seltzer, too, just in case."

Precious laughed as she funneled her hand and let the little nuts slide into the neck of the bottle. She'd already instructed Eva to take three sips to make room. Handing the bottle to Eva, she said, "Go ahead."

Eva hadn't been prepared to like it, but after she took the first salty-sweet sip, she couldn't stop. "It's not bad," she admitted. "I'll let you know if I still have energy after I've shown ten frocks, but it's surprisingly drinkable." Smiling at her friend, she asked, "Are you ever wrong?"

"I'm sure I am, but I tell myself that being wrong is just an opportunity to look for another answer. It makes decisions a whole lot easier to live with—that's for sure." Precious put her own bottle to her lips and tilted her head back. Eva did the same. Precious leaned toward her, her gaze scrutinizing. "The makeup on your neck has rubbed off, and you can see the little dark spot. Personally, I think it gives you an air of mystery. You shouldn't bother covering it up."

Eva's hand immediately went to her neck in an attempt to cover the dark birthmark. Although it was no bigger than a sixpence, she'd been afraid that Madame Lushtak would notice it. She placed her empty Coke bottle on the table and stood. "I'll go find Mr. Danek. I hate it, and I don't want to have to look at it every time I see my reflection."

"All right. I'll save you some peanuts."

Eva nodded distractedly as she knotted her belt over her dressing gown and left. The show wasn't scheduled to start for another hour, but Mr. Danek had already finished painting the faces of the six models and was having a rare break before the mayhem began. He sat, leaning back in his chair, the front legs off the floor. He was reading the newspaper and smoking a cigarette, a scowl on his face.

"Mr. Danek?" The scowl remained as he looked up, but when he saw it was Eva, he smiled. "I need a little touch-up, if you have a moment."

"For you, always." He stood, took her chin between his thumb and forefinger, and turned her face from side to side. "I only see perfection."

"Then you need glasses. Just a little more makeup on my neck, please," she said as she sat and lifted her chin to show him.

"It is invisible already, but if you insist, I will do my best." He sat down on a stool next to her and began searching through the piles of cosmetics on the table.

She scrutinized the jars as he searched. "Why were you scowling? The birds are singing and the flowers are blooming, and I can't imagine there's anything that would make me frown right now with spring going on right outside my window."

He picked up a small jar and gave Eva an exasperated look. "You should try to be more informed, Eva. There is a lot going on in this world that you should know about. Poland is continuing to refuse to capitulate to Germany's demand to annex Danzig and the Polish Corridor. Herr Hitler does not like to hear the word 'no.'"

"But that's so far away," Eva said, tilting her head so he could apply the makeup. "I'd rather wait to worry about it when—or if—I have to."

His dark eyes bored into hers. "That's what the sleeping fly said before the newspaper hit it. Has your Graham said nothing to you about what's going on? He works in Whitehall, yes?"

She smiled softly. "We don't talk about things like that. He takes me to lovely buildings in the city and tells me about their history and design. We go on long walks and talk about things we like and the people we know and sometimes nothing at all. And we're going to Kew tomorrow to see the cherry blossoms. You see? There's so much more to life than worrying about Hitler. I say, thank goodness for the English Channel separating us from Europe."

"I'm afraid Mr. Hitler views the Channel as a mere pond he can wade through to get what he wants." Mr. Danek pulled out a powder puff and dabbed it on Eva's nose and neck. "Sometimes I wish I had the ignorance of youth. How much happier I'd be."

The sharp edge of his voice made Eva regard him warily. "I'm not ignorant, Mr. Danek. I'm just trying to be happy." She winced, realizing how that sounded. "I'm not frivolous—I know there is real suffering and danger in the world. But I lived in misery for the first eighteen years of my life, and I finally have real happiness within my grasp. I don't want to let it go."

His eyes were sad when he spoke, and Eva remembered his dead wife and how little she really knew about Mr. Danek. "I have found that happiness is simply the absence of all other emotions. Remember, it's best to always keep one eye open. Bad things usually happen when we're not paying attention."

"Is that why you had to leave Prague? Because you weren't paying attention?"

He straightened. "It's one of the reasons."

"And your friend from the café, Mr. Zeman. What does he say?"

"Jiri thinks we should work with the Germans, that our economies will prosper if we all go along with their demands."

"Wouldn't going along with the Germans be more peaceful, then?"

Mr. Danek smiled at her, lifting just a corner of his mouth. "Ah, the näiveté of youth. You are like a cat, I think. You will always land on your feet no matter what happens."

She wasn't sure if that was a compliment, so she

didn't say anything. Instead, she reached into the pocket of her dressing robe and pulled out her new cigarette case. "Do you have a minute to look at something? I'm trying to find out what this means."

He took the case, raising an eyebrow as he felt its heft. "This is very nice. Expensive. Did your young man give it to you?"

Eva couldn't meet his eyes, knowing she'd see disappointment in them. "No. It was given to me by another gentleman—someone I met at a dinner party."

He was silent. When she didn't look up, he continued to examine the silver case. "It's very beautiful. But I hope you are planning on returning it to him."

"Why?" But she already knew. She'd been hearing the words in her mother's voice ever since Alex had given it to her.

"Because only a certain type of gentleman gives an expensive gift to a woman who is not his."

Now their eyes did meet. "I'm not married or even engaged, Mr. Danek. Therefore I didn't feel as if I should refuse."

His eyes remained on hers for a long moment. Finally looking down, he flipped over the case. "Are these the words you need translated?"

She nodded. "Do you know what language it is?"

"Latin—from an old proverb." He studied the case, then read the words out loud. **"'Nil credam et omnia cavebo.'"**

She repeated the words, loving how the rounded vowels felt on her tongue.

"You really have an excellent ear, Eva. Your pronunciation is perfect."

She blushed at the compliment. "But what does it mean?"

"Betray before you are betrayed. It's not an exact translation, but that's what it means more or less." He lifted his gaze to her face. "An odd gift to a young woman from a virtual stranger, don't you think?"

Eva agreed, but she didn't want to admit it. "Maybe it was already engraved when he bought it. I doubt he knew what it meant. But the bee on the front is so lovely. He said it was exquisite and unique and that's why he thought of me when he saw it."

"Did he?" Mr. Danek pressed the button, and the case popped open, exposing Eva's Matinée cigarettes.

"Yes. I found it charming," she said, sounding defensive.

"As I'm sure was his intention." He snapped the case shut. "Be careful, Eva. It is sometimes hard to recognize wolves because they are wearing sheep's clothing."

"Thank you for the warning, Mr. Danek, but I'm too old for fairy tales. I'm quite capable of taking care of myself."

"Yes, you are, my dear. But you have a fondness

for beautiful things. Some might see it as a weakness and use it to their advantage. That is all I am saying."

He placed the case in her hand, and she closed her fingers over it, then stood. "It's only a cigarette case. He meant no harm."

"Is that so? And what did your Graham say about it?"

Eva shook her head, flustered. "I haven't had a chance to tell him yet, but he'll understand."

Mr. Danek stood, too, his face unsmiling. "I am sure he will."

Eva nodded. "Thank you for fixing my makeup. You're a genius."

"Thank **you**, Eva, for giving me such a beautiful canvas upon which to work." He gave her a mock bow.

She said good-bye, then walked hurriedly back to the models' room, which had erupted into a volcano of silk stockings, garters, and step-ins as the girls began dressing in their first outfits. She dressed, too, and chatted with Precious and the other models, their voices shriller and higher than usual because of nerves and excitement. Madame Lushtak had sent in champagne, and the atmosphere was almost festive as the girls sipped and offered one another encouragement. Even Freya had kind words for Eva, making Precious raise her brows.

"Graham will be in the first row, remember,"

Precious said to Eva. "So look there first. He'll give you all the confidence you need. You'll walk on air for the rest of the show."

Mrs. Ratcliffe entered. "All right, ladies. Settle down, please. Eva, you're first, in the beaded evening gown. Girls, you know the order, so please line up behind Eva and follow me."

Eva trailed her through the hallways to the showroom door, the other models close behind, waiting in anticipation for the door to open. They'd rehearsed everything—when to turn; when to drop a wrap to highlight a neckline; when to stick hands in pockets to show them off. Eva pressed her hands to the beaded bodice of her gown, amazed that she wasn't nervous.

She could hear the murmur of voices quieting as Madame Lushtak greeted the guests. Staring at the closed door in front of her, she thought of Graham, in the front row, next to Sophia and her fiancé, David. The door began to open, and she took a step forward, her gaze trained on the spot where she knew he'd be.

The bright lights glinted off Graham's light hair, giving his head an aura like a halo. He smiled at her as she walked in the direction of the front row, taking in Sophia and David sitting in the two seats next to him. She stifled an inexplicable and unexpected pang of disappointment, her smile slipping slightly as she tried to figure out why. She'd made it around the room once and was in the middle of her second pivot before she realized she'd been hoping to see another face in the crowd, one with silver eyes and a mocking mouth, one belonging to a stranger who thought her exquisite and unique.

CHAPTER 14

LONDON
MAY 2019

I sat amid the piles of letters and photographs at the dining table in Precious's flat, watching the sun rise over the London skyline and bathe the buildings outside the large bay window in buttery light. Morning had always been my favorite time of day, the chatter and static of life briefly held inert. When I was little, I'd wake up early and go sit with my mama on the front porch swing while she drank her coffee. We'd talk about nothing in particular. Sometimes we wouldn't talk at all. But when I looked back, I felt as if we'd spoken volumes, that our time together on that swing had been the most profound hours of my life.

I'd heard Colin leave an hour before. Now George

was lying at my feet, snoring loudly while Oscar sat nearby, eyeing me. I turned at the sound of tapping on the doorframe and smiled at Laura, who held out a double leash.

"I was wondering where the dogs were. It's time for their morning walk and breakfast." She bent down to affix the leash to the dogs' collars.

"Is there a printer in the flat that I can use? I could go to Arabella's office, but it's a bit far."

"There's a nice one in Colin's room—on the big desk. He lets me use it all the time, so I can't imagine why he wouldn't allow you to use it, too."

"In his bedroom?"

"Yes—but it's perfectly all right. You can text him, if you like."

"All right—I'll do that."

"I'll see you later. Call me if you need anything. Precious is still asleep. Usually she doesn't have breakfast until eleven, so she shouldn't need anything before then. Listen for her bell, though, just in case." Laura gave me a thumbs-up and led George by the leash but picked up Oscar, and the little dog peered at me over her shoulder. I could have sworn he was narrowing his eyes like Clint Eastwood in a gunfight.

I usually viewed and organized my photographs and notes on my laptop, but for this project, I felt the need to print everything out. I wanted to get a better idea of how everything would fit together and which holes could be filled if we found Eva. There was something about Precious's story that defied containment, that made me think I was on a circuitous path with no beginning or ending. I sent Colin a text, asking for permission to use his printer. And when I hit "send," I immediately heard a ping from under a pile of newspaper clippings on the other end of the table.

Carefully, I removed the papers and saw Colin's phone. I picked it up, and as I held it, it rang. No name or picture was attached to the number, so I assumed it was Colin calling from someone else's phone in an attempt to find his. I swiped to answer and said hello.

A woman's voice said, "You're not Colin."

"No, I'm not, but I have Colin's phone. Who's this?"

"I'm Imogen Smith."

I tried to place her accent—not quite cabdriver Cockney but not without some of its idiosyncrasies and odd inflections. Like someone pretending not to have a particular accent. It reminded me of how my aunt Cassie had sounded when she'd returned to Georgia after working in New York for more than a decade. "He's not here."

"Are you his new girlfriend, then?"

"No." I shook my head, even though she couldn't see me. "Definitely not. Colin's at work. Why don't you call him there or text him so he can reply when he collects his phone?"

She paused. "Are you sure you're not his girlfriend?"

"Quite sure."

"Good. Because I'm the old girlfriend, and you seem rather nice, so I wouldn't want to hate you without having met you. Besides, you're an American. I never thought Colin was especially fond of Americans. What did you say your name was?"

"I didn't. But it's Madison Warner."

"Oh! You're **that** Madison."

I shouldn't have been having this conversation with a complete stranger, but I had to know. "You mean he talked about me?"

"Yes. Quite a bit, actually. He talked about how you two didn't suit, and how you had appalling taste in men and a sense of humor that bordered on childish. I'll have you know that I had to do a lot of distracting to get him to stop talking about you. It was very frustrating."

"I'm sorry," I said, eager now to get her off the phone. "I'll tell him you called, but send a text just in case. . . ."

"It's better I don't communicate with him, or I might start crying again. Could you please just let him know that I still had the key to his house in Cadogan Gardens, so I put it through the post slot in the door?"

"I'll tell him."

I was about to end the call when she said, "Has he mentioned me?"

I paused a moment before answering, deciding that the blunt truth was what she needed. "No, Imogen. He hasn't."

Her voice with that odd accent seemed resigned. "I suppose I already knew it, deep down. Sometimes we just need to have someone else say an unpleasant truth out loud for us to believe it, don't we?"

"Probably."

"Thank you, Madison. Good-bye, then." She'd ended the call before I'd had the chance to say good-bye.

I stared at the phone in my hand, her words ringing in my ears. **Sometimes we just need to have someone else say an unpleasant truth out loud for us to believe it.** The words unsettled me, and I found myself staring out the front window for a long time, watching as morning bloomed around the buildings across the road.

Eventually, I fished out my own phone again and called Aunt Cassie. She picked up on the second ring.

"Maddie, sweetie. Is everything all right?"

"Yeah—it's all good."

"Can I call you back? I'm about to start a conference call."

"No need. Just wanted to hear your voice. And to tell you to go ahead and make that appointment with Dr. Grey for the week after the wedding. Yes, it can wait that long—it's just more tests. Nothing urgent. I've got some projects coming up before then, and I don't want to be distracted."

"Now, Maddie, are you sure you want to wait . . . ?"

"I'm sure. Just make the appointment, please, and we'll go from there. No sense borrowing tomorrow's troubles for today, right?"

I heard the smile in my aunt's voice. "Your mama used to say that all the time."

"I know."

We said our good-byes, and when I looked up, I saw Arabella in the doorway. "Everything all right?"

I nodded, avoiding her eyes. "Everything's fine."

She walked into the room, not looking entirely convinced. "I had a bit of time between meetings and I was curious about your two a.m. e-mail. You said you'd found something interesting?"

I stood and led her toward the corner where a stack of hatboxes waited. "These belonged to Sophia. I was hoping that even if we can't find anything about Eva, there'd be something about Graham, right? Sophia and Graham were siblings, so it makes sense. And if we find one, we should find the other."

"One could hope." The clothes racks had spilled over into the dining room, and Arabella stroked the sleeve of a fur coat, its nap flattened by years in storage. "Look at this beauty. Precious has a few pieces of Chanel from after the war. You know I'd love to showcase them in the exhibition, too, but she's not keen on talking about her time in France."

"I did ask her why she went. I thought maybe it'd be a gateway to my questions about the Resistance, her experiences modeling in an occupied Paris, and all that."

"What did she say?"

I considered not answering. When Arabella held her ground and didn't look away, I said, "According to her, she went for the same reason I left Georgia. To escape her ghosts. She's wrong about me, of course. I left to pursue my education."

Arabella dropped the sleeve to face me. "Why do you think she came back after all that time—and to London, not Memphis?"

I shrugged, uncomfortable with my friend's scrutiny. "Why indeed? Maybe her ghosts found somebody else to haunt."

"Perhaps. I'm curious what makes a person leave their home for so long, and then what it is that eventually brings them back."

Eager to change the topic, I grabbed Arabella's arm. "Come on," I said, leading her to the hatboxes. "This is what I found."

I lifted the top box and moved it to a clear spot on the dining table. "I was assuming these all had hats in them, which is why I didn't go through them right away. But I was very excited to find pictures instead. Early nineteen forties—don't you think?"

The box was half-filled with black-and-white

photographs. I recognized the bright blond hair in the images on the top layer and wondered if Precious knew these existed.

"Wow," Arabella said, lifting the top photo. It showed Precious walking down an aisle surrounded by chairs filled with well-dressed women and a few men. She wore a long gown in a shiny material. A matching stole was draped around her creamy shoulders, her face soft and open, wearing an easy smile. Of all the expressions I'd seen on Precious so far, I'd yet to see that particular one.

I did a mental calculation and figured she'd have been in her late teens or early twenties. Maybe that was the look most young women wore before time and life etched themselves on their innocent faces.

"I love this one," Arabella said, reaching in to pull out a photograph of Precious sitting on what appeared to be a park bench. Her hat was in her lap, her head turned toward the right. It looked as if she was laughing with someone just out of the picture frame.

"It's one of the very few that hasn't been cut." I reached inside the box again and retrieved three more photos, each one with a clean edge, the white border of the print conspicuously missing. "This reminds me of something my sisters did to photos of them and their exes. They'd cut out the boyfriend instead of destroying the photo because they were good shots of my sisters."

"And you never did that?" Arabella said absently, digging through the box.

"Hardly. Mostly because I'm the one who does the jilting." I plucked up another photograph from the top, one of Precious seated at a white-clothed table, a glass of something raised to her darkened lips. "Although, since these belonged to Sophia, that theory doesn't really makes sense, does it?"

"No, not really."

"You know," I said, running my finger down the smooth edge of the photo, "I don't think the damage to these photographs was done in anger—it was more of a planned thing."

"What do you mean?"

"Well, they're not torn, are they? This looks like it was done very calmly. Assuming it was Sophia, it looks like she had time to think about what she was doing. And it's so precise. My guess is she even used scissors."

"Have you found the other halves?" Arabella leaned over and picked up one of the smaller black-and-white photos.

"No, but I haven't gone through everything here yet."

Arabella nodded, studying the photograph in her hand. It showed Precious from the waist up, her head nearly hidden by a hat with an enormous brim. A dark-haired man in a black silk top hat, a waisted black coat, and a white cravat stood next to her. They were both looking into the camera, and Precious was smiling the kind of smile that made me think of a woman thrilled with her life.

The man was smiling, too, but it had nothing to do with joy or happiness. It was a smile someone planning to rob a bank might have worn, part cunning, part deception. As I looked closer, I couldn't help but think he had the look of a satisfied squirrel, one who'd hidden all of his acorns and wasn't planning to share.

"It looks like they're at Ascot! But that man—who do you suppose he is? Definitely not Graham—wrong hair—and I don't think it's Sophia's David, either. But he's a looker for sure." Arabella grinned at me, excited. "Have you looked in all the hatboxes? Silk top hats like he's got on here are rare—they're made from hatters' plush, and there just aren't any looms capable of producing that material anymore. Vintage models in good condition can go for tens of thousands of pounds. I would kill to have one for the exhibition."

"I haven't come across one, but be my guest. I was more interested in these photographs. I'd love to know why Sophia would have cut them."

"How peculiar," Arabella said, turning over a picture of Precious, with a darker blond woman who looked like Sophia, leaning against an old-fashioned car. "I wonder why they weren't thrown away. I mean, they're all damaged, so it's not like they can be framed or put in albums, so why keep them?"

"I agree." I took the photos from Arabella and put them back in the hatbox.

"By the way," she said, leaning across the table, "Aunt Penelope called me yesterday. Her friend Hyacinth Ponsonby from the WI volunteers at the National Archives, and Penelope said Hyacinth is thrilled—her exact word—to help dig for information on Colin's great-uncle Graham. A lot of new information has recently been released to the public, and Hyacinth is very excited to delve into the mystery. Aunt Penelope did say she was scolded for not having asked sooner. Even explaining that Colin's father never heard Graham's name mentioned while growing up didn't exonerate Penelope's oversight. Apparently, genealogy is Hyacinth's passion, and she says that Colin's branch of the St. John family is quite illustrious. Sadly, unless he has children, he's the last of them. And at this rate, I'm not sure that's ever going to happen."

"I have to ask—what is the WI? And is Hyacinth Ponsonby a real person, or did you just make that up? If I were writing a cozy British mystery, I'd probably use that name for the old lady who accidentally solves the murder. I bet she has cats, too."

Arabella let out a heavy sigh. "The WI is the Women's Institute—a women's organization that provides a lot of services to the community. It's been around for ages and was virtually mandatory if you lived in the country during the war. The WI made sure the home front was operating efficiently, that gardens were growing food, not flowers, and all sorts of other things. Penelope and my mother are members. So am I, but I don't have a lot of time for meetings. Mother said at the last one, one of the members made a fruitcake in the shape of a corgi in honor of the queen's birthday."

"Wow. Sorry I missed that."

"Me, too." She plucked a yellowed clipping from the table and handed it to me. "Oh—look at this! It's from **The Tatler**, July 1939. Really just a huge gossip rag then and now, but very illuminating."

I looked at her. "Illuminating?"

"Yes. A recent headline accused Meghan Markle of being the next Wallis Simpson, which I thought rather brilliant. But that's not what I'm referring to." With a manicured finger, Arabella tapped on the clipping page. "Recognize the photo?"

I frowned down at it, wondering why it seemed so familiar. Then, brightening, I straightened. "Of course—it's Sophia's wedding photo. Still without the entire wedding party." I tried to keep the disappointment out of my voice.

"True," she said. "But look—it lists names of those in attendance."

I quickly scanned the paragraphs printed beneath the photograph.

> Miss Sophia St. John of Hovenden Park in Guildford and Mr. David Eliot of Stoke-on-Trent were married at the bride's home on

the 10th of July. Bridesmaids were Miss Eva Harlow of Devon and Miss Jeanne Dubose of Memphis. The groom's best man was the bride's brother, Mr. Graham St. John. Also in attendance was fellow Harrovian Alexander Grof of Prague.

"Well," I said, "we now know Eva Harlow was from Devon. That should help our search."

"True," Arabella said. "Precious will be so excited that she doesn't have to remember some of these details. I asked Aunt Penelope to see if there are any of Sophia's photograph albums at Hovenden Hall, and she said she'd look. There are dozens of course, probably going back to the invention of the camera, so it's just a matter of finding the right one."

"I'd like to think that a house that managed to hang on to a panel of Henry the Eighth's banqueting tent would probably still have photographs taken only eighty years ago."

"You're being sarcastic, aren't you?"

"Definitely," I said. I pointed to my laptop. "I need to use Colin's printer. Laura said she was sure it was fine, but when I texted him to check, I discovered he'd left his phone here. Should I go ahead, or will Colin have a hissy fit?"

A male voice said from the doorway, "Colin's not sure what a hissy fit is, but probably not."

We both turned to see Colin. He wore a navy suit and tie, looking like the quintessential British businessman. Except for the cleft in his chin and the smattering of freckles on his nose and cheekbones, which hinted at the boy Colin tried his best to hide. He held a brown paper package tucked under one arm.

"Sorry—we didn't know you were there," I said.

"Apparently. I came to fetch my phone."

"I know. I texted to ask if I could use your printer, and it pinged." I picked his phone up from the table and handed it to him. "Also, you missed a call from Imogen. She said she put the key to the house in Cadogan Gardens in the mail slot."

His face might have paled a bit under his tan. "You spoke with her?"

"Of course I did. It would have been rude not to."

He looked at me expectantly, but I was enjoying myself too much to say anything else.

We continued our staring war until Arabella interrupted. "What's in the parcel?"

Colin's gaze shifted, and he looked at the bundle under his arm as if he'd forgotten it was there. "It was downstairs by the postboxes. I didn't look at the address, but I'm assuming it's for Madison." He handed the parcel to me.

A paper grocery bag had been cut and taped together as wrapping, and there were probably twenty or more small-denomination American stamps plastered in the top right corner. Crayon pictures decorated the front and back, and my name and the address had been written in alternating colored crayons in clear block print. I brought the package to my nose, smelling the unmistakable scent of Ravished, the signature perfume of the cosmetics line that Lucinda sold door-to-door and from her shop, Lucinda's Lingerie.

"I wonder why they used a grocery bag instead of a corrugated box," I mused.

Colin actually smiled. "That's your first question?"

Arabella laughed. "I think it's adorable."

I turned the package around in my hands, looking for a way to get through the tape. "This looks like it was wrapped at Fort Knox. I'm going to need a chain saw. I'll open it later." I turned to Colin. "If it's all right with you, and you have a few minutes before you have to get back to the office, I'll go ahead and start printing while Arabella shows you what we've discovered so far."

"Sure. The power is always on."

Although I'd passed by Colin's bedroom door each time I went to Precious's room, I'd never glimpsed inside. The door was always closed. Now I reminded myself that I had his permission, and there was nothing weird about this at all. I picked up my laptop, shoved it into my backpack, and juggled it with the bulky package as I walked down the hallway, then paused just a moment before I turned the knob.

It was a large room, about the same size as mine, with a big bed—neatly made—in the middle. The plain glass window faced the same side as the spare room, where we'd stored most of Precious's clothes. I reminded myself that his accommodations in Precious's flat were only temporary, and that was why the space was devoid of personality—which I appreciated. It was easier to work if I could pretend I was in a hotel room.

I set my laptop on his desk—clear of clutter, of course—opened up the picture folder, and selected the best photos I'd taken so far. After loading the printer with my photo paper, I hit "print" and sat at the desk to wait. I pulled out my phone to scroll through e-mails; finding nothing important enough to open, I placed it on the desk and noticed for the first time Colin's few desk accessories, which added personality to the room.

A well-worn Rubik's Cube sat within easy reaching distance, next to a mouse pad—minus the computer—with an image of Darth Vader battling Luke Skywalker with glowing light sabers. A stack of ancient leather-bound books held up a brass lamp. I leaned forward to examine the lamp, smiling to myself as I realized the object in the middle of the brass stem was a Golden Snitch of Harry Potter Quidditch fame. A monogrammed notepad on the corner of the desk contained doodles of interlocking circles, surrounding a pencil drawing of a dog's face, maybe a whippet, its eyes full of expression, its ears on alert. It was pretty good, and I wondered if Colin had drawn it.

The printer stopped, and I stood to replace the

photo paper with regular paper for my notes before returning to my seat, noticing as I did a wood-and-leather frame lying on its back behind the stacked books. It looked as if it had been placed there while someone had cleaned the desk, and then forgotten.

I picked it up to put it back, bumping something over with my arm as I lifted it. A small metal soldier wearing a red coat and a tricorn hat and carrying a musket lay on his face where I'd knocked him, an old-fashioned toy cannon sitting next to him. I actually apologized to the toy as I stood it up. The little soldier's red paint was chipped, and his musket wobbled, as if he'd been well played with.

The printer continued to whir. I glanced down at the frame in my hand. A younger version of Penelope was pictured standing with a man, presumably her husband, James, and a little boy about three or four sitting in a stroller. He wore socks with sandals—acceptable only in the very young, in my opinion—and a plaid newsboy hat, and clutched a purple Barney dinosaur doll. The arm wrapped around the toy was almost painfully thin and pale, like the bare legs showing between his navy blue shorts and his knee socks. A dark brown suitcase was partially visible behind the stroller.

The three faces were smiling, but they weren't the kinds of smiles one would see on a family vacationing at Disney World. They looked more like survivors who'd witnessed a tornado ripping the roof off of their house and were happy just to be alive. I stared at the photo, trying to figure out what seemed so familiar to me about it.

Then I noticed the blurred **Welcome to Atlanta** sign in the background. I remembered Penelope saying that they had spent time in Atlanta, and this photo must have been taken at Hartsfield-Jackson Airport. It wasn't a great picture of any of the subjects, and I wondered why it alone was the photo Colin kept on his desk. I set it next to the Rubik's Cube and then decided the tin soldier and his cannon belonged with the picture, too, and moved them to the other side.

Satisfied, I picked up the package, trying to find my way through the tape. I glanced around for scissors, and saw a slim, lidded rectangular box being used as a paperweight. Not wanting to appear nosy, I nudged up the hinged lid with my pinkie, excited to see the glint of brass from the handle of a pair of scissors. I pulled them out without completely opening the lid.

With enthusiasm I stabbed at the paper wrap and tape, spending a good five minutes just trying to make a hole that I could dig my finger into and tear off the rest of the wrapping. Another five minutes later, I found myself surrounded by strips of paper grocery bag and a box from Lucinda's Lingerie. Hoping it wasn't something from the store, I lifted the lid.

Layers of scented lilac-colored tissue lined the

box. I had to carefully dig through them to make sure I didn't miss anything. A Lego fireman fell to the floor, most likely a stowaway hidden by my cousin Sam Junior, and a broken red crayon dropped into my lap before I reached the bottom of the box.

A bundle of magnolia leaves covered the bottom, shiny and green and unmistakably real, their scent carrying with it the memory of long golden summers. I imagined Aunt Cassie neatly snipping them from the old tree in her front yard. She and my mother had grown up under its sheltering arms, chased lightning bugs around it, and shared secrets beneath it.

Confused as to why she'd sent the leaves, I went through the tissue again, shaking it until a small piece of notepaper drifted into my lap. I recognized Aunt Cassie's handwriting and felt a hard tug in my chest as I read the note.

Home is the place that lives in one's heart, waiting with open arms to be rediscovered.

A noise erupted from deep inside me, a sound that was part laugh and part sob, my shoulders shaking with unnamed emotion.

"Madison? Are you all right?" Colin stood in the doorway, a look of concern on his face.

I quickly put the lid on the box, not wanting to explain. Not even sure I could. "I'm fine," I said, standing. "And it looks like the printer's done, too. Thanks for letting me use it."

"You're welcome." He was staring at the scissors, his face unreadable. "Are those mine?"

"Yes. I borrowed them to open the package. It was harder than breaching the beaches on D-Day." Noting again his expression, I said, "I hope you don't mind."

When he didn't say anything but looked at me oddly, I added, "Sorry. I guess I should have asked. But I saw this box on the letter tray. . . ." I lifted the lid with my finger, and this time it flipped all the way open, revealing a framed photograph, the subject faceup.

"Oh." I met his gaze, understanding now why he was looking at me like I'd just kicked his dog.

The black-and-white photo was one I'd taken when we were at school, during my portrait phase. The young woman—a girl, really—was staring into the camera lens with the intensity of someone trying very hard not to smile. Her face was more interesting than beautiful, the hair not light or dark, her freckled nose a little too long, but just like her mother's. The most arresting part of the photo was the look in her eyes. It was so open and honest; at the same time, it seemed to belong to someone completely and utterly lost. I remembered that girl. I still saw her every once in a while when I looked into a mirror.

Colin cleared his throat. "You left it behind in your dorm room. Arabella gave it to me."

It took me two tries to find my voice. "I meant to throw it away. Self-portraits were never my forte."

"Really? I thought it quite good."

He held my gaze, and I couldn't look away. "Is that why you kept it?"

"No."

We continued to stare at each other silently, both of us relieved when Arabella appeared beside Colin in the doorway. "Are you two done in here?"

"Are we?" Colin asked, his voice casual.

"Yes, I'm done printing," I said, hearing the relief in my voice. "Why?"

"I have something I thought you'd want to see." Arabella walked to the desk, holding her phone. "Aunt Penelope found Sophia's wedding album. She wants to know if she should send it to you or if you'd like to come by and look at it there."

"I suppose I do owe them a visit," Colin said. "We can bring Precious. Let her know that I'll call her as soon as I check my calendar."

"Smashing. She said she found Sophia's wedding gown, too—that will certainly be in the exhibition." Arabella looked at the floor where the torn pieces of the grocery bag lay. "Did you open your parcel?"

"I did." I pressed my hand to the gift box, making it clear that I wasn't interested in revisiting their contents right then. "My aunt Cassie sent me leaves from a magnolia tree in her front yard. I'm not sure what she wants me to do with them, but maybe Precious would like me to decorate her mantel? Mama used to do that when I was growing up, and she'd spray-paint them gold at Christmas."

"Interesting." Arabella raised her eyebrows. "Look, I've got to get back to the office—can you join me there around two? I want the whole team gathered so we can finalize the clothing selections. I'd like to begin photographing the outfits and coming up with a story order for them."

"Sure. That will give me some time to speak with Precious first, to make sure I haven't left out anything that she wants to include."

I kept my head down, taking my time stacking the photographs and closing my computer, trying to gather thoughts that wouldn't come, trying to think of all the reasons why Colin would have kept my photograph in a box on his desk. But when I finally found the courage to lift my head and meet Colin's gaze, the room was empty.

CHAPTER 15

LONDON
APRIL 1939

The bell rang downstairs, and Precious ran to the intercom of their new flat, then pressed the "entry" button when she recognized Graham's voice. Breathlessly, she turned to Eva, who was tying a silk scarf around her neck just in case Graham wanted the windows open in the motorcar.

"Should we offer refreshments? Maybe some of my sweet tea?" Precious asked. "I wasn't sure, so I didn't prepare a serving plate. . . ."

"Really, Precious. He's just coming up to escort us downstairs. He wouldn't hear of us meeting him outside."

Precious frowned. "Maybe he's worried about the neighborhood and wants to make sure we're safe."

"Well, Marylebone isn't Belgravia, surely, but it's

not Stepney, either. And David lived here. It's quite respectable and safe."

Eva's gaze took in the elegant cornice moldings and the leaded glass casement windows. She thought of her mother, even imagined her standing in the foyer and seeing where Eva now lived. She'd call it grand; by Graham's standards it wasn't, but Kate Maltby would have seen it that way. Her mother might even have been proud of her daughter. Assuming she knew what that was like. Her emotions had been whittled down over the years to simply wanting food and shelter. There was no room for anything else.

Eva swallowed down the unexpected lump in her throat as she heard the lift door open.

She ran past Precious to the front door and threw it open, wanting to propel herself into Graham's arms. They'd had little time alone since the fashion show due to his work travel. She felt a physical hunger in his absence, needing to see him. To touch him. To hear her name on his lips.

She stopped at the threshold, registering the other people crowding around the lift. Graham took her hand and kissed her cheek, then stood back so she could greet Sophia and David. Her smile faltered slightly when she caught sight of the man sliding shut the metal gate of the lift, then turning to face her. A sharp stab of shame jabbed at her ribs as she recalled her reaction to his empty seat at the fashion show. She hadn't wanted him there. Not really. She simply couldn't make herself forget that he thought her exquisite and unique.

"Miss Harlow," Alexander Grof said with a slight bow. "So we meet again."

Staying by Graham's side, she said, "So we do."

Sophia kissed Precious on the cheek as if they were old friends. "David and Alex, I'd like you all to meet my friend Miss Jeanne Dubose. But her friends call her Precious."

Eva noticed how Alex bent over Precious's hand to kiss it, making her blush, which, Eva was sure, had been his intention. She found it odd that he didn't mention how Precious and he had met before, outside of Lushtak's.

Sophia greeted them both warmly. "I hope we're not intruding, but I so wanted to see what you've done to the flat. Not that I was ever allowed see it before, as it was David's bachelor quarters and Mother would have had a fit of apoplexy if she'd heard I had been here."

Precious laughed. "You're not intruding at all. Come on inside." She beamed at the guests, enjoying her role as hostess. "You can poke around if you like while we go fetch our coats. Please, excuse some of the mess. We haven't finished putting away all of our things yet. The furniture is very nice, although I think we'll want to add our own personal touches to the flat. But I think it's a lovely home, and you are our very first visitors."

Sophia stepped past Eva and Precious and stood in the middle of the foyer, turning around to admire the space. "This is splendid. Really splendid. We couldn't have hoped for better tenants."

"Thank you," Eva said. "We haven't been here very long, but we're already feeling a bit house-proud."

"You have every right to be," Sophia said, and she began pulling off her gloves finger by finger. "It's really perfect, isn't it?"

"It is," Precious said, closing the door.

Eva led the group into the large front reception room. "I know David has already seen this, and Graham likely has, too, but do come see our lovely view of St. Marylebone Parish Church. And while you're admiring the view, I will retrieve my coat."

She left the room and headed toward the first bedroom, where she and Precious kept their coats and any overflow from their armoires. She had just opened the armoire door when she heard Alex's voice behind her.

"I trust you received my gift?"

His voice startled her, but she didn't want to give him the satisfaction of knowing that, or knowing how his mere presence unnerved her. Instead, she reached up, pulled her new blue cashmere coat from a hanger, and stepped back to close the door. "Yes, I did. I'm sorry I haven't had a chance to thank you. It's been rather hectic with the show and our move. But I'm grateful. It's lovely."

"Aren't you going to tell me that you can't accept such a gift from me? That it was very presumptuous of me and you want me to take it back?"

Her gaze met his. It was as if his eyes were laughing at her. She drew in a breath, not enjoying whatever game he thought to play. "No. I have no intention of giving it back. It's far too beautiful. And besides, I needed another cigarette case. My old one was quite useless."

He smiled in a way she was beginning to recognize, a movement of his mouth that had nothing to do with mirth. "I agree," he said, taking her coat. "Allow me."

He stood behind her and held up her coat as she carefully slid her arms through the sleeves, not wanting to wrinkle the sleeves of her frock.

He didn't move away as she began to button the front of her coat, nor did he touch her, but she was as aware of his presence as if he'd just kissed the back of her neck.

"Your accent is getting better, Eva." His words were soft, almost a caress.

Her fingers froze on the last button, her throat tightening. She opened her mouth to speak, but an invisible hand seemed to have stolen the words.

"Does Graham know the truth? Who you really are?"

"The truth?"

"Ah, so he doesn't. You've worked hard to play your part, the orphaned daughter of a country doctor from Devon. I applaud your skill. Very impressive."

"I'm sure I don't know what . . ."

"Yes, you do." His finger stroked her neck, making her shiver. "I'm very good at finding out things about people they'd rather keep secret. I know a man who got himself into a spot of bother in Prague. I was the one who paid enough people to look the other way, and we got him out of jail and into this country. Nobody knows this but me. This makes him very useful to me. You see, Eva, I have a habit of surrounding myself with useful people. And in today's uncertain world, it's a good habit to have."

"Is it?" She looked down at her fingers, trying to remember what she was supposed to be doing with them. "Why are you telling me this?"

Instead of answering, he said, almost jovially, "Eva Harlow isn't your real name, is it?"

"Of course it—"

He cut her off. "Don't bother—several of my useful people are quite good at digging. And you've already told me you're from Muker, in Yorkshire. I would guess that finding a tall, blond, beautiful girl from Muker won't be difficult, even if we don't know her real name. Yet."

"I don't know what you mean. Of course it's my real name." Eva managed to keep her voice steady, even as her fingers fumbled with the same button, her brain frozen with fear and warning, rendering her helpless.

Alexander continued, his voice conversational and without a hint of malice. "Of course, Graham is besotted, and I doubt who you really are matters very much to him—except for the lying part. Most men don't appreciate being lied to, regardless of how in love they imagine themselves to be. But I'm doubtful Mr. and Mrs. St. John will be as forgiving. Graham may be the second son, but he's still a blue blood, yes? And you, clearly, are not. They have plans for him and his future, which no doubt include his marrying someone of his class."

He paused, resting his hands on her shoulders, feeling her traitorous shudder. "A word of advice, Eva—do not underestimate the pressure a family can place on a man when he is choosing a life partner. Eventually, he will be forced to let you go. Assuming you haven't let him go first. As a second son, he's not as rich as you'd like him to be."

Her fingers continued to refuse to work the top button into the buttonhole. Giving up, she clenched her hands into fists, holding them at her chest. "Why are you saying all this to me?" she asked, ashamed of the tremble in her voice.

"Because I like you, Eva. I think we could become quite . . . useful to each other."

Precious's footsteps came down the hallway, and Eva stepped away, relieved to feel Alex's hands slip from her shoulders.

Precious paused in the doorway and looked in. "Are you ready?" Her gaze moved from Eva to Alex, her expression not registering anything out of the ordinary.

"I'm ready," Eva said hastily, exiting the room to join Precious. She didn't look back to see if Alex followed, but sensed him behind her.

Sophia emerged from the reception room with David and Graham. "You're right, Eva. The view is spectacular, and the scale of the rooms is perfect. I know a darling man who would love to help you with draperies and whatnot. No insult intended to David's taste, but the flat most certainly needs a refresh. I intend to hire the same fellow to replace much of what's in the town house after we're married. I don't think anything has been changed for an age."

"May we have whatever you're getting rid of?" Precious asked excitedly. "Eva and I are very good with a needle and thread. We can remake curtains and cushions so that they look like new—just what we need to make the flat more our own."

There was an uncomfortable silence, and Eva found herself carefully putting on her gloves to avoid meeting anyone's eyes.

"I do love an industrious woman," Sophia said, hooking her arm through Precious's. "And what a brilliant idea. I will be happy to let you choose what you'd like. If I had that sort of talent, I'd probably do the same."

Sophia and Precious headed out the door while the men gathered their coats and hats. Eva stayed close by Graham's side, needing not only to be near him, but to be as far away from Alexander Grof as she could manage.

She kept thinking of what he'd said to her, wishing she'd misunderstood. Yet no matter how many explanations she could think of, she knew that she had understood exactly.

She stayed back so that she and Graham were the last to exit. Standing behind the open door so no one could see, she reached for him. "Kiss me, darling. I can't wait another minute."

The light in his eyes that she loved gleamed as he leaned down to kiss her, his lips lingering over hers. "I wish we were alone," he whispered. "Then I could kiss you properly."

"Come on, old chap," David called from the outside hall. "Before you've ruined Eva's reputation." His words were followed by a hearty chuckle, and a laugh from the women, but Eva registered Alex's silence like a shout.

"Coming," she managed, handing Graham the key so he could lock the door behind them.

When they emerged into the lobby downstairs, Alex led the way through the two sets of double doors and down the steps to the front drive, where a silver roadster was parked at the curb. He opened the passenger-side door and, with his eyes focused on Eva, said, "Ladies first."

Eva shook her head, looking at Graham for an

explanation. "We can't all fit in that—there's only room for four of us."

"Not to worry, Eva," David said. "I brought my own motorcar for my lovely fiancée and me. We don't see nearly enough of each other, what with all those blasted engagement parties and so forth. I'm afraid I won't know the woman approaching me down the aisle."

"I daresay she'll be the only one wearing white," Graham said with a grin. "So, what sort of machine is this, Grof? It's nice to look at, but can it move?"

"Oh, yes," Alex said. "It's a brand-new four-and-a-half-litre Vanden Plas Tourer. My own vehicles were left behind in Prague, unfortunately, so I thought I'd make the best of it here."

"And you have," Graham said. "It's certainly attractive. I'll admit to being quite envious."

He took Precious by the elbow and began leading her to the front passenger seat. But she put her gloved hands on top of her small, brimmed straw hat with its extravagant bow; she'd modeled it just the previous day. "Oh, no. I can't sit up front with the top down. My hat will blow off, and I will just die if I lose it. Let me run upstairs and get another one."

"Or," Alexander suggested, "you can sit in the rear with Graham, and Eva can sit in the front. I see she's brought a scarf."

"I'm really fine sitting in the rear seat with Precious," Eva protested.

He looked genuinely disappointed. "And here I was hoping to show off my new car by driving with a beautiful woman in the front."

"I agree," David said. "No better way to display a new toy, right, old chap?"

He slapped Graham on the back. Graham's smile never slipped. "Of course," he said, his hands tucked casually in his pockets. "As long as the lady agrees."

"Oh, go on," encouraged Precious. "Alexander's being kind enough to drive us all the way to Kew Gardens—it's the least you can do." She gave Eva a playful shove on her back, propelling her forward.

Seeing no way to escape without appearing rude, Eva allowed Alex to help her into the front seat while Graham and Precious settled into the rear. It was a gorgeous day with a bright sun and a cloudless sky, but Eva found herself praying for rain.

The wind made it difficult to carry on a conversation, but every time Eva turned around, she saw Graham's and Precious's heads bent together, and twice she heard Graham laugh out loud. Alex leaned toward her.

"I don't believe I've told you yet," he said, "but you look beautiful today."

Eva quickly glanced at the rear seat to see if Graham had overheard, but he appeared to be listening intently to what Precious was telling him. She turned to Alex, facing him only long enough to thank him.

"Do you like how it rides?" Alex shouted over the

wind in an attempt to get Graham's attention, but Graham didn't turn his head or respond in any way, as if he hadn't heard. "And you, my dear Eva. Do you like it?"

"It's nice," she said, adjusting her scarf as it fluttered against her face. She focused on the road in front instead of those silver wolf eyes that she felt upon her.

"If you have need of transportation, it is at your service. As am I. I'm aware of how difficult it is to rely on public transportation every time you want to go somewhere. Especially when wearing beautiful clothes that might get soiled or creased. I'm living at the Savoy. All you need to do is send word."

"It's no bother." Eva smoothed the skirt of her dress, then clenched her gloved hands in her lap so he wouldn't see them tremble. **Your accent is getting better.** It was as if he'd just whispered the words again into her ear. "And Graham is more than happy to escort me wherever I need to go."

"I'm sure. Except his work takes him away quite a bit, doesn't it?"

She turned her head to look out her side window, pretending she hadn't heard.

"He works at Whitehall, yes?" Alex pressed. "What exactly does he do at the Home Office, Eva?"

She turned on him, angry. "If it's so important to you, why don't you ask him? While you're at it, ask him what his income is, too. Believe me, you're the only person who cares."

He surprised her by throwing back his head and laughing. "You amuse me, Eva. You really do. Because I am quite sure that you don't want me talking too much with your St. John, do you?"

She was startled by a tap on her shoulder. Turning, she saw Precious leaning forward from the backseat. "Hey, you two. What's so funny? We can't hear a word back here."

"Nothing," Eva said. "Nothing at all." She looked past her friend's shoulders to Graham. He smiled at her, his eyes showing an odd light.

She managed to ignore Alexander for the rest of the drive, and when they arrived at Kew Gardens, Graham was quick to claim her. They paired off, leaving Precious with Alex. And when Eva and Graham walked into the glass-and-iron Victorian Palm House, its tropical air sticky and wet, he pulled her into an isolated corner behind a towering palm, the odd light in his eyes gone now, leaving behind something dark and earthy. He kissed her with a new hunger, a need she reciprocated, and told her he loved her.

"And I, you," she said, meaning it. She pressed her mouth against his, feeling his sweat mingling with hers, and tried to pretend that everything Alex had said wasn't true.

CHAPTER 16

LONDON
MAY 2019

"Are you ready to go, Nana?" Colin asked solicitously as he settled a peach-colored shawl over Precious's shoulders.

She patted his cheek. "Of course. I've always loved a weekend at Hovenden Park. Your grandmother Sophia used to throw the most elegant house parties back in the day. I love Penelope and James, but their entertainments are smaller. And don't tell your mother I said this, but they aren't as swanky as Sophia's, either."

Colin gently took hold of her arm and led her toward the front door. "They don't have a staff of fifty, Nana. It's hard to pull off 'swanky' without that sort of help."

"Ah, yes. The good old days," Precious said, her voice wistful.

Colin looked at me, and I stifled a laugh. With her arm on his, he carefully led Precious out to the lift.

"I've got the newspaper clippings," Arabella said, emerging from the dining room. "All organized by date, thanks to Colin's diligence. And the hatbox of photos is already in the Rover, next to the groceries for the dinner you're preparing tonight, Maddie. Takeout is a bit dodgy up there, so I threw in some canned beans and bread. Aunt Penelope and Uncle James eat much too healthy for my taste."

I lifted the small cosmetics case I was carrying. "I've got all of Precious's makeup and her pills—thanks to Laura. I don't know which one Precious would be more upset about us forgetting."

"The makeup," we said simultaneously, then followed Colin and Precious out to the lift.

As we descended, Colin said offhandedly, "George is waiting in the backseat. Since Nana is sitting up front with me, I'm afraid you two will have to share with him. I hope you don't mind."

"If we do mind," I said, "can we make you run alongside while one of us drives?"

His response was a raised eyebrow. He opened the lift gate, then held the door while Arabella escorted Precious through the lobby and down the steps. In the car, George was clearly excited, his large head held out of the rear window, as an impressive amount of slobber dripped down the glass.

We settled the rest of the luggage into the back of the Land Rover, then took our seats, Arabella and I fending off an exuberant greeting from George that lasted for the first few miles before he settled down in the middle, his head on my lap, looking very pleased with life.

Arabella picked up a wadded towel from the floor—probably used for window wipe downs after car trips with George—and handed it to me. "You might want to put this under his head, so it doesn't look as if you've had an accident."

I did as she'd suggested and grinned wryly as I stroked George's big head while he looked at me goofily. "I wish Oscar was here to see this," I said.

I met Colin's amused gaze in the rearview mirror for a moment, then turned away. Remembering the photograph of me that I'd been pretending I hadn't seen on his desk, I focused my attention out the window as we made our way through London's Friday afternoon traffic.

The week had been typically drizzly and chilly, but there were gaps in the clouds and the weather forecaster promised warmer temps and blue skies for the weekend. I knew better than to believe it and would check my weather app often, but it was a nice hope after a week of rain.

The scent of Precious's perfume drifted from the

front seat, a sweet floral scent that might have been jasmine warmed with deeper and darker woodsy notes. Something exotic. It wasn't a perfume I recognized or even a scent that might have been popular with today's preference for louder, bigger fragrances and celebrity spokespersons. It was the kind of perfume that made me think of old movies and women smoking cigarettes with lacquered red lips, wearing long, elegant dresses, and looking fabulous while they managed to save the day as the world fell apart around them.

I recalled the scent that had risen from the pile of clothes when I'd retrieved my buried jacket the other evening, and thought it might have been the same one.

"I love your perfume, Precious. What is it?"

The side of her mouth turned up. "It's Vol de Nuit. My model friends and I used to stop by the perfume counter at Selfridges to spritz on a sample before going out, which is why I don't buy it anywhere else now that I can afford it." She gave a little laugh. "I suppose I feel obligated."

I leaned forward, putting a hand on the back of her seat. "Did Eva wear it, too?"

After a long pause, she said, "Yes. It was her favorite. She told me that the perfume had been created for adventurous women. That's why she liked it."

"And was she?" I asked. "An adventurous woman?"

I heard something in her voice, as if she were telling a memory of ghosts. "She wanted to be.

She thought life was supposed to be like the movies she loved. I think she played a character, someone she wanted us to see. I don't know if anyone knew the real Eva Harlow."

"And her family—where were they?"

She shook her head slowly. "She had a difficult childhood, and she didn't like to talk about her past. We'd both been very poor. But being that poor and hungry damaged something inside Eva."

"What do you mean?" I asked, aware of Colin trying to meet my eyes in the rearview mirror.

Precious's hand, with its beautifully painted peach nails, stroked the shawl on her shoulder like a child petting a security blanket. "Eva never really knew what she wanted, until it was too late. I think that's what broke her heart in the end."

"In the end?" I prompted. "When she left London?"

As if I hadn't said anything, Precious went on. "At some point, either Eva or I—I don't remember which one of us—obtained a bottle of Vol de Nuit. We shared it, but that bottle remained nearly full because we were both so careful not to use too much." She tilted her head. "I wonder whatever happened to it."

"Maybe Eva took it with her when she left," I offered.

"Maybe." She turned her head away. "Have you had any luck finding her?"

"We're working on it, Nana," Colin said.

"Mother's friend Hyacinth Ponsonby works with the National Archives. She thinks she should be able to find something about Graham. We're hoping something in his records will lead us to Eva."

She nodded. "I do hope they ended up together, wherever they are. They were so in love." She turned toward the window, ending the conversation.

In the backseat, Arabella began fanning through the folder of yellowed news articles and chuckling to herself. "Colin—Sophia was apparently a big reader of **The Tatler** and **The Bystander**. Most of the clippings your mother found are from those—and then after nineteen forty, it's **The Tatler and Bystander** because they merged. Still very gossipy, but also literary, so I'll try not to hold reading tastes against Sophia. Daphne du Maurier published her first short story in **The Bystander**, after all. And I'm reading some of these articles, and they're quite brilliant."

"Really?" I asked. "How so?"

After waiting for me to pull out my notebook, she said, "Here's an article entitled 'From the Shires and the Provinces,' dated February 1939. It's all about how sad it is that something as inconvenient as a war might interfere with hunting season and British lives in general. Listen to this." Arabella cleared her throat and began to read.

Political uncertainties no doubt have an effect on hunting and it would be quite possible to

> work ourselves up into a terrible state of jitters if we allowed ourselves to think of such things as our horses being taken from us, our hounds being destroyed to save food and money, our homes filled with strangers, etc.

"That's February, did you say?" Colin asked.

I nodded. "Yes. Precious—you were living in London then, right? Great Britain didn't declare war against Germany until September, so I'm curious—what was it like for you and your friends earlier in the year? Were you all worried about what was happening in Europe?"

She was silent for so long that I thought she hadn't heard me. When she did speak, she kept her gaze on her folded hands. "We were busy living our lives." Her shoulders lifted in a tired shrug, as if the burden of memories had become too heavy. "Europe seemed so very far away. It wasn't until men we knew signed up to fight that it suddenly became real to us. It was as if I'd left my house unlocked. When a thief came and stole everything, I shouldn't have been surprised. But I was. Those are the worst kinds of surprises, aren't they? The ones you never see coming."

The last word caught in her throat. I sat back against my seat, something that she'd said echoing uneasily in my head. Maybe it was her reference to a thief and how I'd always felt my mother and my childhood had been stolen by the same stealthy intruder. But there was something else, something dark moving behind Precious's words—something in the way her voice changed in the telling, something even more devastating than a declaration of war.

"You Yanks will find this amusing," Arabella said, breaking the tension. "You're always joking about British understatement. Here's an article in that same gossip rag. The title is 'And the World Said.' It's dated September 13, 1939—so a little over a week after the declaration of war. There's a photo of a wedding party, and the caption reads, 'Among the many marriages that have been hurried up by the current spot of bother . . .' Ha! That might be the first time I've ever heard the Second World War condensed so spectacularly. Even I'm impressed, and I'm British."

Colin turned his head briefly toward Precious. "Was my grandmother's wedding one of those that were 'hurried up'?"

Precious shook her head. "No. It had been planned well in advance. The war was the reason why I was in the wedding party, though. Sophia's original bridesmaids had been quickly married. One got pregnant right away and was very ill from the start, and the other was whisked away to an island off of Scotland to stay with family while her soldier husband was in training. I hadn't known Sophia for long, but we were already good friends. I was happy to be there on her wedding day."

"And Eva, too?"

A brief pause. "Yes. And Eva."

I thought for a moment. "Precious, do you know if Graham and Eva were ever engaged?"

She turned her head away, toward the side window. The only sound in the car was the thrum of the tires against asphalt. When she finally spoke, she was looking again at her hands, folded tightly in her lap. "I think they both wanted to get married." Her chin dropped to her chest. "But then fate intervened."

"By fate, do you mean that the war intervened?"

"Some might see it that way. But Eva believed that fate was something that happened to other people. As if she could control anything at all."

Colin sent me another glance in the rearview mirror. I sat back in my seat. I wanted to ask her about Sophia's cut-up photographs, but I could tell that Precious wanted to change the topic. "I think Arabella has more clippings to share. I'd love to hear your comments about them and how the times you were living through affected your choices about what you wore."

"I suppose," she said quietly before turning her head toward her side window again for the rest of the drive.

The spring breeze had pushed the clouds away by the time we arrived at Hovenden Park, the afternoon sunlight painting the fields in shades of sage, lime, and olive. Fieldstone fences meandered over the landscape, which was punctuated by the occasional farmhouse, pasture of sheep, or field furrow. It was so different from the landscape of red Georgia clay beneath parched summer grass and the fields of cotton and soybeans I was familiar with. It was as if someone had dipped a paintbrush into two separate palettes and painted two soothing interpretations of what home should be. The effect on the viewer was the same—a pulling at the heart that returned a person to their childhood, at least for a moment.

Colin parked the Land Rover in the drive as the front door flew open and a dog that looked a lot like George burst out down the front steps, rounding the SUV to my side of the vehicle. George went crazy, pawing at the door, and I immediately opened it so I wouldn't get slobbered on to death.

"Sorry," said Colin, his expression not reflecting the apology as he pulled my door open wider. "That's Charlotte, George's sister—yes, as in Princess Charlotte. You didn't get to meet her last time you were here because she was with my dad. They'll probably find a good mud puddle or cowpat to roll in, but as long as they're happy . . ."

"Right," I said, and climbed out, hoping there'd be a chance for a dog bath before the drive back to London on Sunday. I followed Colin to the passenger side, where his parents were helping Precious exit the vehicle. I watched Precious kiss Colin's father on the cheek and for a brief moment cup his jaw with a veined hand, her rings catching the light. It was a touching exchange, reminding me of how Precious had adopted Sophia's family as her own. I couldn't help but consider that the adoption might have been mutual.

I greeted Penelope, who turned to the man beside her.

"Maddie, this is my husband, James. He's been eager to meet you after hearing so much about you."

I slid a glance toward Colin, who was patently looking away, and shook his father's hand. "It's a pleasure."

Colin's father was tall, fit, and lean, despite being in his seventies, with the rugged good looks of someone who spent a lot of time outdoors. His blond hair had threads of gray at the sideburns, but it was still thick and wavy and entirely unfair to the majority of the female population.

I stopped midshake, studying his face closely, unsure of what I thought I'd seen. He and Colin shared the same build and coloring, but James's eyes were hazel, not blue, and no freckles decorated the bridge of his nose. His smile was all Colin's, though. Full lips that still managed to be masculine in a smile that could have been mocking but for the tilt of the head and the dimpled chin that was both charming and devastating.

"Is something wrong?" James asked.

"No, not at all." I slipped my hand from his but continued looking at his face. "I guess I'm trying to figure out who Colin favors."

"After looking at the photo you discovered in Sophia's things, Penelope and I think he's a dead ringer for his great-uncle Graham."

I nodded. "Yes, but there's something in your face that's so familiar, too. I'll have to go back over Sophia's photos from when she was younger. Maybe it's there."

"Certainly. And Penelope has pulled out the wedding album for you to look at in the library. Hunting for photos has been a nice distraction from the newly discovered roof leak in the west wing, so thank you for that." He grinned. "And welcome back to Hovenden Park. We're delighted you're able to stay for the weekend, and we thank you for bringing Precious. I understand that you'll be dazzling our palates with a few Southern dishes tonight. I know we will all enjoy them, but especially Precious."

We turned to see her hanging on to Colin's arm in front of the steps, staring up at the facade of the house, the light from the sky hiding the ashy tone of her skin and making her appear young again.

"This house always brings back memories," she said.

"Good ones, I hope," Colin said, leading her up the steps.

"Mostly." She looked straight ahead as she walked

into the foyer, almost as if she were walking back in time, expecting to see someone inside waiting for her.

While James and Colin brought in the luggage and the assorted bags of food, Penelope escorted Precious, Arabella, and me past the Henry VIII tent panels and through an arched doorway into the library. A blazing fire roared in the large fireplace. The smell of woodsmoke made me think of home again and cold winter mornings spent at my grandfather's house.

"It's been chilly at night, and the cold will permeate these walls and linger until we get a longer spell of warm days and nights," Penelope said as she situated Precious in one of the two facing sofas near the fire.

I looked up at the vaulted, beamed ceiling and the large front-facing window. The small glass panes reached almost from floor to ceiling. The heavy velvet curtains were opened to let in the light, but I wondered if, even closed, they could really help stave off the chill hovering beyond the circle of warmth from the fireplace.

"This must be a bitch to heat," I said. Then, realizing I'd spoken out loud, I looked in horror at Penelope. "I am so sorry—I didn't mean to say . . . It's just that my aunt Cassie used to say that about my grandfather's house, before she decided she was going to stay and live in it, and the coziness of this room reminded me of it."

Penelope looked amused. "Does she still say that?"

"I haven't lived there for a while, but she probably does, if only to prove her point."

"Well, she's absolutely correct, and I wouldn't be truthful if I told you I'd never thought those exact words. I could feed a third-world country for a year with what it costs to heat this house for a month in winter. It's one of the reasons why we opened up the dairy to the public, for school group tours and the like. It keeps us warm, at least."

Anna, the young woman who'd waited on us out in the garden when we'd come for lunch, appeared with a tea tray. Turning to Penelope, I said, "If you'll excuse me, I'm going to get started battering the chicken. I just need you to point the way."

"I'd be happy to take you," Colin said, entering the room with his father. "Every once in a while, we find skeletons of visitors in random passageways. They lost their way and were never found." I knew he was joking, but his face was so serious I had to look twice.

"And I can show you how to use the AGA," Anna offered. "She's a bit temperamental."

We excused ourselves and headed toward the kitchen, passing through a door almost hidden in the paneling of the great hall, then down passages that were more maze than hallway. Eventually, we burst into a large, brightly lit room that was surprisingly modern despite the deep fireplace with centuries-old soot staining its bricks. Shiny white subway tiles adorned the walls behind the counters and AGA; all the appliances were stainless steel. It could have been cold and industrial, but a cozy bench with embroidered pillows and a scarred wooden table with six chairs in front of the fireplace warmed the room. A large bowl full of water sat on the floor by the back door, of which a doggy panel took up most of the bottom half.

Anna spent a good ten minutes showing me how to operate the AGA. Once she was satisfied I knew what to do, she said, "Can you find your way around the kitchen by yourself? I've got some tidying up to do, but I'll be happy to stay until you get the lay of the land."

"I haven't got any plans, so I'll stick around for a bit," Colin offered.

"That's really not necessary . . . ," I began, but he'd already started to unload the grocery bags onto the counter, organizing the food by type.

Satisfied, Anna smiled and said good-bye, then left. I turned to see Colin holding up a bucket of Cool Whip. "I'm almost afraid to ask what this is."

I yanked it from his hands and placed it on the white stone counter. "Be careful with that—it's not easily found in London. But oh, the uses of Cool Whip are legendary. Most involve food in the kitchen."

"Most?"

I faced him and felt blood rush to my cheeks,

suddenly remembering the picture of me on his desk, and how since I'd seen it I hadn't been able to relegate Colin to the shadowy corner of my memory where he'd existed since I'd left Oxford.

I grabbed a grocery bag and began to empty its contents so I'd have something else to look at. "Yes, well, it's basically processed whipped cream but sweeter. I've read somewhere that it has uses outside the kitchen."

"Um-hm," he said, carefully folding up one bag before turning to another. "I'm assuming you'll need the Wi-Fi password so you can contact your aunt Lucinda to help you with the dinner preparation?"

I nearly dropped a can of crushed pineapple. "What do you mean?"

He leaned against the counter and casually folded his arms across his chest. "You hate to cook. You had to go online to find out how to boil eggs when we were at Oxford. And you used to Skype with your great-aunt quite a lot as I recall. But please, forgive me if I'm being presumptuous."

Without another word, I pulled my laptop from my backpack and opened up the settings. "Go ahead," I said primly.

He managed to give me the password without a single smirk. "Do you need me to stay? Not that you've ever asked, but I do know my way around a kitchen."

The accusation stung, but I busied myself by

focusing on opening up the Skype app. "No, but thank you. I'll let you know if I need any help."

I felt him watching me and forced myself to lift my gaze to meet his.

"Are you ever going to ask me why your photograph was on my desk?" Colin said softly.

I was too stunned by his bluntness to think of an answer.

"I kept it because it was the only thing you left behind. Not even a good-bye. I thought—stupidly, it turns out—that you might come back for it."

I nodded, the only response I could muster.

And then I remembered the other photo, the one of him in a stroller with his parents at the Atlanta airport. I wanted to let him know that I'd noticed, that he wasn't invisible to me no matter how much I wished he were. "You were a really cute little boy," I said, wondering if my words sounded as stupid to him as they did to me.

He tilted his head in question.

"The other frame on your desk—the one of you with your parents. It looks like you're at the Atlanta airport. You were so adorable in your little socks and shorts." My smile fell quickly at his pinched expression.

"That wasn't me," he said. He pulled himself away from the counter. "I'll ask Anna to bring you tea."

I started to tell him not to bother, but he'd already gone.

CHAPTER 17

Despite the sunshine gilding the house and landscape in a buttery sheen, the afternoon had turned cool, forcing us to eat in the banquet-sized dining room instead of outside. Not that there was anything wrong with eating fried chicken with mashed potatoes, black-eyed peas, and corn bread in a room where Queen Elizabeth would have felt at home, but still . . . If I'd been the gambling type, I would have wagered that it was the first time in the dining room's history when gravy was poured over biscuits and a Jell-O salad was served as a side.

I wore the only dress I'd packed, a simple navy sheath dress made of a material that wouldn't wrinkle in a suitcase. Precious had insisted on lending me a silk scarf—Hermès, I was sure—to dress it up, and had tied it in an elegant bow on the side of my neck. I'd earned appreciative comments from everyone except Colin, whose gaze only glanced off me before he turned to the food on the table.

Precious and I sat across from him and Arabella, making me grateful that I had someone to look at besides Colin. Anna moved behind us, serving from the large platter of fried chicken. She paused behind Precious, serving fork in hand. "White meat or dark meat, Miss Dubose?"

I refrained from smacking my lips, something we'd done as children when fried chicken was served, no matter how many times Mama told us to stop. "Not to unduly influence you, but I personally love the drumsticks."

"Me, too. I'd like a drumstick, please."

Anna hesitated, unsure. When Precious didn't clarify, I said, "A leg. Because they look like drumsticks."

"Yes, of course," the young woman said, placing one on Precious's plate. "And here's a thigh since the legs don't have a lot of meat."

I selected two drumsticks and reached for the mashed potatoes. I realized that everyone seemed to be watching me for cues, so I made sure to explain my process. "After you scoop a big helping of potatoes, you make a little dimple in the top with your spoon before the gravy comes your way. And then you just fill it up and let some spill over the sides, like this. Make sure you get enough gravy to cover your biscuits, too."

Next, I told them how to butter the corn bread, stopping short of how my daddy liked to mix together his black-eyed peas, corn bread, and potatoes in a kind of side dish casserole. That would have to wait for another time—the whole eating fried chicken with fingers was clearly almost too overwhelming, despite the fact that Anna had helpfully set each place with a small finger bowl of lemon and water.

"If you want to eat with a fork and knife, go on ahead. I'm not going to judge," I said. "But if you ever find yourselves in the South again, use your fingers. I hear that it's illegal to use utensils to eat fried chicken in Gainesville, Georgia, and might be elsewhere in the South, too."

I picked up a drumstick with my fingers, watching everyone, including Precious, hesitate, their hands suspended over their silverware. I put the chicken down on my plate. "And I'm perfectly happy to use a fork and knife, too. When in Rome and all," I said, feeling self-conscious.

"Nonsense," James said, picking up a piece with his fingers. "You've gone to all this trouble to make this delicious meal for us, and we should enjoy it in the way it's intended."

Penelope followed suit, taking a bite with pinkies extended.

"I've always wanted to eat with my fingers," Arabella said, almost gleefully tearing into her chicken.

"When in Rome," Colin said, meeting my eyes for the first time as he, too, succumbed to the joys of eating with one's fingers.

Precious was the last to give up her utensils, her fingers hovering over her plate.

"Really, Precious," I said, "if you're more comfortable with a fork and knife, that's fine. You've been overseas so long. Eating habits are hard to get over, especially after almost eight decades."

"Actually," she said as she carefully picked up her fork and knife from the table, "I just hate messing up my makeup." She smiled as she began cutting into the thigh.

When everyone was finished, and I'd received enough compliments that I almost called Aunt Lucinda so she could be thanked in person, Penelope suggested we have dessert in the library.

"Good idea," I said. "I'll need that long walk across the house after such a big meal. I'm full as a tick."

James surprised me by laughing. "How very accurate, Maddie. I imagine we're all of a similar mind."

"Oh, she's got loads more where that came from, I'm afraid," Colin said. He stood, then pulled out his mother's chair. "What is the one about someone being so annoying it's like thumping something off?"

I kept my face as expressionless as his as I turned

to him. "I'm sure I have no idea what you're talking about." I helped Precious from her chair, then linked arms with her, moving slowly as we left the dining room. "We're having ambrosia for dessert," I whispered to her. "I've been keeping it a surprise, but since you're about to find out, I thought I'd go ahead and spoil the secret."

"Ambrosia. How wonderful." Her voice was neutral, making me wonder if she disliked ambrosia and was too polite to tell me.

To make it sound more appealing, I said, "My aunt Lucinda always added maraschino cherries and pecans, too, since she usually made it at Christmastime and she thought the red made it more festive."

"I am sure I will enjoy it."

I patted the hand that rested on my arm. "I thought MoonPies might be nice to serve, too, but they're hard to find in the UK, from what I could tell, and I didn't have time to have them overnighted from home."

We entered the library, and I situated Precious on the sofa by the fire.

"I don't know what a MoonPie is," Penelope offered, "but it sounds rather decadent."

"Oh, believe me, they are. Chocolate, marshmallows, and graham crackers. Made right in Precious's home state of Tennessee for over one hundred years. It's quite the Southern icon. In Mobile, Alabama, they even have a giant MoonPie replica dropped on New Year's Eve to welcome in the New Year."

"And I thought the midnight tolling of Big Ben was exciting. Who knew?" Colin braced himself with one elbow on the mantel and accepted a brandy from his father, who was busy distributing glasses of amber liquid around the room to "help with digestion."

"I do remember MoonPies," Precious said. "They used to send them to the American troops overseas during the war. I must have had one or two in this very house. Those nice American flyboys from Mildenhall—that's the base not too far from here—would come from time to time. Sophia did know how to throw a good party."

She looked down with a secretive smile, her powdered cheeks softened by the glow from the fire. "She adopted a squadron of Polish airmen, I recall. Always felt it was her duty to entertain them, to keep up their morale. They were instrumental in winning the Battle of Britain, did you know? The unsung heroes, never getting the credit they deserved. I think that's why Sophia tried so hard to show them a good time between missions."

"May I?" I asked as I held up my notebook.

"Of course. I like talking about beautiful clothes and MoonPies and Sophia's parties. Because despite all the hardships of that time, there was beauty and goodness, too. A friend once told me that love and beauty were the only things worth holding on to. That they are what shine light in a dark world."

"Who said that?" I asked. "Eva?"

She trained those flame-filled eyes on me. "Yes. A wise man who did our makeup at Lushtak's said that to her. Eva thought it important enough to share, and I'm glad she did. It got me through some of the dark times that were to come." Taking a deep breath, she straightened her shoulders as if reverting to her model persona and preparing to go out on a catwalk. She smiled, her eyes clear again, her face changing as I watched. "I thought of something else that might be interesting for the article."

Arabella sat up as I held my pencil over my notebook.

"You need to have a Royal Air Force uniform in the exhibit."

"Why is that?" Arabella asked.

"Because there's a marvelous story attached to them. When they were originally designed for the brand-new air force in nineteen eighteen, a firm in Yorkshire suggested using leftover blue-gray woolen cloth that had been ordered to make trousers for the tsar's Cossacks. The poor tsar didn't need it anymore, and happily the RAF agreed it was the perfect color. My former employer Madame Lushtak told me that."

"That's a splendid story," Arabella said. "We could

use Graham's photo with it. We'll have to see if his uniform is stored in the attic."

"Sadly, we've given the attic a rather good going through, and we didn't find it," Penelope said. "But I'll have James look again, just in case."

Precious studied her lap, her beringed fingers clasped tightly together. "It should be displayed with the lovely green cotton day dress with the bow at the neck and the cinched waist. That belonged to Eva. I remember her wearing it once when she was with him."

"Got it," I said, writing her suggestion down in my notebook. "It's a great uniform. I've never seen one up close, but judging by the photograph of Graham, I'd have to agree it was a good choice. Of course, it's hard to tell color in a black-and-white photograph. I'm curious, Precious, and it's possible you might not recall, but what color were Graham's eyes?"

Before she could answer, Anna appeared, pushing a cart filled with a coffeepot, cups and saucers, and small glass bowls of ambrosia. As Anna handed them around, I watched everyone eye the dessert suspiciously, using their spoons to lift the sticky mass to the surface and then cutting it in the middle to see what might be hiding.

"I'll take the first bite to show you it's not poisonous." I scooped a mouthful onto my spoon and ate it, chewing and smiling simultaneously. "Trust me—it's delicious."

One by one they all ate their dessert, although I noticed Colin washed his down with the rest of his brandy. Precious tried two bites and then rested her spoon, saying she had to watch her figure. I stifled a laugh, my gaze rising to see Colin doing the same thing.

Arabella opened the folder of clippings she'd left in the room before supper. "These articles are so fascinating—a real insight into people's lives during the war—exactly what I was hoping to tie in with what was going on in the fashion world, Aunt Precious." She slid one out and rested it on top of the folder. "Like this one."

Precious kept a smile on her face as she focused on Arabella, but her eyes changed, adjusting as if she were trying on different glasses to see which ones looked best.

Arabella held up a yellowed page. "This is from a column entitled 'Pictures in the Fire'—not sure what that means but it talks about the Special Branch of Scotland Yard taking definite measures against, and I quote, 'the refugee racket.' Apparently it wasn't so much the new refugees they were worried about, but the ones who'd been planted in Britain for years, completely overlooked because they were so entrenched." She cleared her throat. "'This class of agent is very often not an alien at all, which naturally makes things much more difficult. He may be in the clubs, the pubs, the offices, the services, the trams, the tubes, and the taxis.'" Looking up, she said, "That sounds a bit terrifying, don't you think? Aunt Precious, were you aware of any of that going on?"

Precious took a sip of coffee, her expression thoughtful. "There was an Italian girl, Rosalie, at Lushtak's. She didn't show up for work one day, and Madame Lushtak told us she'd been deported along with just about every Italian waiter in the city. She may have been a spy, though I doubt it. And we couldn't really discuss matters. Most of us models were aware of what was going on in the world, of course. It was hard not to be, what with the black-outs and rationing and all the men we knew being called up or signing up."

She tilted her head. "Even dear Sophia called it the 'unspeakable summer.' Quite literally, women of her class weren't allowed to speak about politics at home. Most were very sheltered. There were posters everywhere, of course, warning us to watch what we said in public, but I don't know if any of us took it seriously. Our conversations certainly weren't about state secrets."

She took another sip from her cup, then set it down delicately. "I wouldn't mind something stronger in my cup, James. If you don't mind. Just don't tell my mama." She grinned as James approached with the brandy, and I was once again reminded of an actress playing a part and wondered if Precious Dubose had missed her true calling.

An old-fashioned phone, one with a very long

spiral cord plugged into the wall, rang out with two pulsed shrills. Penelope rose to answer it. The woman on the other end—definitely a woman from the high pitch of her voice—spoke at length while Penelope nodded and sent us apologetic looks.

"Hang on, Hyacinth. Let me write this down so I don't get it wrong." Pulling the cord toward the desk by the window, she took a notepad and a pen and then, cradling the phone between her shoulder and jaw, said, "All right. Go on."

I used the time to finish my brandy and go over my notes, putting my pen down just as Penelope was following the cord back to the phone's cradle and hanging up.

"I do apologize, but that was my friend Hyacinth Ponsonby from the National Archives. She'd hoped to drop by tomorrow, but her daughter is in labor with her first grandchild at this very moment! Hyacinth and her husband are racing to the city to be there in time. She isn't sure when she'll be returning, so she wanted to get me the information before she left. It's about James's uncle Graham. Hyacinth said she'll be happy to scan the e-mail once she's back if we'd like to see the written record, too."

Arabella sent me a look of self-satisfaction. "I **told** you I hadn't made up her name."

"Who, Hyacinth?" James held the bottle of brandy over my coffee cup and waited for my nod before adding a hefty dollop. "She is most definitely real. Lovely lady and a rather formidable leader of the Women's Institute, isn't she, Penelope?"

"Indeed. We should probably clone her and put all the Hyacinths in charge. World order would commence immediately." Penelope pulled up the pair of readers dangling from the chain around her neck and settled them on the bridge of her nose.

I glanced over at Precious. Her face remained calm, one hand placed over the other in her lap. A slight tremor went through her, bringing to mind a warrior preparing for battle.

Impulsively, I reached over and took her hand. Graham wasn't just a name on a list, or in a photo caption, or a spot on a family tree. He'd been someone she'd known, a very real connection to a dear friend who'd disappeared from her life. I understood and was grateful when she accepted my hand and squeezed back.

"This could lead us to Eva," I said.

Her eyes were blank for a moment, and then she smiled. "I really hope so."

Grief is like a ghost. We waited for Penelope to speak, and we tightened our grip, as if to ward off the relentless spirits that never seemed very far away.

"'Squadron Leader Graham Neville St. John was born March 12, 1907, and educated at Eton and Oxford. He worked for the Diplomatic Service in Rangoon, Burma, before returning to London to work for the Home Office. He resigned his government position in July nineteen thirty-nine and signed up for the Royal Air Force; following training, he joined Nineteen Squadron at Duxford in May nineteen forty, before being transferred to Hornchurch prior to the Dunkirk evacuation. He flew at Dunkirk, and received the Distinguished Flying Cross, with five kills to his name.'"

Precious's hand tightened in mine. "Are you all right?" I asked.

Her expression was rigid, a sheet of ice in danger of cracking. "Does it say anything else?"

We both looked at Penelope.

"Nothing conclusive, I'm afraid." She cleared her throat and read, "'He was shot down over the Channel during the Dunkirk evacuation on thirtieth of May, 1940, and admitted to Queen Victoria Hospital in East Grinstead, West Sussex, with severe burns and broken bones.'"

Penelope took off her glasses and let them dangle from the chain. "There is no more information about him anywhere—whether he survived after being admitted to hospital or where he might be buried. It's very curious, isn't it?"

"I'm assuming Hyacinth is still looking into it?" James asked, his gaze on Precious. A part of her seemed to have shrunk, even while her body took up the same amount of space on the sofa. "My parents never spoke of him, except to tell me he'd been lost in the war. Mother always grew quite sad, as

I believe they'd been close. Eventually, I stopped asking."

Penelope nodded. "Well, Hyacinth is still digging. She's like a dog with a bone—and I mean that in a good way." She turned to Precious. "Do you remember seeing Graham after August of nineteen forty?"

"I don't . . . ," Precious began, her hand still in mine. "I might have. But that was during the Blitz, remember. There was so much confusion. He came back on leave at some point. I do remember that. To see Eva. And then after he'd recovered from his injuries and returned to London." She shook her head. "But I have no idea when that was—sometime during the Blitz."

"Which ended in May of nineteen forty-one," Colin said. "But there should be some record of his death—whether he died during the war or after. Have you asked at our local parish, Mother?"

"I went down myself to check not only the church graveyard but the records, too, since Hyacinth told me that they don't always match. I found the death records and the graves for both of his parents and his brother, but there are no such records for Graham. Just his baptismal record, so at least we know he existed."

"Of course he did. And so did Eva." Precious turned her head toward the fire, away from me, and watched the flames twist and twine like lovers. "I remember them dancing in this very house. They were so very happy." She pulled her hand from mine and took a deep breath. "I'd like to leave it at that. And now"—she pressed her hand into the arm of the sofa—"I think I will go to bed. I'm plumb wore out."

Colin stepped toward her, taking her elbow and helping her stand. "Of course, Nana. I'll take you to your room." She looked into his face, and her smile transformed her, giving me a glimpse of the young woman she'd once been. The woman she might still believe herself to be.

Penelope stood. "Allow me. I have your medications, and I can help you get dressed for bed."

Precious sent her a grateful glance. "Thank you, dear. It was a lovely evening. Good night, everyone." She allowed Penelope to take her arm and lead her from the room. But she paused in the doorway and looked back, her eyes focused on James. "Sweet dreams."

We listened to their footsteps slowly fade, the sentiment reminding me of the mother who'd uttered the same wish each night of my childhood, leaving me to wonder when it had happened that I'd stopped dreaming at all.

CHAPTER 18

LONDON
JUNE 1939

Eva took great care with her appearance, selecting a green cotton day frock with a large white linen bow at the neckline. The belt cinched her small waist, the narrow skirt emphasizing her height and slender build. It was from this year's line at Lushtak's, but Madame had let her buy it for a reasonable price; she said that Eva wore it better than any of their well-heeled customers.

Looking at her reflection in the mirror, Eva quickly pinned on her hat, then left the room, walking down the long hallway to the foyer. Precious had begun lining the walls with photographs of the two of them that had appeared in Lushtak's advertisements. She'd become friendly with the photographer, who had been charmed into giving Precious the photographs she requested. Ever since Sophia had announced that Eva and Precious would be attendants at her society wedding, photographers appeared at every social engagement and even at Lushtak's. It had been very good for business, and Madame showed her gratitude with increased salaries and deeper discounts on clothes.

Eva followed the sound of voices into the front parlor and found Graham and Precious at the large front window. They were standing very close, and Graham pointed out the architectural details of St. Marylebone Parish Church across the road. "You really missed your calling," Eva said to announce herself. "Is it too late to change careers and become an architect?"

Graham walked toward her with a grin. "I'm of the firm belief that it's never too late to try something new." He kissed her gently on the lips, his eyes warm. Turning to Precious, he said, "Are you quite sure you don't want to come with us?"

Eva held her breath, willing Precious to say she was. She was desperate to be alone with Graham. Between his traveling for work and Sophia's social invitations, it had proven nearly impossible.

"I know you're just being kind, and I thank you. But I think I'll stay in and catch up on some letter writing. My daddy can't read or write, but my sister can, and she tells me that it does Daddy a world of good to get a letter from me. So you two go have fun. If the mood hits, I might watch a film later with some of the girls from Lushtak's, so don't worry about me."

Eva tried to hide the relief in her voice. "All right, then. I'll see you later." She tucked her hand into Graham's proffered elbow and allowed him to escort her downstairs and out into the early Sunday afternoon sunlight.

"Aren't you going to ask me where we're going?" Graham said.

"You said it was a surprise, and if I ask and you tell me, then it's not a surprise anymore."

"So if I put a blindfold on you now and didn't remove it until we reached our destination, you'd be all right with that?" His lips twisted up in a half smile.

"Absolutely. I like holding off on surprises until the very last moment. Because once it's revealed, it's over. Like unwrapping a birthday present. I always found the anticipation of opening the present much more rewarding than the present itself." She recalled her mother's intermittent attempts at birthday and Christmas gifts, obvious hand-me-downs or discards from her customers, the wrapping paper old newspaper she'd found in bins, but always tied with extravagant bows made from fabric scraps. The bows were intricate sculptures of loops and curls, and Eva had hated to pull the strand that would unravel them, unspooling her mother's hours of focused concentration and effort with a simple flick of her wrist. She'd much rather have kept the bow intact, the present unopened, a single object of beauty and hope. But her mother would make her open her present, seemingly intent on destroying the one thing that separated them from desperate obscurity.

"Duly noted," Graham said. "Which is a shame, really, since I've brought you a small token of my esteem."

"A present?" She clasped her hands together, then dropped them immediately when she realized how childish she must have appeared.

He noticed, which made him grin even wider. "I do appreciate your enthusiasm, Eva. It's what I love about you the most, I think. The way you treat each experience as something brand-new. So many women exude a studied ennui so that it's impossible to tell what they really like. But with you, I know exactly. You're not afraid to show your excitement. And sometimes I might even say that I know what you're thinking."

She wanted to tell him then how each experience **was** new to her, how she was still studying how to pretend it wasn't. How she'd lied to him, because Ethel Maltby wasn't worthy of Graham St. John, but Eva Harlow could be.

But the sun was bright and warm on her skin, and at that moment, Graham was hers. Not Ethel's or Eva's, but **hers**. She would tell him the truth. She would. Just not at that moment, when the sort of happiness she never thought she could claim was clamoring through her veins like racing horses, causing her heartbeat to thunder in her chest.

They stopped walking at the corner of Marylebone Road and Park Square West and stood in front of the heavy black iron gates surrounding Park Square Gardens. Eva smiled up at Graham, the small brim of her hat shading her eyes. "And what am I thinking now, sir?"

He leaned closer, his green eyes darkening. "You're thinking that I should kiss you."

"Is that all?"

His face became serious. "Do you want that to be all?"

"No," she said without thinking. Because it was the truth. Because she was finally beginning to understand the great passion she saw on the big screens at the theater. "I don't."

He kissed her right there, on the sidewalk, while people walked past them and pretended not to see. Then he took her hand and led her across the street to the crescent of white stuccoed buildings she admired each time she passed them on her way home from the Regent's Park tube stop. "Where are we going?"

"I thought you didn't want me to spoil the surprise."

"But what about my present?"

He spread his arms wide. "What if I said this was my present? To introduce you to the great architect John Nash. He was a friend of the prince regent and the grand designer behind Regent's Park and these beautiful terraces, as well as eight villas. The summer palace planned for the prince was never realized, but what was actually built is perfect, in my humble opinion."

"In your humble opinion? Is there such a thing?" Eva was laughing now, enjoying his boyish exuberance and his apparent joy at sharing his passion for buildings.

He pretended to be offended. "Yes, my dear. I've been known to have a humble opinion every once in a while." He looked up at the columned portico with the ram's-horn capitals. "The color is called crown cream, and it's not meant to be changed, even by those who live in the residences."

Eva bent her neck backward so she could admire the entire building before turning back to Graham. "I think this is what I love most about **you**—the way you notice all the details. Most people walk past this piece of history every day and never see it. But you see everything."

"Yes," he said, his grin dimming a little. "I do."

They stared at each other, seemingly oblivious to the Sunday strollers who passed by.

"Thank you," Eva said.

"For what?"

"For my present. It's lovely, and I will never be able to pass any of these terraces in the park and not think of John Nash and you."

"You're welcome. Although this isn't really your

present, you know. I do have something else. It's not wrapped, so there won't be any anticipation. No chance of being disappointed." He raised his eyebrows in jest, but there was seriousness to his eyes.

"I'll love it because it's from you."

Without dropping his gaze, he reached into his pocket and pulled out something small that he kept hidden in his fist. With careful hands, Eva turned his fist over and began to gently pry open each finger, revealing a small ivory carving in the middle of his palm. She picked it up and held it carefully over her own open hand. "It's lovely. I think it's the most lovely thing I've ever seen." She thought briefly of the cigarette case Alex had given her, of the heavy silver and intricate carvings. But it wasn't like this. Not a gift given from the heart and cherished because of it.

"It's an Irrawaddy dolphin—highly regarded in Burma. According to an enduring myth, the Irrawaddy dolphin was a fair maiden endowed with the body of a fish. Unfortunately, an attempt by her parents to make her marry a magical python saw her proudly cast herself into the Mekong River. Her suicide bid failed, and instead, she was transformed—her enchanting contentment forever immortalized in the dolphin's upturned mouth. Irrawaddy dolphins exude a timeless affability, and when I found myself missing England, I'd look for one of the smiling dolphins to cheer me up. A Buddhist monk I met during my travels abroad made this for me as a sort of happiness charm. It certainly seemed to work."

"How delightful," Eva said, her voice thick. "But how can you bear to part with it?"

He held her close to him, uncaring of where they were or who might be walking by. Eva kept the figure carefully guarded in her hand like one might cradle something as precious as an infant. "I have you now," Graham said. "I suppose that means you're my new happiness charm."

"I hope so." She stepped back so she could open her purse and carefully tuck the dolphin inside. "I don't want anything to happen to it."

They linked arms again and continued strolling into the park. "Were you sent to Burma because of your job with the Diplomatic Service?"

"Yes. I was sent to work in the governor's office after Burma separated from British India and became a proper colony. It was more of a peacemaking mission than anything else, and I enjoyed my time there. I believe I was chosen because I'm rather good with languages. I read Persian and Arabic at Oxford and have picked up several more since."

"I imagine that's a good skill to have if you enjoy traveling out of your native country."

"Indeed." He was silent for a moment. "You know, I don't think he remembers me, but I met Alexander Grof once in Burma. I never forget a face, and I'm quite sure it was him."

The mention of Alexander's name sent a chill

down her spine despite the warmth of the day. "Really? And he didn't recognize you?"

Graham shook his head. "Apparently not, and I didn't want to call his attention to it if he didn't, so I didn't mention it. It was at the Pegu Club in Rangoon. Grof was visiting an uncle, a German aristocrat whose family owns one of the largest teak exporting companies in Burma. I spoke to him only briefly, so I don't expect him to remember me."

"But you remembered him."

Graham was silent for a moment. "Yes, I did. It's a special talent of mine."

"As is selecting the perfect gift," Eva said, eager to change the conversation away from any thought of Alexander Grof.

He squeezed her arm against his side. "I do hope you like the dolphin," he said, sounding uncertain.

"I don't just like it—I love it. Although it's not the first thing you've given me, you know."

"It isn't?"

She shook her head. "Your embroidered handkerchief, remember? From the day we met. You gave it to me to protect my purse in the rain."

"Right before you ran away." His eyes held reproach, as if accusing Eva of finding him lacking on the night they met. As if that wasn't as far from the truth as the sun from the earth.

"I wasn't running away from you," she said. "I was . . . nervous. I wasn't dressed to meet . . ." She almost said **someone like you** but quickly changed it. "I wasn't dressed to meet anyone in my bedraggled state. I didn't want you to think I was a street beggar."

He halted so he could look her in the face. "Do you think that would have mattered to me? From the moment I saw you, I thought you were special. Not just because you're beautiful, Eva. That's the obvious part that most people don't bother looking beyond. I think it's because I recognized a hunger in you. A hunger that I share. A hunger to be something more than what others expect from us. It's why I went to Burma—horribly disappointing my mother in the process. But I needed to go. To test my mettle. To prove—to myself mostly—that I'm capable of being more than the life into which I was born."

They continued to walk toward the park and the new Queen Mary's Gardens, and Eva returned her hand to the crook of his elbow. "Why did it disappoint your mother?"

"Oh, Mother has certain ideas. She's from an old and aristocratic family, and she married beneath her station—or so she reminds us, and our father, often. She has quite lofty ambitions for my brother. Poor William."

"Poor William? He inherits everything, yes? The house and property? I'd say he's quite lucky."

"Yes—the estate will go to him upon our father's death. But that means Mother is watching him like a hawk to make sure he marries someone suitable. She's already chased off several girls who weren't up to snuff. William was actually heartbroken over the last. He's still in recovery."

Eva's tongue felt frozen with the ice from her heart. "It's a good thing you're a second son so you have the freedom to choose."

He smiled down at her. "In many ways, yes. Except, well, William has signed up for the Royal Air Force. I think it's partly to get over his heartbreak, but also because he's convinced war is inevitable. And therefore our mother and father are convinced that something will happen to him." He shrugged. "It's the way with parents, I'm afraid."

She tried to keep the brittleness from her voice. "So now they're focusing their attention on you, to make sure that you're safe."

"Yes. They'd like me to leave my Home Office job and rusticate in the country with them, see how the war plays out."

"But that's not who you are, is it?" It was the part of him she loved, the adventurous man who willingly left the comforts of home to experience life in a country a world away, who befriended a Buddhist monk and recognized the charm of a smiling dolphin.

He shook his head. "No, it's not. Still, it seems Mother has quite elaborate plans for my future. They're very different ideas from mine. But my father is ill, which is one of the reasons I returned from abroad, and I don't want to upset him. Especially so close to Sophia's wedding. So I pretend to agree with Mother's plans so as not to upset her or my father."

"I'm sorry. I didn't know your father was so ill."

He was thoughtful for a long moment. "There is quite a lot we haven't shared with each other. I think it's because you're so special to me. I don't want the realities of the rest of our lives to intrude and spoil all of it. Does that upset you?"

She shook her head, her throat tightening. It was a moment before she could respond. "No, actually. I do understand. I don't have any family, but I can imagine how important it is to remain close, especially in times like this."

"I knew you would, Eva. I want to introduce you to my parents, to let them know that you're special in my life. But I can't right now. It will be hard enough for them. To me, it doesn't matter that you're a country doctor's daughter—I love you as much as if you were the daughter of a duke. But I'm afraid they don't see it that way. Can you be patient with me?"

"If you're asking me to wait for you, you know I will."

He kissed her. "Just until my father gets better. The doctors are hopeful, so that's something."

She swallowed, attempting to sound cheerful. "At least your job now is quite tame in comparison. I expect that must be a relief to your parents."

Graham didn't answer right away, making Eva look at him sharply and recall how Alex had correctly assumed she knew nothing about his job. It shamed her how easily Alex could read her, that he knew how unsophisticated her world experiences were. She'd simply imagined Graham sitting at a desk with piles of papers and a telephone. It was juvenile, but she had no experience or knowledge to imagine anything different. "I know you work at the Home Office—but what exactly do you do there? You're gone so much. I'm imagining it's not Burma, but still quite exciting."

"No, it's not Burma." She waited for him to say more, watching his thoughts darken his face, but instead he smiled unexpectedly. "We're not here to talk about work. Now that I've shown you not one but two surprises, I'd like to take you to the boating lake. It was too cold the last time we tried, but it's nice and warm now. Shall we?"

She took his hand and entwined his fingers with hers. They walked slowly, enjoying the rare time spent alone together. Couples stretched out on the green lawns on blankets, their white skin like the underbellies of fish as it pinkened in the sun.

Wanting Graham's playful mood to return, Eva said, "I'll only get in the boat with you if you do the rowing. I'm afraid my arms are too sore from holding them up all day yesterday to be fitted for an entire wedding trousseau for Daphne Wigham. They've moved up her wedding—her fiancé's joined the Royal Navy. It's as if the whole country thinks we're at war already."

Graham was silent as they walked down a manicured path toward the boating lake, already dotted with rowboats cutting through the dappled water. "I will admit to being worried about what's going on in Europe. But today is just you and me. Let's pretend that the rest of the world doesn't exist."

He pulled on Eva's hand and nearly ran across the lake on the steel bridge to the boat stand. As promised, he took the paddles but pretended to rock the narrow boat as the attendant seated Eva. She gave him a mock frown, which made Graham lean forward to kiss her, causing the boat to violently swish from side to side. Eva gave a shout, and Graham put a steadying hand on her leg, the heat of his touch sinking into her bones. His green eyes sparkled in the sun. "Don't worry, Eva. I'll keep you safe. I wouldn't let anything happen to you."

He pushed off from the boarding dock, and they coasted between geese and fellow rowers until they were clear enough that he could begin rowing. Eva had never been to Venice but had listened intently to the stories the Italian girl Rosalie told at Lushtak's, tales detailed enough that she felt she could see the ancient city in her mind. She could imagine being with Graham in a gondola, transported by a singing gondolier through the beautiful waterways.

But being with Graham in Regent's Park was its own piece of magic, the sky as blue as it must be in Italy. Eva leaned back, allowing her fingers to dangle in the water, still cool despite the heat of the day. Closing her eyes, she sighed. "Please don't wake me. I think I might be dreaming."

She could hear the smile in his voice. "What do you dream of, darling?"

She smiled, keeping her eyes closed. "Of you."

"Really? What else?"

Eva thought for a moment. "The house I will one day live in."

"Ah. And what does it look like?"

The rhythmic slap of the oars was a lullaby, the sound of his voice hypnotic. "It's high on a cliff, overlooking the sea. I can hear the crash of waves through my bedroom window."

"Are you alone?"

The soft sounds of other people in the boats around them and the movement of water against the boat seemed very distant, lulled as she was by the heat and by the warmth of Graham's voice. "No." She opened her eyes to mere slits, his image through her eyelashes like a mirage. "I'm with you."

She closed her eyes again, felt the pull of the little boat through the water, thought of her house on the cliff by the sea, and remembered how Graham had promised to always keep her safe.

CHAPTER 19

LONDON
MAY 2019

We sat in silence after Penelope and Precious had left the room. Then Arabella jumped up. "Who wants to watch the sunset? It's my first night in the country in ages, and the sky is crystal clear." She held out her hands to me. "Come on, Maddie. I promise you've never seen anything like it. Bring your camera." She looked beyond me to her cousin. "You, too, Colin. When was the last time you watched a sunset?"

Colin drained the rest of his glass and set it on the mantel. "Not since university," he said matter-of-factly, an odd note to his voice. He turned to his father. "Dad? Would you like to join us?"

"Thank you, but I've got correspondence I need to see to. You go ahead." James looked at his watch. "Best hurry—the sun sets in about forty-five minutes. The best place is up on the chalk ridge, which is a decent walk from here. Take torches so you can find your way back. It's only a crescent moon tonight."

After running upstairs and quickly changing into jeans and a sweater, I followed Arabella and Colin through the house, grabbing flashlights from the kitchen before heading out through the door to the back garden. The scent of flowers weighted the air with a lightness that almost made me forget the look on Precious's face when she'd turned away from my scrutiny, the sense I'd had of a pen being held over paper, a story with no ending.

But it did end. It had to. Every story had a final act, a place under which the words "The End" could be written. I'd lived my entire adult life on that premise, on the knowledge that some endings were known before the stories even began.

Tonight, there had been something about the way Precious had said **sweet dreams**. Something almost challenging, a hook thrown into water to see what might be caught. Not that it was an unusual sentiment. I recalled the same handwritten words on the back of Graham's RAF photograph. Maybe that was what was niggling at my brain, the sheer coincidence of two things that shouldn't have been related.

Beside me, Arabella stopped, rubbing her hands up and down her arms. "Brrr. How did it get so cold? I'm afraid I don't have a jumper." She looked genuinely disappointed. "And if you wait for me, you'll miss the sunset." Flicking her hand at us, she said, "You two go on. Take pictures so you can show me what I missed."

George and Charlotte, who'd apparently been cooped up during dinner, were eager to escape captivity. "Keep them out of the cowpats," Arabella warned before swiftly retreating, leaving Colin and me alone.

The dogs leapt and bounded around us like gnats, making me grin despite myself.

"Don't worry—we haven't let the cows on this hill for a bit so the grass can grow." Colin looked down at my Keds. "It's a gentle hill, but it might be slippery. Are you all right in those?"

"Probably not," I said, slipping them off, then rolling my socks inside them so that I was barefoot. In response to his blank expression, I explained, "Growing up, I only wore shoes to school, church, and birthday parties. It might be mostly a Southern thing, which means there's a whole mess of people missing out. There's just something magical about grass under your bare feet." I looked pointedly at his loafers. "You should try it."

He hesitated for only a moment before he took off his shoes and placed them neatly next to mine. "It is nice. A bit cool, though. Won't my feet get cold?"

"Don't worry—you'll get used to it. Your toes will be too happy to complain."

"Come on, then," he said, indicating a path leading from the garden to a grass slope interspersed with trees. He whistled to the dogs, who immediately began trotting in our direction.

We walked in silence, the dogs panting as they raced past us and then circled back when they reached the cow gate ahead, prancing impatiently as they waited for Colin to open it. I kept replaying our conversation in the kitchen, hearing Colin's words about the photo of the boy in the stroller on his desk who wasn't him. I wanted to ask him who it was but couldn't find the right words, words that would show an indifference I no longer felt.

"I've been making inquiries regarding Eva Harlow," Colin said, breaking the silence.

"Oh. Great. Have you found out anything?"

He shook his head. "Not a thing. I did find her on the roster of models at House of Lushtak from nineteen thirty-nine through the end of March nineteen forty-one. Then she disappears. Absolutely nothing—from death notices to hospital and marriage records. It's like she never existed."

"But we know she lived with Precious—did you check the building's history?"

"I tried to. There aren't any tenant records for Precious, because my grandparents owned the flat."

"And when she returned to London in the seventies, she moved back in. I wonder why she didn't find a small flat, since it was just her. Maybe it was so Eva could find her after all those years away."

"Curiouser and curiouser, I'd say," Colin said, his thoughts matching mine. "I'll see what I can find in the Devon records—Precious said Eva's father was a doctor and that both her parents were killed in an automobile accident. Those details should help narrow it down. We have an intern at the office to make phone calls; she can see if there are any newspaper accounts of the accident, that sort of thing. It's a long shot, but at least it's a shot."

The hill had become steeper, and I found myself breathing more heavily. Even the dogs had slowed their pace, although Colin continued with his long strides, slowing down only when he realized he was in front of me.

As we reached the crest of the hill, the light in the sky began to shift, and we stopped with the dogs to admire the view. On the south side of the slope, shadows were beginning to cover the bright green patchwork fields; on the north side, a dense forest claimed the landscape. And in the distance, beyond more rolling hills, the shapes of London's skyline projected dark shadows into the horizon like greedy fingers claiming the sky.

Colin pointed toward the trees. "Some of the yews in the forest are over five hundred years old. When I was a boy, Nana would take me for walks and tell me what a particular tree had witnessed in history, depending on its girth." He fell silent, pondering his next words. "Nana said she wished they were time capsules, that she could peel back the layers of bark to relive parts of her life. I never asked her which parts. Perhaps I should have."

Our eyes met. "Perhaps. Although I think you're running out of time. Arabella says her doctors feel as if she doesn't have much longer, yet except for the pallor of her skin, she seems perfectly fit to me."

He sucked in his breath, then let it out slowly. "That's why it's so hard to believe. She has congestive heart failure, and it's getting worse. She doesn't want to be resuscitated if anything happens, so yes, we're running out of time to reunite her with Eva or at least let her know what happened to her friend. And regardless, my father would like to learn his uncle's fate. But even he seems reluctant, as if the reason why Graham was never mentioned is because his parents were keeping something dark and sinister from him." He paused, his eyes staring steadily into mine. "What is it about all of our pasts that we're so unwilling to confront?"

I looked up into the purpling sky, like a bruise on the day to show it had been lived and survived. It might have been the fading light, or maybe the brandy made a confession seem less rash. "It's odd, but when I think of my past, I see it as a younger version of myself. The me I can't quite forgive for making so many mistakes."

I felt him waiting and turned to meet his gaze. He said, "But, Madison, all of your mistakes have made you who you are. And from what I can see, you're rather wonderful. Except for your inexplicable aversion to going home to a place you apparently love and a family who adores you."

"You think I'm wonderful?" I hadn't meant to say that, but his words had taken me by surprise.

"You have your moments."

I looked away. Uncomfortable under his scrutiny, and confused by the rush of blood to my face, I breathed in deeply, the air redolent of spring and growing things and the soft fug of barnyard animals. "I do love the smell of a farm," I said, eager to change the subject. "Pretty much in the same way I love the scent of the south Georgia swamps. I guess it's like loving the sound of bagpipes—you're either born with it or you're not."

"So you like the sound of bagpipes, do you?" Colin smiled reluctantly.

"I do. I can't tell you where I've heard them, but I have often enough to know. There's just something—I don't know—majestic about them. Haunting, almost. And you?"

"I've lived in Great Britain my entire life, so I've heard my share of bagpipes. And yes, I do enjoy them. I don't believe one is allowed to be British and not at least give a show of liking them."

The distant sound of a cow lowing rolled over the hills, making me nostalgic for something I wasn't aware I was missing. "How could you ever leave such a place?"

When he didn't answer, I looked up to find

him watching me closely. "Because I know it's always here. It's where my childhood memories live, good and bad all mixed together." A shadow passed behind his eyes, the kind I saw behind my own. He looked away, as if aware he'd given away something he hadn't been ready to share. Turning to me again, he added, "But that's what makes it home."

I stared at him in the gathering dusk, feeling the tiny night insects brush against my cheeks. "Home is a place that lives in one's heart, waiting with open arms to be rediscovered."

He tilted his head slightly. "What incredibly intelligent person said that?"

I smiled. "My aunt Cassie. She's right about most things."

"She's certainly right about that."

I thought about what he'd just said, about home being a mixture of good and bad, and remembered the photograph of the boy who wasn't Colin. "The photograph on your desk—the one of your parents with a little boy who looks like you. But it's not you." I let the unasked question float in the night air, unseen, its weight heavy between us.

Colin regarded me in silence for a long moment before turning away. Looking up, he pointed to the first stars appearing in the ceiling of sky above us. "In the winter, Gemini and Orion are visible. I've spent many a frigid evening with my telescope on this very spot."

I followed his gaze to the pinpricks of light above us, the brandy and the wide-open sky making me dizzy. "When I was little, I was afraid of the dark, so my mama told me that the stars were little cracks in God's curtains he'd use to keep an eye on us at night. After that, I wasn't afraid anymore."

"She sounds like a very smart woman, too."

"I come from a long line of intelligent women. If I didn't look exactly like my aunt Cassie, I would think I was adopted."

"You're right, you know."

I looked at him in surprise. "About what—being adopted?"

He smiled, his teeth bright in the gathering darkness. "About going barefoot. I rather like it."

I gazed out over the fields. The vanishing sun had begun to tuck the hills into shadow blankets for the night, the light loosening its hold on the day and shifting from gold to purple. "It's beautiful," I whispered, not wanting to disturb the silence.

"It's not the first sunset we've watched together," Colin said close to my ear, and I realized he'd moved to stand next to me.

"It's not?" I turned my face, his own near enough to touch.

"At university. Arabella arranged for a group of us to view the sunset from Headington Hill Hall, and you and I were the only two who showed up."

"I'm not sure I remember," I said, although that wasn't completely true. I didn't remember the scenery, but I did remember him standing next to me, carrying my camera bag.

"You tried to kiss me," he said.

I looked at him, recalling it clearly now. "No. **You** were the one who tried to kiss **me**."

And before I could register that he was smiling, Colin leaned toward me and pressed his lips against mine. I was too startled to pull back right away, too aware of how nice it felt, appreciating the warmth of his mouth on mine, his hands gently resting on my waist, the dusky air that settled on our shoulders and seemed to push us together. The kiss deepened, and I found myself responding to him, to his touch, to the perfect melding of two bodies embracing. I was about to stretch my arms around his neck and pull him closer when I realized what I was doing and stopped, stepping back so quickly that I nearly lost my footing.

"I'm sorry. This . . . No. I can't. . . ." I couldn't formulate the rest of my words, no longer even sure why I was telling him no.

"Is it because of me? Or because you believe yourself to be living with a death sentence?" He didn't look away, holding my gaze and forcing an answer.

The intimacy of the falling dusk and the taste of his lips on mine made me brave. "It's not you."

He sucked in a breath. "Good." He paused a moment, considering his words. "I'm not trying to make light of what you're dealing with, but I've done a little reading to understand all of this a bit better. Surely you know that having the gene doesn't mean your life is guaranteed to be shortened or left unlived."

I watched his face in the gathering gloom, doing my best to ignore the warmth in my chest his words had created. **I've done a little reading to understand all of this a bit better.** As if he truly cared. It was possible that he did, but only because he didn't know the full story. I shook my head as if to erase his words. "But it **might** be. And then I'd be putting the ones I love through the same trauma we went through when my mother died. I can't do that to them. I **won't** do it." I stepped back, needing to create space between us. "You couldn't understand."

His arms fell to his sides, his blue eyes reflecting the last light of day. He didn't speak right away, and when he did, it wasn't what I was expecting him to say.

"The little boy was named Jeremy. He was my twin brother, and he died of leukemia when we were nine years old." He picked up my flashlight, which I'd dropped on the ground, and whistled for the dogs. "Come on. Best use your torch. If you twist an ankle, I doubt I could carry you all the way back, and I'd hate to have to leave you out here all night."

With that, he flicked on his own flashlight and led the way, the dogs loping alongside. I trudged along behind them, the darkness nipping at my heels and chasing me down the hill.

CHAPTER 20

LONDON
JULY 1939

The perfect weather for Sophia and David's weekend wedding in Surrey appeared to have been ordered along with the crisp linen invitations and champagne. Sophia had left for the country the week before, and Graham was in France until late Friday; he would barely make it in time for supper. Even Precious had been delayed in London by a late showing and wouldn't be arriving until the following morning, leaving Eva to take the train to Surrey alone. Thankfully, a car was waiting for her to take her to Hovenden Hall when she arrived.

Sophia greeted her on the front steps, and Eva did her best to express nonchalance at the opulent surroundings of the manor house. She'd seen the bored expression on Sophia's friends' faces and had no problem imitating it and playing the part of a woman to the manner born. But to herself, she was gape-mouthed and wide-eyed, struggling to imagine growing up in such a place and calling it home.

"You're positively glowing," Eva told her friend. "Shall I call the vicar and tell him no candles or electric lights will be needed in tomorrow's ceremony?"

Sophia laughed. "You are too kind, Eva. I've given you and Precious the best guest room, and your frocks have been pressed and hung inside the wardrobe. Mother said you wouldn't need a maid, since there are two of you and each can help the other, but I will lend you my Lucy if you do."

"I'm sure we'll be fine," Eva said, her nerves jumping at the mere mention of Mrs. St. John. She wished desperately that Precious was with her.

A footman carried Eva's valise upstairs—the respectable leather monogrammed valise that Madame Lushtak gave to all of her models after three months' service—while Sophia tucked her hand into Eva's elbow, leading her toward the grand staircase. "Mother is receiving guests in the drawing room. Why don't I bring you to your room, where you can freshen up, and then I'll introduce you?"

"Of course," Eva said, nodding as if she were looking forward to meeting Graham's mother. They began to ascend the stairs. "Does she remember me from Lushtak's?"

"She didn't recognize the name, but she might

recognize your face. It's not forgettable, is it? Although I daresay Mother might not have noticed. She was more focused on the clothes."

"So who does she think I am?"

They paused on the landing, and Sophia turned to face her friend. "I didn't want anything to upset her, not with Father still being so very ill and all her responsibilities for her only daughter's wedding." She paused. "I hope you don't mind too terribly, but she believes you and Precious are school friends of David's sister, Violet—my third bridesmaid. Happily, Violet is always up for a laugh and thinks the subterfuge is all in good fun. She's already told Mother that we've all been friends for ages."

Rather than feel insulted, Eva felt a tinge of relief. "I understand. I do."

Sophia squeezed her hand, then resumed climbing the stairs. "I hoped you would. Mother is terribly old-fashioned about things. I'm sure once she gets to know you, she will love and accept you as much as Graham and I do. It will just take some time."

Eva felt reassured by Sophia's words but didn't miss her friend's grim smile as she turned away.

A half hour later, she and Sophia stood outside the drawing room door. Sophia squeezed Eva's hand. "It can't be any worse than Daniel facing the lions, right? And he survived."

Before she could tell Sophia that her words

weren't helping, a footman opened the door, and they walked in. Three matrons sat chatting over teacups and looked up as they entered.

"Mother," Sophia said, moving to Mrs. St. John's side, "may I introduce you to one of my bridesmaids, Eva Harlow?"

Eva smiled as she approached, feeling as if she were being presented to the queen. "So nice to meet you, Mrs. St. John."

Pale blue eyes flickered over Eva but showed no sign of recognition. Eva kept her knees locked so they wouldn't collapse with relief.

After Sophia had made the rest of the introductions, she indicated that they both would sit on the small settee by Mrs. St. John.

"I am so glad you are here," Sophia's mother said after tea was brought in by a uniformed maid and plates of little cakes were offered. "Perhaps you can talk Sophia into adjusting the neckline of her gown. I have tried to convince her that it is too low for a young lady from a good family, but my words seem to be falling on deaf ears. The dressmaker was absolutely worthless, considering what we spent. I asked for the neckline to be raised, and she did not do as I instructed."

"She most likely didn't understand proper English," said one of the other women, whose name Eva had already forgotten. "You should be glad she didn't leave her dirty fingerprints all over the white satin. Who knows where their hands have been?"

A bite of cake stuck in Eva's throat. She forced it down with a sip of tea. Her hand shook so badly that she almost dropped her cup, the sound alarmingly loud as it tapped the saucer. She felt three sets of eyes on her, but Eva managed to continue to smile and pretend that she belonged there. "I would be happy to take a look," she said, sliding a glance to Sophia for help. "It might be easily remedied."

"Oh, Mother, don't be ridiculous," Sophia interjected. "The neckline is quite modest. I daresay David won't be shocked, and he's the only person whose opinion matters to me."

Mrs. St. John raised an eyebrow as she sipped her tea, her gaze lingering on Eva before returning to her daughter. "I disagree. You have two eligible brothers. It is important there is no stain on your reputation, as it will reflect badly on them. As a matter of fact, Lady Duncan's daughter, Aurelia, is coming to supper tonight. I was hoping Graham would be here in time. I have instructed that her place card be set next to his."

Lady Duncan, the woman whose name Eva had forgotten, smiled, showing slightly protruding teeth. "It would be lovely if our families were united in marriage, wouldn't it?"

"Indeed it would," Mrs. St. John agreed, her gaze drifting back to Eva.

As if anticipating more questions, Sophia stood abruptly. "If you ladies will excuse us, we have so much to do." Eva stood, too, while they said their good-byes, then followed Sophia out of the room. They didn't stop walking until they'd passed down enough corridors to find an empty room.

"Are you all right?" Sophia asked, her eyes solicitous.

"I think so. Thank you for rescuing me."

"Actually, I should be thanking **you** for rescuing Graham from the likes of Aurelia Duncan. She has teeth like her mother's and not a brain in her skull. Graham has been avoiding her ever since her debut two years ago, when our mothers started throwing them together. I think that's half the reason he went to Burma."

Eva remembered what Graham had told her about his reason for going so far away. Something he said they shared. **A hunger to be something more than what others expect from us.**

"Perhaps," Eva said instead.

"That wasn't so beastly, was it?" Sophia asked.

"It was, but I survived. And it's over."

"That it is. Now, I suggest we go upstairs and rest before the other guests arrive for tonight's supper. It's only a small group because of Father still being so ill, but I will need to look my best. David's parents and sister will be here, and they will adore you. I'll make sure you're sitting near them. I can't switch place cards for you and Aurelia, or Mother will get suspicious. You do know that Graham has eyes for no one but you?"

Eva nodded. "And David, you."

A pretty flush dusted Sophia's cheeks. "Then we're in good company."

They linked arms as they returned to the corridor, walking past a housemaid on her hands and knees next to a broken vase, blotting up water and picking up stray pieces. Eva started to smile at her but stopped when she noticed Sophia walking by as if the maid weren't there at all. Averting her gaze, Eva followed Sophia down the hallway, the sound of the scrub brush seeming to chase her until Sophia closed a door behind them.

Mr. St. John was conspicuously absent at the Friday night supper. Graham took his father's place at the head of the table, as William was training with the RAF and would miss the entire wedding weekend. Graham and Eva hadn't had a moment to talk before supper, and Aurelia had monopolized him during the meal, but as soon as the orchestra began, Graham claimed Eva for the first dance, earning a disapproving look from his mother.

Eva hoped Mrs. St. John would be quickly distracted by her guests and wouldn't notice the way Graham looked at her. Not that it mattered. As soon as she was in Graham's arms, nothing else mattered.

The terrace doors had been opened, allowing dancers to waltz in and out of the ballroom. Graham led them outside, dancing to the strains of "Begin the Beguine," and they remained, the sounds of the orchestra and the warm night air caressing her bare shoulders as they swayed.

Eva smiled up at him. "I missed you. Am I allowed to ask what you were doing in France?"

"Isn't it enough to know I missed you?"

"For now. I just hate being without you, knowing you're far away. The nights are the hardest."

The moonlight made his eyes gleam. "Even if you dream we're together in your house by the sea?"

"Even then," she whispered. She moved her hands to his shoulders to bring him closer. He winced, and she pulled away.

"What's wrong?"

"I'm all right. Just a minor accident. You know the French—never paying attention to where they're going." He smiled, but his eyes were hidden in the darkness. "I have a bit of a bruise, but that's all."

"Thank goodness," Eva said, breathing in the scent of him. "I couldn't bear knowing you were hurt."

"I know. I promise to be extra careful in future."

The notes of the orchestra died, but they continued swaying to their own music. They were dancing on a precipice, and Eva was ready to fall.

When he came to her room that night, she was waiting for him in the dark, the full moon outside pouring into the open window, painting her skin with opalescent light. She rushed to him, and he took her in his arms.

"I couldn't go to sleep without wishing you a

proper good night," he said, his lips placing small kisses on her neck and jaw.

"I wish you could stay."

"Me, too." He held her so they could be face-to-face. "But I would never dishonor you, darling. You mean too much to me."

He kissed her, and the room disintegrated beyond her closed eyelids as she allowed her world to become only the two of them.

After he left, Eva lay in bed and stared up at the ceiling for a long while, watching the shadows move across the room, imagining she and Graham were together, listening to the crash of waves far below their house by the sea.

CHAPTER 21

LONDON
JULY 1939

Eva stood at her open bedroom window, wearing only her silk step-in and trying to catch the breeze, looking past the roofs of the park terraces toward Regent's Park. Throngs of people continued to flock there due to the spell of hot summer weather, and they exposed as much pale skin as decency allowed.

Her thumb rubbed the ivory dolphin Graham had given her, her nail having memorized each curve, each notch. She carried it with her always, even slept with it on her bedside table to keep Graham near. Drawing on her cigarette, she closed her eyes, feeling utterly exhausted.

Ever since the fashion show at Lushtak's, Eva and Precious had found themselves thrown into a social whirl that neither had anticipated or prepared for.

They were in demand at work, too; the number of private showings for which they'd been requested had added to their paychecks as well as to their confidence.

Then there had been the near-nightly entertainments and dinner parties with Graham—when he was available—Sophia, and David. Because of uncertainties in Europe, the newlyweds had postponed their wedding trip, which meant Sophia was available and happy to orchestrate everyone's social lives. Sophia never wanted Precious to feel like a fifth wheel, so she always included Alexander Grof, ensuring there would be an even number at every dining table. Of course, Eva wanted Precious to be a part of their group, but Alex's presence always seemed like the fly in the sauce, unappetizing and out of place.

Although, judging by the way Alex joked and conversed with their entire party, Eva was the only one who noticed his silver eyes that missed nothing; who saw the way he always managed to seat himself next to her, close enough that she could smell the starch in his shirts. He was the cat and she the mouse, waiting for him to pounce.

Alex had been at the wedding and the reception at Hovenden Hall, but thankfully there had been enough guests and commotion that he'd managed to get her alone only once, cornering her in the main hall as she'd returned from helping Sophia change. He'd been waiting for her, with the pretense of giving her a glass of champagne. She'd wanted to refuse, to walk past, but she didn't want to call attention to herself and him. To have him say something she didn't wish anyone else to hear.

"You're looking splendid as ever, Eva. Sophia is a beautiful bride, don't you agree? Of course, she couldn't hold a candle to you."

"What do you want, Alex? What could I possibly have that you might find useful?"

He smiled, took a sip from his champagne glass. "Why was Graham in France?"

His question caught her off guard. "What?"

"He just returned from France. I was wondering why he was there."

"Why would you care?"

"Curious, I suppose. Just curious."

She drained her glass, then handed it to him. "Excuse me, won't you?" She walked away, feeling those silver eyes on her back like pinpricks of fire.

For the remainder of the reception, Eva had felt Alex's stare, seen the mocking grin on his face, the knowing look in his eyes that told her he was aware of her charade and capable of blowing it up into as many pieces as wedding confetti. She hadn't been able to eat anything; even a bite of wedding cake had tasted like sawdust in her mouth. She'd been more than relieved when he'd left with the other guests who wouldn't be staying overnight, grateful for the touch of Graham's hand on her back as they'd said good-bye.

Eva drew another drag from her cigarette, absently continuing to watch the people in the park, the warm air stagnant and cloying, fitting her mood. They'd been to the Eton–Harrow cricket match at Lord's earlier in the day, standing in the heat with thousands of well-heeled spectators. Although it was usually a two-day affair, Eva, Precious, and Sophia had opted out of the entire spectacle and made only a Sunday appearance. They were present at the final pitch, when Harrow defeated Eton for the first time in thirty-one years. The resulting brawl would have been amusing if Eva hadn't had to pretend to be as shocked as Sophia.

Precious knocked on Eva's door. "Are you decent?"

Eva stabbed out her cigarette in an ashtray. "Yes. Come in."

Precious entered, already dressed and made-up for the evening. She looked at Eva with surprise. "You're not ready yet? They'll be here in less than half an hour. David is bringing his motorcar and driver, so we'll all fit together. We'll be like bugs in a rug." She grinned, then held out a small package beautifully wrapped with pale blue paper and white silk ribbon. "This just arrived for you by messenger."

"From Graham?" Eva asked as she sat down on the bed and searched for a gift tag.

"Of course," Precious said. "Who else could it be from?"

Eva's hands stilled for a moment. "Who indeed?" she said as she pulled on the ribbon and began tearing at the paper. She eagerly lifted the lid of the box inside, smiling with relief. It was a bottle of Vol de Nuit, her favorite perfume. The one she'd told Graham about.

"Is that . . . ?" Precious's blue eyes widened.

"It is. It's a large enough bottle, so we can share." Eva took it out of the box and unscrewed the glass top. After dabbing the perfume behind each ear and on her wrists, she handed the bottle to Precious.

"Are you sure you don't mind? I know this is your signature scent, and I don't want to confuse Graham." Precious grinned.

"I don't mind sharing with you. We're like sisters, remember?" Eva smiled up at her friend. "Besides, I do believe Graham is familiar with me by now. I doubt he'll be confused."

While Precious applied the perfume to her neck, Eva dug through the box, looking for a card of some sort, wanting to see Graham's handwriting. A folded ivory-colored linen note lay at the bottom of the box. She reached for it, then froze, remembering another folded note. One that hadn't been from Graham.

"Is it from him?" Precious asked, leaning over Eva's shoulder.

Eva pressed the note to her chest. "Of course. And if you'll give me some privacy, I'd love to read it."

"Sorry." Precious managed to look remorseful. "But do hurry—they'll be here soon." She placed the perfume bottle on Eva's dressing table on her way out. Eva waited until she heard her friend's footsteps disappearing down the hallway before unfolding the note. It wasn't signed, and there was no salutation, but none was needed.

Please accept this gift as a small token of my esteem. Its creator, Jacques Guerlain, said it was designed for a demanding and charismatic woman with a sense of adventure. It was as if M. Guerlain had you in mind when he blended his fragrance. I do admire a woman with a sense of adventure.

She read the note several times before tearing it into hundreds of pieces, then scattering them outside her window, shameful little secrets fluttering toward the ground. Turning toward her dressing table, she spied the bottle, noting the front of it was designed to look like an airplane propeller. She picked it up, ready to toss it away as if it were rubbish to show Alex that he didn't know her at all.

Except he did. Otherwise he wouldn't have sent her such an expensive gift, something he knew she coveted yet couldn't afford. Something she would find quite impossible to return. She twisted off the stopper and smelled the cocktail of flowers mixed with vanilla and spices. She knew what the bottle cost, just as she knew it was too much for her to afford unless she didn't want to eat for a week.

Reinserting the stopper, she replaced the bottle on her dressing table, and her fingers lingered just for a brief moment before she pulled them away. **It's just a gift,** she told herself. And Alex wasn't asking anything in return. **Not yet,** her inner voice warned. **But he hasn't,** she argued back. It could be that he was simply an admirer who found her charismatic and appreciated her sense of adventure. What harm could there be in accepting this token of his regard?

She recalled something Mr. Danek had told her, how some might see her fondness for beautiful things as a weakness and use it to their advantage. He was wrong, of course. It was a weakness only if she couldn't walk away. She would if she had to.

She took out her gown from the armoire and finished getting dressed, taking special care with her cosmetics and hair. They were going to Café de Paris in Leicester Square for dinner and dancing. The band was always good and the dancing lively, and it was usually so crowded that one could press more closely than necessary against one's dance partner without anyone noticing.

Eva stifled her disappointment when David appeared at the door of the flat instead of Graham. Sophia waited in the car with Alex, and Graham would meet them at the café, as he'd had pressing business. She allowed David to place her stole around her shoulders, then walked with Precious toward the lift.

Alex stood by the side of the car as they approached, his eyes giving her an appreciative once-over. His black evening clothes suited him, and she recognized the expert fitting and cut of his dinner jacket. It was one of the things she'd learned at Lushtak's. It was how she could tell which of their clientele could afford to buy and which were there just to look.

Alex held the door open for Precious and then for Eva, leaning close to her ear. "You smell divine," he whispered. She almost stumbled as she stepped into the car, but managed to hold on to her composure and greeted Sophia with a wide smile. David and Alex took the jump seats facing them, Alex directly in front of Eva.

Sophia seemed unusually subdued during the drive to Leicester Square. She was usually the one to lead conversations, and after she assured Eva that she felt fine, Eva was at a loss. David, his expression changing by the minute from pent-up excitement to confusion when he looked at his bride, kept time with the rhythm of the tires, his fingers tapping nervously on his knees.

Alex seemed to notice, too, and raised his brows at Eva. Desperate for a distraction, Eva opened the green box bag and pulled out her cigarette case. Precious had finally given the purse to her as an early birthday gift, seeing as how she'd never used it because it was always on Eva's wrist.

She had barely placed the cigarette between her lips before Alex offered a match. She reluctantly met his eyes, his mocking smile seeming to remind her that she was using the cigarette case and wearing the perfume he'd given her. **You have a fondness for beautiful things. Some might see it as a weakness.** Her hand shook as she pulled back, belatedly offering cigarettes to the other occupants.

Precious refused, as she always did. She was the only one of all Eva's friends who didn't smoke, seeming almost virtuous as everyone else puffed away while she blew the smoke away from her.

"I say, that's a very nice case, Eva. May I see it?" David reached across the car, and Eva had no choice but to give it to him. He tested its heft in his hand. "Sterling, yes? It's quite heavy. But it's the bee on top that caught my eye. A queen, isn't it?"

"Is it?" Eva asked, blowing out smoke in an attempt to appear nonchalant. "I hadn't noticed."

"Oh, yes. Definitely a queen. She has a stinger, see? She's not a worker bee, as she's quite wide." Eva tried not to wince as he flipped it over in his palm and saw the inscription. **"'Nil credam et omnia cavebo,'"** he read out loud. He looked up at Eva, his head tilted. "Extraordinary. Wherever did you find this?"

The pause was so long that Alex finally spoke up. "I believe you said you found it in an antiques store on the high street. Isn't that right?"

Eva felt Precious's gaze on her but wasn't worried

her friend would blurt out the truth. Precious was very good at keeping secrets. Eva looked over at Alex, too wary to be grateful. "Yes. That's correct. My other one broke, and I thought the bee was pretty."

"Ah," David said, satisfied. He handed the case back to her. "I wonder who the original owner might have been. That's a rather prophetic inscription, isn't it?"

"Yes, I suppose so." Eva stuffed the case back into her purse and snapped the lid shut. "I just found it pretty," she said, smiling as she looked up, aware of a pair of silver eyes watching her.

Precious turned from the car window. "I love London at night," she said, smiling. "All these lights! And people everywhere! At home we lived so far down a country road that we might not see another person until church on Sunday. I think that's why I always had this antsy feeling that I was missing something. I guess that's why I'm here."

She turned to look at her seatmates. "I hear the band at the Café de Paris is the best in town. I swear my feet are already jitterbugging."

As if to add credence to her words, her feet moved to their own beat beneath the hem of her long gown. Her accent had become stronger when talking about home, causing Alex's lips to turn up in a sardonic smile. "You're from Tennessee, is that correct?"

Eva wanted to tell Precious not to respond, that

she doubted Alex was simply making idle conversation. Everything he did and said seemed to have more than one purpose.

"Yes. I always say Memphis, but we're really from a tiny town in the sticks about an hour away. Nobody knows where that is, so I just say Memphis."

Alex sat back, crossed a leg over his knee. "You're so very far from home. You must miss your family very much. Do you think they'll ever come here to visit?"

The brightness in Precious's eyes faded slightly. "I'd love that, but they don't have a lot of money, and my daddy has to take care of the farm. My little sister is too young to make the trip by herself. I sure do miss them."

Alex nodded, appearing sympathetic, but Eva felt something cold slithering up the base of her neck. "Well, never say never. I'm a strong believer in making the seemingly impossible possible." He turned to Eva. "Don't you agree? Wouldn't you love to see your family from Devon again?" A look of mock sadness came over his face. "Oh, Eva, I am so very, very sorry. I didn't mean . . ." He almost sounded genuinely apologetic. "I hope I didn't bring up unpleasant memories." He brightened. "Of course, now you have good friends, and I daresay sometimes one prefers friends to family, anyway."

He sat back with a satisfied smile as if he'd just solved the world's problems. But all Eva felt was icy cold. She glanced over at Sophia and David, who seemed to be aware only of each other and the strange staticky hum vibrating between them.

Sensing her discomfort, Precious reached over and squeezed Eva's hand. "That's very true. Although sometimes good friends can become more like sisters. Isn't that right?"

"Absolutely." Eva smiled and nodded, avoiding Alex's gaze by stabbing her cigarette out in the ashtray in the door of the car. "Yes, I'm very lucky that Precious found me. For many reasons. There I was, standing on the train platform, having no idea what I should do next. I hadn't thought any further than getting to London. And there was Precious, asking if I needed a roommate. I wouldn't even have my job if she hadn't introduced me to Madame Lushtak." She gave her friend a warm smile. "She's been a good friend to me."

"I think **I** was the lucky one," Precious gushed. "Eva has taught me so much."

"Really?" Alex asked, his eyebrow raised. "How so?"

"Well, how to act and how to talk, for starters. I was just a country girl from Tennessee, so I stuck out like a sore thumb. Eva polished me up like a new penny."

"How interesting that someone from Devon would know so much about polish."

Eva glanced over at the couple on the opposite

side of the car. Sophia was staring out the window, lost in her own world, but David appeared to be listening intently.

"Have you been to Café de Paris?" David asked, and Eva felt her shoulders relax with relief at being removed from the center of attention.

"Not yet," Precious gushed. "But I've heard so much about it. All the models at Lushtak's are perfectly envious of us. Anyone can go, of course, but Sophia said we'll be sitting at one of the best tables, near the band. Freya said we might be seated next to a Mountbatten or Cole Porter. Maybe even the Aga Khan! If we are, I won't be able to dance a lick. I'll be too frozen to move, but it will still be exciting."

Alex laughed. "It is said that at the Café de Paris, all the men are extraordinarily handsome and the young women so very beautiful. At least part of that statement is true, judging from this very car."

Precious blushed prettily, then turned her attention out the window. "There's a line of cars—and photographers on the sidewalk." She looked excitedly at Alex. "Do you think we might be in the papers? My daddy and sister would be over the moon if I sent them a picture of me with this fancy car."

"Would they?" Alex asked, his smile brightening. "How utterly charming."

Precious didn't seem to hear, transfixed by the throngs of people waiting to get into the famous subterranean dance club and by the lights flashing from cameras as their driver pulled up to the curb. The door opened, and Alex stepped out, offering his hand to Precious. "May I?"

She eagerly accepted his hand, then carefully stepped from the car. Cameras flashed as photographers crowded the curb, capturing the occupants inside the cars and then on the pavement. Alex offered his hand to Eva, too, and after a brief hesitation, she allowed him to help her out. He held her tightly, even when she attempted to pull away. Aware of the photographers, she remained smiling. "What game do you think you're playing?"

His smile never wavered. "I don't play games, Eva. You'd do best to remember that." He let go of her hand, leaving her stranded in the crowd as he lifted his elbow to escort Precious inside.

Eva kept her shoulders back and pasted on her smile—the one she'd learned to wear during fashion showings, the one meant to convey sophistication and a knowledge of unmentionable things—as she waited for David to escort her and Sophia through the throngs of onlookers and into the dark and smoky club. The percussive blast of brass instruments led them down one of the two wings of red-carpeted curved stairs that wrapped the stage. Tables circled the perimeter of the room and the dance floor, almost all occupied by men in dinner jackets and well-clad women wearing dark lipstick. It was a kaleidoscope of color and sound, reminding Eva of a county fair she'd once been to. Except here she was inside the fence instead of pressing her face against it.

Wearing a white dinner jacket that emphasized his dark skin, the famous bandleader Ken "Snakehips" Johnson snapped his fingers in rhythm to Benny Goodman's "Let's Dance." The band behind him swayed in time to the music, their brass instruments catching the light, shining as if they'd caught fire.

Eva felt everyone looking at them and focused on staring ahead, chin forward, pretending it was just another show. Except her fingers felt clammy, her stomach unsettled. They were escorted to an empty table right in front of the dance floor, and it wasn't until she was seated that she began to search for Graham, feeling a desperate need to hear his voice, to touch him. To see the light in his eyes and the quirk of his smile when he looked at her.

She turned to place her purse on the chair next to her, to hold the seat for him, but Alex was already pulling it out for himself, having seated Precious on his other side.

"Hello, beautiful." Graham's voice came from behind her, and she felt his warm lips on her cheek. She looked up at him, not caring if he saw the relief or the hundreds of emotions she was feeling.

"I thought you'd never get here," he said. He greeted their friends, even giving Alex a pat on the back. "But I'm very glad you did. It's a mad crush but always good fun." He waved at a passing waiter.

"A bottle of champagne, please—it's a night to celebrate."

The waiter nodded. Graham took a seat across the table from Eva, allowing his fingers to brush the nape of her neck as he left. A delicious shudder ran through her, ruined only by Alex's mocking eyebrow.

"What are we celebrating?" Precious asked, hardly able to keep her focus on one place, scrutinizing the nearby tables for anyone famous.

Graham's face sobered as he considered David. "Have I overstepped?"

David shook his head, then reached over to take Sophia's hand. "Not at all, my good fellow. I'd meant to tell everyone earlier, but"—he looked gently at his wife—"I'm afraid my dear bride hasn't quite reconciled herself to it yet."

"Are you expecting?" Precious leaned forward, tense with excitement. "I do love babies."

Eva wished her friend were sitting close enough that she could pinch her leg under the table. Such a topic was definitely not appropriate in mixed company.

Sophia blushed. "Really, Precious. It's too early. David and I were only recently married."

"Yes," Precious blundered on. "But everyone knows . . ."

"I've signed up," David blurted, either to get Precious to shut up or to get it over with.

Eva looked at him with confusion, not because she didn't understand what he meant, but because she couldn't understand why. "Signed up . . . ?"

"Territorial Army. I've decided I can't idly stand by while waiting for the inevitable. War **will** happen. Chamberlain said we'd have peace in our time, but I'm afraid Hitler doesn't want peace, and he's neglected to inform our prime minister. Whatever happens in the future, I want my children to be proud of me, to know that whether we win or lose, their father fought to save England. That I fought for them."

A champagne cork popped behind them, and they watched as the waiter filled glasses, an oddly silent and still tableau amidst the swirls of color and sound around them. When the waiter left, Graham raised his glass. "To king and country."

"Hear, hear," Alex said loudly, as if he were speaking of his own king and country. As if any of it mattered to him. They all took sips from their glasses, except for Sophia, who was a statue of misery as she sat next to her husband, her hand a ghostly white where it grasped David's arm on the table.

"Dulce et decorum est pro patria mori," Alex said quietly.

Graham sent him a sharp look. Sophia stood, knocking the table and shaking the champagne, the bubbles rising like angry fists. Without a word, she left, heading for the stairs. Eva rose to go after her, but Graham had stood, too.

"She's my sister. Let me talk to her."

Eva nodded, understanding but wanting to console her friend. It was as if David's announcement had punctured the bubble she'd been living in, and she could hear the air slowly beginning to leak. She wanted to call Graham back, to get his assurance that he wouldn't do anything so foolish as signing up to fight before war was even declared.

"Shall we dance?"

Alex was holding out his hand to her. Eva looked across the table at David for an escape, but he was downing his glass of champagne and reaching for the bottle to pour another.

"I'll stay and keep David company," Precious said. "You go dance."

"But . . . ," Eva protested.

"I'll have plenty of time to dance later—you two go on and have fun."

Reluctantly, and not wanting to explain her reason if she refused, Eva accepted Alex's hand and allowed him to lead her to the dance floor. The band had slowed the tempo, and couples were dancing closer now, holding one another in intimate embraces. Alex expertly swept Eva into a waltz, the steps familiar to her because she and Precious had practiced endlessly in their flat for Sophia's wedding. They'd wanted it to appear as if they'd been taught the rudiments in the schoolroom, just like properly brought-up young ladies.

"It means, 'It is sweet and fitting to die for one's

country.' From Horace's **Odes**." Alex spoke very close to her ear, his breath brushing against her neck. "I know you don't speak Latin, so I thought I'd translate."

"Why would you presume such a thing?" Eva asked, her mouth suddenly parched.

"Because the girl with the name Ethel Maltby, raised by a laundress in Muker, wouldn't have had the chance to learn Latin, I'd wager."

Eva stumbled, but Alex skillfully danced her through it.

"Where did you hear that name?"

"I told you, my dear. One associate in particular takes inordinate pride in digging up the truth. Putting money in the right hands always loosens tongues. And you gave us some very large bread crumbs, so it wasn't even that difficult. Granted, your mother moved quite a bit to get away from your father's fists, didn't she? Didn't want him to find her when he was released from jail. The neighbors were only too happy to share that little fact. But she never moved too far away, did she? Didn't want to lose her best customers by straying too far from the source of her income. It made it almost too easy to find her."

Eva tried to pull away, but he held tight. "Don't make a scene," he said quietly. "People are always watching. Remember that, Eva. You might find it useful."

That was the second time he'd said that word in

reference to her future. "Useful." She had begun to hate the word.

"I'm assuming you asked someone to translate the Latin on your cigarette case, yes?" Alex swept her around the dance floor as if they were speaking of nothing consequential, even though her heart thumped inside her chest. **Betray before you are betrayed.**

"I did. I assumed you'd purchased it already inscribed."

"Why would you assume such a thing?"

"Because the words have nothing to do with me." She looked around, trying to spot Graham, wanting him to rescue her.

"Not yet," he said, his tone prophetic.

For the first time, she met his eyes. "Why? Will they be useful to me someday?"

"Precisely." His serene smile made it look as if he were talking about nothing more than the weather. "I like your friend Precious. It's the perfect name for her, don't you think? And of course, she's quite beautiful. I do believe she has an **entichement** for me. How delightful. I'm always looking for a new toy."

Eva stumbled again, and he caught her, righting her steps without slowing down. "You leave her alone," Eva hissed. "She's good and kind and doesn't deserve any toying by you or anyone else."

"Ah, spoken as by a true friend. Would you be so forgiving if she set her cap for your St. John?"

This time she tried to stop dancing altogether,

but he kept moving, carrying her along with him. "That would never happen."

"Never say never, my dear. Did you know that Precious actually comes from an old Southern family—lots of property and illustrious forebears, including a signer of the Declaration of Independence? Remarkable, really. Sadly, they had a reversal of fortune following their Civil War, but still, a much more palatable background for someone in Graham's position, don't you think?"

"What do you want from me?" she said through clenched teeth.

"Smile, dear. People are watching, and photographers are taking photos. You want to look your best."

She forced her lips into a grimace.

"To answer your question, I knew you had something to hide from the day we first met, when your accent veered off course. And people with something to hide can always be useful."

"Stop using that word. People aren't meant to be **useful**."

"**Au contraire.** It's an excellent survival device. Why my exiled Czech government relies on me here in London, for instance."

"They find you useful?" she asked, not bothering to hide her sarcasm.

"And I find them more so," he said with a smile.

"What do you want from me?" she asked again, the fight gone from her words.

His eyes, clear and calculating, regarded her closely. "Oh, I think you're doing nicely on your own. With St. John, I mean. He seems genuinely enamored of you. At least until he finds out you've been lying to him."

His hand was warm on her naked back, but an icy chill swept through her, as if he'd just laid bare her future and it wasn't what she wanted to see.

"And he won't find out if you do a little something for me."

She forced herself to breathe. "Like what?"

"Like telling me where he's going when he travels."

She stared at him, not understanding. "Why would you want to know that?"

His smile almost looked genuine. "That's not anything you need to concern yourself with. Just tell me where he's going and when, and I'll keep your little secret. Just a simple little thing."

He held her close as they continued to dance. Whispering in her ear, he said, "And if he asks you to marry him, say yes. You'd be even more useful if you were his wife. I'd be ever so grateful."

She pulled back in surprise. "But then you'd have no more hold on me."

"No, my dear. If he should find out you'd lied about your identity, he could have your marriage annulled. Even should he not want to, his parents would certainly demand it."

Feeling suddenly ill, she jerked her head to the side, spotting David and Sophia on the dance floor,

Sophia's head resting on David's shoulder. And right beyond them, she saw Graham and Precious, dancing closely, his hand on her back, her head thrown back in laughter at something he'd said.

Now she succeeded in wrenching away from Alex. Quickly, she made her way from the dance floor and up the stairs, not stopping until she was outside on the sidewalk, past the dwindling crowds of onlookers. She put her hand on the brick side of the building to steady herself and took deep, gulping breaths.

"Eva—darling!"

She turned at the sound of rapid footsteps and saw Graham coming toward her, the button on his dinner jacket loosened, his hair flopping against his forehead. Her heart seemed to stop and start, constricting and expanding just from looking at him.

"Are you all right?" He took her in his arms and held her head gently against his shoulder.

"I am now," Eva whispered. "Now that you're here." She held on to him tightly, as if he might vanish without her to keep him earthbound. "Just . . . hold me."

She looked up, and Graham turned his head, the streetlight making odd shadows in his eyes. The fear returned, a fistful of lead in her stomach. If she could breathe, she knew she would smell it.

He spoke softly into her ear. "I need to tell you something."

She held her breath, knowing what he was going to say, helpless to stop the words.

"I've signed up, too. The Royal Air Force. I already know how to fly, and they'll need pilots. War is coming, Eva, and I must do my duty."

Surprise mingled with relief stole her breath. "Your duty? But you already work for the government—isn't that duty enough?"

"No, it's not. Please understand."

An eerie calm settled over her. She did understand. She did. She just couldn't stop the horrible sense of finality. He was speaking again, but she was having trouble comprehending the words, as if they were coming from too far away.

She blinked up at him, slowly grasping the intensity of his voice. "What?"

"Marry me, Eva. We don't need to tell anyone, not yet. But I can't wait anymore. Please, marry me."

She was stunned; she could only stare at him and blink. **And if he asks you to marry him, say yes. . . . You'd be even more useful if you were his wife. I'd be ever so grateful.**

"You do love me, don't you?" His eyes held an uncertainty that was too painful to see.

"Yes, of course, but . . ."

"Then say yes."

I'd be ever so grateful. She wanted to scream with the unfairness of it. To have everything she'd ever dreamed of standing right in front of her yet so out of reach. But she couldn't let Alex win. Even if it meant breaking her own heart. She looked into Graham's eyes, needing him to see the love and the truth in them. "I promised you that I would wait for you. Isn't that enough?"

He pulled back, his eyes narrowing as if he were trying to decipher foreign words. "Enough? Hardly. I want to go and fight knowing you're mine."

"I already am," Eva said, the tears thick in her throat.

"It's not enough. Not for me. Please, Eva. Say you'll marry me now."

"No." She shook her head. "Think how awful it would be if your father found out, Graham. Could you forgive yourself—or me?" She leaned forward and kissed him, taking her time, letting him know what would be waiting for him. "Let's wait until your father is better, and this war is won. It will give us both something to look forward to."

His hands dropped to his sides. "Is it Alex?"

"What? Of course not. How could you even think that?"

"Because I don't understand you right now. You're not making any sense. What else am I to believe?"

"That I love you. And I will wait for you. And we can dream together, of our lives after the war, of our beautiful house by the sea. I want to be able to hear the waves from the bedroom, so you and I can wake up together, listening to the ocean. Won't that be lovely? You can build it so it's just what we want. People will be amazed. They'll think you're the next John Nash."

He took a step toward her and held her head in his

hands, his eyes glittering in the lamplight. "I want more than just dreams, Eva. Tell me you love me, and that will give me something to come back for."

"I love you, Graham. More than I can say. And I promise to keep your ivory dolphin close to my heart every day. It will be a good-luck charm for both of us."

"I don't believe in luck. But I do believe in you." He kissed her, soft and sweet, sealing their promise and almost making her believe that it would all work out in the end.

Later that night, after Eva and Precious had shared their ritual cup of hot cocoa before bed, they talked about the evening and Sophia and David, about the music and how Precious found Alex to be the most handsome man she'd ever met. Eva pretended not to feel ill at the mention of Alex's name or at the memory of his hateful words.

"Sweet dreams," Precious said at last, as she always did. She left Eva's room, softly closing the door.

Eva stared up at the sky outside her window, by turns feeling happy and troubled. She'd thwarted Alex this one time, even though it had broken her heart to tell Graham no. And she wasn't naive enough to believe she'd won. But Graham was hers, she told herself, and they would be married eventually. That was the one thing she would focus upon. Everything else would work out. Somehow, it always did.

When she finally fell asleep, the ivory dolphin clasped in her fist, Eva dreamed of a house high on a cliff overlooking the water that she and Graham would share, of waves crashing against the shore before pulling back to the sea, and of the endless and futile attempt to remain whole before collapsing on the sand once more.

CHAPTER 22

LONDON
MAY 2019

Despite my comfortable bed and beautiful bedroom, I'd slept fitfully, tossing and turning and replaying the evening over and over in my head. Mostly I focused on Colin's kiss, but then I'd loop back around to the after-dinner conversation and Precious telling us to have sweet dreams as she left the room. Eventually, I'd thrown on a sweatshirt and jeans and grabbed my backpack, then attempted to make my way down to the kitchen in search of coffee just as the sun rose. I stumbled through the house, turning down wrong hallway after wrong hallway.

My phone beeped with a text from Aunt Cassie as I crossed through the dining room. I stopped to respond, knowing I couldn't text and figure out the maze of hallways simultaneously. It was the middle of the night in Georgia, but my aunt sometimes worked best in the wee hours on the creative aspects of her job as the partner of an advertising agency.

I made your appointment with Dr. Grey.

Thanks. I think.
How's it going?

Fine. Confused.

Is it Arabella's cousin?

???

Sorry—Sarah Frances told me about him. What's his name?

I ignored her second question. Yes—Arabella's cousin. I paused, wondering how much I should tell her. And then I remembered this was my aunt Cassie, who knew me better than most. I took a deep breath. He kept a photo of me on his desk all these years.

Wow. Did you remember him?

I held my thumbs over my phone, not sure how to answer. Finally, I tapped, Sort of. More than I thought.

A smiley face emoji appeared on my screen.

I answered with ???

It was that way with your uncle Sam and me, too. Turns out I remembered a lot more about him than I thought. And then I married him.

I stared at my screen, wondering how to respond. I'm not marrying anyone so tuck that thought back where it came from.

Sure. Call me later. Although I like texting you.

Why?

Because you type in full sentences. And tell me his name!

I sent her an eye-rolling emoji, then closed my screen and returned to my hunt for the kitchen, imagining I smelled coffee as I opened yet another door and found myself in a broom closet. I wondered if lack of caffeine made people hallucinate as I opened the second doorway to my right, which finally led me into the kitchen.

Sun streamed through the tall windows over the sink, reminding me of home. I could picture my mother standing at our kitchen sink, washing out the endless Tupperware Popsicle holders to make sure that each of us had his or her favorite color. She always wore pink rubber gloves to protect her hands. The last time I was home, I'd found a box of them tucked in the back under the kitchen sink. They must have made the move when my dad and Suzanne relocated to a new house after they married. The rubber had probably disintegrated by now, but no one seemed to have the heart to throw them away.

"Good morning."

I jumped at the sound of Penelope's voice. She sat at the kitchen table with a cup of steaming coffee and the hatbox of cut photographs, surrounded by newspaper clippings. A rectangular black box and a thick leather-bound album I hadn't seen before sat next to the hatbox.

"Sorry—I didn't mean to startle you." She looked closely at me. "I expect you're needing some coffee." She indicated the pot on the counter by the sink. "Please, help yourself."

"Thank you. I thought I was imagining the smell." I pulled out a mug from the glass-fronted cabinet.

"I love my tea," Penelope said, "but I need coffee first thing in the morning. It's a habit I picked up on our first trip to Atlanta."

I brought my cup over to the table and sat down. "Were those trips to Atlanta for Colin's brother?"

She nodded. "He told you, then? He doesn't usually tell people."

"I saw the picture of Jeremy in a stroller at the Atlanta airport and asked him about it. All he told me was that it was his twin brother and that he died of leukemia when they were nine."

Penelope took a sip from her cup, flicking through the photographs on the table with an unvarnished nail. "Jeremy was diagnosed when he and Colin were four. Ever since, Colin has had survivor's guilt, which I think is especially hard since they were identical twins."

"I'm sorry. I can't imagine anything more difficult than losing a child."

Her clear blue gaze settled on me. "I imagine it would be a lot like losing one's mother when one is still a child." She smiled sympathetically. "Colin told me. I hope you don't mind."

I shook my head. "No. It's all right. I just never liked telling classmates. I didn't want to be known as the girl whose mother died."

Penelope sat back in her chair, her hands wrapped around her mug. "Colin was the same way." She took a deep breath. "I wish I'd handled it differently. For Colin, I mean. We were older parents, and I knew we wouldn't have any more children, so I became a bit overprotective. I believe that's why he's so cautious now. It's not that he's afraid of getting hurt himself. He worries about us if something happens to him." She looked down into her mug. "I think that's why he admires you so much, Maddie. The way you don't hold back. How you aren't afraid of how other people might perceive you. Even your silly pranks. They always made him laugh—especially the time you put a Teletubbies theme on his laptop before a PowerPoint presentation. He thought that quite brilliant, although he pretended otherwise."

"I can't take credit for my sense of humor—blame my aunt Cassie. My whole family, really—I'll let you listen to my ringtones sometime. But Colin's worry over what might happen if he should be hurt is just . . ." I started to say "ridiculous" but stopped. "I wondered why he was always so cautious. It's not like his chances of survival can change just by worrying about them. My aunt Cassie says that worrying is a lot like sitting in a rocking chair. It keeps you busy, but it doesn't get you anywhere."

"Brilliant observation."

The voice came from the doorway, and we both turned to see Colin, who looked annoyed. I wasn't sure how much he'd heard, but I assumed it had been most of it. He filled a kettle, then put it on the AGA, his movements jerky.

"It is, rather," Penelope said, turning back to the table. "It's something we should all adhere to, I think. Worrying about things that may or may not happen reminds me of riding a horse with the reins always pulled in tight. A person might admire the scenery along the way, but they won't experience the joy of a full gallop."

She was looking at me as she said this, her eyes kind, but her expression that of a person trying to explain something complicated to someone who speaks a different language. Colin waited for the kettle to boil, then sat down at the table across from me with his cup of tea, his eyes meeting mine as he took a sip.

I couldn't help but remember our kiss, and the way I'd pushed him away, and how all night long I'd wished I hadn't. Flustered, I studied the items on the table. "What are these?"

"Arabella brought these in here last night. The clippings and photos from the hatbox you've already seen, I believe. The album and box came from the attic—I missed them in the last go-round when I was collecting things for you and Arabella to go through. It's Sophia's scrapbook from her debutante season in nineteen thirty-nine and other related materials in the box. I discovered a leather valise up there, too. It's too bulky for me to bring down, but I believe it belonged to Sophia. It must have been put there prior to her death—I don't remember seeing it in her rooms when we redecorated afterward. You're welcome to bring it down if you think it might be helpful."

I nodded absently, studying the photographs

from the hatbox, their carefully cut edges, once again wondering why. "Any guess as to why these have all been cut?"

Penelope shook her head. "I was hoping you'd have some theories about that."

"Sadly, no. Have you by any chance found the missing halves? Those might give us a better idea of why they were cut."

"No, I haven't," Penelope said. "And I have no theories as to why Sophia would save these. We've already got so many photographs of Precious. Have you asked Precious? She might know something."

"Not yet—I will. You said you found Sophia and David's wedding album. Can I see that before I get into these?"

"Of course. It's in the library—on the window seat. Colin—would you take Maddie? I don't think she's had enough coffee yet to find it herself." She smiled, the glint in her eyes reminding me of Colin.

Colin stood. "If only to protect these walls from being knocked down by Maddie taking wrong turns and bumping into them. The house will thank me."

"Very funny," I said as I stood to follow him.

No fire burned in the grate, and despite the warmth of the day outside, a distinctive chill hovered about the room. I took a moment to admire the tall bookcases and the highly polished paneling in the prisms of light streaming from the multipaned window.

Colin sat down on the window seat and opened

the album on his lap, leaving me no choice but to sit beside him. He opened it to the first photograph, the one I'd already seen of Sophia and David with the full wedding party. Except this one showed Precious staring into the camera instead of looking away, a bright smile on her face. I leaned closer.

"I know this is an old photo, but look at her smile. The way her eyes match the joy in the rest of her face. She looks . . . different." I had struggled to find another word before settling on that one.

Colin leaned forward, too, his thigh pressing into mine. I told myself that the flash of heat that shot up my leg was simply gratitude to him for sharing his body warmth in the chilly room. "I see what you mean. In all the years I've known Nana, I've never seen her smile that way with her whole face." He squinted, leaning even closer. "Of course, she's lived through a war since then, which could account for it."

"Very true." I pointed at the even edge, which neatly sliced the woman standing next to Precious in half. A woman with blond hair the same brightness as Precious's was partially visible, their shoulders at an even height, showing that they were of the same statuesque build, both slightly taller than the groom in their high heels.

I tapped Precious's face, wondering what it was besides the smile that was bothering me.

"What is it?"

I shook my head. "I'm not sure. It'll come to me—usually it does when I'm not thinking about it. But there's something about the jaw. . . ." I stopped, turned the page. "Don't worry—I'll figure it out. I always do."

We looked at the next page, a photo of the bride and groom with two older couples, most likely the parents. One of the men leaned heavily on a cane, his face pained as if it had taken all of his energy to get out of bed.

Colin pointed to his face. "That is my great-grandfather. He was very ill and died within a year of the wedding, according to Sophia. She showed this album to me when I was a little boy—not that I really paid attention at the time. There are a few more formally posed photographs of the happy couple and family groups at the church, but the rest are unposed shots from the reception at the house. Looks like most of the photos in Grandmother's debutante scrapbook, I think. Formally dressed people having a good time. Hard to believe they were on the brink of war."

He turned the pages slowly. He was right—the smiling, beautiful people in the pictures looked as if they didn't have a care in the world. As if Poland wasn't on the verge of being invaded, and Hitler hadn't already set his sights on Great Britain.

"But isn't that the British way? To ignore the obvious so as not to appear rude?" I said, reaching over to turn a page.

"I wouldn't say it's solely a British trait," he said very close to my ear, so close that I fought hard not to turn my head.

"Where are the missing photos, do you think?" I asked, noting the blank spots between photos, as if several had been randomly removed.

"I just assumed that's how the album was created." Colin lifted the book and shook it. "Nothing."

I nodded slowly, then leaned forward, studying the faces. "I'd hoped to find more photos of Eva, but there aren't any. I wonder why."

My phone beeped on the ledge behind us, making us both turn.

I read the screen. His name is Colin, right? It was Aunt Cassie again. I reached for my phone, but Colin was quicker.

"How should I reply?" he asked.

"Don't reply at all. That's the only way to get her to stop."

Turning his back to me, he began to text, avoiding my reaching hands. I heard the swish sound of a text being sent and then he handed the phone back to me, a satisfied grin on his face.

I looked down at my screen with one eye closed. Yes. He tried to kiss me last night. I wanted him to, but I pushed him away because I enjoy being impossible to understand.

My phone immediately began to ring, and I sent a quick text back. Call you later. Looking up at Colin, I said, "She'll never believe I wrote that."

He crossed his arms. "Really? Who else texts in full sentences?"

I wanted to ask him how he knew that I did but didn't bother. I stood and began walking toward the door.

"Aren't you going to argue with me?" he asked, following close behind.

"No." I headed down what seemed to be a familiar hallway.

"Because you know I'm right."

"I don't want to talk about it." I'd reached a door that I thought should take me back to the kitchen.

"Madison, stop."

I tugged on the doorknob. "I said I don't want to talk about it."

"Fine. But that's a coat closet. The kitchen is two doors to your right."

I dropped my hand and walked toward the kitchen with as much dignity as I could muster.

Arabella had joined her aunt at the table and was going through the black box. "Good morning," I said, as I slid into the seat next to her. "Anything interesting?"

"Just odds and ends, really. Train tickets, invitations—that sort of thing. Leftovers that didn't fit in Sophia's scrapbook, I think. Nothing from Eva showing a return address."

"What about Graham?" Colin asked. "Surely he would have written to his sister."

Arabella shook her head. "Nothing so far. That doesn't mean he didn't write, though. If it was during the war, the letters he sent might have been so heavily censored that Sophia didn't deem them worthy of keeping. There are a few from William before he was killed. Nothing very informative, sadly. Just a lot about nearly getting frostbite when flying at higher altitudes."

I turned to the cut photographs again and tapped my fingers on one showing Precious with Sophia wearing pretty spring hats and linking arms in front of the glass house at Kew Gardens.

"Did you by any chance grab the folder of photographs I printed at Colin's?" I asked Arabella. "I need to look at them again."

Arabella chewed on her bottom lip. "I think so. Might be in one of the totes I brought in. Let me go look."

A small bell from a row of bells on the wall behind the table rang. Penelope stood. "That's Precious—she still believes we have a houseful of servants. She'll probably want help dressing and breakfast brought up. I'll be back eventually."

She excused herself, then left the room with Arabella. I pulled the scrapbook over to me and began thumbing through the pages, thick with mementos of 1939. The first contained a pressed orchid, still in its wire corsage frame, next to an invitation for a coming-out ball at Blenheim Palace. The pages were full of invitations, race cards, dance cards, train tickets, and photographs of Sophia at boat races and horse races and relaxing on lawns in front of castles with groups of beautiful young people.

"It's amazing that all this entertainment happened right up to war being declared."

Colin moved to stand behind me. "Gives a whole new meaning to 'Eat, drink, and be merry, for tomorrow we may die,' doesn't it?"

"Look at this," I said, pointing to a clipping from **The Bystander**. Under a subhead entitled "Women in Uniform" was a picture of Red Cross volunteers showing women how to put on their gas masks. It was dated June 1939. "Some people were prepared, at least," I said.

"Someone had to be," Colin said as he began rifling through the black box. "Looks like there are a few things that either fell out or were never put in."

A matchbox cover from the Café de Paris caught my eye. "Isn't that the club that was bombed during the Blitz? I read that somewhere. A bomb found its way through a ventilation shaft and killed lots of people."

"The bandleader was decapitated, if I remember correctly," Colin said. He picked up a yellowed menu from the Savoy. "I wonder when she got this." He turned it over in his hand. "The Savoy was a hotbed of intrigue during the war. Exiled European heads of state living cheek by jowl with spies, MI-Five operatives, and Nazi sympathizers." He handed me the menu. "They also had a very luxurious bomb shelter beneath the building—it was known for its five-star accommodations. Apparently, the Savoy believed their guests wouldn't want to bunk with the average Londoner in a public shelter."

"Can't imagine why," I said, turning the menu over in my hand, noticing the pretty print of a woman with a fan on the cover before replacing it where I'd found it.

"Found the folder," Arabella announced. She entered the room and slapped it on the table in front of me. "Is anyone hungry for beans on toast?"

"Just coffee for me, thanks," I said as I opened up the folder. It contained the candid shots of Precious I'd taken as we chatted in her flat. She had the sort of face that looked good from any direction, in any light. Even at nearly one hundred years old, her bones hadn't softened, as if time's chisel had sharpened the planes of her cheeks and nose instead of blunting them.

"These are really good," Colin said over my shoulder. "I especially like this one." He pointed to the photo I'd taken of Precious sitting in the front drawing room of her flat, looking at the windows as the rain pelted them. She'd been telling me that she'd always imagined Eva and Graham together, in a house by the sea.

"Thank you. I like it, too. It tells its own story, I think."

I felt him nod, but I didn't look away from the photograph. There was something about it that drew me in, that tugged on a sense of recognition, a piece of information that kept sliding away from me as I reached for it.

"Oh, and Aunt Penelope would like you to come out on the terrace," Arabella said. "Precious is skipping breakfast and wants to have coffee outside. She said to bring your notebook."

I met Colin's eyes, then stood. "I'll go get it." I started to leave, then turned back to grab the menu before rushing out of the room.

"Turn right and then left," Colin shouted after me as I tried to enter the broom closet again.

When I finally managed to find the terrace, Colin was already out there with Precious, sitting under an umbrella in the bright morning sun. Coffee sat next to her in an untouched china cup I remembered from my previous visit, the steam leaking weakly into the air. Sparkling dew capped the leaves and flowers of the garden; it looked magical enough to make a person believe in fairies.

"Good morning," I said as I approached.

Colin sent me a worried look, and as I bent to kiss Precious's cheek, I realized why. Her skin seemed blanched under her makeup, the peach lipstick almost garish against the stark whiteness. Her gold hair sat atop her head in lackluster strands like unpolished brass. When she turned to me, her blue eyes were pale and watery, her smile weary.

"Good morning, Maddie." She spotted the menu I'd laid on the table. "Where did you find that?"

"With Sophia's scrapbook. We also found a hatbox full of photographs. Penelope said they'd belonged to Sophia. All of the photographs appear to have had something or someone cut out of them, but we haven't found the missing halves. Do you know anything about them?"

Precious sighed, the weary sound bone-deep. "I don't." She placed her fingers on the menu. "Sophia did love her photographs. And her mementos. But then, she had the sort of charmed life she'd want to remember." Her eyes met mine. They held a wariness I hadn't seen before. "Do you ever fear, Maddie, that your past is the most important part of your life?"

"Every day," I said without thinking. I felt Colin's gaze on me but didn't turn. "I can't seem to help it."

Her voice sounded weighted with time, each year marking its passing with invisible force. "Oh, you dear girl. Your past should never become your present. When you live your life looking backward, thinking of all the ways you could have or should have done things differently, of the infernal unfairness of life, you end up running into the brick wall of old age, having learned nothing but the futility of it all."

I shook my head, not sure what I was disagreeing with. Maybe I was just so used to telling people I couldn't change that it had become a rote reaction. "It's different for me."

"Is it?" Her smile looked ghostly against the pallor of her skin. "I lost the two people I loved most in the world. Colin lost his twin brother. The only difference I can see is how we go about atoning for whatever we blame ourselves for. I don't think we're allowed to die until we figure that out. In fact, I believe that's why I'm still here. No offense, you understand, but I surely don't want to be. Old age is nothing but a cruel thief." She kept her eyes on me. "Do you know what atonement is, Maddie?"

I frowned. "Sure. It's making amends for a past transgression."

"No. That's selfishness. That's like committing a crime because you know you'll be forgiven."

Colin sat very still. "Then what does atonement mean to you, Nana?"

She closed her eyes. They were bare, without eye shadow or the false lashes I was used to seeing, giving her the appearance of innocence. "Living one hundred years. So that I might hear their voices and see their faces every time I close my eyes."

An odd note in her voice caught me by surprise,

making my eyes sting. "You once told me that grief is like a ghost."

"I am glad you were listening, Maddie. Maybe that's why I'm here—to shake up your sad life."

I sat up, ready to argue, but Colin placed his hand on my arm. "Who did you love and lose, Nana? Eva and who else?"

She shook her head slowly. "Not Eva. It's because of her that I lost the other two." A sad smile crossed her face. "Have you found her yet?"

"No. Not yet. But we're still trying."

A soft smile touched her lips. "When I dream of Eva and Graham, I always dream of them together." Straightening her shoulders, she said, "I hope you don't mind, but I'd like to go home now. I left something behind."

I kept my voice light, but I was worried by the color of her skin and how, for the first time since I'd met her, she looked her age. "I'd be happy to go back to London and get whatever it is. I know Penelope and James had hoped you'd stay the week."

She shook her head. "I want to go back. I don't dream when I'm here."

Colin took her hand. "Did you have a nightmare?"

She surprised us by smiling. "My nightmares follow me everywhere. In London they're more vivid, and for good reason."

"Are you referring to the Blitz, Precious? Were you in the flat when it was bombed?"

"We all were."

"'We'?" Colin prompted.

She stared down at her hands as if she hadn't heard the question.

Gently, I asked, "Is that why you left London for France?"

She waved her hand at me weakly. "I went to France hoping I'd die. I wanted to do something for the war effort and there was nothing left for me here. David had connections and helped me get across the Channel. I didn't think I'd survive six months fighting with the Resistance, but God had other plans for punishing me, however, so I lived. I still live." She braced her hands on the arms of her chair. "I'm feeling poorly. I'd like to go home now."

As I watched Colin lead her to Penelope, who was hovering in the doorway, I thought of the dozens of questions I still had. I had learned next to nothing today except that I didn't know the meaning of atonement and Precious didn't want to be one hundred years old. Slowly, I began to gather up my things and shove them into my backpack.

"I'm sorry," Colin said. "I know my parents were looking forward to your stay."

"I'm sorry, too," I said. "Is Precious going to be all right?"

"She has spells like this sometimes. Mother's called Laura, who will be expecting her. She'll let us know if anything is amiss." He tilted his head, regarding me like I was a problem to be solved. "Are you all right?"

"I think so. I'm just . . ." My gaze fell on the menu. "There's something you said, about the Savoy. About it being a hotbed of intrigue during the war." My eyes met his, and I focused on keeping my gaze steady and not thinking about our kiss. "And about reasons why a person's records might be missing."

He folded his arms across his chest, his eyes widening as he reached the same conclusion I had. "Do you think Graham might have been involved in espionage?"

I nodded. "It's not out of the realm of possibility, is it?"

"No, I suppose not. I'm just disappointed that I didn't think of it, too. Makes sense, though, doesn't it? And it's actually a bit of good news. Recently—twenty seventeen, I believe—the National Archives released top secret files of MI-Five and MI-Six operatives during the war."

"Really? So Hyacinth might be able to tell us more?"

"If there's something in those records about Graham, she'll unearth it. I'll let Mother know so she can call. It might be a few days, if Hyacinth is on baby watch with her daughter. Although it wouldn't surprise me if Hyacinth had her laptop and phone with her in the labor and delivery room. She's a general at multitasking."

"That sounds terrible, but I hope you're right. If what we suspect is true, it would certainly answer a lot of questions."

"And raise just as many," Colin said. "Although it might mean you have to stay longer."

"Is that a problem?"

"No. Maybe it will give you the chance to lose that accent of yours."

I frowned at him as we passed through the terrace doors, my mind spinning with unanswered questions, wondering what ghosts haunted an old woman's reflection. And which voices spoke to her in her dreams.

CHAPTER 23

LONDON
SEPTEMBER 3, 1939

Eva pushed open the door to Horvath's Café, breathing heavily, desperate to hear the voice of reason. She'd been keeping her fear and apprehension at bay, practicing a cool demeanor in the flat and during her clothes showings at work. She dared not allow even a stray thought into her head, or her fear and worry over Graham would crush her.

He'd been sent to an RAF base in Gloucestershire for training. He'd written to her twice, letting her know that his previous flying experience had helped him bypass some of the training the other chaps were doing. He told her not to worry, that he was a good pilot. And he reminded her that he loved her.

And everything he'd written she'd given to Alex.

She'd told herself it would be only that once, that

Alex would see how pointless it was and not ask again. But he had, and again she'd given him the letter. He'd insisted on keeping both, not explaining why, telling Eva it wasn't her place to question him. So she didn't, the persistent threat of exposure binding her tongue but not her mind. She might have thwarted Alex by refusing Graham's marriage proposal, but it wasn't enough. That was what kept her up in the middle of the night, tossing and turning, trying to think of some way to escape her predicament, the niggling thought always pressing on her brain that she'd brought this on herself.

You have a fondness for beautiful things. Mr. Danek had been right, of course. If only she'd known to be different or to hide it. But that would have been like a leopard changing its spots.

That morning at Lushtak's, instead of the usual conversation about the best lipsticks and mascaras, or whose gentleman had been seen at the most shows, all the models had been talking about the news, how Germany had invaded Poland. How England and France had sworn to stand with Poland and how the prime minister, Neville Chamberlain, had given Germany an ultimatum: Pull out or risk war.

Eva had seen in the past few months the growing number of sandbags stacked against hospitals and government buildings, the barrage balloons being flown in the sky to deter enemy aircraft. She'd even seen lorries delivering Anderson shelters to houses with back gardens big enough to contain them. But today's news had shaken her, had made her run from Lushtak's and vomit in the back alley behind the showroom. The thought of the inevitability of Graham going to battle, and the thought of all that was still unsaid between them, had loosened her fear like rocks in a landslide.

She'd seen Graham only once since his proposal at the Café de Paris. It had been the night before he left for training, at a dinner party organized by Sophia at the Savoy as a send-off. She had had barely a moment alone with Graham all evening and no opportunity to tell him she loved him. To remind him that she was already deeply and completely his. That she wanted to marry him.

Instead there had been long looks across the dining table and then just enough time for a quick embrace and a stiff good-bye as David's car waited at the curb to drive Eva and Precious back to their flat. Eva had been struggling ever since through shadows cast by self-doubt and her fear for Graham, fighting them in dreams that were no longer sweet, no matter how many times Precious wished it otherwise. She was lost, left to holding the tiny ivory dolphin against her heart each night, hoping Graham could feel its strength, too.

Now Eva paused in the doorway of the familiar café, looking for Mr. Danek. He was there, at his usual table, but he wasn't alone.

Alex stood and gave her a sharp bow. "What a

delightful surprise, Eva. And how beautiful you look today. I believe you've already met my friend Jiri Zeman. I told you about him, remember? Although I don't think I mentioned his name."

She jerked her head to stare at Jiri, recalling Alex's words: **I know a man who got himself into a spot of bother in Prague. I was the one who paid enough people to look the other way, and we got him out of jail and into this country. Nobody knows this but me. This makes him very useful to me.**

Jiri was smiling as if he had been told an enormous joke but didn't want to share it. At least not with her. Her gaze traveled to Mr. Danek, who sat smoking a cigarette that was nearly down to its butt. She turned back to Alex. "What . . . ?"

"Sometimes Mr. Zeman and I need to hear our native tongue, so we come here for news and gossip. How delightful to know you are also a patron of Horvath's."

He pulled out a chair; the waiter brought Eva's coffee and placed it in front of her. She looked at Mr. Danek. "You never mentioned you knew Mr. Grof." She forced a laugh she didn't feel. "What a funny coincidence."

"Not so much when you consider how few Czech cafés are in the city." He said this with an unconvincing smile, his eyes on Alex. "Will you excuse me for a moment? I see a friend with the latest newspaper." Without waiting for a response, he stood and moved to a small table occupied by an older man, a newspaper spread out in front of him.

"I believe these are yours," Jiri said with a smirk. He slid two envelopes across the table. Eva stared at them in surprise, then pulled them closer. After a brief hesitation, she opened one and took out the letter to be sure. It was one of Graham's, the paper singed and brown between each line.

"What happened to it?" There were so many other questions she wanted to ask, but that was the first one she could force through her mouth.

Jiri grinned. "To see if there was more than meets the eye."

Alex reached over and snatched the letter from her, then refolded it and stuffed it in its envelope. "I suggest you put these in your purse and read them in private."

"I don't understand. What did he mean? And how did he get these . . . ?" She saw Mr. Danek returning and stopped. She didn't want him to notice the letters, to ask her why she'd given them to Alex. She couldn't stand to see the disappointment in his eyes.

Eva shoved the letters in her purse, then looked up as Mr. Danek slapped a newspaper onto the table and sat down again, a new weariness in the curve of his shoulders and around his eyes. She looked down at the newspaper, the headline glaring in bold black ink. BRITAIN SENDS LAST WARNING TO GERMANY. Mr. Danek crushed his cigarette into the nearly full ashtray and leaned back with a weary sigh.

Eva blinked, not ready to believe it until she heard Mr. Danek's confirmation. "Is it true? There's to be a war?"

"Undoubtedly," Mr. Danek said, his voice calm. "Herr Hitler is not fond of ultimatums. He has until eleven o'clock today to respond, but I do believe Mr. Chamberlain knows the response already. One can only hope that he has started assembling his war cabinet."

"Surely your St. John has plans to tuck you securely away in the country?" Alex spoke slowly, as if they were discussing the weather. "Although I heard from David that Sophia has already signed up with the Women's Voluntary Services. At this very moment, she's helping escort the last of the children who are evacuating London for the country."

Eva nodded. "Yes. She told me. Precious and I signed up for the WVS, too, to help in the shelters, but we haven't had our first meeting yet." She had followed Precious and Sophia into the building and signed her name to a document. But she'd done it as if she were an actress in a play, with no meaning behind her actions. No belief that any of it would matter. But those words splashed on the front of the newspaper suddenly made it all so startlingly real.

She stood, recalling the bolts of fabric Precious had procured and sewn into blackout curtains. The two gas masks sitting on the foyer table. Precious had picked them up and made Eva practice putting hers on.

"I should go. We should all go. And prepare ourselves."

"Surely you've already started?" Alex said with mock surprise. "Our friend Precious said she needed someone to help hang your blackout curtains. I suggested Graham since he's so tall—although he's training somewhere with the RAF, isn't he?"

His eyes sparkled with some inner joke that Eva didn't find amusing. Ignoring him, she turned to Mr. Danek and said, "Thank you for your honesty. You always put things in perspective for me." She made the mistake of glancing at Jiri, saw his look of feigned concern as he blew out a plume of smoke. She turned blindly toward the door, stumbling in her heels. "I've got to go."

Alex put a hand on her arm, steadying her. "I'll walk you home."

Eva wanted to pull her arm away, to tell him no, but she wasn't sure if her legs were strong enough to carry her back to her flat.

"Co oči nevidí, to srdce nebolí," he said to Mr. Danek and Jiri as he held the door open for Eva.

She had a glimpse of Mr. Danek's bland face looking toward her as the door shut.

"What does that mean?" she asked, standing on the sidewalk. Her head spun; she forgot where she was or where she was headed.

"It's an old Czech saying. It means 'What eyes don't see, heart doesn't hurt.' You are so good at pretending, Eva. You even fool yourself."

She pulled away from him, running down the sidewalk. But her heel stuck in a grate, and broke. She pulled off both of her shoes and kept going, aware of Alex managing to keep up with her without even breaking into a run.

She needed to barricade herself in her room, to calm her thoughts. Inside her building, she ran up the stairs, unwilling to wait for the lift, feeling Alex climbing behind her. Pausing in front of the thick mahogany door, she tried to catch her breath as she dug through her purse for the key, dropping the purse and all of its contents in her haste.

"Damn!" She bent down to gather up her items just as Alex reached her floor, not out of breath at all.

"I believe this is yours," he said, handing her the cigarette case.

She took it without thanking him, then jabbed her key into the lock and pushed open the door. She was about to tell him that he could leave now, that she was fine, but froze at the sound of Precious's laughter. And a man's voice. A voice she knew.

An RAF uniform cap hung from the hat rack inside the door.

"Graham?" Eva called, dropping her shoes and rushing into the front reception room, stopping at the threshold as she registered Graham, wearing his smart new bluish gray RAF uniform, and Precious sitting together on the sofa.

Graham stood, his smile fading as Alex came to stand behind her. Eva moved across the room toward him. He hesitated only a moment before taking her in his arms, not caring about their audience. "You're here. You're really here," Eva whispered. She buried her face in his neck, smelling the scent that was uniquely his, now mixed with that of new wool. She wanted to stay there forever, to make Precious and Alex and the rest of the world disappear so that it was just the two of them.

Instead, she heard Alex crossing the room, felt Graham moving her aside, his hand firmly planted at her waist as he took Alex's hand. "Pleasure to see you safe and sound, old man," Alex said, his voice jovial. "We didn't expect you back in London so soon."

"Nor did I. I managed to pull in a favor and get one night's leave." Graham's gaze flickered over to Eva's stocking feet, before returning to Alex. "Tomorrow they're sending me to another base for further training."

"Where, Graham?" Eva asked. "Closer to London?"

He paused for a moment, his eyes never leaving hers. "I'm not at liberty to say." He dropped his hand from her waist and looked at Alex. "I wasn't expecting to bump into you." He kept his voice light but there was something about the inflection that made Eva wince.

"I ran into him at Horvath's Café. It was quite by accident." Eva was babbling, and she wasn't sure why. Maybe it was the guilt of sharing Graham's letters with Alex. It wasn't as if she'd had a choice or she'd planned on meeting Alex or she'd even wanted to. But something in Graham's expression made her want to explain.

"I'm sure it was, Eva." Graham's voice was almost curt, although he continued to smile.

Eva's heart fell. "When do you have to be back?"

"Tonight. I'll have to catch the three ten from Euston."

"But that's not even a full day." Eva felt horribly close to tears, although her heart sang with the knowledge that he'd come such a long distance just to see her.

Graham cut a glance toward Alex and Precious. "Sadly, yes. And if Germany ignores Chamberlain's ultimatum, I'm afraid we will be at war."

"We should all stay here and listen to the wireless," Alex suggested. "We have less than an hour."

Graham glanced at the small carriage clock ticking away on the mantel, a flicker of annoyance crossing his face. "So we do."

"I'll get refreshments," Precious offered as she stood. "I made chess pie and sweet tea. I'm thinking sugar will top the ration list, so we might as well enjoy it."

Eva jumped up, too, unwilling to sit still and listen to the clock tick by the wasted minutes—time she and Graham couldn't spend alone, waiting for the news that would seal all of their fates. "I'll help," she said, following Precious into the kitchen.

As if feeling the same nervousness, Graham moved toward the wireless to turn it on. From the kitchen, Eva overheard the announcer describing the evacuation of London's children, which was going on at that very moment, as if war were already a foregone conclusion.

When Precious and Eva returned, the men were standing by the wireless, an air of tension thick in the room, although both Alex and Graham retained their calm demeanors. Precious laid out the refreshments, and they all politely took plates and glasses that would remain untouched.

The minutes continued to tick by. Eva sat on the sofa and was immediately joined by Alex. Graham appeared not to notice; he took his own seat next to Precious in one of the two matched club chairs Eva and Precious had received as a gift from Sophia.

Restless, needing the fresh air and the blue sky, Eva jumped up again to open the casement windows at the front of the room. The sound of traffic below would prove that life was continuing as usual. Because surely it was too nice a day outside for a declaration of war. She kept the thought to herself, knowing how absurd it was, but all the same, she couldn't stop herself from wanting to believe such a thing was possible.

A church bell tolled nearby, announcing the eleven o'clock hour. Still nothing from the prime minister as the minutes continued to tick by without anyone attempting conversation. And then the anonymous male announcer, his impeccable accent one Eva had studied night after night, said, "This is London. You will now hear a statement from the prime minister."

Eva met Graham's gaze across the room. She wished she were sitting next to him, holding his hand. Feeling the solidity of him against her side. She glanced at the clock. A quarter past the hour. As if by unspoken agreement, they returned their attention to the wireless, looking at it as if the prime minister had suddenly joined them in their drawing room.

"This morning the British ambassador in Berlin handed the German government a final note stating that unless we heard from them by eleven o'clock that they were prepared at once to withdraw their troops from Poland, a state of war would exist between us. I have to tell you now that no such undertaking has been received, and that consequently this country is at war with Germany."

"God Save the King" began to play, and the foursome found themselves staring at one another in stunned silence. When the song ended, Graham stood and flipped off the wireless, his face pale. "And so it has begun."

The air raid siren began to wail only minutes later. They were still in their places, their untouched plates of food in front of them. Graham moved first. "Quickly, grab your gas masks. We'll go to Regent's Park Underground for shelter."

Alex looked as if he wanted to argue but stayed silent. With shaking hands, Eva slipped on a pair of shoes; then Alex, Precious, and Eva obediently followed Graham out of the flat, not even pausing to lock the door. Eva felt an odd stillness inside, as if everything were happening to someone else.

They rushed out of the building. The sirens continued to wail, and people emerged from the surrounding buildings, looking around in confusion as traffic on Marylebone Road slowed.

Eva felt Graham take her hand. As he led her away from the crowd headed to the tube station, she scanned the clear sky above for planes, unable to forget her wishful thinking: that such an awful thing couldn't happen on a perfect Sunday morning. Graham pulled her to the left, separating them from Alex and Precious. When Eva looked behind her, she saw her friend and Alex were together, part of a throng of people headed toward the tube.

"Where are we going?" she asked, nearly jogging to stay next to Graham.

"The nanny tunnel under Euston Road—not many people know of it."

In silence, Eva followed him down a steep path on an embankment beside the sidewalk and through an iron gate completely hidden from the road. She barely had time to register where they were before he pulled her into a short white brick-walled tunnel. She could hear the traffic and the horns of the motorcars and buses on the road above them.

She was breathing heavily, from the exertion of running and the terror of anticipated explosions. Fear, too, that war was now certain and Graham would be leaving her. The hand that clutched his shook uncontrollably, and she couldn't get it to stop.

"It's just a drill," Graham reassured her. "That's the all clear sounding."

Eva nodded, willing herself to calm down. Willing herself not to beg him to stay.

Graham pulled her to him, close enough that she felt the buckle of his jacket press against her, felt the brass buttons on his chest and smelled the wool of his uniform, felt the embroidered wings against her cheek. Eva closed her eyes, committing him to memory. "Don't go." The words came from her heart before her head could stop them.

"Eva." He breathed her name into her hair.

"Promise me."

"Anything, darling."

"Promise me that you'll come back to me."

He pulled away, his eyes dark like the shadows of the tunnel. "I can only promise that I love you, Eva. That I always will."

She stepped away, then stumbled out the other side of the tunnel into a deserted corner of the park, a secret garden. The air seemed saturated with the scent of fresh-cut grass and the heat of the late-summer day. "Well, then," she said, her heart aching with every word, "I suppose that means I shouldn't promise you that I'll be waiting when you come back."

He stopped behind her. "I know you don't mean that."

She choked out a sob. "Of course I don't." She kept her back to him so he couldn't see the tears streaming down her face.

He put his arms around her and rested his chin on top of her head. "I'll write as often as I can."

She gave him a quick nod, unsure where her voice had gone, unsure even if she wanted more letters from him, letters she'd be forced to share with Alex.

"Just promise me . . ."

When he didn't finish, Eva turned around. "What?"

"Promise me that you'll be careful. London is a dangerous place right now."

"I know," Eva said. "We're at war."

"Not just with bombs." He paused, his eyes searching hers, a cold light in them that chilled her blood. "Just know that not everyone is who they say they are."

The sound of nearby traffic seemed amplified, along with the buzzing of insects and the tweets of a bird on a branch above. It took a moment for her to respond. "Really?" she said, trying to keep the ice from her voice. "Then I promise to be very careful."

She held her breath, waiting for his response.

"Good."

She waited for him to say more, deciding that if he told her he knew who she was, or if he asked her to marry him again, she'd confess everything. But he didn't. Instead, his fingers slipped beneath the rolled curls at the back of her head. "I wish we had more time."

Desire like an ocean's wave consumed her, threatening to pull her under. Maybe it was a natural response to having one's life threatened, or maybe it was simply because he was Graham and he was looking at her with those eyes, and they were utterly and blissfully alone in this green oasis in the middle of London. Standing on her toes to press her face into his neck, she whispered, "We have enough." She felt his pulse jump under her skin, and it seemed that hers raced to match his. As if they were already one.

Then she slipped her hand into his and led him back to the empty tunnel, her need for him overpowering her fear and uncertainty. And her sure knowledge that he was absolutely right about people and secrets.

She didn't go with him to the train station, wanting his last memory of her to be not of a tearstained face on a crowded rail platform but of a tousled and thoroughly satisfied woman who'd promised him that she'd wait for him and that she would love him forever.

And all through that first long night of the war, as Precious cried herself to sleep in the room next to hers, weeping over a world that suddenly seemed too big and too evil, and as Eva clutched the ivory dolphin in her fist and prayed to a God she wasn't sure even existed, Eva remembered the scent of freshly cut grass on a late-summer afternoon and the feel of blue-gray wool against her bare skin and beneath her trembling fingers.

CHAPTER 24

LONDON
MAY 2019

I awoke in the middle of the night, a noise or movement bolting me out of bed before I could remember where I was. I flipped on the bedside light and blinked uncertainly, taking in the unfamiliar furniture, the open wardrobe crammed with vintage dresses opposite the bed, each piece labeled with a neat hangtag of Precious's description, all moving gently, as if someone had just walked by. I blinked and waited for my eyes to adjust to verify everything was still.

Even then it took me a moment to realize I was in Precious's Harley House flat, the one that she and Eva had shared before the war. A moan came from the bedroom next to mine, soft and muffled.

I quickly crossed to my door and pulled it open to listen.

Laura and Oscar slept in another bedroom, only a bell ring away, and there was no sound from their end of the hallway.

I crossed to Precious's door and, after a brief tap, let myself into the empty sitting room, which was lit by a small lamp. After another brief tap with no response, I entered her bedroom. All of the windows were open, allowing in the smell of cut grass from the park and the gentle sounds of stirring birds. Although the front of the building faced Marylebone Road, the back of the flat, where our bedrooms were, could have been out in the country for all the absence of traffic sounds.

Moonlight spilled into the room, falling on the white sheets of the empty bed. I started, then rushed over, expecting to find Precious on the floor. Instead, I heard the moaning again from a chair by the window and blinked, trying to accustom my eyes to the moonlit room.

Precious sat utterly still. She had something in her lap, her head bent over it. Her hair had fallen undone around the shoulders of her pale nightgown, and the moonlight bleached it to cottony whiteness. She looked at me, and the moonlight made her twenty-two again.

"Are you all right?" I asked, moving to her side and kneeling. "I thought I heard you calling." That wasn't exactly right, but I thought it was easier for her to accept than **I heard you moaning**. Because that would have construed weakness, and there was something about Precious Dubose that defied that word.

"I'm fine," she said, although the wetness on her cheeks told me otherwise.

A cool breeze blew through the windows. "Are you cold? I can close these."

I made to stand, but she put a hand on my arm. "Don't. I enjoy the fresh air."

"What are you doing out of bed?"

"I suppose I should ask you the same thing." She reminded me so much of my aunt Lucinda that I smiled.

"I wanted to see if you needed anything. It's three thirty in the morning."

"Is it?" I heard the weariness in her voice. Not exhaustion or tiredness, but something bone-deep, something that had festered for years. "Time isn't the same to me now. I know it's there, waiting. It's like watching a stopped clock, but I can still hear it tick." She tilted her face, flooding it with soft light, erasing the faint lines around her mouth and eyes. "Like you do, Maddie. But I'm old, so I'm allowed."

Her words stung. "What do you mean?"

I heard the sound of rustling cotton more than I saw the small shrug of her shoulders. "You're too young to think you know how your story ends. You haven't yet figured out that life holds more than one story. Each with a separate ending. The end of one doesn't mean you're done."

I forced a lightness I didn't feel. "And it takes ninety-nine years to figure that out?"

"It took me seventy, but I suppose I can be a slow learner. Imagine all those who never figure it out at all. Of all the tragedies in the world, I think that's the worst."

I swallowed my unformed response. It was too late at night to be arguing about the meaning of life. Mostly because I had a terrible suspicion that she might be right. "It really is late. You should be getting some sleep."

As if I hadn't said anything, she asked, "Have you ever been in love?"

"No," I said quickly, ignoring the flash of Colin's face in the back of my mind, his beautiful eyes and the way his smile always started like an accident. Maybe it was because of the darkness, or because my confessor was nearly one hundred years old and had probably heard worse, but I added, "My grandmother and mother died young, and I'm probably going to die young, too. It wouldn't be fair to have a relationship just to share my misfortune with someone else."

The room was silent except for the soft ticking of a clock somewhere nearby. I felt her watching me, considering. "My sweet Maddie. Life is about **reinvention**." She emphasized the word, as if I might misunderstand or confuse her meaning.

"If you don't like what life's dished out for you, turn on the oven and start baking something new."

I surprised myself by smiling. "Did your mama tell you that?"

Her gaze shifted away from me. "Yes. And she was absolutely right." Slowly, she picked up a dark shape from her lap. "If you'd be so kind as to put this on my dresser, I should probably lie down and get some beauty sleep. Careful—it's full of memories."

I took it from her, recognizing the boxy contours of the old embroidered silk purse. Something moved inside as I settled it on the dresser. **The cigarette case,** I thought, **with the Latin words and the bee on the front. The case that once belonged to the elusive Eva.**

As I helped her into bed and tucked her under the sheets, she said, "You need to find Eva, Maddie. She's the only person who can help you."

"Help me?" I wasn't sure if she was confused and babbling, if she even knew what she was saying. Either way, I was afraid to hear her answer.

"Eva was a formidable woman. She always knew who she was. And she understood that reinventing herself was always better than giving up."

I kept my voice gentle. "You know, Precious, it's possible that Eva isn't alive. I'd be happy to record her stories, too, while I'm here. Beyond the modeling and the fashions. I want to hear about two women coming of age in a time of crisis. That would be a great way to preserve your memories for future generations."

The corners of her mouth turned down. "Hogwash. What's the point in reinvention if a person can't leave their past in the past? I never intended to parade mine around like a new outfit."

I studied her, saw the unyielding jut of her chin, and found myself wondering what parts of her past she was hiding. In my experience, it was the darkest ones that were buried the deepest. "Is that why you don't talk about your work with the Resistance? Sophia believed you to be a hero, but nobody knows the story. Surely that's worth sharing."

Her silence stretched, the space punctuated by the ticking clock. When she spoke, I had to lean forward to hear.

"'His little, nameless, unremembered, acts of kindness and of love.'"

I frowned, knowing I'd heard those words before.

"Wordsworth," she said. "They're lines from a poem. Eva used to recite it over and over to practice her accent and pronunciation."

"I don't understand. . . ."

"Unremembered acts of kindness and love. You see, Maddie, some grand gestures and heroic moments never make it into the history books. But that doesn't mean they didn't happen."

"But don't you want the people who love you to know?"

"No. Because then they'd ask why." She looked at my chest, where my heart necklace hung. "You kept your family together after your mother died. Was it because of guilt? Because of something you did or didn't do while your mother was alive? Did you think you could have changed the outcome?"

My chest burned with smoldering memories of the last months of my mother's life, and all of the truths Precious had just voiced. "Why are you saying that?"

"Because no heroic deed is done for the simple act of heroism. There's always some payment due, some penance owed. Some wrong to right."

As I leaned closer, I heard my own breaths keeping time with the ticking clock. "What wrong were you trying to right?"

She smiled at me in the moonlight. "You first."

I sat back, trying to regain control of my feelings. I cleared my throat, searching for a neutral topic so I could sleep. "My aunt sent me magnolia leaves from home. If you like, I can use them to decorate the flat."

She stared at me blankly.

"For your mantel or dining table. I'm not really good at that kind of thing, but my mama was, and I'll just copy what she used to do."

"Of course. Please—decorate away." She flapped her hand, her fingers like a bird's wings in the moonlight. "This place could use some freshening up."

"Has it not changed since the forties?"

"A bit." I felt her eyes on me, heard a fluttering outside the open windows. "The rooms that were destroyed in the Blitz had to be completely refurbished. Sophia took care of that—she always had such a good eye for that sort of thing. Happily, our clothes were stored in rooms that didn't sustain much damage, although Sophia said it took a long time to air them out."

"It's a good thing that Sophia and David didn't sell the flat and you could live in it when you returned."

"Yes." She closed her eyes.

"I'm just curious why it took you all those years before you came back to London."

She smiled without opening her eyes. "I was waiting until I was ready to face the past. Like you, Maddie. It's hard to return home when the memories aren't all happy ones."

I straightened, felt the zing strike me in the chest. Pretending I hadn't heard, I said, "Did you ever consider returning to Tennessee?"

"I would have been returning to strangers. London was my home. I wrote to my family, right after the war, so they wouldn't worry. I let them know that I had survived but wouldn't be returning to Tennessee."

Her chest rose and fell, and I waited a moment for her to say more. When she didn't, I stood, prepared to leave.

"Don't wait too long, Maddie. Face your fears.

Walking through the flames is always less painful than anticipating them."

I stopped, turned around. "Excuse me?"

But Precious's eyes were closed, her chest rising and falling as if in sleep. I waited another minute, then moved to the windows to close the curtains. Without the moonlight, I turned on my phone's flashlight to guide me out of the room. I'd taken a couple of steps when the beam caught on a small rectangle of white on the carpet. I bent to pick it up and took it to my room to get a better look.

When I flipped on the light, an unexpected jolt of **something** shot through me before I realized it was the photo of Graham in his RAF uniform. It had seemed, just for a moment, that it was Colin. They shared the same shy grin and dimpled chin. The same light-colored hair. Even the pattern of freckles on their noses seemed to match. Not that I'd paid that much attention to Colin's freckles.

I leaned down to get a better look. Genetics was a funny thing. Colin resembled his great-uncle more than his own parents or grandmother. I looked a lot more like my aunt Cassie than I did my mother, so it wasn't so far-fetched. Yet I remembered when I met Colin's father, how I thought he looked familiar. Something in his face must have been a throwback to a shared ancestor.

I flipped the photo over, saw the feminine handwriting again. **Sweet dreams, darling.** I yawned. It was too late to be up, and certainly too late to be thinking. Yet something about those words pricked at my brain, a slow drip that evaporated as soon as it landed.

A noise from the front of the flat startled me. I flipped off the light, holding my breath as I strained to listen. It could have been Laura in the kitchen, but as I tiptoed to the hallway, I could see no light from the kitchen, and Colin's bedroom door was still closed. I took a step, cringing as the old wood floor creaked beneath me. I stopped, hearing an odd rustling sound. I considered calling the police, but I'd dead-bolted the doors myself and set the alarm.

More curious now than frightened, I crept down the hallway, sticking to the side by the wall where the floorboards didn't squeak as much, an old trick I'd learned from my grandfather's house. My shoulder knocked one of the framed photographs, but it stayed on the nail.

In the foyer, I stopped to listen again, pausing in a bubble of shadow. The moonlight through the leaded glass windows painted willowy patterns on the floor and walls. A dim light shone from the reception room, a triangle spilling from the door left slightly ajar.

Something rustled again, followed by the solid plop of a heavy object being dropped on the floor. Whoever it was wasn't trying to be stealthy. With more confidence, I crossed the foyer and peered around the door.

Colin stood in front of the window at the desk,

Sophia's stationery box by his feet, the desktop littered with old letters. His jacket lay discarded on the sofa, his shirt untucked and hanging loose. As I watched, he pulled his fingers through his hair and let out a groan of frustration.

"What are you doing?"

He turned his head but didn't startle, almost as if he'd been expecting me. "Sorry. I hope I didn't wake you. But I didn't leave the office until eleven. I thought I'd take a few moments to have a look at some of this, in the hopes of finding Graham or Eva." He straightened, then turned around to face me. "I wanted to see if you'd join me, but I don't know what time you go to bed."

"Eleven, usually. Unless I'm editing or facing a deadline. But usually I turn off the lights at eleven."

"I wasn't asking, but thanks," he said.

I felt a blush stain my cheeks, making me glad the only light was from the small desk lamp on his side of the room.

"How's Nana? She didn't look well when we brought her home."

"She seems much better. I just tucked her back into bed." I glanced at the desk behind him. "Are those Sophia's letters?" I asked as I approached to stand next to him, smelling the faint scent of Scotch and noticing the crystal tumbler on the edge of the desk, empty except for two ice cubes.

"Yes." He faced the letters again. "Sophia had so

many friends. It's taken me a while to sort through them all."

"Did you find any from Eva?"

He shook his head. "Besides that note about leaving her purse at Sophia's house, there's nothing. Which is odd. They must have been particular friends if Sophia thought enough of her to have her as a bridesmaid."

"True, unless Eva wasn't a fan of letter writing. Maybe she was embarrassed about her handwriting. Mine looks like a drunk chicken's."

"I've never seen a letter written by a drunk chicken, so I can't comment. Then again, I've never seen one written by you, either, so perhaps you're right."

"That's why I e-mail or text, to save everyone the headache of deciphering drunk-chicken scratch."

"I've never seen an e-mail from you, either, so I'll have to take your word for it."

There was an almost belligerent note in his voice, so at odds with the Colin I knew. "Are you all right?"

He rubbed his hands over his face and then through his hair again, making him look like he'd just gotten out of bed. "Sorry. It's been a stressful day. And all this—it's a bit frustrating. And I'm somewhat drunk, I'm afraid."

I crossed my arms. "I didn't think you drank."

"I usually don't. But desperate times and all that."

I raised my eyebrows. "Desperate times?"

"Desperate times call for desperate measures. Supposedly Hippocrates said it. Do you know Hippocrates?"

"Not personally." I wasn't sure if I liked this version of Colin. There was something electric and bristling about him, and I was pretty sure if I reached across the short space between us and touched his bare wrist exposed by his rolled-up sleeves, there'd be a spark. "Well, you certainly shouldn't drink alone."

He raised his eyebrows, then strode across the room. Two decanters filled with amber-colored liquid sat atop a console table.

"That's not what I meant. . . ."

Ignoring me, he dropped two cubes into a glass before adding a generous amount of Scotch. He crossed the room to hand it to me.

"I'm not a Scotch drinker, and I really don't like drinking alone. . . ."

He took the glass from me and took a gulp before handing it back. "There. Problem solved." Turning to the letters, he said, "There are no letters from Precious until nineteen forty-six. Granted, if she, Eva, and Sophia lived in the same city, there'd be no reason to write, though of course back then there were no cell phones, so a lot of notes were sent." He frowned. "And there are quite a few letters between Precious in France and Sophia between nineteen forty-six and nineteen seventy-one, when Nana moved back to London. They're full of questions and comments about the London flat, and 'our darling boy'—presumably my father, as he was Sophia's only child—but none of them have any mention of Graham at all."

"What about William? By nineteen forty-five, we know he was dead, so if Graham isn't mentioned, either, then . . ." I let my voice stop.

"That's the thing—William is. Rather frequently, in fact. Apparently, Sophia had his body exhumed from the cemetery in France and interred at our home parish. That caused a flurry of questions about William as a child. Apparently, as a boy my father had similar interests as his uncle William, and that's the subject of many of the letters."

"But nothing about Graham." A cube of ice shifted in my glass. I stared at it, then took a sip, trying not to grimace as the Scotch burned my throat.

"Not even a mention. It almost seems as if it were a deliberate omission."

"Maybe. To protect Sophia?"

"Or perhaps Precious?"

The Scotch warmed my blood as I allowed the implications to sink in. I swirled the liquid in my glass, then took another sip. "That would be odd, wouldn't it? Precious told us that Graham and Eva were crazy in love. I can't imagine why Sophia would feel the need to hold back any information about Graham from Precious."

"Curiouser and curiouser."

I smiled. "Alice from **Alice in Wonderland.** I know that one because I read it to my sisters over and over. I practically have it memorized."

A corner of his mouth lifted. "Three sisters, correct?"

I looked at him. "I didn't expect you to remember."

"Knoxie, the one getting married in December, Sarah Frances, and Amanda, I believe." He wasn't smiling or frowning, but his expression wasn't one I was familiar with.

Unsure of what to say, I lifted my glass between us and took another sip.

"I thought you said you didn't like Scotch."

"I said it's not my drink of choice. If you can get past the throat scalding, the aftereffect is kind of nice." I took another sip. Remembering, I asked, "Didn't you bring the valise from your mother's attic? I looked for it but couldn't find it."

"I did," he said, frowning. "But I left it in the Rover. I can bring it up tomorrow, if that suits."

I nodded slowly, my gaze focused on the window and the moonlit night outside. I was reminded of Precious and her box-shaped purse, the feel of something shifting inside it as I moved it to the dresser. I pulled out Graham's photo from my back pocket, and held it in my palm for Colin to see. "I think Precious is using Eva's purse to hold on to special mementos. She was going through it when I came into her room tonight, and this fell on the floor."

Colin took the photograph, narrowing his eyes

as he studied it. "I really don't see the resemblance. Maybe a little around the nose?"

I took the photograph from him, rolling my eyes. "Oh, for crying out loud, Colin. You're the spitting image."

He gave me a half smile. "And didn't you say something about thinking Graham was hot?"

"Actually, that was Arabella. Although I may have agreed with her." He was looking at me oddly, so I quickly took another sip of my drink.

Gently, he wrested it from my grasp. "I think you've had enough, Madison. Especially if you're not used to it."

I wanted to argue, but my mind was whirring with the image of Precious holding the handbag. Her telling me it held her memories. The photograph on the floor. "Do you remember where we put the box of purses? Arabella said she didn't want to see them until most of the outfits had been decided upon, but I think we've reached that point."

"Yes, I already put them back downstairs in the storage unit, but I can bring them back up."

"That would be great. I think we should go through the purses. See if anything was left inside any of them." I grinned giddily, unsure if it was because of the Scotch or my brilliant idea. "I could find all sorts of day-to-day things to complement the exhibition and my article. Do you think you could bring them up tomorrow, too?"

"Certainly. I can even do it before work."

Without thinking, I threw my arms around his neck. "You're brilliant—thank you!"

His face was close enough that I could count the freckles on the bridge of his nose. Four. "And hot, too, don't forget."

I thought I should laugh, that I should throw my head back and make light of our little conversation. But the way his eyes sparked, and the moonlight outside, and the slow ticking of the mantel clock made me pause. Made my gaze drift down from his eyes to his beautiful mouth, forced my hands to pull his head toward mine and kiss him.

He let out a breath, a small surrender, and then his hands were pulling me closer, or maybe it was me pulling him closer, and my hands were in his hair and his lips were kissing me back and my fingers were tugging on his shirt. I wanted to tell myself that it was the Scotch that warmed my blood, that took my heart and held it carefully, that reminded me of the promise of the girl I'd once been.

The mantel clock chimed, breaking the spell, reminding me of the woman I now was. I became aware of the desk pressed against my back, letters falling softly to the floor. And Colin kissing my neck, his fingers sliding up my bare skin. I put my hand on his chest, and he stopped, lifted his head, a question in his eyes.

"This isn't a good idea."

He looked at me for a long moment, then stood,

pulling me up gently so that we faced each other but didn't touch. I found myself looking at his nose, counting to four over and over in my head. Anything to avoid looking into his eyes. "If you think you have feelings for me, don't," I said.

"I believe it might be too late for me to reconsider." His lips quirked, and the blood swished faster in my veins.

I shook my head. "It would be a huge mistake. I'm not . . . meant to have relationships."

"Why? Because you believe you're destined to die young? Even though the science shows that carrying that rogue gene you inherited from your mother is no guarantee of anything?"

I blinked while his words bounced around in my head, trying to find a place to land. But I'd already spent half of my life accepting how it would end, and my conviction was too deeply rooted now to allow alternative thinking. "I'm not meant to grow old. I won't do that to the people I love."

He considered me. "Sounds like you've been doing a lot of chair rocking—or whatever your aunt Cassie calls it."

I almost smiled. "I can't help it. I've tried to change the way I think, but I can't."

He began buttoning his shirt. "It must be difficult to know how the rest of your life will play out at such a young age, Madison." Plucking his jacket from the back of the sofa and tossing it over his shoulder, he said, "Even if you only have nine years to live, you should live them. And let the people who love you decide what they can and cannot endure."

He flicked off the desk lamp, the glow of the moon settling on the furniture, softening the corners. "Good night, Madison." He leaned down to kiss me on the cheek, then left the room. I waited in the slant of the light from the window until I heard the creak of his footsteps down the hallway, and the finality of his bedroom door clicking shut.

CHAPTER 25

LONDON
DECEMBER 18, 1939

Eva sat in the front parlor next to the wireless, reciting from memory her favorite poem by Wordsworth. Graham had given her a book of poetry, and she had done her best to memorize it all so she could surprise him when she saw him again.

Closing her eyes, she spoke out loud, using the inflections and pronunciations she'd been learning from listening to the BBC broadcasts:

With tranquil restoration: feelings too
Of unremembered pleasure: such, perhaps,
As have no slight or trivial influence
On that best portion of a good man's life,
His little, nameless, unremembered, acts
Of kindness and of love.

The wireless sat next to her so she could flip it on and off, giving her time to practice the proper inflections in between. Leaning over, she flipped the "on" switch, and heard now the voice of Winston Churchill. He was the first lord of the admiralty, which Eva knew because of her nearly daily conversations about world events at Horvath's with Mr. Danek. She made sure to stay up-to-date by listening to the wireless so she wouldn't disappoint him.

Eva still saw Mr. Danek at Lushtak's, too, but talking about war was frowned upon by Madame Lushtak, who didn't want her fashions shown by dour girls wearing frowns and depressed by the news.

But Graham's absence and the lack of letters had made Eva hunger for any information at all. Graham had told her he might not be able to write; even if he did, he might not be able to say very much. Sophia appeared to be as ignorant as Eva regarding Graham's whereabouts, so Eva didn't feel left out. And there was a part of her that was grateful she didn't have to lie to Alex about not having any letters to share.

The front door to the flat shut, and Precious came into the room, bringing with her the scent of chilly air and Vol de Nuit on her emerald green coat. Her arms were burdened with gaily wrapped presents from shops on Oxford Street. She marched over to the sofa and let them fall, watching as several slid to the floor.

"Oh, my goodness. I am plumb wore out. Who

knew Christmas shopping could be so exhausting?" She took off her leather gloves and shoved them into her pockets before slipping off her coat and letting it fall on top of the presents. She turned her attention to the wireless. "Is there any news?"

"Something about a British victory at sea—they sank a German ship called the **Graf Spee**. Somewhere near Uruguay."

Eva reached over and turned up the volume in time to hear Churchill say, ". . . brilliant sea fight that warmed the cockles of British hearts."

She frowned. "After so many defeats of our allies in Europe, I suppose this one ship is considered quite the victory. I'd much rather hear the whole German army had been routed."

Eva surprised herself by how much she'd begun to sound like Mr. Danek. In the last few months, he'd become like a father to her, proud of her when she could converse intelligently. But only when Jiri Zeman wasn't there. She hadn't seen Alex again at Horvath's, but Jiri was now a regular, his mocking eyes watching her closely. She suspected that he was the one who'd discovered her real name and learned that her mother had been a laundress, but she was too afraid to confront him. Sitting next to him at Horvath's felt like sitting next to a time bomb. She refused to consider what else he might have discovered.

The sound of the post slot slamming had Precious running to the foyer. "You have a letter," she squealed with excitement. “I think it might be from Graham!”

Eva took the envelope and stared at the handwriting. **Miss Eva Harlow.** Seeing it written like that gave the name veracity, gave her confidence somehow, as if seeing herself through Graham’s eyes made the charade real. She stood, wanting to read the letter in private, away from Precious and her curious eyes.

“I think it is. Excuse me,” Eva said, feeling badly about the hurt look from her roommate as she retreated down the hallway to her bedroom.

She closed the door behind her and sat on the bed. Not wasting time looking for a letter opener, she slid her finger under the flap, ripped it open, and eagerly pulled out the letter. There were no marks from censors, making Eva wonder whether Graham had known what not to write to avoid censorship, or if he’d used his government connections to send her a letter bypassing review. She didn’t care. She was holding his letter, and it took a moment for her hands to stop shaking long enough for her to read it.

12 November 1939

My darling Eva,

I’m sorry this has taken so long to write. Please know that it’s not because I haven’t

wanted to, that I haven't been thinking about you every waking moment, because I have. I'm working dawn to dusk and I'm quite bleary with exhaustion.

I've been assigned a squadron, and there's word that we're being readied for an important operation, and they are asking for volunteers. I can't say more. Just know that I am safe and well, and missing you with every passing moment. I'm eager to hear news from you, but I'm moving bases again. Not sure where, but hopefully I'll be able to be more specific when I see you again.

David writes often. As I'm sure you're aware, he's been assigned to administrative duties, owing to another failed medical evaluation. He's bound and determined to try again, but in the meantime he brings me news of Sophia. He is proud to report that "our girls," as he calls you, Sophia, and Precious, are quite active in the war effort and working with the Women's Voluntary Service. I can't imagine how the führer expects to win Britain with the strength of our women stacked against him. He also mentions how Alexander Grof has been kind enough to fill in as escort in our absence. I will be sure to thank him when I see him next.

I only have a few minutes until I have to report, so I have to cut this short, but I'm writing to let you know that I expect to have leave around Christmas. Because of the uncertainty of our special mission and which volunteers will be selected, everything is unclear at the moment. I won't be able to let you know anything more specific, but that will make it a lovely surprise, won't it?

Just know that you are my last thought before I fall asleep, and the first one when I awaken. I sometimes dream I hear the crash of waves against the shore, and I imagine that's our future I'm dreaming of, and it makes my sleep restful.

I love you, darling.

Yours always,
Graham

Eva looked at the date on the letter—it had been written over a month ago, which meant they might be together any day now. She read the letter again, then hugged it to her chest, worry over the **special mission** warring with her excitement at seeing Graham again. She was reading it for the third time when Precious knocked on her door.

"Is it from Graham?" she asked, joining Eva on the edge of the bed. "He's coming home, isn't he?

You see—I told you if you didn't watch him leave, he'd come back."

Eva nodded. "He's coming home at Christmas. He wasn't able to tell me when, so I suppose I'll just have to say no to every invitation." She picked up the bottle of Vol de Nuit and applied it generously to her neck. "I want to be ready," she said, smiling at her friend in the mirror.

Precious turned a guileless gaze on Eva. "Did you ever tell Graham about the perfume?"

Eva considered lying but said simply, "No. And it's not like Graham isn't the one who is allowed to enjoy it the most."

Precious smiled. "Looks like you figured out how to have your cake and eat it, too. I'm glad, since I love the perfume. Being able to wear it makes me as happy as a hog in a waller."

The relief at not being judged for her decision to keep the perfume loosened the knot Eva had been carrying in the pit of her stomach. She smiled back at her roommate. "I have no idea what that is, but I'm glad it makes you happy."

They both started laughing, from relief more than anything else. They were still howling with laughter, the tears running from their eyes, when the front door buzzer sounded, sobering them both quickly. Eva stood, smoothing her hair in the mirror. "It could be Graham."

Precious pushed her gently. "Hurry. I'll stay here so you two can have some privacy."

Eva's heart raced as she ran to the front door and threw it open.

Alexander stood on the threshold in elegant evening attire, his hat in his hand. "A kind gentleman let me inside so I didn't have to ring up. I do apologize for the late notice, but I would like you to accompany me to dinner at the Savoy this evening."

"No," Eva said, not caring if she sounded rude. "I'm not going out tonight."

He raised an eyebrow. "Is there a reason? Something I should know? I hope you're not keeping anything from me."

She swallowed the nervous lump in her throat, hoping he didn't notice. "No. I'm tired and want to stay in." She began to close the door, but he put out his arm, stopping it.

"That would be a mistake on your part, my dear. I have news of your parents that I think you should hear. Or if you're not interested, I'm sure Mr. and Mrs. St. John would be."

Cold fear slipped through her veins as she let go of the door and allowed him to step inside. "You're very smart, Eva," he said. "It's why I like you. Now, do run and make yourself presentable. I have a job for you this evening, and you need to look your most beautiful self."

"What about my parents?"

He gave her a look of admonishment. "Didn't you learn as a child that you don't get a treat until you've done your work?"

She wanted to tell him that she'd never gotten treats as a child, but knew it wouldn't matter to him. Without a word, she retreated to her bedroom, where Precious waited.

"It's not Graham?"

Eva shook her head. "No. It's Alex. He's quite insistent that I join him for dinner this evening."

"Didn't you tell him no?"

"He's not the sort to take no for an answer. I'm afraid I don't have a choice."

"Of course you do," Precious said. "Just tell him no."

"I don't have a choice," Eva said again in a tone she hoped brooked no argument.

"If you say so," Precious said. She stood. "You take your time. I'll go keep Alex company. I think I'll tell him the story of how my little sister brought a skunk into the house as a pet. That should entertain him for a while." She winked before heading out of the room, her quick footsteps receding down the hallway.

Eva read Graham's letter again, then folded it into her bag to keep it close, to read again later, making herself a promise that she would not share this one with Alex.

Alex made Eva leave her cashmere coat in the flat before they descended in the lift. Despite gas rationing, his car and driver were waiting at the curb when they exited the building. She was surprised to see Jiri Zeman in a chauffeur's uniform, but treated him as if he were just the driver and not someone she knew.

He held out a full-length mink coat. Alex took it from him and draped it over Eva's shoulders. "Your coat won't do on such a cold night, dearest Eva. Wear this and you'll be warm."

Knowing that he really meant her serviceable coat wouldn't do at the Savoy, she accepted the offer after only a brief hesitation, and snuggled into the backseat. She moved her chin against the fur, feeling the unadulterated luxury of it, the heavy weight of all those pelts on her shoulders. She took off her gloves so she could stroke the fur, just like the Hollywood actresses wore, enjoying the sensation of believing it was hers. She caught Alex watching her and immediately dropped her hands, but not before she saw his knowing grin.

On their way to the Savoy on the Strand, they drove past the venerable emporium of Fortnum & Mason. The windows had been x-ed out with tape, and the walls banked with sandbags. All across the city, blackout curtains covered windows; half-painted headlights on cars and the extinguishing of streetlights evidenced a population preparing for an air attack. Thus far, all had been for naught—and an alarmingly large number of pedestrians had been struck and killed at night by motor vehicles. Despite England's having been officially at war with

Germany for nearly four months, not one single bomb had fallen in the British Isles.

Last week, Mr. Danek had shown Eva a map, pointing out where Hitler stood with his armies, poised at borders like vultures waiting for something to die before devouring the carcasses. Eventually they would make it into France, he said, and then onto the coast and into the English Channel. Only twenty miles of water separated England from the Continent. It was simply a matter of time.

"It's a supper and dance cabaret tonight—I hope you enjoy the dancing." Alex's words broke her reverie. "My friends will be quite envious of my partner for the evening."

"I doubt I shall enjoy any of it. Just tell me what 'job' you want me to do so I can get it done and you can tell me about my parents. I'd like to get home as soon as possible."

"All right," he said. "Tonight's job is easy. It's a test for you, to see how well you can follow directions." He pretended to think for a moment. "Though it's a test you shouldn't fail."

She shivered in her mink but was careful not to show her apprehension. "Go on," she said, sounding bored.

"I want you to be friendly with a gentleman who will be introduced to you, Lord Merton. If he asks you to dance, tell him yes. And then, while you are dancing, ask him if he buys his cheeses at Paxton and Whitfield's. He will then escort you back to your seat, where you will pull out a cigarette and ask for a match. He will give you a matchbox and tell you to keep it. You smoke your cigarette and deliver the matchbox to me when we are in my car, but not before."

"May I ask why you need me to do this?" Eva faced him, wanting to read his expression, to see if he'd gone completely mad.

He touched her jaw, caressing it. "My dear, it is not for you to understand. You are merely to do what I ask."

He grinned, the flash of white from his smile seeming detached from his face as it floated in the darkness. She turned her head away from him, eager for the night to be over so she could return to the flat and wait for Graham.

At the Savoy, Eva was introduced to Lord Merton, an older man with muttonchop whiskers and thick hair in his ears and nose, at the beginning of the evening. She didn't see him again until after the dancing had begun.

She endured the long night and the dancing with partners who spoke little to no English. She kept glancing at her purse, on the table, where she'd put Graham's letter, as if to keep him close. She barely tasted the caviar, quail Richelieu, and jalousie Parisienne, and not just because she felt guilty for the rationing that the rest of the city had to withstand.

Eventually, near midnight, Lord Merton appeared at her side and asked her to dance. He seemed drunk, and Eva was afraid his cold, clammy hands would leave marks on her gown. He spoke of the weather while she tried not to look up into the hairy caverns of his pronounced nose. And just when it seemed that the band was about to finish, she asked casually, "Sir, do you buy your cheeses at Paxton and Whitfield's?"

He stumbled, and she had to use all of her strength to keep them both from falling over. Beads of sweat formed on his temples, dripping onto her arms. He offered her a stiff smile. "Yes, my dear. I do."

And when he escorted her back to her seat, she asked him for a light. He gave her a matchbox before excusing himself. As she sat smoking, she caught Alex's approving gaze, and she turned away without acknowledgment. Then, as the praline ices and coffee were served, she pleaded a headache and asked to be taken home.

When the driver pulled up to the curb in front of her building, she handed Alex the matchbox, which he took without comment. "I've done what you asked," Eva said. "Now tell me about my parents."

"Allow me first to escort you upstairs, to see that you are safely home."

Reluctantly, she led him through the checkerboard-floored foyer and into the lift. As soon as he slid open the gate, she stepped into the hallway and turned around. "Thank you for the lovely evening. I can see my way from here. I'm tired and would appreciate you telling me what you promised." Remembering the mink coat, she slid it off and handed it to him. "And thank you for this—it kept me quite warm."

As if he couldn't tell that she wanted to be free of him, he ignored her outstretched arm, stepped out of the lift, and closed the gate and the outer door. "It looks lovely on you, Eva, and I know you enjoyed wearing it. So please, keep it with my compliments."

She didn't relent, keeping her arm outstretched, her shoulder hurting from the coat's weight. "Don't be ridiculous. I can't accept such a gift. It's far too expensive and not at all appropriate."

"I'm sorry to hear you say that." He took the coat, studying it. A smile crossed his lips. "Do you hear much from your mother, Eva?" His expression and tone made him seem genuinely interested. As if he didn't already know the answer.

"I hear nothing from her." She lifted her chin to show that she wasn't embarrassed. "She doesn't know how to read or write."

"Ah, yes. And your father?"

"You know very well that he was illiterate, too. And I haven't seen him since I was a little girl."

"Poor little fatherless Ethel. Is it good news, then, that he's been visiting your mother?"

Eva froze, the food and drink she'd consumed over the evening threatening to come back up. She remembered her mother's arm, crooked where it had been broken more than once and not set properly; her jagged nose, which made it hard for her to breathe; the way her fingers and arm hurt in the cold because of her mangled bones. Remembered, too, her mother's bleeding and bruised face after she'd tried to prevent her husband from taking her wages and spending them at the local pub on drink and gambling. Recalled the way her mother protected her from her father's fists more than once by taking the blows herself.

"He's dead."

"I assure you, he's quite alive. He's been in prison for so long that you and your mother were most likely happy to assume he was no longer living, but he is, and he's been released. If he'd succeeded in killing the man he assaulted with a bottle of gin instead of simply maiming him, he'd still be in prison. Alas, both survived. I was going to suggest that you write your mother when you send her money and tell her she should move where he can't find her. But if she can't read . . ."

"How do you know all this?" The words rushed out of Eva's mouth. She was going to be ill.

His smile disappeared. "Eva, I'm very disappointed in you. I make it my business to know things. And as I've mentioned, Mr. Zeman is very helpful in finding out what people would prefer remained hidden. Haven't you learned that by now?"

Eva desperately began to think about how much

more money she could afford to send to her mother, about how to make her move yet again.

"You're lying," she said, proud that she kept her voice steady.

"I assure you I'm not. Your mother lives near Muker, yes? In Angram. And your father loves his ale but has a special weakness for gambling. He's good at darts, isn't he? When you were a little girl, he won a lot of money in a tournament and spent it all on drink. It was an argument at that very pub about his unconventional rules that got him locked up. And your father went right back to that pub the day he was released from prison." Alex smiled kindly. "You see, Eva, I'm telling the truth."

Her breath was coming in shallow gasps, and she thought she might faint. "Why are you telling me this?"

"Because I think I have a solution. We can move your mother here, to live with you and Precious. Surely your father wouldn't think to look for her in London. Then you could take care of her. I know St. John would enjoy meeting her. Perhaps inviting her to tea with his mother?"

His mock seriousness was worse than if he'd laughed in her face. Eva tasted bile in her throat.

How could this be happening to her carefully constructed world? It was like watching two trains on the same track heading toward a certain devastating collision. She wanted her mother to be safe and well. That was why she sent money each month.

But her mother couldn't come here. She couldn't. And the guilt of that last thought made Eva's knees crumple.

Alex grabbed her elbows, catching her before she fell. She was shivering, as if she were outside in the cold without any clothes. He settled the fur coat around her shoulders, then pulled her into his arms, pressing her head against the lapels of his coat. He patted her back and uttered consoling words as if she were a small child. "There, there, Eva. I have another idea that you might find more palatable."

She wanted to lift her head, to step away from his embrace, but she wasn't sure she had the strength. "What?" she whispered.

"I own a little country cottage in Dorset, in the seaside town of Bournemouth—won it playing cards, I'm afraid. I've never seen it—apparently, it's where the former owner kept his mistress, so it's nicely appointed although quite small. I could set your mother up there, put it about that she's a military widow with a new name. Perhaps Harlow, since it's worked so well for you? Or is that too obvious a connection? I'm sure you'll think of something, and your mother will be too grateful to care. She could retire from washing other people's clothes."

"Why would you do that?" Eva whispered, unwilling to look up into his face. "I could never pay you back."

"Oh, my sweet Eva. I wouldn't ask you to pay me back in kind."

"It's so I'll feel beholden to you so that I can be useful in some way."

"You're very clever, Eva. You passed the test tonight, by the way. Well done." He held her away from him so she could see his face and smell his cologne, sharp and tangy and not entirely pleasant. Graham didn't wear cologne, and she loved that, loved the clean sandalwood soap scent of him.

Alex pulled her closer. "You're almost as clever as you are beautiful." He pressed his lips against hers. His were dry and hard, and she was so surprised that she stood unmoving, unsure of what was happening. Then she reached out her hand and pushed him away, stepping back, gulping air.

"I want proof. Proof that my father is out of prison."

"I will get it—something signed by the prison warden, perhaps? I suppose you don't need proof that he's found your mother. You said yourself that he has established a pattern of finding her wherever she goes. I suppose he's who you got your industriousness from."

She was shaking now, her jaw hurting as she clenched it, trying to keep her teeth from chattering. "And I will come up with a surname for her. I will at least do that."

Alex smiled. "Good night, Eva. It's been a most pleasurable evening." He tipped his hat and headed down the stairs, his footsteps stealthy on the carpeted runner, then clicking as he reached the marble of each floor. It reminded her of the disembodied smile in the car, as if Alex were an invisible man choosing the moments in which he wanted to appear.

She heard a small sound behind her, and she swung around to the closed front door of her flat. She stuck her key in the lock, opened it, and looked down the long hallway, hearing a door softly click shut. Eva waited for a long moment for Precious to reappear so she could explain what her friend might have seen through the small peephole. Or maybe the noise had been Eva's imagination.

The fur coat fell from her shoulders, puddling on the floor. She stared at it, feeling ill, and left it where it lay and made her way to her bedroom at the back of the flat. She hesitated outside Precious's door, listening for movement, for any excuse to knock and try to explain. But she heard only the creak of a floorboard from the flat above and the sound of old water pipes burbling in the walls.

When she reached her room, she kicked off her heels, sat down on her bed, and opened her purse, needing to see Graham's handwriting, to read his words. But when she peered inside, the letter was gone.

CHAPTER 26

LONDON
MAY 2019

I sat next to Arabella on a crowded Jubilee Line tube carriage, our impressive collection of shopping bags tucked behind our legs, and I tried hard not to look like a tourist. I wasn't wearing a fanny pack, which put me ahead of the game, and I was traveling with a bona fide Brit, but she said my face shouted "American." She thought it had something to do with my perpetual tan and my straight white teeth, courtesy of fluoride in the water and three years in braces.

Arabella was tapping away on her cell phone, a result of being out of the office for an entire day, but I didn't feel guilty since our shopping expedition had been her idea.

She looked up. "When is your lunch with the

historian at the London College of Fashion? I'd like to join you. I'll have Mia clear my schedule."

"Tuesday at eleven thirty."

Arabella nodded, then went back to tapping. The sudden sound of the theme song from **Gone With the Wind** erupted, strident enough to be heard over the sound of the train wheels on the metal tracks. I glanced around, realizing that people were looking at my purse on my lap. Arabella elbowed me. "I believe that's yours."

I fumbled for my phone, yanked it out, and hit "decline" when I saw it was Knoxie. On train. Can't talk right now. I usually kept my ringer off, which was why I hadn't been aware my brother had changed that ringtone, too.

> It's Aunt Cassie—my phone is dead and I'm borrowing your sister's. When are you coming home? Maid of honor is supposed to organize bridal shower.

I resisted rolling my eyes. I don't know. Pick a date and book the Dixie Diner. If I'm not there, Knoxie will know what to do. She's always been bossy.

Two photos appeared on my screen, of iced confections that made my mouth water. A text from my aunt followed. Chocolate or vanilla charm cakes? Or both?

"What's a charm cake?"

I turned to see Arabella unabashedly looking over my shoulder.

"It's a Southern wedding thing. They're little pastries with charms attached to a ribbon hiding inside. Each of the bridesmaids pulls one out to discover her fate." I thought for a moment, trying to recall the meanings from when I'd been Suzanne's maid of honor at my dad's wedding. "Let's see. . . . The anchor charm means a stable life. The ring means marriage, and the airplane means travel and adventure."

"Sounds like a Southern version of a fortune cookie."

"Pretty much," I said, turning back to my phone as it buzzed again.

I'm thinking both.

Great. Sounds like you've got it all under control.

Lucinda wants to throw a lingerie shower at Lucinda's Lingerie. I said I liked the idea if she didn't mind punch and icing being near all that lace and polyester.

All fine with me.

I started to return my phone to my purse when it buzzed again. It sounds like you're not taking your position as MOH seriously.

I held my thumbs over my phone, trying to think of a way to remind her why I didn't want my visit to Walton to be too prolonged. Before I could type the first letter, my phone buzzed again.

How are things with Colin? Tell him I've earmarked the guest room at my house for him for the wedding. It's over the back porch, so easy to access from the trellis. I recall you're good at climbing it.

I pressed the "power" button on the side of my phone, shutting it off, then threw it into my purse.

"Does Colin know he's invited to the wedding?" Arabella asked, unashamed.

"No, because he's not. I have no idea why my aunt thinks he might be."

"Maybe she just has an aunt's intuition. The sparks practically zoom off you two when you're together."

"Or it's wishful thinking."

"I bet he'd go. He'd probably go to Antarctica if you asked him, so Georgia shouldn't be a problem."

The train squealed to a stop, saving me from responding. We joined the throngs of exiting passengers, and I clutched my Harrods and Harvey Nichols shopping bags in both hands as I stood to the right on the escalator at the Baker Street tube station.

Industrious Brits jostled by on the left, climbing the steep steps. I turned to Arabella, who was equally burdened with shopping bags.

"It's so civilized here. I wish they'd adopt the whole 'queue to the right' thing in the States. Although most motorists haven't yet got the hang of faster traffic to the left and slower traffic on the right on the highway. At least driving through Atlanta gives me the chance to practice all my cusswords."

"How lovely." We reached the top of the long escalator and lifted our bags as we left through the turnstiles to Marylebone Road, emerging into a steady drizzle.

"There's a Marks and Sparks to Go here if you want something sweet."

I pulled the hood of my raincoat over my head. "We just had lunch, Arabella. How someone as small as you can eat so much, I'll never know."

We walked past the M&S shop sign toward the long line of tourists waiting in the rain to get into Madame Tussauds wax museum.

"Have you heard from Colin?" I asked, keeping my voice nonchalant. "Last night he said he would bring up a box of handbags from the storeroom and the valise from Penelope's attic this morning before he left for work."

"Actually, yes. He called to let me know both box and valise were in the guest room. He seemed . . . upset. No, that's not the right word. Confused, I think. He was very heavy-handed with the pronouns instead of using your name. It was all 'she,' 'her,' and 'that woman,' so I could tell he was quite confused about something. What on earth happened?"

My face reddened, and I tried to hide it by walking faster. Arabella quickened her pace and grinned when she peered under my hood. "You're blushing! Does that mean he kissed you?"

I scowled at her. "No."

If I'd thought that would shut her up, I was hugely mistaken. Instead she squealed, "You kissed him! Oh, that's marvelous, Maddie."

I marched silently beside her as we passed the Royal Academy of Music, the muted strains of a trumpet solo coming through a window that was partially open despite the drizzle. She was practically running, trying to keep up with me, but I didn't slow until we'd reached the steps to our building and the porter was holding open the door. I did take a moment to scan the front drive to check for Colin's Land Rover. I couldn't decide if I was relieved or disappointed when I didn't spot it.

Never one to miss anything, Arabella said, "It's not here. I could message him if you like and tell him—"

"No." My voice sounded harsher than I'd intended. I smiled my apology. "We don't need him right now. We're two intelligent women who are more than capable of sorting through old purses and a dusty valise."

She grinned. "Agreed."

We stepped out of the lift, and I followed Arabella into the foyer—then nearly ran into her. She'd stopped three paces into the room and was focused on Laura standing in the doorway to the reception room, watching something.

Laura faced us with a finger to her lips before turning her attention back to the room. Moving silently, we peered inside. Precious stood at the window, in front of the desk strewn with Sophia's letters. She wore a midnight blue sequined gown. A hang-tag I remembered making dangled from a shoulder strap. Arabella had already decided that she wanted the dress front and center in the exhibition, but I'd yet to get the full story behind it from Precious. It still fit her tall and slim body, but the opening in the back showed the soft pale skin of an old woman. It made her seem vulnerable somehow, like an animal showing its belly in surrender.

Letters lay scattered on the floor and chair, the drawers of the desk pulled open like turned-out pants pockets. "I can't find it. I can't find it." Precious muttered the words over and over, her hands swiping through the messy pile on the desk, scattering the remaining letters.

"I'll give her another moment, see if she calms down on her own," Laura said quietly. "This happens sometimes, and I've found that if I interrupt her, it upsets her more."

"Where is it?" Precious shouted, slamming one of

the drawers shut before pulling it open again, surprising me with her strength.

"Is she dreaming?" I asked.

Laura shook her head. "No. She's completely conscious. Just . . . off in her own world. She's been looking for something for nearly fifteen minutes. She must have had a dream last night that jarred her memory."

I dropped my packages on the ground. "I think I know what she's looking for." I walked silently into the room, toward the fireplace mantel, where I'd left Graham's photograph. I carefully picked it up, then approached Precious.

She looked at it for a long moment, then took it from me. "Thank you." She blinked as if just then realizing who I was. "It's not mine. I've been keeping it for a friend."

"For Eva?"

Precious nodded. "Yes. When you find her, would you please make sure she gets it?"

"Of course," I said.

She flipped the photo over in her palm and looked as if she was seeing the writing on the back for the first time.

"I'm curious," I said. "It's a woman's handwriting. Is it Eva's?"

She glanced down at the photograph, then looked up at me with a wobbly smile. "Do you like my gown?"

I shared a quick look with Arabella. "It's beautiful. And it looks beautiful on you."

She smiled. "I wore it that Christmas. Before . . ." She frowned, searching for her words. "Before the bombs started."

"And it still fits you so nicely," Laura said, bustling into the room. "Now, let's go get you changed into something more comfortable, all right?"

We watched as Laura led Precious from the room, Precious's shoulders as straight as if she were getting ready to walk down the runway of a designer's showroom.

Oscar, apparently alerted to my presence, bounded into the room and began growling at me. Arabella picked him up and put him in the kitchen before returning and grabbing my arm. "Come on—let's go open up those purses. Going through my own out-of-season bags is its own trip down memory lane. I can only imagine what Precious's might be like."

Leaving our shopping bags in the foyer, we headed toward the first bedroom. "My little brother Joey once kept a chicken breast he'd dissected in science class in his backpack over the summer," I said. "It took my dad three months to find out where the smell was coming from."

Arabella wrinkled her nose. "I can't tell you how happy I am at this moment that I have only sisters."

In the spare bedroom, the antique leather valise lay opened on the bed, displaying a mishmash of clothing, papers, costume jewelry, and cosmetics.

It all looked like something you might find in the back of a dresser drawer, an excavation by layers of someone's past. I could imagine Colin opening the valise to verify that its contents weren't anything important, and then leaving them for Arabella and me to sort through.

Arabella picked out a pair of high-heeled sandals from the valise, slipped off her own shoes, and tried to put her foot into one of them. "Too small—you try."

I slipped out of my flats and buckled the sandals on my feet, then winced as I stood up. "Some of the shoes we've found have fit me perfectly, and others have been a little too snug. Sadly, these are of the snug variety, which is a shame. They're almost brand-new and really swanky."

"Swanky?" Arabella said with a smile as I handed them back to her.

"It's what my aunt Lucinda says to describe anything she considers fancy enough for her to wear, usually involving ruffles and sequins."

"I'll remember that," Arabella said as she placed the shoes next to the door. "This is my keeper pile—items that I think should be considered for the exhibition." She turned back to the bed and surveyed the piles. "Aunt Penelope is always threatening to clean that attic. It will take an absolute age—some of the stuff has been stored there for aeons. There's an actual suit of armor in the back. I remember Colin making it talk when we were children playing up there when we weren't supposed to. Scared the wits out of me."

The image of Colin playing ventriloquist with a suit of armor made me grin, and I wasn't fast enough to hide it from Arabella.

With a matching grin, she spun the case around so it faced her. "Looks like there were initials stenciled on here at some point, but they've been rubbed off. Can't tell what they were."

I looked where she indicated, examining the smooth leather of the case and the heavy marks of the mostly scratched-out gold-stenciled monogram. "It looks old but not worn. Definitely not worn enough to justify the monogram being scratched over like this."

"Almost like it was deliberately removed." Arabella straightened, examining the contents more closely. "A bunch of junk, really. Look—more menus." She reached into the valise, pulled up a small stack, and screwed up her eyebrows as she flipped through them. "It makes me think that whoever this belonged to might have been a tourist—or, if not a tourist, then someone new to the kind of life one would have to dine frequently at these hotels. Look—the Dorchester, Claridge's, the Ritz, and several from the Savoy. I can't imagine anyone who wasn't starstruck thinking to collect them."

"Good point. Which makes me think it wasn't Sophia. She likely ate at places like that on a regular basis. Plus, she had her memory box from her debutante year and her album full of mementos, so I don't think this is hers."

"Apparently the owner of the valise was also a memento keeper." One by one, Arabella plucked out loose ticket stubs from theaters and cinemas, a telephone charge receipt from the Savoy, two ticket stubs from the gardens at Kew, and a vintage Selfridges receipt for a pair of kid leather ladies' gloves.

I pulled out the remaining items and placed them on the bed next to the first pile while Arabella put her hand inside to make sure we'd removed everything. "There's a label stitched into the lining at the top." Arabella bent her head to see better. "Hand me your phone."

She peered inside, shining the flashlight upward, then stood, shaking her head. "Whoever stitched this on was a very good seamstress—I've never seen such tight stitches that weren't done by a machine. It's especially hard when one has to look upside down while stitching. I'm afraid if I try to pull it off, it will rip the entire lining out. I'll need scissors."

"I just bought a pair—I'll be right back."

When I returned, Arabella had her hands on her hips and was frowning at the valise.

"What's wrong?" I asked, handing her the scissors.

She dipped her head into the opening of the bag. Her voice was slightly muffled as she sawed at the threads. "It's just odd that the address label is hidden. Usually people put it in a more visible spot, so that if the case is lost, it can be returned to its owner."

I waited a moment. Then she shouted and straightened, holding something in the palm of her hand. She stared down at a rectangle of fabric, her brows knitted in concentration. "I have no idea who this is. What do you make of it?" She handed it to me.

K. Nash, Quayside Cottage, Bournemouth, Dorset

"Well, it's definitely an address label of some sort—written long before postal codes."

"I think those started in the late fifties or early sixties," Arabella offered.

I nodded, studying the block letters. "It's hard to tell, but I'd say this looks more like it was written by a woman than a man."

"Although because they printed, it's impossible to tell if it matches the handwriting on any of the letters we've seen."

"It might not even be related to Sophia or Precious at all. But we should still check it out, don't you think? Maybe this is the missing link to finding Eva."

"Unlikely, but never say never, right?" Arabella beamed. "I think you and Colin should take a holiday weekend to Bournemouth, see what you can find. It's beautiful this time of year, and you can show Colin what you look like in a bikini."

"For your information, I don't own a bikini. Besides, I'm sure we can find out about Quayside Cottage and K. Nash online, without having to actually get in the car."

"Not nearly as much fun as a road trip." She stuck her hand back in the valise. "I guess it's a good thing you and Colin aren't speaking to each other. You can't tell him that I accidentally cut a hole in the lining."

"I wouldn't worry about it. It doesn't look like it's valuable, and as you pointed out, it's not really visible, anyway. Chances are that K. Nash is long dead, too. He or she won't be looking for it."

"True." She leaned over and lifted a bundle of silk stockings from one of the piles. "I don't think it's a he. These are real silk—can you imagine the luxury of wearing silk stockings?"

"No," I said. "But until you forced me to go shopping today, I couldn't imagine wearing anything but jeans." I frowned, looking at the bundle. "Wasn't silk rationed during the war? So it could be used as parachutes or something? And women drew seams on the backs of their bare legs, so it looked like they were wearing something."

"K. Nash must have been a hoarder, then," Arabella said matter-of-factly. "Or maybe she dealt in the black market." She raised her eyebrows. "These look like they've never been worn. Maybe she was a model, like Precious or Eva. Didn't Precious say that Madame Lushtak required them to wear silk stockings?"

"Yes, she did. Let's ask her if she knew of a fellow model named K. Nash. Not sure why her valise would be in the attic at Hovenden Hall, but it doesn't hurt to ask."

Arabella picked up the empty valise to put on the floor, then quickly set it down. "We missed something—there's a paper stuck between the bottom and the side. Hang on."

She reached inside and pulled out what looked like another receipt, folded in half, the ink bleeding through to the back. Arabella's eyebrows arched. "K. Nash certainly had money to burn. This is from a furrier on Bond Street—one mink coat, for the very reasonable price of three hundred pounds sterling."

I took the paper from her and scanned it, focusing my eyes on the amount at the bottom, double underlined. "Seriously? That's a lot of money—now and then. Whoever this K. Nash was, she appears to have been rolling in the dough. No date but definitely before PETA, right?"

"Definitely." Arabella brushed her hands together as if she were finished. "Come on, Maddie—let's go hang up your new clothes and put away those blue jeans."

"We're not done, Arabella, remember? We still have the purses."

"Oh, right. I'd like to match some of them up to the outfits we've already chosen for the exhibition. A nice contrast to the gas masks that Mia has managed to secure on loan from a military museum. Some are in brown boxes with strings for straps. Not very attractive but necessary. Others are a little more high-end and decorative. Mia managed to find an Arden pigskin holdall—worth a small fortune even then and so pretty. Gas masks were carried everywhere, regardless of what a person was wearing. Definitely a fashion look for the period."

We restuffed the valise and placed it on the floor, then picked up the box full of old purses—lots of sequins and velvet and paste jewels—and dumped them on the bed. There were about twenty or so, mostly small, evening-sized. Apparently the oversized-bag craze wasn't yet a twinkle in a designer's eye.

The first three purses we opened were empty, but the fourth and sixth yielded lipsticks, both red, and chalky with age. Arabella found a compact and a lacy white handkerchief in a black velvet ball-shaped purse with a rhinestone clasp and a gold chain strap.

"This is lovely," Arabella said, placing the strap on her wrist and parading the purse about. "Definitely one for the exhibition. Then I'm going to beg Precious for it. It's very 'swanky.'"

"Aunt Lucinda would approve." I reached for a beaded bag with most of its beads missing, leaving red satin bald spots on one side. Inside, I found a single page of card stock, folded in half. "It's a cocktail menu from the Savoy," I said, admiring the bold vintage fonts and the ingredients and instructions for an absinthe cocktail. "I wish it hadn't been folded—now there's a crease in the middle. It's so pretty, and I'd love to have it framed."

"What's that on the back?" Arabella asked.

I flipped it over. In the white space between the Washington Cocktail and the Waterbury Cocktail someone had handwritten in ink: **Jsi v nebezpečí. Utíkej!**

Frowning, I asked, "What language is that? Hungarian?"

Arabella shook her head. "I don't know. I think it might be Czech." She met my gaze. "Isn't there an app for that?"

"There is," I said, pulling out my phone. "I don't know how accurate it is, but I will say it's been useful in my travels." I opened up the translation app and pointed my camera at the words, waiting for the miracle of modern technology to do its work.

Then I stared at the screen for a long moment before Arabella moved to stand next to me.

I forced the words out of my tightening throat. "It says, 'You're in danger. Run.'"

Our eyes met before we both turned toward a sound in the doorway. Precious was there, in one of her peach-colored lounge sets, her face the color of the walls. She seemed to melt where she stood, her legs collapsing under her. I caught her before she hit the floor, a name on her lips as she fell. **Alex.**

CHAPTER 27

LONDON
DECEMBER 30, 1939

Eva nearly skipped down the steps of her building on her way to work at Lushtak's. The air stung with an icy chill, but the sun was shining, Graham was coming home on leave, and she hadn't seen Alex since that night at the Savoy when he'd told her she'd passed the test.

He'd sent a note informing her that her mother had been moved and was using the name Eva had given to Alex. Inside the same envelope had been a letter attesting that her father had indeed been released from prison.

Eva hoped this meant that she was done with Alex, that she had returned a favor and their accounts were perhaps settled.

A horn blew, startling her and making her turn. When she recognized Alex's car, Jiri Zeman behind the wheel, pulling up beside her, she froze inside her wool coat. She considered ignoring it and running, but that was stupid; there was no place she could run where Alex couldn't find her.

The door opened. "Good morning, Eva," Alex called from the backseat. "It's cold—get in, and we'll drive you to work. You have a ten o'clock showing, yes?"

It bothered her that he should know that, but she supposed she shouldn't be surprised. With only a brief hesitation, she got inside the car, turning her face away as Alex reached across her to close the door.

"You're looking lovelier than usual, Eva. You must have good news."

She kept her face still as she looked out the window. She had no doubts that he'd taken Graham's letter from her purse and knew that Graham would be coming home soon.

"I have news, too." He placed the morning's **Times** on her lap, crisp and ironed by some nameless maid so that the print wouldn't smudge onto his fingers. "Page five, first column on the left. I think you might find it interesting."

When she didn't move, he plucked the paper off of her lap and began turning the pages. With great fanfare, he found the proper one, then folded the paper in quarters to make it easier for her to read. "There you are. I believe you'll recognize the gentleman in the photograph."

Curious, Eva bent her head—and froze. It was the man she'd danced with at the Savoy, the one who'd given her a matchbox after she'd asked him where he bought his cheeses. She read the headline.

Lord Merton, MP, found dead in hotel room from apparent botched robbery

"That's horrible. Why are you showing me this?"

"Because you need to know."

She looked up, saw Jiri looking at her in the rearview mirror, that familiar smirk on his face. The bile rose in her throat. "Was this about the matchbox?"

"More or less. Lord Merton made the mistake of confiding to the wrong person that he'd been paid a large sum of money for handing over government information. They killed him because of it."

She looked down at the photograph, remembering how Lord Merton had tried very hard to avoid staring at her cleavage while they were dancing. She felt a pang of regret—a sorrow that she hadn't known him well enough to grieve his passing.

She shook her head. "They . . . ?"

Alex grabbed her arm, making her wince. Eva tried to pull away. "Let go—you're hurting me."

He squeezed tighter, leaning close so that she could feel his breath hot on her face. "That is what happens to people who can't follow the rules. Such as talking about things they shouldn't to people they shouldn't trust." Alex's grip tightened. "And not sharing letters when one has been asked to do so. This is a dangerous game, Eva. Don't think you can make up your own rules. Just do as you're told."

He let go of her, and she rubbed her arm, staring at him. Her lungs felt frozen, making it hard to breathe, to think.

Without looking at her, he said, "Just do as you're told, and don't talk to anyone about anything you discuss with me or that I ask you to do—not anyone. And don't think you can withhold information or a letter from St. John from me. Because I will find out. There are worse things than your secret being revealed, Eva. That would be the lesser punishment, believe me. Let's not forget that I know where your mother lives. And I wouldn't like to see Precious or Sophia suffering the same fate as the unfortunate Lord Merton. The ax swings both ways."

He turned to her and smiled the smile of a fox circling a chicken coop. "Now do you understand, my dear Eva?"

Eva thought she might throw up. Or faint. But she wouldn't. She never wanted to give Alex the satisfaction of knowing he'd frightened her.

She swallowed the bile that had risen in the back of her throat. "Yes. I understand," she said, somehow managing to keep her voice calm.

The car stopped at the curb in front of the House of Lushtak. Jiri stepped out to open her door. Eva quickly moved to the edge of the seat, eager to get away from Alex. But he grabbed her hand, pulling her back.

"One more thing. Be careful, Ethel. Your accent slips when you're frightened."

She yanked her hand out of his grasp and started across the sidewalk.

"I'll pick you up at nine o'clock on New Year's Eve," he called after her. "We're going to a party."

Eva knew she couldn't say no. The photograph of Lord Merton and Alex's threats danced in her head. Without acknowledging that she'd heard, she hurried across the sidewalk, nearly colliding with Freya in her rush to get inside and shut out the rest of the world.

DECEMBER 31, 1939

Eva stared at her face in the mirror, at her reddened and swollen eyes, the pallor of her skin, which couldn't be disguised by pancake makeup or rouge. Precious stood behind her, twisting and curling Eva's hair into an elaborate evening style.

The newspaper, its war news almost two weeks

old, lay faceup on the dressing table, the bold headlines shouting at her with each glance.

RAF SUFFERS HEAVY LOSSES,
12 ENEMY PLANES SHOT DOWN

The first major air battle had taken place on the same day Eva had read Graham's letter, the eighteenth, on the North Sea at the mouth of the Elbe River in some godforsaken German port called Heligoland Bight. It had been Sophia who'd told her. She'd rushed to Eva's flat wearing her nightclothes under her fur coat. David, working in administration at the War Office, had come home, reassuring Sophia that despite the losses, some of the bomber crews had managed to return to England.

Eva had sat on the sofa with Sophia, holding her hand, a glimmer of hope spreading as she recalled something Graham had said. "But Graham isn't a bomber pilot. He flies Spitfires and other fighters. There must be some mistake. . . ."

Sophia had shaken her head. Keeping her head down and speaking quietly, she said, "This is in strictest confidence, you understand. David told me. It appears that Graham volunteered for a mission. A secret mission involving the bombing, something to do with advance reconnaissance. He may have run out of fuel before he made it back." She choked, squeezed Eva's hand harder. "David says they believe he may have crashed into the sea. They found the wreckage of his plane, but they're still searching for him. Because this was a covert operation, the information has been weak at best and will have been intentionally delayed. Even though David is in the War Office, this operation was out of his jurisdiction, so to speak."

"So there's still hope," Eva said, wishing her head would agree with her heart, with the sure knowledge that Graham was still alive.

Sophia nodded, then swallowed, trying to regain her composure. "Until we hear differently, we can assume that he has been picked up by one of our allies and that he is safe. David will let us know as soon as there is confirmation."

Eva, Precious, and Sophia had huddled together and wept, clinging to that one hope, emptying the vodka from the decanter before starting on the as-yet-untouched Scottish whisky Alex had given Eva. In that moment, Eva hadn't cared where the alcohol was from. She wanted only to numb herself. To be rendered senseless until the moment Graham walked through the door and put his arms around her.

But Sophia had eventually left, and then Precious reluctantly returned to Lushtak's, agreeing to tell Madame that Eva was ill. And Precious had made Eva promise that if she heard news, any news, she would let her know immediately. Believing she wasn't alone in her grief and anxiety brought Eva some comfort, at least until she closed her eyes and the images of broken pieces of a plane floating in the water made her heart bleed again.

Now Precious dropped a golden lock of Eva's hair from the curling tong so that it bounced against her neck. "I don't know why you're going out tonight, Eva. Alex knows that Graham is missing—surely he'd understand if you said you'd rather stay home?"

Eva didn't miss the note of disapproval in her friend's voice. It had been there ever since the night when Alex kissed her and gave her the mink coat. Eva wanted to pretend that it hadn't happened, because she couldn't explain the reason for it. Nor could she explain why she continued to see Alex, to meet his friends, to go out dancing with him. She had become her lie; and to unravel it now would leave only empty air at its center, erasing Eva Harlow as if she'd never existed.

So Eva tried desperately to smile, looking instead like a grimacing clown, all red lips against white skin. "It makes me feel better—to be around happy people. And it's New Year's Eve. You should come, too." She heard the desperation in her voice. She didn't want to be alone with Alex. Precious, with her incessant chatter and drawling accent, was the buffer Eva needed.

Precious pressed her lips together in disapproval. "Well, it's not right. It's not right at all. Graham could be hurt, and you're out there dancing with another man." Her accent was always more pronounced when she was agitated.

"Stop it!" Eva hardly recognized the harshness in her voice. It was the sort of voice her father had used when he roared at her and her mother after a bout of drinking and heavy losses. But the lack of sleep, the nightmares when she did finally close her eyes, and the constant worry had all shot holes in the social niceties she'd worked so hard to attain.

She stood, pulling out the curl that Precious had been wrapping around her finger. "It's not any of your concern. Graham's mine to worry about, Precious. Not yours. Mine." She jabbed her finger into her own chest, scratching the skin.

They stood staring at each other in shock, the angry words seeming to remain in the room like an echo. Eva dropped her hand, the fire of her anger extinguished by the hurt look on Precious's face.

"I'm so sorry . . . ," she began, but Precious was already retreating, shaking her head.

"No, you're right. I shouldn't intrude. Worrying grabs people in different ways, and I understand. I really do. I just wish . . ."

The buzzer rang, and Precious threw up her hands. "He's here, and I'm not quite done with your hair. I say we make him wait while we take our little ol' time about it."

Eva managed a real smile. "Thank you," she said,

closing her eyes. She felt Precious tug on her hair and begin to wrap it around her finger again. She dressed carefully in the sequined gown with the open back she'd borrowed from Precious. If she pretended she was dressing for Graham, Eva had found, she could get through the evening. It was her private act of revenge against Alex. At least until she figured out a more permanent solution.

Atop the dress, she wore a white fox fur cape; Alex had sent it over with a note instructing her to wear it that evening. It was one of several furs she'd been forced to accept. To alleviate her guilt over the expensive gifts, Eva had offered them to Precious to wear, but her friend always deferred to her own wool coats, as if the furs were tainted, which, Eva knew, they were.

As Alex handed her into his car, she affected a bored tone. "And where are we headed tonight?"

He waited until he'd joined her in the rear seat before answering. "To the Embassy Club on Bond Street. There's someone I'd like you to meet. A woman, Georgina Simmonds, formerly Sedlak. We are old friends—our uncles on our fathers' side were close school friends in Munich, and our mothers are both British, so we have a lot in common. Georgina and I grew up together in Prague. Our families always wanted us to make a match, but she fell in love with a fellow Harrovian, and I was left to lick my wounds and remain eternally single."

"Is Georgina also a thief? The kind who digs through another lady's purse while she's dancing, and removes precious items?"

He didn't even blink. "Perhaps a lady shouldn't be offended when it is she who breaches a verbal contract to share certain documents."

The fox cape at her throat seemed to suffocate her, the weight of it like dirt on a coffin. "As soon as the clock strikes midnight, I want to leave."

"Fair enough. Just be nice to Georgina and dance with whoever asks, and I will take you home as soon as the last bell tolls. But there are several gentlemen I want you to be particularly friendly with. Do you understand? I need you to be amiable, to let them know you're someone they can trust. Someone they can confide in. War makes strange bedfellows, I find. Everyone joggling for position, trying to be the one on top."

She felt his gaze on her, and abruptly turned her head.

New Year's revelers flooded the streets of the capital long past midnight, and Eva didn't return to the flat until nearly half past two, exhausted and drunk, her feet blistered and sore from dancing with men who held her with too much familiarity and spoke in languages she couldn't understand. She'd met Georgina, an attractive brunette who smiled and laughed and conversed like the rest of Alex's friends, except Eva couldn't help but feel as if she was also being judged. Georgina's flat dark eyes followed Eva as she moved on the dance floor, her expression one of consideration, as if judging a match of skills.

As usual, Alex escorted her to the door of her flat, kissing her hand in farewell. She turned away to open her door, then swung around again. She hadn't wanted to be the one to bring it up, to make him believe she cared enough to inquire. But she needed to know. "You haven't mentioned my mother. Is she safe?"

"She is. And quite happy, I might add. She wants to see you so she can thank you for saving her from your father. You've seen the corroboration that he was released from jail, so you know I can be trusted."

"Trust you? Are you mad?"

He was suddenly very serious. "No, my dear. Simply a realist." He gave her an appraising look. "And you forgot to cover this." He reached out a finger and touched the small crescent-shaped birthmark on her neck.

She recoiled as if he'd burned her.

"I prefer perfection." He took her hand, kissed it again, then left, taking the lift this time.

It took Eva several tries to get her key in; she finally succeeded on the fourth try. The door swung open and she stumbled inside, kicked off her shoes, and began to undo the clasp on the fox fur cape.

Then she stopped. All the lights were on in the flat, and music from the gramophone came from the drawing room. She recognized the song, remembering it from when she and Graham had danced at Sophia's wedding at Hovenden Hall. "Begin the Beguine."

But it wasn't the lights or the music that seemed to sober her. It was the scent. Of cold wool and sandalwood soap. **Graham.** Eva ran into the drawing room, stumbling once and almost falling before catching herself on a club chair.

Precious stood alone in the room, swaying to the music. Through the alcohol haze, Eva noticed that she wore a silver evening gown that fit her curves like a second skin. The mink coat lay on the sofa as if carelessly discarded, not in the wardrobe where Eva knew she'd left it.

She blinked. "Where's Graham?"

Precious stopped swaying and lifted the needle off the record. "He was here. He had only a few hours, and he wanted to see you. To let you know that he's all right."

"But . . ." Eva couldn't form the words she wanted to say.

"Graham wanted to celebrate the New Year, so he asked me to get dressed and pour the champagne. David and Sophia apparently stockpiled a whole bunch of it." She offered a wobbly smile. "He said it might be his last New Year's, so he wanted to do it in style. I borrowed your mink—I hope you don't mind." She attempted another smile, but it failed quickly. "He wanted you, Eva. He did. I just happened to be available."

It was then that Eva noticed the bottle of champagne on the console table, the two empty champagne glasses, the lipstick mark on one of them.

"He was here." The relief removed the bones from Eva's legs, and she collapsed on the sofa. "He's alive."

Precious sat down next to her, grabbed her hands. "Yes, Eva. Sophia didn't find out until yesterday, and she didn't want to spoil the surprise. But isn't that the best news? He parachuted into the water and was picked up by a Danish fishing boat. David believes the mission was compromised, that the Germans were somehow alerted and expecting them. The Danish had to hide Graham until they could get him back to England. They weren't allowed to broadcast his name or confirm he'd survived until he reached British soil."

Eva nodded, her heart constricting in her chest, making it difficult for her to breathe. "Did you tell him where I was?"

Precious's smooth brow furrowed. "He guessed. But I told him you didn't want to go."

Eva wanted to laugh at the earnestness in Precious's face, but she was so very numb. "Is he coming back?"

Precious shook her head. "He said he might not have leave for some time."

A sob escaped from Eva's throat. Precious put an

arm around her shoulders. "He dropped something on the way out. I think it might have been meant for your Christmas gift."

Eva thought of the gold cuff links she'd bought Graham at Selfridges, how she'd saved her money to get him something special. They were shaped like dolphins, and she'd known they'd be perfect. But they were still in her wardrobe, wrapped and beribboned, waiting. "He did?"

Precious stood. "It wasn't wrapped, so I can't be sure it was meant as a gift—but it definitely seems like a present to me."

Eva's eyes stung as she remembered the day in the park when Graham had given her the ivory dolphin, and she'd told him how she felt about surprises.

Gently, Precious placed the object in Eva's outstretched palm. A small brooch in the shape of an airman's winged patch, sparkling with pavé diamonds and the letters "RAF" across the top in red stones. Eva looked at it and wanted to cry.

"It's lovely. I wish he knew that I loved it."

Precious chewed on her lip. "He . . ." She stopped.

"He what?"

"He asked me about the mink—where it had come from. He guessed it was from Alex. It was pointless to lie. He wouldn't have believed me."

Eva began to shake. "And what did he say?"

"He said . . ." Precious closed her eyes, as if she wanted to make sure she remembered correctly.

"He said for you to give his regards to Alex. That he hoped you'd be happy together."

Eva stood abruptly, her head swimming. "I've got to go to him. To explain. Where did he go?"

Precious shook her head, her eyes pooling with tears. "They're moving him to a new air base. He said he wasn't sure where."

"And then he left? He didn't say anything else?"

"Just . . ." Precious swallowed, lowering her head so the light of the chandelier turned the tips of her hair to gold.

"Just what?"

"I didn't understand it. Something about . . ." Her brow furrowed. "Something about a house by the sea being only a silly dream. I wanted to ask him what he meant so I could tell you, but he didn't wait."

Eva felt the room begin to sway and spin along with her heart and her head. Soundlessly, she slipped to the sofa, the brooch clutched tightly in her hand, cutting into the skin until she bled.

CHAPTER 28

LONDON
MAY 1940

Throughout the winter and early spring of 1940, Eva barely slept, floating through her days and nights like a ghost. She recalled her mother saying she felt dead on the inside the year they'd spent in the poorhouse. Eva had never understood how a person could continue to draw breath but feel as if they were dead. But she did now.

She spent her days at Lushtak's modeling, perfecting her acting skills by portraying a woman without any cares. The work kept her busy; it seemed the prospect of war and the new rationing hadn't yet reached Madame's clientele. They still purchased clothes for the upcoming social seasons, including appropriate hunting outfits for Scotland in the fall.

Mr. Danek would shake his head, then pocket his paycheck. One had to eat, he said.

Eva also pocketed most of her paycheck, saving larger and larger portions for her mother. She gave the money to Alex on his promise it would end up where it was intended, but he wouldn't divulge the address. It was one more thing he held from her, another tie binding her to him. One more thing for which she had no recourse. She was completely and utterly at his mercy. And she had to trust him that he was telling her the truth. She had no other option.

On her days off, and in the evenings when Alex didn't require her company, she worked side by side with Precious and Sophia in the Women's Voluntary Service, serving tea to the night wardens and running the canteen at Paddington Station for soldiers and sailors.

And waiting. Waiting for bombs to fall, for shelters to be used for more than just drills.

She had not received any word from Graham, not a letter or even a message passed on through Sophia. Sophia did keep her apprised of his whereabouts and what he was doing—as much as he was able to share—but that was all. He'd been made squadron leader, was tolerating the food, and complained of being cold when up in the air for extended periods of time; would Sophia please send him extra gloves? It was impersonal, curated by

Sophia, Eva was sure, in order to placate both her brother and her friend.

She longed to hear his voice, to hear him tell her even the dullest parts of his life. She dreamed of boating in Regent's Park with him again, reciting the poetry she'd memorized for him. Eva had written a letter a day for the month of January and had Sophia promise she'd send them on. By February she stopped, clinging to what little pride she had left and not wanting Sophia to see how pathetic she was. But she still slept with the ivory dolphin in her fist, held against her heart. Not because she thought Graham might forgive her for the transgressions he knew and those he didn't know, but to keep him safe. She could do that, at least.

As the weeks went by and Denmark, Norway, and then Belgium and the Netherlands toppled like Hitler's dominoes, newly exiled governments settled into London. Alex became more demanding of Eva's time, needing her to accompany him to various entertainments throughout the city.

There were no more matchboxes to retrieve. Instead Alex asked her to dig through the pockets of discarded evening jackets on the backs of chairs or to distract a man with her low décolletage while they danced so Alex could do the same. These men were nameless to her, the retrieval of odd bits of paper and other items seemingly meaningless. She knew she should care, that it wasn't insignificant. But she was too dead inside for any of it to matter.

"I have something for you."

They were in the backseat of his chauffeured motorcar after another interminable evening at the Suivi Club. Despite private automobiles being banned due to petrol rationing, Alex usually had his chauffeured car available to them. He pulled out a slim black velvet box, and impatiently opened it when Eva showed no inclination to do so.

A diamond bracelet sat on a bed of black velvet, the lovely gems catching the stray pieces of light in the darkened city, shimmering like an electrified snake.

"It looks expensive. Is it real?" She said it to annoy him, knowing that to question his generosity was to question his manhood.

He frowned, giving her immense satisfaction. "Of course it is. A small token to thank you for all of your good work."

"Is that what you call this petty theft? Surely you can find a pickpocket in Piccadilly Circus who's more skilled and who could be bought with a mere shilling."

He pretended to consider. "Ah, yes, but a pickpocket wouldn't be nearly as charming as you. Or have such a weakness for beautiful things."

She hated herself then. Hated recognizing the truth as she held out her arm so he could place the bracelet on her bare wrist, leaning close so he could close the clasp. She felt the weight of the diamonds, could imagine how they'd twinkle like stars under the crystal chandeliers of the places they dined and danced. The part of her that was still Ethel Maltby wanted to raise her arm to show everyone, to prove that she was more than who she'd been. But the new Eva wanted to howl with her own disappointment that she hadn't changed at all.

Alex looked up, meeting her eyes without drawing back. "Do you like it?" he whispered.

"Yes."

She let him kiss her then. She kept her eyes open and didn't push him away. But she didn't kiss him back. He lifted his head, and she felt the unspoken question.

"I'm not a whore who can be bought."

He sat back in his seat, straightened his cuffs. "Everyone has a price. Even you. It's only a matter of time. Just know that I'll be waiting. Anticipating your surrender."

He turned to face her, his expression hidden in the shadows of the backseat. "You do know what you're doing isn't petty theft, yes? That this is all much more serious."

Something in his tone made her shiver in her fur. When she didn't respond, he settled back against his seat. "You remember Lord Merton, don't you?"

"Of course. He was killed in a burglary." She closed her eyes, saw the photograph in the paper. Remembered Alex's threat about Precious or Sophia ending up like Lord Merton. How she'd told herself she didn't understand, refusing to acknowledge an inconvenient truth.

"He was a Nazi spy. He was killed by his own countrymen for passing secrets to the enemy. Secrets hidden in a matchbox."

Eva began trembling violently, her frozen bones crackling in her skin. She took two deep breaths, focused on keeping her voice steady. "So I was responsible?"

She could hear the smile in his voice. "In one way or another, yes."

She was silent, searching for the right words. The right question. Knowing the answer before she voiced it. "But I gave the matchbox to you."

Now he laughed out loud. "Yes, you did. And I made good use of it. I paid Lord Merton a good deal of money for it, too."

She faced him, staring through the darkness, swallowing back the sob she knew he wanted to hear. "I don't want to do this anymore. I've paid my dues. Tell Graham what you want. I don't care anymore. Just tell me where my mother is. She and I will find another place to live, and you will be done with me. Please, release me. Please. I can't be a part of this."

A slow, throaty chuckle emerged from the darkness beside her. "I'm afraid it's too late, darling Eva. You're already a woman without a country. That makes you the enemy to everyone. If you were to walk away, you'd meet the same fate as Lord Merton. Your friends, too, just to prove a point. Even your St. John wouldn't be safe."

She was light-headed, sparks of light like diamonds shooting across her eyes. "How do you live with yourself?" she asked, no longer able to keep the tremor from her voice.

He leaned closer to her, and she could feel his anger. "Because I know which side I stand on, which is always better than straddling a line. Something to remember, Eva—feigning innocence does not make you innocent."

She turned her face to the window so he couldn't see her tears.

When it was time to get out of the car, he turned to her again. "Listen carefully. I have a new job for you."

She looked at him, hating him. Hating herself. "What is it?"

He smiled, knowing he'd won. "I need you to visit the London Library in St. James's Square tomorrow morning after ten o'clock. Check out **Alice's Adventures in Wonderland**. It will be misshelved. The location is written on the piece of paper you took from the purse of the woman seated next to you tonight. If you believe someone is watching you, come back later in the day. There will be an envelope inside. I need you to deliver the envelope to thirty-seven Chester Terrace. Slip it into the mail slot on the door, and do it at night so no one sees you. You'll do this every Thursday, each week a different book and a different time of day, always misshelved. The pickup time and the location of the next book will be written in invisible ink on the title page of each book. You will need a heat source to read it—Jiri will show you. Destroy the page when you've memorized it."

She felt the driver's eyes on her in the rearview mirror, and a violent tremor made her jaw ache. She recalled the letters from Graham she'd given to Alex, which then had been returned to her with singe marks between the lines, and she thought she might be ill.

"And if I say no?"

The gleam of his teeth in the moonlight mocked her as he smiled. "Oh, my dear, we both know you won't."

The door shut, and the car pulled away. Eva stood still for a long time, watching it disappear until she could no longer hear the engine, feeling an unfamiliar weight on her arm. She looked down and saw Alex's bracelet, the diamonds throwing back the reflected glow of a dimmed headlight like stars in the black, black night.

On a rare day off, Eva walked with Precious into the Palm Court of the Ritz Hotel to meet Sophia for tea. As always, when the two of them were together, heads turned; people stared as if they'd never seen two tall blond women together. It made Precious giggle, but Eva remained pointedly unaware of the attention. It was something she'd learned from watching Sophia and her debutante friends, the women who'd been taught proper deportment from the cradle.

Besides, she was completely and gloriously drunk. She'd found it was the only way she could face each day and the reality that Graham could have been in the midst of an air battle, that she might not see him again. At one of the dinners she'd attended at Sophia's, an obnoxious guest had mentioned that the fatality rate for airmen in combat was fifty percent. At Sophia's look of distress, David had asked the gentleman to leave.

She also needed to forget why she went to the London Library once a week to check out a new book. How she'd find an empty envelope between the pages and slip it through the mail slot of the house in Chester Terrace under cover of darkness.

The only way to make her self-loathing go away was to drink the endless supply of fine Scottish whisky Alex presented her with. She neither knew nor cared where or how it had been procured. When drunk, she could speak without slurring her words and could even manage walking in a relatively straight line. As could her father—up to a point. She supposed that was the one useful thing she'd inherited from him.

The opulent Palm Court, with its glass ceiling,

enormous Corinthian columns, and full-grown potted palm trees, bustled and thrummed. Waiters sped to and from full tables as if a war weren't being waged on the other side of the Channel.

Sophia stood to greet Precious and Eva, kissing them each on the cheek. She smiled warmly, pretended that she didn't smell the whisky on Eva's breath, and chattered through tea. But she kept rattling her cup in its saucer and adding sugar to a cup already oversweetened.

Eva caught her arm as Sophia reached for the sugar bowl for the third time. "What's wrong? Is it David?" He'd applied for active duty more than once, but he'd failed his medical examinations twice on account of a minor heart condition that wouldn't affect day-to-day life but exempted him from active duty. He'd been permanently assigned a desk in the War Office, which he took as an affront to his manhood. He'd already applied for yet another medical examination, just to be sure.

Sophia shook her head. "No. It's not David."

Eva's blood froze. She'd been at Horvath's just that morning with Mr. Danek. Again he'd shown her the map of Europe, the defensive Maginot Line on the French–German border that many were calling impenetrable. But with Germany's invasion of Belgium on the tenth of May, it was entirely conceivable that the German armies could bypass the line completely by cutting through Belgium. And once they got through Belgium, France and the

English Channel would be the only things standing between England and the Germans.

Despite the early hour, Eva had gone back to the flat and poured a healthy serving of whisky. She remembered what it had been like when Graham had been missing before, and that was for only a short time. She couldn't imagine a lifetime of missing him. Of knowing she'd be given no more chances to tell him she loved him. To tell him the truth. To ask his forgiveness.

She'd fallen asleep on the couch and woken hours later to Precious telling her she needed to get ready for tea. Precious had fixed Eva's hair and makeup and helped her dress, her hands gentle, her words consoling and free of any criticism about the empty glass on the table or the stale stench of whisky on her breath. And now, staring across the table at Graham's sister, Eva was grateful for the alcoholic haze. "It's Graham, then."

A waiter appeared, bringing more tea, fussing over setting out the cakes and sandwiches, making Eva want to scream at him to stop.

Sophia waited until he left, keeping her gaze down, her voice quiet. "You're not to know this—I heard it from David. The RAF is sending fifteen squadrons to France. It's all a disaster, and our boys are trapped on the coast. They've started an evacuation."

"But those are the foot soldiers," Eva said quietly.

Precious put a hand on her arm. "They need air

cover. To protect the men being evacuated. It's what Graham's been trained for. He's ready."

Eva turned to Precious. "How do you know that?"

Precious shared a look with Sophia before taking Eva's hand. "Graham was on leave, a week ago."

"Graham was here—in London?" The joy of knowing he'd been safe a week ago was quickly tempered by the fact that he'd been so close to her and hadn't let her know.

"Yes," Sophia said quietly. "It was only for two days. He stayed with David and me."

"And you didn't think to tell me?"

"I'm sorry, Eva. I don't know what happened between you two, but I know he's hurt, too. I begged him to let me tell you, but he wouldn't allow it."

"I see," Eva said, and did a remarkable job of sipping her tea and replacing the cup without rattling it in the saucer. "Did he . . . ?"

"I could tell that he wanted to ask about you," Precious said. She chewed on her lower lip. "I went to Sophia's to pick up a pair of her old drapes for my bedroom, and he was there. He—"

"He thought it was you," Sophia interrupted. "Precious walked into the drawing room, and the light from the window altered the shade of her hair, and she looked so much like you. He thought it **was** you until she spoke. He seemed happy at first. And then . . ." She stopped, looked at Precious as if for encouragement. "He became despondent, although he didn't tell us why."

"And you didn't tell me." Eva carefully replaced her teacup on the saucer; the smell of the delicious cakes was making her nauseous.

"He asked us not to," Precious said, her large blue eyes filling with tears. "He said he couldn't afford to be distracted."

"He didn't want to . . . ," Eva started, wishing she had the choice not to see Graham's face every time she closed her eyes. "And he's flying over France. Right now."

Sophia nodded. "Somewhere over the Channel, at least. Many of the British Expeditionary Force and their allies are stranded on the coast in a place called Dunkirk. Graham's been there for two days already to protect the British ships." She stared at her cup of tea, grown cold, the curdling milk floating at the top. She glanced around the table, ensuring nobody could eavesdrop, before adding, "David said that the navy has requisitioned private vessels to help rescue as many men as they can. It's all quite . . . bewildering."

Sophia's eyes glistened, and Eva looked away, unwilling to share that particular weakness. She stared at her empty teacup, wishing it were full of numbing whisky.

"Don't, Eva. Drinking is not going to help."

Eva looked into Precious's wide, innocent eyes. "It's all I've got." The last word ended on a sob.

"We'll get through this together. Just like we have since we first met."

Eva nodded, but only so Precious would stop talking. Stop looking at her with pity. She hated to be pitied. She was meant to be envied.

Sophia made a small strangled sound in her throat, and the three of them turned to the entrance of the Palm Court. David stood there, dark and morose, his hat in his hands, his gaze moving about the room until it settled on their table. He greeted them somberly, kissing his wife on the cheek before pulling out the fourth chair and joining them.

"What is it, David? Is there news of Graham?" Sophia's voice was steady, belying the trembling in her fingers.

He nodded, just once. "I'm afraid it's not good."

They remained seated, as if this were no more than a passing conversation. David placed his hand on his wife's shoulder. Precious reached for Eva's hand and held it tightly while Sophia looked stoically at her husband.

"This is premature, you understand," David said quietly. "We won't receive confirmation until tomorrow, and the public . . ." He looked down at his feet, embarrassed. "The War Office will decide how much to release to the press and when to release it."

"Please, David. What is it?" Sophia did her best to put on her brave face, but her lower lip trembled.

"Graham and two other Spitfire pilots in his squadron were in a dogfight with a Messerschmitt over the Channel last evening." David paused, collected himself. Cleared his throat. "Witnesses saw

Graham take a hit. His plane caught fire. He jettisoned the canopy in time, and his parachute was seen hitting the water. A British vessel rescued him from the burning wreckage, and he's being transported to hospital. There has been no confirming information, but his injuries are reported to be quite severe. Queen Victoria Hospital, where he's being sent, is the absolute best for burns. I made inquiries and have been assured there is no better place for him to recuperate."

Sophia remained ramrod straight in her chair, the only sign of her distress the handkerchief pressed to her mouth. "Does Mother know?"

David shook his head.

"Good. Let us allow her a few more hours of peace, shall we?" She focused on the plate in front of her. "I'll have to take the train up to Surrey so I can tell Mother in person. I don't have enough ration coupons for petrol and besides, our chauffeur has left us for the army, so it will have to be the train," she said matter-of-factly. "Mother won't want Father to know. It could kill him."

A delicate frown marred her face as she looked up at David. "I should go to Graham—he'll need someone. They do say that patients heal sooner if surrounded by loved ones."

David gave his wife such a tender smile that Eva had to look away. "Darling, I understand, but is that wise in your condition?"

Sophia blushed prettily, avoiding looking at her

table companions. She had already lost two pregnancies, and her doctor had given her strict orders not to exert herself. She'd cut back her hours with the WVS without telling Eva why, and Eva had been too distracted to guess.

"I'll go," Eva said without hesitation. "I can put to use all of my good training with the WVS, wrapping wounds and such. I can be useful." She almost bit her tongue on that last word.

Both Sophia and David looked at her with alarm. David spoke first. "That's very generous of you, Eva, but considering . . . Well, I don't think he'd welcome your presence right now. It might even hinder his healing."

Sophia nodded, her face strained. "I'm afraid David's right, Eva. I know your heart hurts as much as ours do, but we have to think about what's best for Graham. You do understand, don't you?"

Eva wanted to argue, to tell them that she loved him, that surely her love would be healing. But he'd been in London a week ago and hadn't wanted to see her. If she continued to press, they would undoubtedly remind her of that, and another piece of her heart would break off, and that would surely kill her.

"Then I should go," Precious said.

"No," Eva said, not thinking of how it might sound, glad for the whisky to blunt the sharp edges. She shook her head to emphasize the one word, the world spinning around her. She understood why they were saying she shouldn't be the one to go, yet she couldn't even voice the reasons why she didn't want Precious to go.

Precious spoke with a soothing tone, as if to a child. "Graham considers me a friend, and I'd be a familiar face. I've learned how to bandage wounds alongside you and Sophia, and I'm not squeamish. I might be able to help him get better sooner so that he can return to you."

Eva had stopped shaking her head, realizing that neither Sophia nor David was going to agree on her behalf.

Precious continued. "You can fill in for me at Lushtak's, Eva, since we wear the same size. Madame is quite patriotic and will do whatever we ask if it's to help the war cause, right?"

Eva forced her head to nod, afraid that if she moved it more than that, it might shatter.

Sophia smiled tentatively. "That's very generous of you, Precious, but . . ."

"I know it's not ideal—you or Eva would be much better at this than I am. But that's just not possible right now. Please, let me help. You have been so kind to me. Please, let me do this for you. Please."

Her gaze moved among Sophia, David, and Eva. As if Eva had any say at all.

"We'll have to arrange transportation and accommodation, get permission and that sort of thing . . . ," David began.

"Which you will take care of. It's what you do

best." Sophia smiled at her husband, softening her words. "It's settled, then. I'll go shopping for a few things I know he likes. . . ."

"May I?" Eva asked. "May I do that one thing so that I'm left not feeling quite so helpless?"

"Of course, dear. He likes . . ."

"Sandalwood soap." She could smell him, the softness of his neck as she pressed her lips there. She hadn't meant to say that right there. But she caught the scent of him, as if he were sitting at the table next to her.

David cleared his throat. "I'll go see his man at Truefitt and Hill and pick up a few shaving things he prefers. They have the sandalwood soap Graham has used since I've known him."

Eva swallowed, forcing a smile that hid how utterly and completely cut off from Graham she felt. "That's a wonderful idea. I'm sure familiarity is just what he needs." She pictured him in a hospital bed as Precious slathered shaving cream on his chin. Precious, not her. Her chest stung, and she wondered if she might be bleeding.

"All right, then," Sophia said, standing while David solicitously helped her out of her chair and took her arm. "It's settled. We'll let you know as soon as the arrangements are made—which could be as early as tomorrow morning. Can you be ready?"

Precious nodded eagerly. "Yes. I'll pack tonight."

They said their good-byes, leaving Precious and Eva on the sidewalk, staring into the verdant expanse of Green Park across from the Ritz. People walked their dogs and strolled amiably as if everything were in order. But it wasn't. It never would be again.

Precious let out a loud sob, not even trying to hide it. Eva put all of her energy into feeling scornful for the outward show of emotion, for not understanding the proper etiquette for such a situation. But was there any to begin with? She was only just realizing that if she focused on things outside of herself, she could walk quickly away from the hotel, listening to the click of her heels as they propelled her forward. Hear the sounds of the traffic. The whistle of a policeman. She was a spectator at the cinema, watching this person on the screen, watching her behave as if everything were fine.

"Eva, stop. Please."

She turned, dry-eyed, and waited for Precious to catch up to her. Precious reached for her hands, but Eva shook her off. "We should hurry. I'm sure you've got washing to do. I'll help you."

Precious nodded, sniffling. The only handkerchief Eva had in her pocket was Graham's, the monogrammed one he'd given to her on the day they'd met. She wouldn't give it to Precious. She couldn't.

The following day when David arrived in a government car to collect Precious, Eva walked down with her, cheerful and optimistic. Acting, always acting. She was getting quite good at it.

When Precious turned to hug her good-bye, Eva handed her the book of Wordsworth poetry

Graham had given her. "He might enjoy this being read to him if he's not up to reading himself yet." Eva hesitated before pulling the ivory dolphin from her pocket. "I want you to take good care of this and bring it back. Do you understand? Let Graham know that you have it, that it will be his good-luck charm until he gets better. And tell him . . ." Her composure slipped, but just for a moment. She smiled brightly. "Tell him that I will expect him to return it to me personally when he's back in London."

Precious started crying again, and Eva wanted to shake her, to let her know that tears were worthless. "I'll take good care of him for you," Precious said. "I promise. I'll make sure he returns to you. He does love you, Eva. I know he does."

Eva forced a reassuring smile. "Just make sure he gets better and bring him back to me."

Precious nodded once, then slid into the car next to David. Eva turned her back on the departing car, remembering what Precious had told her, how you should never watch a person leave because then you'd never see them again. She climbed the steps without turning around, but stood waiting at the front doors until the sound of the car's engine had been absorbed by the thrum of the morning traffic.

CHAPTER 29

LONDON
MAY 2019

I sat next to Colin and his parents in the well-appointed waiting room at Princess Grace Hospital in Marylebone. It was a strangely soothing room with tasteful furniture and an appealing lack of clown paintings and other medical office art on the quiet silver-gray walls. The absence of cracked orange vinyl chairs and linoleum tiles made it easier to pretend that I wasn't in a hospital. If it weren't for the worried faces of Colin and his parents, I could have easily imagined I was anywhere else.

Arabella had called for the ambulance after Precious collapsed. She had been breathing, and conscious, but not entirely lucid when they'd placed her in the ambulance. I kept asking every medical professional we encountered if she would be okay, the reality that she might die hitting me with a force I hadn't expected. I knew she was old, and I couldn't completely forget Precious telling me that being old was her punishment. But it was still too soon. Her story was not yet completely written.

Colin looked at his watch again, the third time in thirty minutes. "I wish they'd tell us something more conclusive than that she's stabilized and sleeping comfortably."

"They said they'd let us know as soon as she wakes," Penelope soothed. "Although it's quite late. She might sleep until morning. You two should go home and get some rest."

"Just a while longer," Colin said. "In case she wakes up and needs reassurance."

Penelope smiled at her son. "Your father and I are here—and we promise to call you when she awakens. You should have left with Arabella. You both have to be at work in the morning, and there's nothing you can do here."

"I'd like to wait, too," I said.

Penelope tapped her index finger against her chin. "Did you notice any mental confusion prior to her collapse?"

I thought for a moment. "Earlier in the day she had put on an old evening gown and was frantically looking for that photograph of Graham and not making a lot of sense. She calmed down once we found it. And last night she was reciting poetry from memory—a Wordsworth poem." I frowned.

"But she also said something strange. When I asked her what took her so long to come back to London, she said she waited until she was ready to face her past."

Penelope frowned. "Whatever could she have meant by that?"

"I have no idea. She went to sleep right afterward, so I couldn't ask her." **And then I threw myself on your son and forgot all about Precious.** I looked away, feeling the heat rising up my neck.

Colin's father stood and began pacing, his hands shoved deep into his pockets. I remembered from school that Colin had done the same thing when we'd been studying together, saying it helped him think.

"What was the name again? The name Precious said," James asked. "Was it Alec?"

"Alex. I think she was referring to Alexander Grof. I saw his name in some of the captions of pictures from **The Tatler**. He was photographed several times with Precious at several social functions. He was at Sophia's wedding, too."

James nodded slowly, silently contemplating. I studied him, wondering again what it was that was so familiar to me about him. "Any idea who he was?"

I shook my head. "She had quite a large social circle, so someone from her 'set,' as they used to call it."

Penelope looked up from a magazine she'd been flipping through. "I don't remember Sophia ever mentioning him, so he might have been just a hanger-on. The gossip pages aren't always the best source for determining who's actually a friend."

"True," I said. "Although if he wasn't important, why was he Precious's last conscious thought before she collapsed?"

"That's a very good question," Penelope agreed. "And one that we can all contemplate tomorrow after we've had a good night's sleep."

"I think you're right. I'm so bleary headed, I feel like a bagel in a bucket of grits." I stood, vaguely aware of Colin suppressing a laugh as his parents stared at me. "Just promise you'll call."

Penelope stood, too, and kissed me on the cheek. Then she faced her son. "Colin, please, make sure Maddie gets home safely?"

"I'm fine, really," I said. "If you want to go out with friends or whatever, I can find my way back on my own." I'd avoided meeting Colin's eyes the whole night, replaying over and over in my head the events of the previous evening. I had almost called Aunt Cassie for her advice, had reached for my phone multiple times before I talked myself out of it. Because she would only tell me what I already knew—that I was confused and unsure, not willing to let go of a lifetime's worth of self-denial and a strongly held belief that my life had a known outcome and a specified number of years assigned to it. She would have couched it in different terms, though. She would have just called me an idiot.

Colin was already moving toward the exit. Not wanting to argue in front of Penelope and James, I said my good-byes and followed him out into the cool spring evening.

"You don't have to talk to me if you don't want to," he said, already looking for a taxi, striding ahead with his hands shoved into his pockets.

I rubbed my hands on my bare arms. It had been warmer in the afternoon when we'd rushed Precious to the hospital, and I was wearing a sleeveless blouse.

"Here," Colin said, slipping his sweater over his head and handing it to me. "I remember you always being cold and never having the proper clothing. It must be an American thing."

He wore a long-sleeved shirt underneath, so I didn't feel guilty accepting the sweater. "Probably more of a Southern thing," I corrected. I pulled the sweater over my head, feeling his body heat against my bare skin, smelling the clean, soapy scent of him that clung to the fibers. I resisted the impulse to bury my nose in the knit and breathe deeply. The sleeves were way too long, and I let them dangle.

"Can we walk back?" I asked. "I'm exhausted, but it's not that far. I need to clear my head."

"Yes, that bagel in a bowl of grits must be difficult to overcome."

I gave him a playful elbow in the ribs, and he groaned with exaggerated pain.

"Sure," he said, falling into step beside me as we made our way to Marylebone Road.

We walked in silence as I breathed in a lungful of air, trying to calm my racing thoughts. I loved London's deep purple sky on clear nights, the city's glow creating a bruised halo on the horizon. But over Regent's Park, where there was no competition from artificial lights, I could see the stars.

"Do you think she'll be all right?" I asked, finally voicing the thought that had been pecking at my head since we'd rushed Precious to the hospital.

"She's almost one hundred, Madison. It wouldn't be out of the realm of possibility that it's simply her time. And believe me, I hate saying that as much as you probably hate hearing it."

I swallowed, nodded. "She told me she went to France to escape her ghosts. And that living this long has been her punishment. I'm not sure what to make of that."

I felt him looking at me, but I didn't turn my head. "Neither am I. I've never heard her say that."

"I'm wondering if bringing up all these old memories hasn't been good for her health."

"Arabella said the same thing." A car passed by, the sound of an orchestra pealing out from an open rear window, then fading as the car sped away.

"Do you agree?" I asked.

"No. I actually think Nana's relieved. It's cathartic. You seem to have given her a new purpose, something to achieve before she dies."

Now I did look at him. "How have **I** become something for her to achieve?"

"Well, imagine living most of your life holding on to some burden, something for which you believe you need to be forgiven. You plan on taking it to your grave. And then, just when you think it's too late, you see the opportunity to unburden yourself. To perhaps make dying not so hard to contemplate."

"But she could have chosen anyone—you or Arabella, for instance."

"True. But maybe she chose you because you're blood related. Or she just saw an opportunity to help someone avoid the same mistakes she's made."

I stopped walking and faced him. "Just stop right there. Regardless of what Precious does or doesn't think, you can't make assumptions. You know virtually nothing about me."

A cool breeze lifted the hair from his forehead, making him look somehow boyish. Vulnerable. "I know you more than you think."

I turned away and resumed walking, faster than before. "We're not talking about this now."

"Later, then?"

I shook my head vigorously. "No."

"All right. But can we talk about something else? We have about eight blocks to go."

"Depends—about what?"

"I didn't get to tell you earlier because of what's happening with Nana, but Mother heard from Hyacinth Ponsonby. About Graham. We found him post–nineteen forty."

I slowed down. "And? Where was he? What was he doing?"

"Do you want the official title or what he was actually doing?"

"They're not the same thing?"

"Not exactly. After Graham was shot down over the Channel, his injuries prevented him from returning to the RAF, so he secured a position in the War Office. He was assigned to work in the map room in Churchill's basement war rooms."

"How did he do that? Doesn't a person have to know someone to jump from flying planes to that sort of position?"

"Well, he came from an aristocratic family, but you're right. One doesn't 'get a job' at the War Office without some sort of background. Or, as you said, knowing someone. Apparently, Great-uncle Graham had both. Hyacinth, bless her, did some digging into his life before the war. She discovered that he read Persian and Arabic at Christ Church, Oxford—apparently he was quite proficient with foreign languages; his government files show that he spoke at least six, including German." He raised his eyebrows at this last. "He also learned to fly at Oxford, as a sort of hobby, I suppose. Following Oxford, he joined the Diplomatic Service and was sent to Burma. He also flew while he was overseas. His earlier training meant he was able to jump through some of the basic RAF training requirements. He flew his first mission—reconnaissance, not actual fighting—in December nineteen thirty-nine, after joining the RAF in July of that year."

"Smart guy or a fast learner?" I asked.

"Most likely both. I am related to him, after all."

I pressed my lips together so I wouldn't laugh, and rolled my eyes. "That was his official position. But what was his real role post–nineteen forty?"

He turned to me and grinned. "It's what we suspected."

I stopped in the middle of the deserted sidewalk, making Colin stop, too. "Get out! MI-Six? Like James Bond?"

"Close. MI-Five. Roughly speaking, MI-Six were our spies overseas, whereas MI-Five operatives were here in England looking for **their** spies. Graham's 'cover,' so to speak, was the War Office."

"Wow," I said. "I didn't expect that. Although . . ." I smacked my forehead, remembering the box of purses. "Was one of the languages he knew Czech?"

"I believe so. Why?"

"Arabella and I found a scribbled note on the back of a Savoy menu, stuck inside one of the old purses. We found it right before Precious collapsed, so I completely forgot about it until just now, when you said 'MI-Five.' It was written in Czech, and it said something like 'You're in danger—run.' According to the translation app, anyway. Maybe Eva was Czechoslovakian?"

He rubbed his chin. "Could be. There were a lot

of Czech refugees in England during the war, so it's certainly possible. But why the cryptic note?"

"There's no way of knowing, is there? Unless Precious tells us."

Our eyes met in mutual understanding. "Then we'll wait until she fully recovers and ask her." Colin spoke so matter-of-factly that I could have almost believed the world would unfold the way he predicted.

We resumed walking. "So, when did Graham die?" I asked.

"Now, there's a good question. Precious told us that she saw him off and on in nineteen forty and early nineteen forty-one, and then he and Eva disappeared from her life. Hyacinth can't find anything related to an Eva Harlow, nor can she find a date or a place of death for Graham. She hasn't given up, of course. She's quite keen on the challenge of finding out what happened to him. She believes it's very untidy of the government archives to be missing this information, and she is bound and determined to put it to rights."

As we approached Harley House, my steps slowed. "Just out of curiosity, when did William die? I keep thinking about Sophia's parents, losing their elder son in the war and not knowing what happened to the second one. It must have been awful. I guess that's why it wasn't spoken about around your father."

"Most likely—how very British of us. But from what I remember, William was killed toward the beginning of the war. He wasn't married and had no children. My father said it was lonely growing up without siblings or cousins."

"And your father was born in nineteen forty-one, correct?"

"Yes, that's right. And then waited until he was practically in his dotage before getting married and having children. My mother is a good decade younger than he is. But according to my parents, their late start wasn't for lack of trying. Not that I wanted them to elaborate, of course."

"Of course." I placed my hand on the outside railing of the steps leading up to our block of flats and led the way inside, choosing the stairs instead of the lift, unwilling to be with Colin in a confined space. I put my key into the front door and walked inside, almost tripping over George, who had apparently been waiting for Colin. I scratched behind his ears, happy to have something to keep my hands occupied. "I'd offer you some Scotch, but I remember what happened last time."

"Would that be such a bad thing?"

The small hallway lamp illuminated his smile, and I had the sudden impulse to kiss him. Instead I slipped his sweater over my head and handed it back. "Yes, it probably would." I paused, trying to remember the name on the valise label. "By the way, are you familiar with the last name Nash?"

He thought for a moment. "Not personally, no. Just the famous architect of Regent's Park, John Nash, but he died nearly two hundred years ago. Why?"

"I'll show you tomorrow. I'm feeling more and more like that bagel."

He smiled. "Well, then. Go get some sleep." He didn't move away. "Are we ever going to talk about last night?"

"I'd rather not."

"That's very British of you, you know."

"Yeah, it probably is. I guess London is rubbing off on me."

He nodded. "I'm going to take George and stay at my parents' town house in Cadogan Gardens. I need to get more clothes."

I wondered if that was the whole reason and felt a little satisfaction in knowing it probably wasn't.

"Well, then," he said again. "Good night, Maddie."

"Good night, Colin."

I latched the door behind him and was halfway to my room when I realized he'd called me Maddie.

CHAPTER 30

LONDON
AUGUST 1940

Throughout the summer, while Eva worked double the hours at Lushtak's to fill in for her friend, Precious dutifully sent letters to both Sophia and Eva detailing Graham's condition. Eva had a newfound respect for her American friend, admiring her carefully chosen words, which were meant to truthfully inform and not alarm. The letters arrived biweekly, Precious's surprisingly bold yet elegant handwriting sprawled across the envelopes.

In the beginning, Precious spent more time discussing Graham's injuries and the doctors' hopes for his recovery. He'd suffered burns to his back and to his hands as well as a broken arm, smashed ribs, and a broken nose. And a crushed leg. It wasn't until her third letter that Precious informed Eva that the doctors were afraid that the injuries to his leg were extensive enough to cause permanent debilitation. Graham might never walk again.

Eva had rushed to Sophia's to console her, only to be told by David at the front door that Sophia had been ordered by her doctor to stay in bed for the duration of her pregnancy, and that David had deemed it best to keep any bad news from her.

Alone, Eva had gone back to the flat and drunk half a bottle of Alex's whisky. Before showing up for work, she gargled with lavender water and spritzed on a heavy dose of Vol de Nuit. It wasn't that she couldn't bear to think of Graham never walking or dancing again. Or driving a car or flying a plane, all those things he loved to do. What mattered was that he was alive. And as long as he was alive, she would be waiting for him whether he wanted her to or not.

"You're not fooling anyone, you know," Mr. Danek said as he dipped a brush into a mascara pot.

"What do you mean?"

"I still smell the whisky, and the perfume hides nothing. You shouldn't drink alone, my dear. It's bad for the soul."

Taking his words to heart, Eva brought the rest of the bottle to Horvath's after work, and she and Mr. Danek shared it while she sat, dry-eyed. He plied her with coffee and food, dishes placed in front of her by seemingly invisible hands.

"You need to eat," he said, pushing yet another plate forward. "When St. John returns, he'll need you to be strong for him."

"But he doesn't want me."

"Of course he does. The heart remains faithful even when the head tells it otherwise." He patted her hand. "Have you written to him?"

"Yes." She looked down at the table to hide burgeoning tears. "Only short postcards—Sophia said we shouldn't tire him overly much. But he's never written back." She choked on the last word.

Mr. Danek patted her hand. "He is injured, yes? It could be very difficult for him to write. Have you considered that? But he will surely want to hear your words. They will help him heal."

Eva felt a glimmer of hope somewhere in her alcoholic haze. "You're right. Thank you, Mr. Danek. I will. I will! I'll write to him right now." She stood and hugged the older man, then kissed his scruffy cheek, making him blush.

She rushed back to the empty flat and wrote her first long letter to Graham. She took her time, discarding precious paper as she perfected her penmanship, trying to make it look as refined and feminine as Sophia's. She'd been practicing, and it looked more natural than her earlier attempts, more graceful.

When she was done, she sealed the letter in an envelope and enclosed it inside a larger one with a letter to Precious, instructing her to give it to Graham when he was capable of reading it himself. Her words were meant for Graham alone; she hoped he would feel the love expressed in each line, hoped he would forgive her. That he would write back.

She waited each morning for the slam of the post slot in the door. But as the days, and then weeks, and finally two months passed, she began to lose hope. Even Alex commented on her despondency, which she didn't bother trying to hide from him. Whether or not he guessed the reason for it, he never asked, and she didn't offer an explanation. To cheer her, he plied her with more and more expensive gifts—jewelry and perfume, black-market items such as French champagne and silk stockings. She accepted them, unwilling to use any of the gifts but equally unwilling to reject them. It was as if the two persons inside of her were at an impasse, fighting over who would survive.

In desperation, Eva wrote to Precious, asking for reassurance that Graham had received her letters. Precious's response was quick and precise, offering only that he had gotten them. Eva's despair was tempered by the news in the same letter that Graham's recovery was going better than expected, that much to the surprise and delight of his doctors, he was already up and walking with crutches. Graham had become a hero to the other wounded men, an example of what will and fortitude might accomplish.

Eva wrote one more letter, her fifth, knowing she couldn't write any more and retain what pride she still possessed.

My dearest Graham,

Precious tells me you have made miraculous progress with your recovery. I expected no less from you, darling. My only wish is that I could have been the one to nurse you, but I'm not going to spend time thinking about what-ifs and if-onlies and will just be grateful that you are well on your way to recovery.

I love you so very much, and only wish for one letter, one word from you, to let me know you haven't forgotten me. That you still love me. Please, darling. Forgive me for any sins I have committed, whether imagined or real. I can say with a clear conscience that I have never willingly done anything to hurt you. My heart is yours and always will be.

You promised me once that you would always love me. Do you remember? That day in the park, when the sirens were sounding and we were alone in our secret

tunnel. You promised me, and I know you to be a man of your word.

I still dream of our house by the sea. Promise me that you dream of it, too. And that when this war is over, we will build it together. Come back to me, darling. I will always love you. It will always only be you.

Yours forever,
Eva

The only response she received was from Precious, letting her know that Graham continued to recover and was expected to be sent home soon. With that hope in her heart, she rushed to visit Sophia, who was still on bed rest but who always welcomed visitors.

Sophia sat up in her enormous bed cushioned by dozens of pillows and wearing a white fox fur bed jacket. She looked thin and drawn, not at all like a happy expectant mother should. Her hands were cold and clammy, almost clawlike as she gripped Eva's. Eva kissed each rouged cheek, trying to remain cheerful.

"You're looking beautiful," Eva said, sitting on the edge of the bed.

"Liar," said Sophia with a warm smile. "But I'll take it. You and David are all I need for my ego."

"Is everything . . . all right?" Eva asked, always

unsure how to approach Sophia regarding her pregnancies. With each one, Sophia had grown more and more hopeful, and with each loss, her grief had been deeper and longer.

Sophia waved her hand, as if refusing a selection of desserts. "My doctor remains optimistic, as does David." She smiled bravely.

"And you?"

Her smile waned. "I try not to think about it. I don't think I could bear it again. And we do so want children."

Eva smiled. "And you shall have them. Determination seems to be in the St. John blood."

She waited while a maid arrived to set up tea on Sophia's bed tray. Eager to continue the conversation, Sophia dismissed her and asked Eva to pour.

"Isn't it marvelous news that Graham will be coming home soon? Could we have hoped for a better miracle?"

Sophia's smile faltered. "Did you not hear?"

"Hear what?" Eva remained composed, unsure of what Sophia might say.

"Oh," she began, and paused as she spent a longer time than necessary preparing her tea and stirring it. Avoiding Eva's gaze, she took a sip and said, "Graham returned yesterday, via a military transport. And just as marvelous, David has found him a flat on Tufton Street near Whitehall, where he'll be working alongside David in the War Office."

"Graham's here? In London?" Eva welcomed

the sound of the blood rushing through her ears, because it meant she couldn't hear the small voice telling her that he'd been in London for a day and hadn't let her know.

"Yes, I would have thought Precious might have told you."

Eva shook her head. "She hasn't. And where is Precious? She hasn't returned to the flat."

Sophia frowned. "Surely she wrote you? Has the morning post not yet arrived?"

Eva felt an odd sense of relief as she shook her head. "No."

"Precious left a few days before Graham. She volunteered to escort a blinded airman back to his home near Bristol. Horribly out of the way, but she thought it best to take the place of a Red Cross nurse who has more training, since all the man needed was someone to be his eyes for a few days. She should be back any day now."

Eva's throat burned as if she'd swallowed molten lead, but she kept smiling. "How thoughtful of Precious—sounds just like something she'd do."

"It does, doesn't it?" Sophia squeezed her eyebrows together. "I am sorry to hear that Graham hasn't been in touch. If I were up and about, I would have had a welcome-home party and invited you, but . . ."

"No, of course. I completely understand. You should rest and not worry about anything but keeping yourself and your baby safe."

Sophia smiled, placated. "I'm sure he'll come around." Carefully replacing her cup in its saucer, she said, "Dear Eva, I don't know what happened, but I do know Graham still loves you. I can tell because he won't talk about you." Her lips lifted slightly. "That's what Esme Moncrieffe—one of the girls presented at court with me—always said was how she could tell when a man was truly in love. And you still love him?"

Eva nodded, too close to tears to speak.

"Then it will all work out. Mark my words. Love always finds a way." She made a small grimace and put her hand to her stomach.

"Are you all right?" Eva moved to the door. "Should I go fetch someone?"

Sophia shook her head. "No, no. I'm all right. Perhaps I overindulged, but Cook has been doing her best to tempt me with all of my favorites." She gave Eva a smile. "If you could ring for the maid to remove the tray, I think I'll get some rest now. That's probably all I need."

Eva looked at her with worry as she reached over and rang the silver bell on Sophia's bed stand. "Only if you're quite sure."

"Quite sure. You are such a dear, Eva." Sophia paused. "Would you like me to tell Graham that you were asking for him?"

Eva almost said yes. But she still had her pride, for what that was worth. It seemed to be the only thing she did possess anymore. "No. He's read my letters, and he knows where I stand. If he wants to see me, he knows where to find me." She leaned down and kissed Sophia on the cheek. "But thank you. You are very kind. I want you to rest and not worry about anything but your baby, all right?"

Eva passed the maid on the way out, pausing only long enough to see Sophia close her eyes.

Precious's letter detailing her decision to detour through Bristol arrived the next morning, followed shortly by Precious herself. There was no mention of Graham.

When Eva returned to the flat after a full day of fittings at Lushtak's, Precious was in her room, unpacking. Eva stuck her head around the open door. "You're back." She felt silly somehow, stating the obvious.

Precious straightened from where she'd been hanging a dress in her wardrobe. "Yes. I am." She smiled and gave Eva a hug, something so American and unfamiliar now that Eva found herself laughing.

"It's good to have you here. I let one of the newer models from Lushtak's stay in the spare bedroom for two months before she found her own place, so I haven't been too lonely. Still, it's nice to be back where we were."

"Yes, it is." Precious turned to her valise, pulled out a dress. "You're looking good, Eva. Thank you for your letters, for keeping me up on all the news from Lushtak's. I can't say I was upset to hear that Mrs. Ratcliffe left."

"It was a relief to everyone except Madame Lushtak, I'm afraid. She's taking up one of the supervisory salaried positions with the WVS. Who knew that Mrs. Ratcliffe held such patriotic fervor in her considerable bosom? God help the women who serve under her. I hope they all have thick skin."

"Isn't that the truth?" Precious said as she placed a folded jumper in her chest of drawers.

She seemed, to Eva, different somehow. More grown-up. More beautiful, even. With more than just a hint of a suntan on her face and bare arms. Precious saw Eva looking and laughed. "I know. It looks like I've been on vacation, doesn't it? When the weather was nice, several of the nurses and I would take the patients who could walk down to the gardens to sit in the warm sun."

"Did Graham go?"

Precious nodded, focusing on placing her hairbrush and comb in the right spot on her dressing table. "When he was well enough. He seemed to enjoy it."

"Did he talk about me at all?" Eva hadn't meant to ask, hadn't meant to seem as if she cared.

Precious shook her head. "I don't really recall. I think he was focused on getting better. He was in such bad shape when they brought him in. You can't imagine what he had to go through."

"He never responded to my letters. Not once. Did he tell you why?" Eva felt her voice rising, felt herself beginning to lose the self-control she'd become so good at. She fumbled in her pocket for her cigarette case, and her hand shook as she lit one, an Abdulla. That was the brand Sophia's friends smoked, so she'd switched. Her thumb brushed the engraved bee on the silver case as she shoved it back in the pocket of her skirt.

Precious looked troubled. "I'm sure he has his reasons. You know how men are." She attempted a smile. "The important thing to remember is that he's alive. We should all be grateful for that."

"I am. Of course I am." Eva took a deep drag from her cigarette, watching the smoke rise. "I didn't even know he was back in London until I went to see Sophia yesterday." She couldn't hide the accusation in her voice.

Precious concentrated on shutting her valise and moving it into the bottom of her armoire. "I assumed he'd see you before you received a letter from me, so I didn't write. I'm so sorry." She put her arm around Eva's shoulders and squeezed. "One of the sailors I met at the hospital is here now on leave. He wants to take me dancing tonight. Come with us, Eva. You might even meet someone new."

Eva pulled away. "Someone new? There will never be anyone besides Graham. He's not an old frock I don't want to wear anymore!"

"What about Alex?" Precious's voice was quiet, her eyes wide and searching. "Surely you have feelings for him."

"Alex? Oh, yes, I have feelings for him." Eva took a final drag from her cigarette, then stubbed it into the ashtray. "But not the kind you might think."

"What do you mean?"

Eva pulled out another cigarette, though what she really craved was a drink. "He's not a nice man. Just stay away from him. Promise me."

Precious blushed. "Sure, but . . ."

Eva studied her friend closely. "But what?"

"I've met someone. The sailor I mentioned—Paul Watkins. He's very . . . special to me."

Eva tried to feel happy for her friend, but the news somehow made the weight in her chest tug even harder on her heart. "Good for you," she finally managed. "I hope he deserves you. A lot of disappointed gentlemen have called for you at Lushtak's while you've been gone. This Paul Watkins had better know what a prize you are."

"Thank you, Eva." Precious surprised her with another hug. "You're a good friend."

"You, too," Eva said, blinking back the sting in her eyes, desperate for the moment she could leave and throw back a shot of whisky. She had two hours before Alex would arrive to pick her up for another insidious evening, two hours to numb herself so she could perform.

"Well, I'd best let you get rid of all that travel dust

and get ready." She smiled. "Like I said, it's good to have you back."

"It's good to be back."

Eva was halfway through the door when Precious called her name.

"I forgot something. From Graham. He asked that I give this back to you."

Eva looked at the small object Precious held out, and her vision blurred around the edges. "Thank you," she said, her tongue thick, as Precious placed the ivory dolphin in the palm of her hand. She closed her fist around it, the ivory like fire against her skin. Then she left the room in search of the only way she knew to ease her pain.

CHAPTER 31

LONDON
MAY 2019

I lay awake most of the night, imagining I could hear the echoes of the past that lived within the walls and between the floorboards. Whatever haunted this flat seemed like apprehension, a feeling of waiting. I remembered the first time I'd been here, when I'd stood in the foyer and felt that suspended breath, the expectation of someone about to walk through the front door.

It unsettled me enough that no matter how much I tossed and turned, sleep eluded me. The fact that images of Colin kept crossing my mind didn't help much, either. Eventually, I threw off my covers, slid my laptop from my backpack, and made my way down the creaking hallway to the front room. I flipped on the desk light and opened my laptop on the desk. Someone—presumably Laura—had neatly stacked the letters in precise piles on the back edge.

I sat down and stared at them, wondering again why there wasn't a single letter from Eva, and why there were no letters from Precious prior to 1946, and no mention of Graham at all. There had to be a logical reason, and I shared Colin's frustration at our inability to make any sense of it. I needed to question Precious. She had to know the answers, as well as the meaning behind the cryptic message written on the Savoy menu. I could only hope that we wouldn't be too late.

I was almost done with the article, with the factual aspects of it, at least—what people had worn and where, what had happened to the fashion houses during the war. I had the stories to go along with most of the dresses—where Precious and her friends had gone, what songs they'd danced to. But I didn't have the rest of the story—Eva's story. I needed to find out what had happened to her, for Precious. And for me. Every story had a beginning and an end. I needed to know the rest.

I opened my search engine and typed in "Bournemouth." I felt ignorant, not even knowing where it was. I quickly discovered the town was on the southern coast of England, almost one hundred miles southwest of London, and that it had a large number of new retirement communities.

An old photograph of an impressive villa caught my attention. It had been constructed, along with other villas, in the early nineteenth century, when Bournemouth was a resort for tuberculosis victims seeking to recover their health. I wondered if this was the type of house K. Nash might have lived in, and eagerly clicked the link for Quayside Cottage villas. But, as I'd long ago discovered, nothing was ever easy.

I distracted myself by searching for anyone with the name K. Nash, or anything resembling it, in Bournemouth. Exactly four names met the criteria. I wrote down the four associated phone numbers to call during daylight hours, although I didn't hold out much hope that whoever K. Nash was might still be living.

Of course, Precious had nearly made it to one hundred, so it was a possibility. I flipped back to my original hunt for Quayside Cottage, expanding my search to include the entire county of Dorset, and then focusing on just the words "Quay," "Quayside," and "Cottage." My finger rested against the down arrow key, the screen scrolling by so quickly that I almost missed the word "Quay." I lifted my finger and began tapping the up arrow, reading each line to find it again.

Seventy-fifth Anniversary of German Bombing of Poole Quay, December 16, 1942.

I scanned the article, stopping at a black-and-white newspaper photo of a street with the improbable name of Barbers Piles. One side looked normal, with small seaside cottages nestled against one another like children, jagged and uneven rooflines and chimneys adding to their charm. The opposite side of the street lay in complete rubble, bricks and debris, the odd piece of furniture protruding from the piles. A child's shoe lay in the foreground, making me pause.

Lightning raid by German bombers in broad daylight obliterates an entire row of cottages near the Poole Quay.

I sat back in my chair, deflated, my gaze straying to the shoe again and again. Maybe the reason I couldn't find Quayside Cottage was that it no longer existed.

An alphabetical list of the victims of the attack appeared in the article. There were sixty-seven names, and I examined the list twice, to be sure. No one with the last name Nash had been killed in the attack. Or at least killed and identified. Judging by the photos, some victims might have been completely obliterated.

I blew out a deep breath of frustration, then looked down at my notes, at the four phone numbers. I didn't hold out much hope that they'd lead me anywhere, but they were something. Maybe in the morning, I'd think of something else.

I closed my laptop, then rested my hand on it until it grew cool under my fingers. The gentle swish of traffic against the pavement below soothed me with its rhythmic regularity. I tried to imagine standing at this window and listening to the wireless eighty years before, as war had been declared. Hearing the air raid sirens and having to run from the building.

Precious could. She'd been here, had seen and heard all of it. There was so much more we needed to know, so much more she could tell us. Yet the more questions arose, the more uneasy I became.

. . . no heroic deed is done for the simple act of heroism. There's always some payment due, some penance owed. Some wrong to right.

Goose bumps erupted on my arms, as if Precious and her ghosts were standing behind me, whispering in my ear. It made me think of the purse I'd placed on her dresser. The heft of it. **Just memories.**

Leaving my laptop on the desk, I flipped off the lamp and left the room, telling myself I was going back to bed, no matter how futile my efforts to find sleep would be. I was wide-awake now, my thoughts on an old woman dying and taking her memories with her.

Without intention, I paused outside her door, imagining I'd heard a sound inside. I remembered the open windows from the night before. With thoughts of pigeon poop all over Precious's antiques and lace linens, I pushed open the door, quickly crossed the sitting room to the bedroom, and hit the wall switch.

The small chandelier filled the room with more shadows than light, but at least I could see that the windows were closed, the curtains still. The bed had been made, Precious's peach silk dressing gown placed neatly at the foot, with her slippers waiting for her on the floor. All was as it should have been. I paused, waiting to hear the sound again, eventually realizing it must have come from one of the neighboring flats.

Turning to leave, I spotted the box purse still on the dresser, where I'd placed it the night before. I stood on an especially creaky floorboard, changing my weight from foot to foot, listening as it protested. As if it knew what I was thinking. As if it knew my mama had raised me better.

I took a step toward the doorway, remembering Precious moaning softly as she sat by the window, holding the purse. How she'd told me that she felt as if she were watching a stopped clock but could still hear it tick. There had been a sense of desperation to her words, a dim hope. As if, for the first time, she could see a glimmer of salvation.

I turned back and stared at the purse. Precious could have been dying. Dying right now and taking with her not only her memories, but her last chance for salvation. For atonement.

Before I could talk myself out of it, I reached for the purse and opened it. Very carefully, I began to empty out its contents, placing them one by one on the surface of the dresser. First, the familiar cigarette case. Then I reached into the dark interior of the bag, my fingers finding a small, hard object, pulling it out to study under the light.

The crude carving had angles where there should have been curves, making it difficult for me to determine what it was—until I looked at the front of it, saw the smile, and recognized it as a dolphin. It was white and undoubtedly ivory, made long before ivory became a banned material. It was oddly beautiful, and I held it for a moment in my closed fist, feeling its edges, wondering at its significance.

Placing it next to the cigarette case, I pulled out a wadded linen handkerchief. I nearly dropped it, as I hadn't been prepared to find something rolled up inside. Red and white stones from a brooch reflected the light of the chandelier, the letters "RAF" over a winged emblem I recognized from the patch on Graham's uniform in his picture.

My gaze fell to the yellowed and crumpled handkerchief, the monogram in dark blue. GNS. **Graham Neville St. John.** I recalled Penelope saying his full name after Hyacinth called to tell her she'd found Graham in the archives.

I frowned at the collection on the dressing table, my gaze going from one item to the next as I tried to find some connection. To figure out why these were the memories Precious had hung on to. Especially the pin and the handkerchief. She'd given the purse to Eva, so were these Eva's mementos? How had Precious ended up with them?

Did she know more about what happened to Eva than she'd told us?

A single thought ping-ponged around my tired brain, an idea too outrageous to verbalize, too unreasonable for me to acknowledge as a valid possibility. A single thought that had been floating on the periphery of my consciousness ever since I'd first seen Sophia's wedding photo. I pushed the thought aside, unwilling to confront it, tucking it away to be examined later in the full light of day.

I picked up the purse again and spread the accordion bottom open as far as it would go, then held up the black interior to the light to see better. I was about to declare the purse empty when I caught a flash of white. A slim pocket, nearly invisible against the black lining of the purse. I gently tugged on the zipper, opening it little by little so I wouldn't tear the old satin lining. It slid easily, as if it were used to being opened and closed.

Five small envelopes lay nestled inside, all the same size. I carefully slid them out, already telling myself that no matter what was on the outside of the envelopes, I wouldn't open them. I'd already done enough I'd have to apologize for.

I flipped through the envelopes. They all had the

same careful handwriting, and all were addressed to the same person at the same location.

Graham Neville St. John
Queen Victoria Hospital
East Grinstead, West Sussex

I stared at Graham's name, wondering if it might have been a trick of my tired eyes. All of the searching we'd done to find some record of him, and these five letters had been here the entire time. I blinked, trying to focus on the inked address, on the beautiful penmanship. I thought I'd seen it before, but with all of the letters and handwriting I'd been staring at for the last two weeks, I couldn't place it. I'd have to show it to Colin, see if maybe he could.

There was no postmark or return address, making me think that the letters might have been hand delivered or included in a care package or some other bundle so that they wouldn't have gone through the postal system. I flipped the first letter over and found myself staring again, this time at the back of the envelope.

It was still sealed. I quickly looked at the other four and saw they were all identical, unopened. I checked the edges, looking for a slit that might have been made with a letter opener; I examined the sealed edges, searching for any breach in the seal to show that they had once been opened, but there wasn't any. These letters had never been read.

I carefully replaced them in their pocket, then returned the rest of the objects to the purse, my mind not willing to settle on any one thing. Too many niggling thoughts circled the drain that my brain had become, too many loose pieces that wouldn't settle into place. I remembered feeling this way when I saw the hatbox of cut-up photographs, being unable to put a finger on what bothered me about them.

Taking the purse, I walked back to the dining room, where the cut photos were. I needed to talk to someone about my discoveries, to discuss my theories. I looked out of the window, at the bubblegum-colored sky above Marylebone Road as dawn teased the horizon, and pondered calling Arabella. Just as quickly I dismissed the thought, grabbed my phone, and texted Colin.

Are you up?

It took a minute for him to respond. I was about to text him again, when he replied, I am now.

Great. I've got something to show you. Is now a good time? I thought I'd catch you before work.

Since I don't have to be at work for another four hours, now would be fine.

Okay. See you in about half an hour. Any news of Precious?

Nothing yet. Will call Dad in an hour when he's awake, but no news so far.

As I began to run toward the back of the flat, I had another thought. Does the tube run this early?

Take a taxi. That was followed by the eye-roll emoji, which made me laugh. He'd never seemed the type to know about emojis, much less use them. Then again, I apparently didn't know him as well as he knew me.

I threw on clothes and emptied my backpack so I could fit the box purse and the stacks of letters inside, then tucked the hatbox under my arm. As I walked back down the hallway, I stopped in front of the framed photographs of Sophia's wedding party and the picture of a glamorous Precious stepping out of a car while a dark-haired man stood ready to take her hand. I stared at them for a long moment, my gaze moving from one photo to the next.

Finally, after only brief hesitation, I took them both off the wall and placed them in my backpack, the niggling thought in the back of my head finally beginning to take root.

CHAPTER 32

LONDON
OCTOBER 1940

The Luftwaffe finally arrived on the seventh of September. Like a child who'd placed a winding top on the floor and was surprised to see it spin, Precious looked up at the blackened sky with incredulity. Eva found it odd that the very thing they'd been preparing for and expecting could still come as a shock. With courage found at the bottom of a bottle, she listened to the sirens before she and Precious calmly donned their WVS uniforms, collected their gas masks, and left the flat, just as they'd done hundreds of times before in drills.

Precious headed to the tube station shelter canteen to serve tea to evacuees. Always tea. The British government had sought to buy up the world's supply of tea at the beginning of the war, knowing it would be detrimental to the morale of its citizens should Britain run out in its time of need.

Eva had chosen instead to man a canteen for the fire brigades, who would be working throughout the night and into the morning. It was much more dangerous work than being inside a shelter. That was why she'd chosen it. She found a certain satisfaction in the violence in the air, in the ground echoing with the staccato beat of the bombs hitting in steady succession. The wail of the sirens and the percussion of the antiaircraft fire ripping through the night seemed to feed her, to fill the empty spaces inside of her. She was **doing** something to help with the war effort. Something that almost made up for the nights spent pretending to be merry. To be doing things for Alex she could no longer consider meaningless or innocent. She was a bird in a cage, unable to escape from the prison of her own making. Her days had fallen into a mindless routine from which she could see no alternative, and for which the endless supply of Alex's whisky barely smothered her conscience.

During the day, she went to her job at Lushtak's, showing frocks and gowns to a dwindling clientele, smiling and pretending everything was normal. Once a week, she'd leave work and visit the London Library to check out a misshelved book. As instructed, she'd tear out the title page and decode the hidden message written with lemon juice, using a lit match, and then burn the page after committing the information to memory. She'd fallen into the habit of reading each book she retrieved from the library, to expand her mind, as Mr. Danek encouraged her to do, although now, without Graham, it seemed pointless.

Later, after night fell and the enforced blackout enshrouded the city, she'd drop an empty envelope into the mail slot of the white-stoned terrace house in Chester Terrace before rushing home to change for an evening out with Alex. If she was scheduled for a shift with the fire brigade, she wouldn't drink at all. But for an evening with Alex, she would drink until she was satisfyingly numb.

She felt again the gambler in her blood, the stakes life or death. And as the nights of whisky and ceaseless bombings continued, she no longer flinched at the crying of an approaching incendiary or a nearby explosion. She would survive, or she would not. She couldn't find it in herself to care either way.

On a night in late October, Precious sat on the edge of Eva's bed as Eva prepared for another evening out with Alex. Precious entertained her with stories of the people from the air raid shelter, as well as the gossip she'd heard from the other models about the dwindling number of clients at Madame Lushtak's. Precious speculated on what would eventually happen to all of the employees at Lushtak's should they run out of customers.

Eva was hardly listening, her thoughts occupied with Alex, with his untenable hold on her. Her desperation to escape. As she applied bright red lipstick to her mouth, she caught sight in the mirror of the diamond bracelet on her wrist. She usually didn't wear it, but tonight she'd thrown it on, tired of seeing it on her dressing table. The large stones glinted like eyes, capturing her attention. She'd scraped one of the diamonds across the corner of the mirror to see if it would cut glass. The line could still be seen in the corner. She sat, staring back at the glittering stones. They would be worth a lot of money.

She lifted her eyes, aware that Precious had stopped talking. "I'm sorry—what?"

"I asked if you were happy. You were just smiling to yourself."

"Was I?" Eva put the lipstick on the dressing table, not yet ready to admit even to herself what she'd been thinking.

"So, are you? Happy, that is."

Eva met Precious's gaze in the mirror. "No, I'm not."

"Is it because of Graham?"

Eva nodded, not dropping her eyes.

"You haven't seen him at all, then, since he's been back?"

"No."

Precious was thoughtful, biting her nail, even though both Eva and Mr. Danek had tried to break her of the habit. "I'm sorry. I really am. I just wish . . ."

Her voice broke and Eva turned in her chair to look at her.

"You just wish what?"

Precious blinked hard. "That you'd been the one to go to him. I wish it had been you."

"Why?"

"Because you were the one he wanted."

The buzzer rang, and Precious slowly rose to her feet. "It's Paul. He's on leave for a few days, and he promised to take me out tonight." She hesitated, as if she wanted to say something more. "Maybe we'll have cocoa later and talk like we used to—if the bombs stay away. I've missed that."

"Me, too," Eva said, meaning it, wondering how such a short time could seem to stretch across years, leaving just as many scars.

The sign in the Savoy's lobby reminded all visitors that the blackout would begin at precisely five thirty. It was far later now, but Eva imagined the well-dressed guests passing the sign wouldn't have paid it much attention. They seemed the sort to allow others to take care of things like closing blinds and pulling shades.

After checking her mink coat, Alex led her to the American Bar. Its bar of chrome and rounded edges always made Eva feel as if she were on an ocean liner. The effect had probably been intentional, but she'd always thought it in bad taste to mix alcohol with the potential reminder of seasickness.

It was reported that Winston Churchill had his own private entrance here, as well as a private bottle of coveted whisky held behind the bar. Piano music could barely be heard beneath the din of so many voices, an array of foreign languages that Eva had become adept at not only recognizing but mimicking. Alex called it her special talent. She could now understand and speak French, thanks to her lessons with Odette, and had become familiar enough with Czech and Dutch that she could understand most words in conversations she overheard. She didn't understand why Alex was so interested in the banal chatter of drunkards, their talk of people she didn't know and places she'd never been. Yet Alex wanted to hear every word repeated and would jot it all down in a small notebook he kept in his jacket pocket.

As Alex escorted her to a table in a corner, strategically placed so he could see who entered and who left—and with whom—Eva mentally slid on her mask, a mask that was becoming more familiar to her than her own face, and gave a dazzling smile to everyone Alex introduced. She smiled, she nodded, and she made small talk. She allowed men to stand too close and look down her dress. She didn't mind anymore. She was playing a part, and it had nothing to do with who she really was.

Across the bar, she thought she spotted Georgina,

Alex's childhood friend. They had met only once, and Eva was drunk enough that she wanted to demand to know what she'd been judged for and if she'd come up short.

She began to stand, but Alex put a strong hand on her shoulder. "Don't," he said under his breath, a wide smile on his face, as if he'd just uttered an endearment. And when Eva turned back to where she thought she'd seen Georgina, the woman was gone.

A white-coated bartender approached. Alex never drank, though he always ordered a Scotch, neat. But in this bar, famous for its invention of the cocktail, he felt the need to order something from its famed cocktail menu. "French Seventy-five?" he asked Eva.

She shrugged, then pulled out a cigarette. "Sure. If they still have champagne. If not, I'll take whatever they've got with a kick."

Throughout the evening, they were joined at their table by Alex's friends and acquaintances, many of whom Eva recognized, though she couldn't remember their names. She forgot them on purpose, to aggravate Alex when he asked.

A young French couple sat with them for a time, complaining about de Gaulle's inability to admit the French defeat, instead wasting his time rallying support for the Resistance. They spoke with disdain of the leader of the Free French, as if they themselves hadn't fled to live in exile. As if they were merely waiting for the Germans to leave of their own accord so they could go home.

Eva paused with her glass halfway to her mouth, feeling a pinprick of awareness on the back of her neck, a heatwave of sensation that made her turn. Look up. Graham's green eyes didn't register surprise, as if he'd been expecting to see her. Or had been watching her for a while. Her breath stopped. Colors and movement stilled around her, and it was only the two of them in the crowded bar. Her chest hurt, the heat spreading to her limbs as if he'd touched her. She smiled and began to stand just as Alex slipped an arm around her shoulders and pulled her to him, pressing his lips against the bare skin on her neck.

She quickly pulled away, but when she turned back to Graham, he was gone. With both hands bracing her on the table, she pushed herself up, feeling the gazes of the French couple on her, seeing the interest in the eyes of the passersby. Alex pulled on her wrist, making her sit again. When she saw the Frenchwoman staring at her with pity, she looked away, feeling ashamed.

"Where are you going, my dear?"

"Don't . . . ," she pleaded, just as the air raid sirens began their nocturnal wail. The French couple stood immediately and began to follow the line of people heading out of the bar toward the posh basement shelter, carefully holding their drinks so as not to waste a single sip. As if that might be the biggest concern when German planes were dropping bombs overhead.

Alex remained seated, holding Eva's wrist tightly. He pressed his mouth against her ear. "Perfect timing. While everyone's distracted, I need you to go into the coat check and search the pockets of a dark blue man's overcoat—it's the third from the front. Bring me anything you find. If you're caught, say you've lost your favorite lipstick, and you think it might be in the pocket of your mink."

"You do it," she hissed, trying to extricate her wrist so she could go find Graham. He was **here**. All she needed was to see him again, to tell him that she loved him. That every word she'd written in her letters was true.

He tightened his grip. "I know you don't mean that. Remember Lord Merton. That's what happens when one is no longer useful to those who employ them."

He let go of her wrist. She stood still, watching as the last of the occupants left the room, laughing and talking, sipping their cocktails as if it were all a game. As if the finger of fate weren't at that very moment haphazardly circling, deciding which building would fall tonight, which lives had run out of luck. Her gaze followed the stragglers as she looked for a shining head of sandy-colored hair, the tall, lean form of a man who carried her heart with him whether he cared or not.

"All right," she said, calculating.

She walked briskly across the deserted hotel lobby to the small coat check. The manager stood with his back to her, issuing last-minute directives to employees and guests alike. Eva entered the small room, the sound of the sirens muffled by all the cashmere and fur. She found the coat immediately and with practiced fingers began searching through the silk-lined pockets.

The ghost of a scent wafted up from the soft cashmere, a familiar smell that made her heart ache. She leaned back, studying the coat, wanting it to be his, daring to hope. Pressing her face against the sleeve, she closed her eyes and breathed deeply of sandalwood and soap and the scent of Graham's skin.

"I believe that's mine."

She dropped her hands but didn't turn, wondering if it had been her imagination. But she'd seen him before in the bar. Slowly, she turned around, unable to keep her face from giving away her feelings. It was something Alex had told her she needed to stop, but she couldn't. "You came back," she whispered, afraid if she were too loud he'd vanish.

He stepped forward into the small room, and she saw his cane for the first time, the ivory handle and the silver tip. "Yes. It would appear that I have." Half of his mouth lifted in a crooked smile, reminding her of the afternoon they'd spent on the boating lake. He looked behind her, to where the dark blue coat hung. "If you're looking for the dolphin, I'm afraid I've lost it."

She stared at him, unsure. "But I've . . ." She was

about to say that she had the dolphin on her dressing table. That he had returned it to her.

"The coat," he said. "Was there something you were looking for?" He was staring at her oddly, and for a moment she had the mad thought that he'd forgotten who she was.

She reached for him, placed her arms around his neck, searching his eyes for recognition. A small scar cut through one eyebrow, adding character to his face. His eyes were wary, as if he'd already seen too much. "Graham, it's me. It's Eva."

He didn't touch her, but his lips parted. A breath escaped between them, a word that couldn't form but might have been her name. He didn't step back. She pressed herself closer to him, and placed her lips against his jaw. "I love you. It's only ever been you." She closed her eyes, breathing him in, wanting to melt into him. "You promised me, remember?"

"That I would always love you." His shoulders softened as the tension in him eased beneath her fingers. Something fell behind her—his cane, she thought—and his arms wrapped around her. His lips found her hair, then her temple. "I didn't forget," he said against her lips as he kissed her.

The sirens and the rest of the world faded away as she kissed him back, showing him how much she loved him, how much they'd been made for each other. Reminding them both that he'd come back to her. When they finally pulled apart, she rested her head against his chest, feeling the reassuring beat of his heart beneath her ear. She felt the wasted time of their separation as a solid wall between them, incomprehensible, but real as his heartbeat.

"Why didn't you write back to me?"

He stiffened, pulled away. She wondered if it had been a reaction to her question, but then he took her arm and touched the diamond bracelet. "Where did this come from?"

She opened her mouth to tell him the truth, because she was tired of the lies and all the pretending. She wanted to take his hand and lead him away, to escape to a seaside somewhere. To a house on a cliff.

Alex's voice interrupted her before she could utter the first word. "It was a gift. From me. It looks rather lovely on her, don't you agree? But then again, she looks lovely wearing nothing at all."

He'd come into the room behind them and leaned casually against the doorframe, his eyes hooded and appearing bored. But Eva knew those eyes missed nothing.

Graham didn't drop his arms or take his eyes off her. "Is this true, Eva?"

She met his gaze, wanting him to see the real truth there. The truth that she loved him and was faithful to him and that nothing else mattered as long as they loved each other.

She heard Alex move behind her and then the sound of a hanger being slid over a metal rod.

"Come, Eva. The all clear's sounded. Let me take you home." She felt the mink coat settling on her shoulders.

Graham still hadn't moved, was still holding her gaze. "Is it true, Eva? Did he buy you these things? And you accepted them?"

She thought of the ivory dolphin that she'd cherished above all other gifts because it had been given out of love, and how Graham had returned it to her. "Yes," she whispered as Alex kissed her neck. As if he owned her, which, she supposed, he did. "I didn't have a choice. . . ."

Graham stepped back, picked up his cane, took his coat. "Well, then, I bid you both good night." Without meeting her eyes, he executed a quick mocking bow and left, his limp almost undetectable but for the tapping of his cane.

She moved to run after him, but Alex held on to her arm. "Please, Graham. Please! Let me explain!" But her words fell only on air, her protests as empty as her promises.

Later, when Eva returned to her flat, she grabbed a bottle of whisky, not bothering with a glass, and headed down the long hallway to her bedroom. She heard Precious retching into the basin in the water closet as she passed. She didn't stop. She'd had enough pain for one night.

She stepped out of her dress and kicked off her shoes, leaving them in a puddle on the floor. And when she finally felt numb enough, she laid her head on her pillow and closed her eyes. The image of Graham's face when she'd asked him why he hadn't written her back floated behind her eyelids, chasing her into oblivion.

CHAPTER 33

LONDON
NOVEMBER 1940

Eva stood in the long internal promenade of the Dorchester, watching the elegantly dressed people move in and out of the mirrored ballroom next door, listening to the **ack ack** of the antiaircraft guns outside in Hyde Park.

The bandleader kept nervous dancers fox-trotting and bunny-hugging over the parquet floors with lively music that might have seemed ill-suited to the air raid wardens stationed on the hotel's roof or the gunners in the park across the street.

Because of the nightly bombings, dancing at the Dorchester had been moved to the Gold Room on the ground floor, in the center part of the building, under eight floors of reinforced concrete. The new location hadn't seemed to dim the determined faces of the revelers, who were eager to carry on with their lives despite the chaos beyond the fortified walls.

Eva stood with Alex and a group of men discussing the inconvenience of wartime shortages, something Alex knew nothing about. She suspected he was heavily involved with the black market, but as long as he kept her supplied with the Scottish whisky she'd grown to depend on, she wasn't going to complain.

She felt Graham's presence before he spoke, sensed the shift in the air and the flow of her blood. She hadn't spoken to him since the month before, in the cloakroom of the Savoy, though she'd seen him several times at evening events with Alex. They ran in the same social circles, she told herself. She wouldn't allow herself to believe it had been by design. But she'd avoided him, leaving a room when Graham entered, asking to be taken home as soon as she was aware of his presence. Graham was a constant reminder of all she'd gained and lost, the sight of him too painful to endure.

"Good evening, gentlemen," he said, moving to stand next to her.

Alex brightened, enjoying the drama and the part he played in it. "St. John, you remember Miss Harlow, don't you?"

Green eyes settled on her, not giving anything away. "Hello, Eva. I trust you are well?"

She noticed a scar along his jaw—it must have

been from when his plane crashed into the Channel. She'd missed it in the dimly lit cloakroom at the Savoy. She wanted to touch it, to kiss it. To absorb some of the pain he had suffered.

Graham took a sip from his drink, his eyes never leaving hers. She wanted to tell him that she was dying inside, that everything was wrong in her world. That it had always been him. Instead she said, "Quite well, thank you."

Alex watched them, his smile predatory. "How is our good friend David? I'm afraid I haven't seen much of him of late. Busy at the War Office, I presume."

Eva wanted to tell Graham not to say anything else, that Alex shouldn't be trusted with any information regarding people they cared about. Graham's gaze remained steady. "Yes. And he spends as much time with Sophia as possible. She is expecting a child and hasn't been well."

"I am very sorry to hear that," Alex said with what almost seemed genuine concern. "I'm surprised she's stayed in the city."

"Yes, well, her doctors say it's too dangerous to move her. David has created a rather plush shelter for them in the basement of their town house, with running water and electricity. He carries her downstairs each night to sleep and then brings her back up to her bedroom the following morning."

"A true testament to love, isn't it?" Alex said, as if he were well versed on the subject.

"Yes, it is." Graham took a sip from his drink, his eyes never leaving Eva's face.

Eva looked away, wishing she had a drink but knowing that she could never be drunk enough to dull this pain.

"Dance with me?"

She turned toward Graham, wondering if she'd just imagined it.

"I'm sorry, St. John. Eva has already promised the next dance to me." Alex slipped his arm around her waist. "Didn't you, darling?"

Graham gave them a mocking bow of his head, his eyes never leaving hers, then walked away into the ballroom. His hair shone in the light from the chandeliers and the sparkles of the glass studs set into the mirrored wall. He didn't have his cane, but his limp wasn't pronounced. Eva imagined the leg pained him, kept him up at night after days when he didn't use his cane.

As she watched, he stopped in front of a young woman wearing red chiffon, one shoulder bare, the other nearly covered with a silk georgette rose. She smiled as she placed her hand in Graham's, and they moved together onto the dance floor. Eva watched his hand on the woman's back, remembering what it felt like. Feeling the heat on her own skin.

Alex moved her in his arms, the splash of red on the periphery of her vision a reminder of where she'd rather be. She breathed in the miasma of expensive cigarettes as she half listened to the bubbles of conversations around her, the smoky, insinuating music of the band, all the while pretending she was somewhere else.

They were halfway around the dance floor when the outdoor bombardment began, the noise penetrating the soundproofing of the walls. The dancers paused, looking at the bandleader for guidance. After the second blast, the band struck up the first bars of the "Anvil Chorus" from **Il Trovatore**. The musicians played every other note, timing the gaps to allow the detonating bombs to complete Verdi's lines.

"How amusing," Alex whispered in her ear.

Eva watched as Graham smiled down at his partner, saw the pretty flush that colored her cheeks. "I want to go home."

"All right." Alex leaned close to her ear. "But first, I need you to go to the bar and ask the waiter with the large mustache for a French Seventy-five. When he tells you he has no champagne, ask for a menu. Put the menu in your purse, and then we shall leave."

"Why can't you do it yourself?" she hissed.

"Because they're watching me. You're not of any interest to them. Yet."

"Them?"

He looked at her, then threw back his head, laughing loud enough that fellow dancers turned to stare.

But when she turned her head to see if Graham was among them, he and the woman in red had gone.

The smoky scents of crumbling concrete and burning paper traveled through the clear air of the early November evening. On her stroll around Regent's Park to Chester Terrace, Eva shoved her gloved hands into the pockets of her wool coat, feeling the crinkle of the empty envelope. It wasn't too far a walk from Harley House, and she knew the way well enough now. She carried a small torch, the top half of the glass darkened with nail polish, that she'd flicker on and off to point her way and illuminate any debris or holes. A bus full of people had fallen into a giant crater just the week before, the driver unaware that a bomb had dropped the night before, cleaving the street in half. She carried a white handkerchief to be seen by other pedestrians and drivers so as not to be hit as she stepped off a curb.

Faraway fires to the east created a hellish orange glow on the horizon, the enemy's calling card. Eva's footsteps echoed on the quiet street; she huddled into her coat and walked quickly. She always felt watched when she ran this errand, as if all the darkened windows had eyes, the cracks in the pavement ears. A few times she'd imagined a man in the shadows, a large shape that resembled Jiri's. She'd never approached, not sure if she was more afraid it might be him or more afraid that it wasn't.

A distant dog barked, turning her head. It was rare to see or hear pets in the city anymore; most had been evacuated to safer spots in the country. Or euthanized by their owners in acts of mercy, as Freya had informed her when Eva made the error of mentioning how quiet the city had become.

She passed under the Corinthian arch bearing the terrace's name at one end of the street; she allowed her hand to follow the wrought iron railing, counting the openings until she reached the third. Carefully, she climbed the two steps. She found it almost amusing that she had no idea what color the door was, having ever seen the house only at night.

Pausing to make sure there was no one nearby, she slipped the envelope out of her pocket and through the brass slot in the middle of the door. Her gloved fingers held open the brass flap as she waited for the light slap of envelope on marble, then closed it gently.

She didn't move, listening for the sound of footsteps or any other sign of life on the other side of the door. As always, a tomblike silence answered her curiosity, the quiet almost more disturbing than a shout.

Holding carefully to the railing, she returned to the sidewalk, eager to get back to Harley House and the half-empty bottle that awaited her on her bedside table.

"Eva."

Her hand pressed against her heart as she turned,

her mouth dry. She stuck out an arm into the darkness, her fingers touching the heavy fabric of a coat. "Graham?"

"Yes." He didn't say anything else, but he didn't move away.

Her joy at hearing his voice warred with the fright and surprise his sudden appearance had caused. "What are you doing here?"

"I was about to ask you the same thing." The scratch of a match striking was followed by a brief flame as Graham lit a cigarette, briefly illuminating his face. He still wore his evening clothes, his tie undone, his throat exposed. Eva closed her eyes for a moment, seeing the image imprinted on her eyelids.

She thought of Alex and his threats. She couldn't tell Graham the truth. What was one more lie on top of all the others? "I couldn't sleep. I had to clear my head."

"Me, too," he said, the end of his cigarette glowing orange. "I was admiring the architecture."

And maybe because she'd become so proficient with lying, she recognized the lie he'd just told her.

"In the dark?"

He smiled around his cigarette, as if amused at being caught out. "Did you know Chester Terrace was originally designed by John Nash? Sadly, his plans were altered almost beyond recognition by Decimus Burton. He made such a mess of it that

Nash sought to have the entire terrace demolished and rebuilt, but his efforts were in vain."

"I didn't know."

"Do you know who lives here?" he asked softly. He stood close to her, blocking the chill wind, warming her bones.

She felt relieved that she didn't have to lie. "No."

"Ah," he said, bringing the cigarette to his mouth again before dropping it on the ground and crushing it with his shoe.

"Graham," she said, her voice barely louder than a whisper. "Please." **Please come back to me. Please love me again. Please don't leave me.** She didn't say any of those things, just let the single word float in the dark air between them before crashing to the ground.

"You should go home," he said, his words gentle as if he knew how harsh they would seem to her. "We shouldn't be seen together. I'll stay a block behind you to make sure you get back safely."

She took a step closer instead, felt his breath on her face. Lacing her fingers around his neck, she pulled him to her. He didn't resist, that simple action letting her know that he hadn't forgotten, either. His arms went around her, pressing her body against his, his lips hot and demanding as they claimed her mouth. She wanted to go back to their secret tunnel, to the place where they'd committed their love to each other, but instead Graham abruptly stepped back, his arms holding her for a moment longer before they fell away. His breath came fast, and she imagined the small clouds of his exhalations rising above him in the cold air.

"You should go. London is a dangerous place at night. You never know who might be lurking in the dark."

Hurt and confused, she turned and began walking in the direction from which she'd come. All the way back to Harley House, she heard the uneven tread of his footsteps and the tap of his cane behind her.

As she entered her flat, his kiss lingered on her lips, the feel of his body on her fingertips. She replayed their conversation over and over, recalling that he'd asked her if she knew who lived at number thirty-seven. She hadn't lied, told him that she didn't know. But it was clear that he did. She felt she'd been tested and somehow failed.

Precious's room was silent as Eva tiptoed past her door, and closed her own gently behind her. She reached for the bottle on her bed stand and unscrewed the top, eager to reach her own blackout where she couldn't remember Graham's kisses or see his face. Or wonder why he would have already known who lived at number thirty-seven Chester Terrace.

CHAPTER 34

LONDON
MAY 2019

The taxi drove me into the heart of Chelsea and the tidy residential square of Cadogan Gardens. Tall redbrick mansions clustered together like old men overlooking the private garden in the center, the crisp white moldings on the top window arches of each building rising like lifted eyebrows.

I'd been here a few times with Arabella while we were at Oxford, for tame parties Colin hosted while his parents were away at their home in Surrey. Their town house had not been subdivided into flats, like many of their neighbors', although Colin's parents did rent the basement apartment. According to Arabella, Colin acted as property manager to justify his parents' refusing to accept any rent payment from him.

As we pulled up to the central house on the east side of the square, yellow sun stroked the wrought iron fencing, lending a glancing blow to the sienna bricks of the houses and camouflaging them with coral. Colin met me at the taxi, insisting not only on paying the driver but on carrying my backpack inside. I allowed him, not exactly sure why. It might have had something to do with the way his damp hair curled around the collar of his shirt, and the way his blue eyes smiled in tandem with his mouth. I didn't want to stick around the taxi being forced to look at all that, so I headed up the front steps and opened the door.

George greeted me with his usual unbridled enthusiasm, which made up for Oscar's continued antagonism. My phone vibrated, silenced now, as I was unwilling to discover what other ringtones my brother had gifted me with—and I wasn't surprised to see it was Aunt Cassie. No one else would have been up at three o'clock in the morning.

I answered just as Colin came through the door and George began barking in greeting, as if he hadn't seen Colin in a month. "Good morning, Aunt Cassie. I'm in the middle of something—can I call you back later?"

"Sure," she said, and disconnected.

I'd started to put my phone away when a text appeared on my screen. Who's barking?

That's George, Colin's dog. He likes me.

Good to know. Is it getting serious?

I responded with an eye-roll emoji. I was talking about the dog.

It's a good sign if Colin's dog likes you, though.

Oscar—who belongs to Precious's nurse—hates me.

She didn't respond right away, so I made to put my phone in the back pocket of my new pants—before I realized that my new pants didn't have pockets. "Ugh," I said. "This is why I wear jeans, as I tried to explain to Arabella before she made me buy these."

Colin shut the door and gave George a stern look; the dog immediately stopped barking and sat at attention. "I would have thought you'd realize by now that my cousin doesn't recognize the word 'no.' We're somehow both here helping with her work project, aren't we?"

"Good point." I gave up searching for a pocket and resigned myself to holding my phone. "Dining room or library?"

"Upstairs, actually. I have a work space in front of a large picture window that faces the gardens. There's far more light."

"Sure." I frowned down at my phone as it vibrated.

> That's odd about Oscar. Dogs usually love you. Maybe he's jealous of Colin's feelings for you.

That's ridiculous. We're just trying to do a job. Speaking of which . . .

I didn't get to finish; Aunt Cassie sent me another text right away. Trust me. Dogs are good at sensing underlying tension or emotions.

I sent her an eye-roll emoji, then: I need to get to work. Was there something you needed?

> Beef or chicken?

I frowned. ???

> For the wedding reception. We're having a sit-down dinner at the old bowling alley—it's now an event space. The Dixie Diner is catering.

I guess that explains no

vegetarian or fish options. Either is fine.

And Colin?

"Tell her I'm fine with either as well. But what's a Dixie Diner?"

I spun to find Colin looking over my shoulder. "Seriously? What is it with you and Arabella being so nosy? It's very un-British." I began climbing the steps as I texted, He won't be there, so it doesn't matter.

Before I could turn off my phone, her quick reply popped up. Okay. I'll put him down for beef.

Colin called up to me. "First room on the right at the top of the stairs. You'll see a big table in front of the window. I'm going to make coffee."

"Bring the pot up, if you would," I said, retracing my steps to relieve him of my backpack, dropping my phone in one of the outside pockets. "First room on the right—I'll see you there." I began to climb the stairs again.

"They look nice, by the way."

I stopped, turned. "Excuse me?"

"Your new trousers. They fit you nicely, even if they don't have pockets."

"Thank you," I stammered, feeling my face redden, thankful that he'd already headed back toward the kitchen and couldn't see.

I'd never been upstairs in Colin's house, though

I'd always wanted to know what existed at the top of the curving staircase. I walked slowly, trying not to gawk at the twelve-inch egg-and-dart moldings of the ceiling cornices or the lovely carved pediments over the doors. I wanted to explore more, but dutifully turned in to the first door on the right instead. Out of habit, I tapped on it briefly before opening. A person didn't grow up in a large family sharing a bathroom without learning that one simple rule.

Despite the drizzly day outside, light from the large window opposite the door flooded the high-ceilinged room. A parquet floor softened by Persian rugs made the cream walls and brilliant white trim pop.

I crossed to the window and carefully emptied the hatbox of cut photographs onto the table, then placed my backpack on the floor. Outside, in the gated gardens across the street, an elderly woman was walking two small fluffy dogs with no apparent interest in going in the same direction as their owner or each other.

It made me smile, reminding me of outings with my parents and siblings when we were young, how our parents must have felt the same way with the five of us running around in different directions. They'd probably wished for leashes and muzzles—at least I know that **I** had. Although I remembered it had usually taken only a word or a single look from Mama to get us to behave. Daddy had called it her magic touch; he'd said that of all her many talents, her best was being a mother.

Turning my attention back to the room, I noticed a wall of bookshelves, a comfortable couch upholstered in a subtle check pattern of black and white—probably to help disguise dog fur—and a cozy red wool throw with matching pillows. A leather reading chair with an ottoman; a copy of Harlan Coben's latest thriller sitting on a small table built from what appeared to be airplane parts. Black-and-white photographs of architectural masterpieces—Notre-Dame, the Houses of Parliament, the Taj Mahal—in simple silver frames were placed around the room. A **Star Wars** poster signed by George Lucas hung next to a shadow box with a toy lightsaber. I smiled as I pictured a little Colin playing Jedi warrior.

The room had obviously been professionally decorated but curated by Colin. It was functional and nonfussy but showed parts of his personality I hadn't expected.

An open door on the far wall captured my attention. If it hadn't been ajar, I'd like to think my curiosity wouldn't have been piqued. But it sat open, inviting inspection. And it wasn't like Colin hadn't sent me up here alone to begin with.

I walked over, making an agreement with myself that I wouldn't go any farther than the doorway, and peered inside. A large king-sized bed dominated the center of the big room, flanked by two nightstands.

The bed was unmade, the sheets mostly kicked to the floor, a duvet puddled on the rug, as if having lost a fight with a restless sleeper. A large red blanket with black printed paw prints covered one of the pillows, letting me know that Colin didn't sleep alone.

Looking at the bed felt so intimate, the way it allowed me to picture Colin's nighttime tossing and turning. I'd imagined him to be a focused sleeper, one who remained in the same position all night long without moving. But, as he frequently pointed out to me, I apparently didn't know him very well at all.

I looked around the room, brightly lit by a window matching the one in the adjacent room, and I wondered if they might have originally been two bedrooms, converted at some point into a two-room suite. The furniture in here was all midcentury modern, flat fronts, no ornamentation. It surprised me, as it was so different from the rest of the house, but it fit Colin somehow. Not just that it wasn't fussy or antique, but it showed that he'd cared enough to make his own mark.

I heard the jangling of china and the tread of footsteps on the stairs. Quickly, I returned to my backpack, pulling out the two framed photographs I'd taken from the wall in Precious's flat. I placed them on the edge of the very large table, really looking at it for the first time.

It was almost what I would have described as

rustic, with rough-hewn and weathered wood, rusty screws holding the large rectangular top to the picnic table legs. A thick piece of glass had been placed on top to make it functional, the beveled edges dressing it up to fit the room.

But it was the stack of architectural renderings neatly piled in the corner near a felt-lined box of drafting tools that I found the most interesting. I'd leaned over to get a better look at the drawings when I heard Colin enter the room behind me.

"I've brought coffee, lots of milk, as you like it, and in a cup big enough to be considered a serving bowl in most countries."

I stood back so he could put the tray on the table, rattling the cups as he set it down. "Just in case your job as—" I stopped, unable to fill in the blank.

"Financial analyst," he supplied with a wry look.

"—your job as an analyst doesn't work out," I continued, "you seem qualified to run a B and B. Except you'll have to learn how to make beds."

"Actually, I do know how. And I make my own. Every morning. A habit from boarding school I can't seem to break. It's just that I'm not used to being awakened at the crack of dawn and having to squeeze in my morning run and shower before entertaining guests prior to breakfast. But it's nice to know of your interest in my bedroom habits."

I felt my cheeks heating, but before I could defend myself, he said, "I brought toast and jam, by the way. I thought you might be hungry."

"Ravenous—thank you." I lifted off the silver domed lid and took a slice of thickly cut brown bread for my plate. We both spent a moment slathering black currant jam on our toast and eating; then I reached into my backpack again and pulled out the purse, and placed it next to the array of cut photographs.

I stood, sipping my coffee, washing down the toast and jam, my gaze wandering to the pile of drawings on the corner of the table. "What are those?" I asked.

He wiped his fingers on a napkin from the tray and picked up the stack to move it. "Just a hobby of mine."

"A hobby?" I said, putting a hand on his arm so I could get a better look. "Did you draw all of these?"

"I did," he said.

"You're pretty good, you know. They look like they were done by a professional architect."

He frowned. "Doubtful, but thank you. Nana is actually the one who got me started. She bought me my first drafting set when I was very small. Happily, I seemed to have an affinity for it."

I took one of the pictures from the pile. It was a drawing of a house that had more windows than walls, with wraparound decking and a gabled roof that would allow for soaring ceilings inside.

"It looks like a beach house," I said.

"That's because it is. Besides taking me to see the great architectural masterpieces of London, Nana talked about the house she wanted me to build for her, should I one day become an architect. This is what I came up with."

"It's lovely," I said, imagining I could hear the shrieks of gulls and see the blue reflections of sky in the wide windows. "This is all better than a hobby, Colin. You never thought of architecture as a career?"

"Not really. Even when we were children, Jeremy was always so much better at this than I was. Mother still has some of the drawings of buildings he made as a child, and they show so much promise—much more than I had at the same age. I suppose, as I grew into adulthood, I always thought of it as his career choice, not mine. Since I was better at maths than he was, I followed a different route."

He seemed uncomfortable under my gaze and turned to place the stack of drawings on top of the small table by the chair. "So, what is it that you had to show me so bright and early?"

"A few things." I opened the purse, then placed the ivory dolphin, brooch, and lace handkerchief on the desk. "The handkerchief has Graham's monogram, so I'm going to assume it's his. But the purse belonged to both Precious and Eva, so it's impossible to determine who this all belonged to without asking Precious."

Colin picked up the brooch, rolling it between his long fingers. "From Graham?"

"Again, I can only speculate. But since he was RAF, it would make sense."

He examined the dolphin, then watched as I pulled out the five envelopes.

"These don't appear to have been opened. And they're all addressed to Graham. Which raises the question of whether they were never delivered to him, or if he chose not to open them."

His eyes met mine. "And you didn't steam them open."

"Definitely not," I said, attempting to sound as offended as I felt, as if the thought hadn't occurred to me more than once. "It was bad enough that I opened her purse. If I opened sealed letters, I'd be in a fine pickle trying to explain it to her."

"A fine pickle?"

"It wouldn't be good. My mama would probably come down from heaven and open up a can of whoop ass on me for reading someone else's letters."

"That's a bad thing, then?"

"Very. Mama wouldn't appreciate being called down from her fluffy cloud, where she's probably listening to her favorite eighties music, so let's leave those letters be until we can ask Precious about them."

The corner of his mouth quirked as if he wanted to smile. "All right. But why did you bring these?" He pointed to the framed photographs.

I picked up one and handed the other to him. We took them out of their frames and placed the photos flat on the table. "Something has been bothering me, but I haven't been able to put my finger on it.

I thought I should look at all these photographs to see if I'm right."

"Right about what?"

"Look," I said, studying David and Sophia's wedding photo. "Here's the only photo we can find of Precious and Eva together—well, sort of, since we don't see them both clearly. Remember all those empty spots in the wedding album? Remember how we thought that someone had deliberately removed photographs? I can't help but wonder if they were photos of the two women together since this is the only one I could find."

Our eyes met again, but neither of us said anything.

"That's why I wanted to look at this one more closely." I turned the photo of the glamorous woman stepping out of the car so that it faced Colin. Looking closely at it in the clear morning light, I realized that I'd been right. What I'd thought I'd seen wasn't a spot on the glass. I turned, looking for my phone, but Colin put his in my hand without my asking. As if he'd read my mind.

I flipped on the flashlight and aimed it at the photograph. "There," I said, tapping on the glossy picture. "Look—there."

I kept my finger pointed at the spot, waiting for him to see it, too. Eventually he pulled back. Regarded me. "There's some sort of mark on her neck. It's practically invisible unless one is looking for it."

"That's right." I turned back to the wedding

photograph, pointing to the woman standing next to Sophia, her head turned away from the photographer. "Precious said this is her, right? But her head is turned to the left, so no birthmark is visible. And in every single photograph we have of her, her head is turned or facing forward."

"You could have just asked me if Nana has a birthmark. She's always worn high collars or makeup to hide it, but I've seen it a few times. I think that she simply wanted perfection—she was a model, after all. Maybe that's when it started."

"That totally makes sense. But bear with me." I began sorting through the cut photographs from the hatbox, the ones that had been deliberately sliced with scissors. I trained the phone flashlight on them again, wishing they were digital, that I could simply spread my fingers to make the pictures bigger.

"Without really analyzing all of these closely, I can't say for sure, but from just a random sampling, it appears she's not caring at what angle she's being photographed from. And in the ones where we can see the left side of her neck, I don't see the mark. Yes, it could be concealed with makeup. But it's very odd, don't you think?"

Colin nodded, his face closed in thought.

I pulled out the blown-up candid pictures of Precious I'd taken in her flat, and slid them over. "When I was snapping random photos of her just a few weeks ago, she made sure her face was turned to the left. As if it still mattered. As if she still didn't want people to see it."

When he eventually spoke, his voice sounded tight. "I appreciate your observations, but I think we've already agreed that even at ninety-nine, Nana is still vain, so it's not like it's out of character. And old habits are hard to break."

"I agree. But that doesn't explain the missing photographs in Sophia's wedding album, or an entire hatbox full of cut-up pictures."

"Or these," Colin said as he picked up the stack of sealed letters.

I frowned at them, staring at the large block print of Graham's name on them. Then I turned toward the stacks of Sophia's letters, which I'd placed in bundles, separated by sender. I found the ones written by Precious after the war and placed them on the table in front of us. "Does this look like the same handwriting?"

We compared the two, our heads moving from one to the other like spectators at a tennis match. "It could be," Colin said. "Except on the sealed letters the person printed in block letters. It's really impossible to tell."

"Unless we open the letters and look at the handwriting inside, which I'm not going to do."

"Neither am I—not without Nana's permission, at any rate." Our eyes met, both of us contemplating the chances of receiving it.

I straightened as a thought occurred to me. "Where's the photo of Graham—the one with the writing on the back? It's definitely a woman's handwriting. We can assume that's Eva's, right? Because she and Graham were . . ." I searched for the correct mid-twentieth-century word.

"Lovers," Colin said with the hint of a smile, the word on his lips doing interesting things to my breathing.

"Yes, that. Do you know where the photo is?" I began searching through my backpack, trying to recall where I'd last seen it, and straightened as I remembered. "Never mind. Precious was looking for it, and I gave it to her—right before she collapsed. But I don't think it's in her room at the flat. I would have seen it when I picked up her purse."

"She must have had it with her when she checked into the hospital, then."

"Maybe it's with her personal effects?" I said hopefully. "Or they gave everything to your parents."

He checked his wristwatch—the fact that he wore a watch was one of the things I liked about him. "They said they'd call by eight with any updates. I'll ask when I talk to them."

I nodded absently, thinking about the valise. "I searched online for the name and address on that valise you brought over from your parents' attic. The address doesn't exist anymore—possibly because of an air raid during the war. I've got four phone numbers of people with the last name Nash that I can call, but otherwise I'm afraid it's a dead end."

"Unless Nana knows. Even Hyacinth Ponsonby seems to have run into a brick wall. I'm beginning to think that Nana is the only person alive who holds any of the answers. And we're running out of time."

I picked up one of the cut photographs, looking at the woman's bright, open smile, and felt the same zing of recognition that had nothing to do with knowing what Precious looked like now.

Before I could examine the thought further, Colin's cell phone rang—a normal ring that came with the phone. I found it refreshing. "It's my father," he said as he answered it.

I busied myself picking everything up and returning it all to my backpack. When I heard the word good-bye, I asked, "Any news?" I reminded myself not to hold my breath.

"Nana is awake but not completely coherent. She's asking for you."

"For me?"

"Yes. Come on, I'll drive you."

He took my pack, then placed a gentle hand on the small of my back, leading me out of the room toward the stairs. At the bottom I stopped to face him. He raised an eyebrow in question.

"Precious told me she doesn't like to talk about her time with the Resistance during the war because people would ask **why**."

"I don't follow."

"She told me that no act of heroism is done for truly altruistic reasons. That every good deed is done in penance. To repay a wrong."

He kept his steady gaze on me for a moment. "Every time I think about our questions, all the answers seem to swirl around what became of Eva and Graham. Everything seems to come down to that, doesn't it?"

I nodded. "I'm not sure we'll like where this is going."

"Neither am I. But I think we need to find out the truth. Not for us. For her."

His cell phone rang again. After a brief conversation, he hung up. "Father says they have the photo of Graham. And Nana is asking for the dolphin."

I squeezed my brows together. "It's in the purse—I'll bring it."

I made to move past him, but he gently pulled me back. "There's one more thing."

I met his gaze.

"The photograph of Graham. With 'Sweet dreams, darling' written on the back, supposedly by Eva. That doesn't really make sense, though, does it?"

"What do you mean?" I asked.

"Well, if I were to give you a photograph of me, I'd write something on the back, to you from me. Not the other way around."

"Then why would Eva have written that on the back of Graham's picture?"

Our eyes met in mutual understanding. I swallowed. "Because she knew he was already dead."

He didn't look away. "I'm glad you're here."

"Me, too." It was as much a confession of my feelings as I would allow myself to share.

He continued to regard me closely, his eyes searching mine. I turned away and headed toward the door. I stood on the front steps while he locked up. I stared into the garden across the street without really seeing it, wondering to what lengths a person might go to seek atonement.

CHAPTER 35

LONDON
NOVEMBER 1940

In early November, a day after an evening of heavy bombardment, Eva and Precious walked to work, sidestepping the rubble of buildings and roads closed because of unexploded bombs. They paused at a bare spot on Wimpole Street, where a dress shop had stood only the day before. A woman swept the sidewalk of debris, broken pieces of furniture being used to display what wares she'd been able to rescue. A crudely made sign propped against her make-do sales counter read **BOMB SALE.** Next door, at the damaged greengrocer, another sign read **BUSINESS AS USUAL, MR. HITLER.**

People were going about their daily lives, taking pride in their ability to thumb their noses at the Nazis to prove their unwillingness to surrender at any cost. But the smell of fire and smoke and unspeakable burning things couldn't be erased from Eva's nostrils, no matter how much Vol de Nuit she saturated her skin with. Or how much whisky she drank.

"You don't look well," Eva said as they picked their way through broken glass. Dark circles ringed Precious's eyes, and in the dim light of the overcast day, her skin looked sallow.

"Of course I don't. I was serving tea in the shelter all night. And listening to people complain that the twopence a cup we were charging was twice as expensive as at ground level. I told one man that if he didn't stop complaining, I'd spill hot water on him and give him something to complain about."

Eva smiled. "Oh, Precious—did you really?"

Precious gave her a wan smile. "I did. I'm not proud of it, but I'm just so give out. I can only hope that Mr. Danek can do his magic with his cosmetics."

"I heard you retching again this morning. Are you sure you're well? I can always fill your spot. It's not as if we have many customers right now anyway."

Precious shook her head. "No. I need to work. To take my mind off of . . . things."

"Is it Paul?"

Eva knew that Precious's beau was away now, on a ship somewhere avoiding German U-boats, but when he was able to get leave, he'd come to London. Eva had met him only once. He was large with dark curly hair, affable yet completely forgettable. At least he seemed to make Precious happy. Or if not happy, then at least content.

"No, it's not Paul." She walked ahead of Eva, signaling that the conversation was over.

Eva was glad for Precious's unusual silence, wanting to go over in her mind her own problems. She hadn't seen or heard from Graham since that strange evening in Chester Terrace, and the entire exchange lingered like an unanswered question. She needed to know why he'd been there and why he'd asked her if she knew the residents. Even if she was afraid of the answer.

They reached Hanover Square and stopped, disoriented. For a moment Eva thought they'd turned down the wrong street. Rubble filled one side of the square, the branches of the trees in the central garden shorn and singed, the ground bleeding with leaves. The three buildings were now piles of stone and brick, smoke rising from the ruins like unleashed demons.

A woman stood on the sidewalk, her mouth open like a baby bird's. At first Eva didn't recognize Madame Lushtak, doyenne of the House of Lushtak, the woman whose mere presence instilled fear and admiration in her models. This stranger seemed diminished in size and stature, as if someone had removed her bones and her heart, reducing her to a mere woman.

"Are you all right?" Eva asked. "Did anyone get hurt?"

Madame looked at her with blank eyes. She shook her head slowly before turning to survey the wreckage of her life, her devastation too much to express in tears. Eva held back her own sobs, not just at Madame's shattering loss, but at the disappearance of the place where Ethel Maltby had been transformed into Eva Harlow. Ethel was truly and permanently gone now, buried in piles of brick and ash, erased and removed as if she'd never existed at all.

A man approached, and Eva saw it was Mr. Danek, carrying his bag of cosmetics, his expression grim. "We are lucky the building was empty," he said. "And not filled with customers and models."

Eva turned at the sound of soft sobbing and found Precious crying into her hands. "It's all gone," she said. "All of it! What are we going to do? How will we get by?"

Reluctantly, Eva put her arm around Precious, embarrassed at her friend's outburst. Madame Lushtak had truly lost everything, worst of all the dreams she'd brought from Russia and used to create something wonderful and new. All irrevocably gone.

Mr. Danek gave Precious an unexpected smile. "Stay with Eva, my dear, and she will see you through this. She is a survivor." His smile dimmed as he faced Eva. "Sadly, sometimes surviving is the easiest part."

Precious pulled away and made it to the garden before she collapsed onto her knees and began to retch. When she was done, Eva helped her stand, giving her a handkerchief to wipe her mouth. "Come on, Precious. Let's get you home, where you can rest." She looked worriedly at Madame Lushtak.

"Don't worry," Mr. Danek said. "I will see Madame gets home safely."

Eva nodded, then put her arm around Precious, leading her back the way they'd come, unwilling to turn around and see their past disappearing from view.

The bombs continued to fall each night, the fiery explosions becoming as predictable as spring rain. When the air raid sirens started their bedtime wailing, Precious and Eva dutifully donned their WVS uniforms and draped the straps of their gas masks over their shoulders before venturing out of their flat.

But as November progressed, Eva found it harder and harder to rouse Precious from her bed. It was almost a blessing that Precious didn't have to model each day, although she managed to show up for canteen duty most evenings.

Not going to work had freed Eva to consider her

choices and to find another way to earn income. Freya had been stepping out with a businessman much older than she; he had a contact who didn't ask questions when a fur or a piece of jewelry needed to be sold. Eva was discreet, choosing smaller pieces Alex might not notice were missing. She stashed any money not needed for daily living in a box hidden inside her leather valise, all of it buried in the back of her wardrobe.

She had no specific plan; her fear of Alex and his associates was as real as bars on a prison cell, and she couldn't run away. Not yet. The growing pile of money was simply a thin thread to cling to, a hope of finding her mother and escaping together someplace where Alex could never find them. Mr. Danek had called her a survivor. She only wished he hadn't told her that surviving was the easiest part.

She'd expected to see Graham again or at least to receive a message from him. An invitation to finish their conversation. But it had been two weeks with no word. Her remaining hope drowned in the bottom of a bottle.

In the evenings, Eva continued going out with Alex. She'd become an accomplished actress. She conversed with his friends and acquaintances, answering with smiles and laughter, as if she were a woman without cares, one whose biggest worry was selecting which fur to wear. It broke her inside. She imagined each word like a step on an ice-covered pond, waiting for the cracks to open up and swallow her. But as long as she kept the cracks from showing on the outside, she would survive.

One cold evening in late November, when the sirens above the Savoy began once again to shrill, Eva made her way to the cloakroom. She walked steadily across the lobby, moving against the sea of people drifting toward the basement of the hotel.

Alex had been deep in discussion with a rotund, bearded man with perpetual sweat beads on his forehead—Vladimir or Leonid, Eva thought. Something Russian. She still hadn't been able to master the language but had become quite proficient at mimicking the accent. The men were too engrossed to notice her leave, and she felt a moment of freedom as she approached the cloakroom.

On a recommendation from Alex to the hotel's manager—to help a fellow countryman, he'd told her with grave self-deprecation—Mr. Danek was the new coat check clerk. It was the reason Eva hadn't dreaded her evenings at the hotel as much as usual. And Alex no longer required her to turn out the pockets of the guests. Maybe he'd sensed that she wasn't forthcoming with everything she found, that she sometimes pretended her fingers had missed a ticket stub or a receipt.

Now, as the sirens screamed outside and her heels clicked against the marble floor, she looked for her friend, hoping to go down to the shelter together and talk. But when she neared, she saw that the cloakroom shutters had already been closed. She stopped to search the quickly emptying lobby for Mr. Danek. The floor vibrated under her feet, the lights flickering, scattering people like ants as they rushed for the stairs.

Eva stood still in the middle of the now-deserted lobby, unsure what to do. The floor vibrated again, the chandeliers above swaying as plaster drifted from the ceiling.

A strong hand grabbed her by the elbow. She swung around in surprise, the shout dying in her throat when she saw Graham's grim profile. "Are you trying to get yourself killed?" he said through gritted teeth as he dragged her toward the stairs. He didn't have his cane, but his irregular gait didn't slow him as he pulled her alongside him.

"No, I . . ."

"Are you aware there's an air raid going on?" He didn't look at her, just practically dragged her down the stairs toward the sound of voices. But instead of turning toward the sound, he spun her down a subterranean hallway, all brick walls and concrete floors, and then into a windowless room. A single lightbulb lit the space. Shelves filled with food cans and dried meats occupied three walls, with wooden barrels stacked against them.

"Graham . . ."

He took her by the shoulders and looked at her with eyes that seemed backlit by fire. "What were you doing up there?"

"I was looking for Mr. Danek. My friend from Lushtak's. He works here now. . . ."

"I know who he is. But why were you up there? Don't you know it's dangerous?"

"I was on my way to the shelter . . . ," she began, then stopped, suddenly aware that he wasn't referring to the air raid.

The sound of voices approached, and Graham put his finger to his lips, pulling her against him. They hid in a shadow until the voices passed. Even then he didn't let her go, as if he were as reluctant as she to separate. As if he remembered, too, the way they felt in each other's arms.

He spoke against her hair. "I'm saying that you shouldn't leave your bag in the coat check. People have reported things missing from pockets."

"I don't . . ." Eva stopped, too stunned to think of a response that wasn't a lie.

He looked down into her face, and it was the same Graham that she'd fallen in love with, the man who'd gifted her with the architecture of John Nash, who'd lived in a foreign land to prove to the world he was more than what it expected of him. The man who'd once told her he would love her forever. "You little fool. You beautiful little fool. You don't know how dangerous this game you're playing is, do you?"

"It's not a game, is it?"

He shook his head. "No. It's not."

"Why were you at Chester Terrace that night? Were you following me?"

He hesitated a moment. "Yes."

"Why?" She held his gaze.

"To keep you safe. That house on Chester Terrace is dangerous."

"But you know who lives there."

"Georgina Simmonds. I believe she's a friend of Alex's. She's also dead."

The distant sound of laughter got louder as a door down the passageway opened, then just as suddenly faded, leaving Eva feeling seasick. "Dead?"

"Her body was pulled from the Thames this morning."

She swallowed back the sour taste in her mouth, wishing she had a drink. "Why are you telling me this?"

"Because you need to choose which side you're on."

She dropped her gaze and stared at the top button of his dinner jacket. "Alex . . . knows things about me. He's threatened to hurt people I love. . . ."

Graham put a finger on her lips. "I know. I know everything."

"You know about my mother?"

"Yes. And I know you're not from Devon."

She flushed with shame. "I never meant to deceive you. I only wanted to be better than the girl I was born to be."

Graham closed his eyes briefly. "I wish you'd

known that none of it matters to me. I wish you'd trusted my love enough to tell me yourself."

He stopped speaking as footsteps approached, then retreated.

Eva's eyes filled. "Then Alex wouldn't have found me useful."

Graham raised an eyebrow. "Not necessarily. Men like him always find a way."

"He's dangerous. He's working with the Germans. Lord Merton . . ."

"We know," Graham said.

"'We'?"

More footsteps approached, and before Graham could move himself and Eva back into the shadows, David appeared in the doorway. He gave a short nod of greeting to Eva before turning to Graham. "We've got to go."

David sent Graham a serious look before returning to the hallway, his rapid footsteps echoing against the bricks. Graham turned back to Eva.

"There is so much unsaid between us, Eva. We haven't got time now, but we will. Later, when this business with Alex is over." His arms tightened around her. "Alex doesn't know Georgina is dead, and we need to keep it that way. I need you to continue delivering the envelopes to Chester Terrace. Except they will be collected by one of my people first, before they reach their intended recipient."

Her head was pounding as she moved aside the

endless questions pressing against her skull, trying to get out. "They're empty, you know. The envelopes. There's nothing in them—I checked."

A corner of his mouth lifted. "They're actually not empty. They contain microdots, barely visible to the human eye, stuck inside the folds. Once they're transferred to a slide, they can be read under a microscope."

"What sort of information is it?"

He shook his head. "Just know that the information will be altered before being passed along." He placed a gentle hand on either side of her face, cupping her jaw. "I will let you know when you can stop, but you can't tell anyone. Especially not Alex. Can you do this?"

She nodded. "Yes."

"You are much braver and stronger than you believe you are, Eva. Never forget that you are both. Never forget how far you've come."

"I'm not brave or strong. I'm not." She clutched his lapels, feeling him begin to pull away from her. "Just tell me you still love me," she whispered. "That's all I need."

He responded with a kiss, a hard, searing kiss that made her want to weep and shout at the same time. When he lifted his head, he simply stared at her as if memorizing her features.

"We've both made mistakes, haven't we?" He didn't wait for her to answer. "We can only hope that when this is all over, we will find our way back to each other and learn how to forgive the unforgivable."

"Forgive—"

He cut her off. "Be careful, Eva. I once promised to keep you safe, remember? And I intend to keep my promise." He turned away.

"What side are you on?" she asked through bruised lips.

He stopped, looked over his shoulder. "The good one." And then he was gone, his uneven footsteps disappearing into the darkness.

Eva waited there until the all clear was sounded, then returned upstairs with the other guests, joining a conversation with two women as they climbed the stairs so that it would appear she'd been with them the entire time. Alex met her in the lobby, holding her mink and her bag; then he escorted her to his waiting car. Eva could barely look at him, still tasting Graham on her lips, hearing his words over and over in her head. They were halfway to Marylebone before she spoke. "Why are you betraying your country?"

Alex laughed, an odd hollow sound. "Are you developing a conscience, my darling?"

She turned away, unable to look at him, her loathing making it difficult to breathe. "Would it matter to you if I were?"

He chuckled. "No." They were silent for a long moment. Eva stared out her window, seeing the glow of smoldering fires as wardens rushed to put them out, the piles of rubble where people's lives and histories had been snuffed out simply because they wouldn't give up and surrender. Because they would willingly suffer to prove a point.

As they pulled up in front of her building, when she thought he wouldn't answer, Alex said, "I have too much German blood in me to turn my back on the Fatherland. England will fall. All of their inbreeding has made them weak. And I never bet on a losing horse."

She looked across the darkened backseat, feeling a burning heat rise up from her core, licking at the ice around her heart. "Good night," she said, then stepped out of the car. Alex didn't insist on accompanying her, and she was glad she didn't have to look at him for a moment longer.

It was nearly four in the morning when she let herself into the flat, noticing that the hallway and bathroom lights had been left on, and Precious's door was ajar. She knocked gently and, when there was no response, pushed the door open, then turned on the overhead light.

Precious lay on her side in the bed, sniffling, her face swollen from crying. The room smelled of unwashed sheets and dirty hair and a sour odor that reminded Eva of her mother. Eva had always likened it to the scent of despair, if there were such a thing.

She rushed to Precious's side and placed the back

of her hand against her forehead and cheeks, as she remembered her mother doing. They were cold and clammy enough to cause Eva concern. "I'm going to call for a doctor."

She made to move away, but Precious caught her wrist. "Don't. Please don't. I'm not sick."

"Of course you are. Look at you—you're definitely not all right."

Precious smiled weakly. "I'm definitely not all right, but I'm not ill."

Eva sat down on the edge of the bed, pushing the dull, damp hair off of Precious's forehead. "I don't understand."

Precious closed her eyes and took a deep breath. "I'm not ill," she repeated. "I'm going to have a baby."

CHAPTER 36

LONDON
MAY 2019

At the hospital, Colin and I were joined in the elevator by a woman with a poker-straight spine who held her large handbag in front of her like a battering ram. Her profile reminded me of the carvings on Stone Mountain, except the granite might have been softer.

"Mrs. Ponsonby?" Colin asked as the elevator door opened onto Precious's floor and we all stepped out.

The woman turned to us, and I was surprised to see that she was much younger than I'd thought someone named Hyacinth Ponsonby should have been—in her late fifties or early sixties—and smaller, too. Petite, even. It seemed her reputation added height and breadth to her frame. She wore a pleated plaid skirt, a buttoned-up cardigan, pearls, and loafers, exactly as I would have pictured. I grinned without meaning to.

She turned to Colin with bright blue eyes behind sensible glasses and smiled. "Is that you, Colin Eliot? I don't believe I've seen you since last Christmas, yet it seems like yesterday that you were competing in the local gymkhana with my Jessica. You fell off your horse quite a bit, didn't you? Do you still ride?"

"Sadly, no. I'm afraid I'd break something. Hyacinth Ponsonby, may I introduce my friend, Madison Warner? She's the one who's been interviewing Precious for the article."

Hyacinth shook my hand firmly. "It's a pleasure. I've heard so much about you from my dear friend Penelope," she said with a knowing look. I almost expected her to waggle her eyebrows, but instead her face became serious. "I am so sorry to hear about Miss Dubose. Is there any news?"

Colin shook his head. "She's awake and speaking but not completely herself, according to my mother. Have you come to see her?"

"Actually, I've just come from the maternity wing, where Jessica delivered my new grandson, Henry. I thought I should bring my homemade scones to the nurses there because they were so helpful and kind." She beamed as if she'd just invented grandmotherhood. "And while I was here, I wanted to bring your mother some new information I've just unearthed."

"Wonderful," Colin said. "I believe my parents are in the waiting room."

"I can't wait to tell them that I've found Graham!" She began walking briskly down the corridor. Colin and I exchanged a glance as we followed in her wake toward the visiting room. Despite her short legs, we found ourselves nearly jogging to keep up.

Penelope stood and greeted Hyacinth while James, who'd been staring out the window, turned toward us. I'd been in midgreeting, but I immediately closed my mouth. I stopped hearing what everyone was saying. I knew I was staring at James, but I couldn't seem to stop.

I thought back to when I'd first met him, how something about his face reminded me of someone who wasn't Colin. That something else had kept tugging on my memory, and I still couldn't place it. Not quite.

"Maddie?" I turned toward Penelope, realizing she'd been speaking to me.

"I'm so sorry—what did you say?"

"I was saying that Precious is asleep again, but the nurse has promised to let us know the minute she awakens. Did you bring the dolphin?"

"Yes, I've got it."

"Splendid. And I have the photograph of Graham you were asking about. The one of him in his uniform. Precious did bring it to the hospital—she was holding it when they brought her in." She picked up her purse and pulled out a small sandwich baggie.

"One of the nurses was kind enough to keep it safe until we arrived."

Reluctantly, I turned my back on James. "Thanks." I carefully removed the photo from the bag, then held it in the palm of my hand.

"Well, Colin, I daresay it's your doppelgänger." Hyacinth Ponsonby put her hand on my arm to lower it so she could see better. "The resemblance is really quite remarkable."

"I still don't see it." Colin frowned. "He'd be my . . ."

"Great-uncle," Hyacinth finished. "Your paternal grandmother's brother. I've gone over your family tree and records enough times that I feel as if I'm part of the family!" She laughed—"tittered" would be more accurate—and turned her attention back to the photograph. "I'm always amazed by family genetics. But what a fine-looking man. And in uniform, too. I can see why your Precious would have been enamored with him. And why she has such a fondness for Colin."

"Oh, no, Precious and Graham . . . ," Penelope began, then stopped, considering Hyacinth's words.

I did, too, as I turned the photograph over and looked at the writing on the back. **Sweet dreams, darling.** I met Colin's gaze and knew he was remembering Precious saying those exact words. But many people said that—including my own mother. And Eva had lived with Precious, had probably copied many of her little sayings, enough to feel comfortable writing one on the back of a photograph. When I'd roomed with Arabella, it had taken me less than a month to begin using words like "loo" and "brolly" and putting milk in my cup before I poured my coffee. And yet . . .

As if reading my mind, Colin reached for my backpack and pulled out the bundle of Sophia's letters. A small note, separated from the others, sat on top. It was the single letter we had from Eva, the correspondence she'd sent to Sophia in 1939 after she'd left her purse behind at a dinner party. I remembered the first time I'd seen the handwriting, how I'd thought it looked like a child had been practicing her penmanship.

Colin carefully slid the note out of its envelope and moved to stand next to me. I held the back of the photo next to it, looked at one and then at the other, letting the implications sink in, allowing them to reverberate in the place in my brain that made clowns out of clouds, and boogeymen out of shadows. The place where the improbable became possible.

"It might not mean anything," I said out loud, "but this might."

I pulled out one of the letters written by Precious in Paris and sent to Sophia in the decades after the war, and placed it next to the note and the back of the photograph.

Colin's eyebrows knitted together. "I'm not a handwriting expert, but it looks to me as if all of these were written by the same person." He pointed to the signature at the bottom of the note about the purse. "By Eva Harlow." He slid one of the Paris letters closer. "Or by Precious Dubose?"

"Except Eva Harlow doesn't appear to have existed, according to the archives," Hyacinth said. "We have exhausted all our resources. The name does appear in various records, but none in Devon and certainly none who would be the right age."

James cleared his throat. "Although you did find something new to show us, Hyacinth?"

She tittered again. "About your Graham! I'd completely forgotten in all this excitement. I feel as if I'm the one with mummy brain and not my daughter. Although comparatively, Jessica is much more clearheaded than I am right now." She grinned at Penelope and James, then slid her gaze over to Colin. "You'll understand just as soon as you hold your first grandchild, I can assure you," she said, pulling her purse straps off her shoulder.

"Let me get that for you," James said, placing her large yet efficient purse on the table, exposing the organized sections inside, filled with all sorts of papers and office supplies, as well as a stuffed blue giraffe and a pacifier neatly tucked inside a pocket next to an iPad.

I opened my mouth to say something, my words forgotten as I saw James's profile turned away from me, a smile creasing the side of his face. I stopped breathing for a moment, forgetting all politeness and simply staring at him. "Well, burn my biscuits!"

Everyone turned to look at me. Hands trembling with excitement, I dug into my backpack and pulled out a cluster of the cut photographs. I pointed to the one of a woman sitting on a park bench, her hat in her lap, her face turned so that we saw her profile and the entire expanse of perfect skin on the left side of her neck. "Look," I said, indicating her nose. "Do you see this slight curve at the bridge? It saves her nose from being perfect, but it makes her more interesting. She's still a beautiful woman, so people don't really notice it."

"True," said Colin.

"Hang on," I said. "I'm not done." I reached inside the backpack again and pulled out the framed photograph of the woman stepping from the car, her face also in profile, and then one of the more current photos I'd taken of Precious in her flat. "These two women are the same, see?

"But this—" I slid the cut photograph of the woman on the bench closer so they could compare. "It's a different nose from the one of the woman on the bench. Completely straight and smooth. And look." I tapped the photo, showing the nearly hidden mark on Precious's neck. "There's this, too. It's concealed but not completely. But in all of the cut photos of the woman with **this** nose, it's not visible at all."

"So it's not the same woman?" Hyacinth asked—a little gleefully, I thought. As if she enjoyed puzzles, even personal ones.

"No. It's not." I turned to Colin's father. "James, would you mind turning your head a little, so we can see your profile?"

With a questioning look, he did as I asked. I felt rather than heard the intake of breath of the three people standing behind me. I turned to meet Colin's eyes. "What do you think?"

"I'm not sure what to think. But one thing I do know is that whoever that woman sitting on the bench is, she is somehow related to my father. And to me, too, I suppose."

"But who is she?" James asked. "Is that the elusive Eva?"

I stared at the photo for so long that I began to lose focus. Precious's words echoed in my head. **Just because a person is lost doesn't mean they want to be found.** She'd said that about Eva. And she'd liked to imagine that she and Graham had run away together to their house by the sea.

I recalled the thought that had bounced around my brain when I'd first emptied the purse back in Precious's flat. A thought so outrageous and unbelievable that I had pushed it aside, unwilling to recognize it as the truth that had been dancing around me longer than I cared to admit. It startled me to realize how long I'd known, but had been too immersed in my own drama to look up and acknowledge it. And because I knew it hadn't been my secret to tell.

But the time had come for Precious to explain why someone who is lost might not want to be found. It was time to help a dying woman find atonement.

I looked up and met Colin's eyes. "No," I said. "That is definitely not Eva Harlow."

CHAPTER 37

LONDON
FEBRUARY 1941

In the months following Precious's revelation, Eva waited. Waited for Precious to make some kind of plan for her baby. Waited for the bombs to stop, for the fires and the destruction and the death to end. For Alex to release her, and for the weather to warm.

And she waited for Graham.

She hadn't seen him since November, when he'd kissed her in the Savoy's basement. When he'd told her they had left so much unsaid. That they'd both made mistakes and would need to forgive the unforgivable. She wanted to ask him what he'd meant, to explain. But he remained elusive, a ghost around each corner as she walked to work or headed out at night with Alex. She felt watched, and she found it oddly comforting. She continued to deliver envelopes to Chester Terrace, unsure who would tell her when to stop. And she waited.

She also worried—mostly about Precious and her unborn child, the child Precious thought might be due in April. Despite Eva's furnishing her with pen and paper, Precious wouldn't write to Paul to tell him about the baby. With some shame, Precious had admitted that the last time she'd seen Paul, he'd told her he was married. She didn't want to have any further communication with him. Eva's plan of soliciting help from his parents had evaporated, leaving her with no other option than the hope that Paul might try to contact Precious.

Christmas came and went with little remark. The weather remained dull, wet, and cold; although people were quick to say that it wasn't quite as cold as the previous winter, snow and frost did nothing to raise a Christmas spirit or disguise the rubbled ruins that huddled like frightened children on nearly every street.

The one bright spot had been the survival of St. Paul's during the brutal air raid on the twenty-ninth of December. The WVS had assigned Eva to tea duty for the firemen known as the St. Paul's Watch. She'd sat in the cavernous crypt under a vaulted arch near Lord Nelson's tomb, amid the firemen's coats and hats, with a makeshift tea cart and tins of biscuits and pitchers of milk. She had no idea that Hitler had chosen that night for the Luftwaffe to destroy the landmark cathedral—along with what remained of the British people's morale.

The first wave of planes came as a new shift was suiting up. The lights flickered, and the floor echoed with the impact of shells exploding nearby. Richard Kobylt, a teacher by day at Turner's Free School for Poor Boys, held tight to his hat and looked at Eva with wide eyes. "Hitler's angry tonight, miss. Not going to be many tea breaks for us, I'm thinking."

And there hadn't been. The church was hit that night by twenty-eight incendiaries, each burning ember and piece of falling ash doused by the tireless firemen, who together saved Wren's architectural masterpiece from disaster.

At dawn, Eva climbed out of the crypt, dismayed to see daylight through the east-end wall of the cathedral, but amazed that the church seemed relatively unscathed. As she made her way back home, passing through the smoking streets that surrounded St. Paul's, the dome of the church hung over the pinkening sky of the burning city like a phoenix. It was a miracle in a city desperate for miracles.

As the gray days progressed and her baby grew inside her, Precious became quieter and seemed to turn inward. Eva found herself missing her friend's constant chatter and perpetual good mood; she dreaded returning home from running her daily errands, making a round of the shops clutching her ration books, to see that her friend still sat by the front window, not having moved, an untouched plate of food long since grown cold beside her.

Eva worried about Precious and her despondency, her lack of interest in everything. She was desperate to reach out to Sophia, but Sophia was mourning the loss of her daughter, stillborn during an air raid in their small basement shelter in late January.

In desperation, Eva broke down and confided in David. It was he who told her that Paul's ship had been sent to the northern coast of Africa and sunk by a German U-boat, all souls aboard lost. He couldn't tell her where it had happened, as that was classified, but it didn't matter. Paul was gone and, along with him, Eva's remaining hope of helping Precious and her unborn baby.

She'd dreaded telling Precious, but when she shared the news, Precious simply nodded, then returned to watching sleet fall from the sky.

On a particularly nasty day in February, Eva received a note from Sophia inviting her and Alex to the theater. Though no air raid interrupted the evening, Eva felt on edge, a tremor shaking the air around her. Alex seemed to be watching her closely, measuring her words. They never spoke of Georgina, or Eva's weekly trips to Chester Terrace, or anything that wasn't banal and mundane. Eva still retrieved books from the London Library. And each day she waited to hear from Graham. To learn she was free of Alex. As each day passed without word from Graham, she felt more and more on edge, balancing on a precipice where equal disaster waited on either side.

During the intermission, while the men retired to smoke their cigars, Sophia took Eva by the elbow and walked slowly with her toward the women's powder room. As if anticipating the question Eva wouldn't ask, she said, "Graham is fine. He's working hard, as is David, and has been doing quite a bit of traveling. I don't think either of them is getting enough sleep, but Graham is well." She dug into her evening bag. "I have something for you. I thought you might want it."

She gave Eva a photograph of Graham, an official one of him in his RAF uniform. The boyish grin on his face softened the severity of the photo. It was the way Eva pictured him in her mind, his head slightly tilted, his eyes full of light and humor. This was the man she loved. The man for whom she'd wait forever.

"Thank you," Eva said, pressing it to her heart. "Thank you so much." She opened her purse and slipped it inside, making sure it wasn't next to the cigarette case, as if it might get soiled.

A feeling like the start of a fever crept into Eva's throat, making her dizzy. "To forgive the unforgivable. Graham said that to me."

Sophia gently touched Eva's chin. "You poor dear."

"What do you mean?"

Sophia didn't drop her gaze. "I know things that

I shouldn't. Being confined to bed above my husband's office was quite enlightening." She didn't smile. "I know about Precious."

"I didn't want to tell you. Because . . ." She couldn't finish.

"Because you knew it would hurt me. Here I am, a married, respectable woman with a wonderful husband who would make a wonderful father, and for some reason, we are not permitted to have children. Yet, Precious, well . . . Is she due soon?"

Eva nodded. "Yes. She thinks April. She won't see a doctor, so she's only guessing. She says that her mother had very quick and easy deliveries, and she isn't afraid of childbirth, so she's made no plans."

Sophia studied Eva's face, searching for something. "A woman usually knows these things. With all of my pregnancies, I knew without my doctor telling me when each of them had been conceived." Her eyes hardened, as if she were remembering three babies, dead before they'd had a chance to live. "David says that the baby's father was a sailor."

"Killed in action. And Precious is reluctant to attempt contact with his family. Or her own, for that matter."

"Has she told you much about the baby's father?"

"I met him. Once. He was quite tall, and broad, and had very dark curly hair. That's all I remember of him."

Sophia nodded, her gaze still on Eva's face. "Will you promise to call me when her pains begin? My doctor is wonderful. I'll have him come to her, see her safely through. It's the least I can do."

"What do you mean?"

Sophia seemed flustered, waving her hands in front of her face. "Only that I know how difficult childbirth can be. She'll need a good doctor."

"Of course. That's reassuring, although as I said, Precious believes she won't have any trouble. Not that I have any intention of letting her find out on her own."

Sophia leaned closer. "You will take care of her?"

"Of course. I love her like a sister. I couldn't desert her now. Why might you think otherwise?"

Instead of answering, Sophia stepped back and smiled as David and Alex approached.

"Shall we go back in?" Alex said, offering Sophia his arm.

As Eva placed her hand on David's elbow, she looked up to find him watching her with an expression she couldn't quite place.

Eva stepped out of a small basement workroom off of Oxford Street, squinting in the last bit of daylight. She and Odette had found work as seamstresses; it paid only a quarter of the money they'd made as models, but it kept them busy during the day, and Eva earned enough to buy food for her and Precious without having to use her emergency escape stash.

And she found her new job, creating clothes that

were as functional as they were fashionable, oddly satisfying. **Vogue** magazine dictated all, and Eva found it amusing that, despite paper shortages, the magazine was still allowed to publish. Odette had said it was because the government realized **Vogue**'s importance in communicating messages about domesticity and consumerism to the women of Britain.

In a recent issue, the magazine had urged its readers to swap their usual tweed skirts for trousers—but only if they were under fifty years old and weighed less than ten stone. Shortly afterward, Eva and Odette found themselves stitching women's trousers in their basement workroom, then returning home and making their own, using material ripped from clothing articles they'd once modeled.

"Eva."

A man stopped in front of her, and at first she didn't recognize him. She wasn't used to seeing him in anything besides evening clothes.

"David," she said in greeting. "What a nice surprise."

"Would you walk with me?"

Fear-fueled heat flooded her chest. "Is Graham all right?"

"Quite." He waited with his arm bent until she slipped her hand around it. "He asked me to deliver a message. He thought it best you not be seen with him. You're being watched, you know."

She nodded. Several times she thought she'd seen

the hulking shape of Jiri Zeman in a crowd or walking around a corner as she went about her daily business. Yet when she'd run to catch up with him, to see if it was really him, he had somehow managed to disappear.

"Alex knows that Georgina is dead. Did he mention it to you?"

"No. And he didn't ask me to stop delivering the envelopes."

David frowned. "Well, then, it's a good thing we're ready to move forward. It's not safe to wait any longer."

"Not safe?"

"For you. I'm afraid Alex believes you have exhausted your usefulness."

The heat in her chest rose in her throat. She swallowed it back. "What is Graham's message?"

"He wants you to go to Horvath's Café tomorrow morning. We have a plan to take care of our mutual problem."

"Horvath's?"

"Yes. Graham's been known to visit there on occasion to practice his Czech. He finds listening to native speakers the best way to learn. He speaks several languages fluently, I should add—he's better than I, certainly. It's why he chose the Diplomatic Service."

"He did tell me. It's one of the few things I know about Graham."

"Now, now, there will be plenty of time for that later."

Her steps slowed as she contemplated his request. "What does he want me to do there?"

"You don't need to know anything in advance. It's safer that way."

She looked up at him. "You and Graham aren't really with the War Office, are you?"

He gave her a sidelong glance. "Of course we are."

"You must both think I'm a traitor. And I suppose I am. I wish . . ." She paused. "I wish to be forgiven. I want to do whatever it takes for Graham to forgive me."

David patted her hand where it rested in the crook of his arm. "There's nothing to forgive. These are difficult times, and people find themselves in difficult situations. We do what we can to survive. I have found that acts of heroism are not always committed for unselfish reasons, but to make up for past transgressions. Not all of us are given the chance for atonement."

Eva ducked her head to hide her face, the tears that threatened to fall. "Did Graham say anything else?"

A small smile formed on David's lips. "He wanted me to tell you that he's started drawing the plans for a house by the sea. He said you'd know what he meant."

The following morning, Eva entered Horvath's, wearing the practiced smile of an actress looking for nothing more than conversation and something to drink and eat off ration. She wore an old frock she'd once modeled at Lushtak's to give her confidence, and she was clearheaded.

Ever since that night in the Savoy's basement with Graham, during all the interminable waiting for something she could not name to happen, she'd been drinking less. She'd stopped drinking entirely during the day, wanting to be alert. To be ready. For what, she didn't know.

She was relieved to find Mr. Danek at his usual table, facing the door. He worked the evening shift at the Savoy, and she had half hoped to see him. His expression didn't change as she entered the café, as if he'd been expecting her. He signaled for a coffee as she sat down across from him.

"You're looking well," he said.

"Thank you." She glanced around the room, unsure what or whom she was supposed to be looking for. Wishing that she could do more than simply look the part, that she could be strong and smart. Brave. But she was none of those things. All she knew how to do was pretend that she was. That was the one thing she was very, very good at.

Mr. Danek took a long drag on his cigarette before putting it out in the overflowing ashtray. He sat back in his chair, regarding her. "I hear the seaside is beautiful this time of year."

She looked at him sharply. "Is it? I haven't really thought about it."

"Yes, you have. You've been thinking about going for a while."

Eva kept her eyes on his, wishing David had given her some sort of script. "You're right. I want to go to Dorset. To visit my mother."

"And why haven't you gone already?"

She looked into his calm eyes, felt a small tremor jumping in her fingertips. "Even if I knew where she was, I worry about Precious—she'll need to come with me, but she shouldn't travel now." She pulled out her cigarette case. Mr. Danek's hand fell on it, trapping it against the table's surface.

He tapped on the Latin inscription. "'Betray before you are betrayed.' Have you ever wondered why he chose this for you?"

She didn't remark how Alex's name wasn't spoken aloud. She swallowed. "He told me that I would one day find the words as useful as he found me to be."

Mr. Danek picked up the case and took a cigarette, then held the case open for Eva. He spoke very quietly, as if murmuring to himself, so that Eva had to lean forward to hear. "And have you?"

She considered Mr. Danek's new position at the Savoy, and Alex's part in securing it and Graham's instructions to come to Horvath's began to make sense.

"Yes." She swallowed. "And you, Mr. Danek—are you useful to him?"

He held smoke in his lungs for a long moment, then exhaled slowly. "Not as useful as he thinks."

She placed her hand on the cigarette case, but he stopped her, his strong fingers encircling her wrist. "Be careful, Eva. A tiger is most dangerous when he knows he is trapped." He looked behind her at the almost-empty tables around them, his gaze settling briefly on the only other occupants of the café: a woman and a young girl having tea and sharing a sliver of the sweet Czech breakfast cake **bublanina**, a rare treat because of sugar rationing.

"I don't . . ." She wanted to tell him that she didn't understand what he was saying, that there were no tigers. But she did understand. He was wrong, though. Alex had always been dangerous. She'd just been too weak to believe she could fight back. Until the night Graham had made her almost believe she was both brave and strong enough to choose sides.

Mr. Danek spoke softly. "What would you do to be free of him?"

She'd thought of her answer many times. It never wavered. "Anything."

"Anything," Mr. Danek repeated. He tapped his cigarette against the ashtray, then looked at her with an unfamiliar intensity. "Whose side are you on?"

She answered without thinking. "The good side."

A hint of a smile traced his lips. "I am happy to hear it." He blew out small smoke rings that drifted toward the ceiling. As if he were talking about the weather, he said, "You need to pack a bag for yourself and Precious, and be ready to go at a moment's notice. We might not have the luxury of waiting until the baby is born. Do you understand? I will find out where your mother is, and when I tell you, I want you to write her address inside your bag, somewhere not obvious, yes? Take it to your friend Sophia. She will keep it safe until you are ready to leave."

Sophia? She didn't let the question reach her lips. Of course Sophia. Graham's sister. David's wife.

She pulled the cigarette case to her side of the table, keeping her eyes down, as if it were the focus of their conversation. "How do you know you can find this information?"

"Because I have at times been useful to our friend, and he trusts me. As does Jiri. I don't know for how much longer, however. We will need to move fast."

"I'm ready." She leaned forward.

"Listen carefully." He glanced behind her before returning his attention to Eva, who nodded, exhilarated and alarmed at once.

"A week from Thursday, there will be another Blackout Ball at the Savoy. Tell Alex that you wish to go. Alex's car has been confiscated because he was caught using rationed petrol, so you will take a taxi. That means there will be no Jiri, which is good. When Alex brings you back to your flat, invite him upstairs. To your bedroom."

She hid her revulsion at his implication. "What if there's an air raid?"

"Then we will make adjustments. You will need to be prepared."

"And Precious? She'll be in the flat. I won't do this unless I know she'll be safe."

"Sophia will invite her over for dinner and will then convince her to stay in case of an air raid."

Eva nodded, ready for his next words. "And then what?"

"You won't need to worry about anything after that. Just get Alex upstairs. Someone will be waiting for him. David will be downstairs in a car with Precious. He will drive you to the train station, and you will take the train to Dorset. To your mother. You will be safe from Alex forever."

"You make it sound so easy."

"Because it is. But ask yourself—can you do this thing?"

She thought of Alex's face in the dim light inside his car, calling her Ethel. Giving her the diamond bracelet because he knew she wouldn't say no. And she thought of Graham saying she was strong and brave. She met Mr. Danek's eyes. "Yes. I can."

He looked over her shoulder as the woman and the little girl stood to leave, and noisily pushed in their chairs. "Good." Turning back to Eva, he said, "There is one more thing."

"Yes?"

"You will need a weapon to protect yourself. I have a gun for you. Meet me tomorrow morning at fifteen past six in the ruins of St. Giles Church in

Cripplegate. Don't be late. You may need to walk far, because there is so much bomb damage in the area. I will show you how to use the gun, make sure you can fire straight and not shoot yourself. Be sure you are not followed. I will try to make sure Jiri has another place to be, but our mutual friend has many associates."

She nodded. "I understand. I'm not frightened."

Mr. Danek's eyes darkened. "You should be. Being brave isn't the same as not being frightened. Being brave is feeling frightened and still doing what needs to be done."

Eva hesitated, then stood. "When this is all over, will Graham know where to find me?"

"He'll know. He has made you a promise, yes? To keep you safe. He is a man of his word."

Eva felt the sting of tears at the mention of something she and Graham had shared, how he'd thought it important enough to tell someone else. But determined to be strong, she blinked them back, nodded, then left.

Outside, she paused on the sidewalk and looked over her shoulder, through the window. Mr. Danek was watching her. She almost ran inside to tell him not to, that it meant he wouldn't see her again. But she turned instead and headed down the sidewalk, hoping that what she'd told him and Graham was true.

CHAPTER 38

LONDON
MARCH 1941

On their way to the Blackout Ball at the Savoy, Eva smiled at Alex in the back of the taxi as it slid along the darkened streets. Not too much; she didn't want him to be suspicious, but enough that he wouldn't be taken by surprise when she touched his leg on the ride home. When she asked him up to the flat. When she invited him inside.

She didn't think about what would happen next. Somebody would be waiting in the flat, Mr. Danek had said. All she had to do was go back downstairs and get in the waiting car with David and Precious. She had already given her valise to Sophia, had sewn in her mother's address label. She'd filled it mostly with all the evidence of her life in London—the ticket stubs from the theater, restaurant menus, and the like—to show her mother that she wasn't Ethel Maltby anymore. That she had managed to be more than that.

Eva had also sewn a jewelry pouch into her underpinnings so she could hide the money from the sale of the furs and jewelry Alex had given her. She'd found particular satisfaction in the knowledge that he was helping her escape yet would never know.

Tonight, she wore the bracelet and her new diamond earrings, even though it was gauche; the society ladies never wore anything so showy. But Alex would notice and be pleased. She hoped it would make him amenable. Slipping on her mask, she smiled, like an actress playing the most important role of her career.

The only potential snag in the plans was Precious, who'd complained of not feeling well and thought she might stay in instead of going to Sophia's. Eva stopped short of begging her, not wanting to make Precious question her urgency. In the end, she had reminded Precious that their next-door neighbor Mrs. McCormick had a telephone, and that Precious should call Eva at the Savoy if she didn't feel better within the next hour.

Worry over this unexpected complication nagged at her, and Eva decided she would find David at the Savoy and let him know of the potential problem. Sophia had told her that he'd be there for the earlier part of the evening to make sure everything was in place. He'd know what to do about Precious.

Because nothing—**nothing**—could go wrong tonight. She pressed her hand against her belly, worried Alex might hear the excited flutter of butterflies as she contemplated her escape.

"You seem to be in good spirits tonight," Alex said as he helped her from the taxi.

She sent him a brilliant smile, met his eyes. "I am. I suppose I'm thinking that this war can't go on much longer. That should make all of us happy."

He placed her hand on his arm, his hand pressing against hers. "That it should," he said with his own smile as he escorted her to the coat check.

He'd questioned the absence of the mink when he'd picked her up, saying it was too cold for just a fox fur stole, and she'd had to insist that the fox looked better with her gown. She was relieved when he'd relented; she certainly couldn't tell him she wasn't wearing the mink because she'd sold it and that the money was currently in a small pouch pinned to her garter.

A pinprick of anticipation touched her spine as she caught sight of the strange man in the hotel uniform standing where Mr. Danek should have been. He nodded obsequiously as they approached. "Good evening, Mr. Grof. Madame. May I take your coats?"

Alex lifted her fox stole and her handbag and handed them to the man.

"Where is Mr. Danek?" Eva asked.

The man's face pinched. "I beg your pardon?"

"Mr. Danek. The man who works the cloakroom in the evening. I expected to see him here tonight."

"I apologize, madame. I usually work in the dining room but was asked to work here tonight. I wasn't given an explanation as to why."

She forced a smile. "Of course. Well, no matter." She turned away and slipped her hand back onto Alex's arm, as if she'd already forgotten Mr. Danek. But she hadn't. As they descended the stairs to the subterranean Abraham Lincoln suite, where the best parties were now held, she casually looked around for David. Mr. Danek's absence had shifted the night off-kilter, as if everyone had started walking backward without explanation.

"Are you looking for someone?" Alex asked.

She managed to keep her mask in place. "Just anyone familiar, really. It's easier to eat and converse with someone we already know, don't you think?"

He murmured something too quietly for her to understand. She continued to search in vain for David, the pinpricks of unease becoming more like nails driven by a thudding hammer, impossible to ignore.

As soon as they reached the bottom of the stairs, they were swept up in a crowd of familiar faces and seated at a table in the front, near the bandstand. Eva wore a Cartier wristwatch, the same model gifted to Princess Elizabeth by Mr. Cartier himself, according to Alex, and she surreptitiously glanced at it throughout the interminable dinner, amid constant interruptions to dance and chat and pretend.

She forced herself to eat even though each bite made her ill; she knew that Alex would notice if she didn't. She continued to scan the crowd in vain for David, or Mr. Danek, or even Graham, waiting for eleven o'clock, the designated time she was to beg Alex to take her back to her flat. To tell him that she wanted him to come upstairs with her. Her stomach lurched at the thought, the taste of bile bitter in the back of her throat. Only the thought of being free of him, of knowing her mother and Precious were safe and seeing Graham again, calmed her nerves, made her think again of possibilities.

At around a quarter past ten, Alex excused himself to speak with a friend he'd spotted across the room. Eva was relieved, his absence giving her the opportunity to move through the crowd unimpeded. But by forty-five minutes past the hour, she'd still seen no sign of David or Mr. Danek or Graham, and a full rush of panic consumed her. She lingered by a potted palm, sure she would disgrace herself and throw up her dinner. But thinking of Graham, of showing him how brave and strong she could be, helped her regain her wits and move stoically away, back into the middle of the crowd.

When her wristwatch showed eleven, she went in search of Alex. Not until she'd finished making her rounds and inquiring about acquaintances with no success did the panic overwhelm her, making her knees fail her. She staggered, caught herself on the wall. Forced herself to swallow her fear. Tried to clear her head.

A tap on her shoulder made her jump. A dark-haired woman stood behind her, holding out Eva's purse, the box purse that Precious had given her. It took Eva a moment to realize she was the woman in the red dress who had danced with Graham that night at the Dorchester.

"You left this in the cloakroom. A mutual friend said you might need it."

"A friend? Is Graham here?"

The woman pretended she hadn't heard her, backing away until she was absorbed by the crowd. Eva looked at the purse, remembered checking it alongside her fur stole. Remembered, too, the time she and Graham had been alone together in the cloakroom and he'd told her she should be careful, that people were searching through pockets and purses there.

Walking deliberately, she made her way toward the stairs, remembering to smile and nod. The lobby was nearly deserted, most revelers still in the basement. The coat check man stood with his back to her, and Eva quickly ducked around the corner, out of sight. She wasn't sure why. She was sure only that something was terribly, horribly wrong.

In an empty alcove, she opened the purse, her fingers trembling so that it took three tries. She stared inside, certain the purse couldn't be hers. Yet she recognized her lipstick. Her compact. The white ivory dolphin she always carried, along with the pin, carefully wrapped in Graham's handkerchief. The small key to her flat.

And nestled against the side lay the pistol Mr. Danek had shown her how to use in the ruins of a church. He had kept it, promising to make sure she'd have it when she needed it. It was small, small enough that it fit in her hand, and easy to use. But accurate only if one stood very close to the target.

Eva trembled, wondering why she might have need of it now.

Next to the pistol lay a folded cocktail menu. Eva pulled it out, skipping over the printed items, studying the handwriting. **Jsi v nebezpečí. Utíkej!** It was written in Czech. Between Mr. Danek and Alex, she'd learned enough of the language to understand it, although she could read Czech better than she could speak it. That was what Mr. Danek had said, and that was why he would have written this message to her in Czech so not just anyone could open her purse and read it.

Except for Alex, of course. And she suspected he already knew.

Eva focused on holding the menu still, studying the words, trying to think. The blood thundered in her ears. She slowly translated the third and fourth words, and when she said them out loud, she started to shake. **Danger. Run.**

Somehow, she managed to shove the menu back into the purse. Knowing she shouldn't request her stole or enter the lobby at all, she exited through a side door and walked two blocks before trying to summon a taxi away from the hotel. After ten minutes without a single taxi driving by, she gave up.

Desperate now, she took off her shoes, hoisted up her skirt, and began running toward Berkeley Square, where she'd find Sophia and sanctuary, where she could ask David what to do next. She'd made it only a block before she stopped.

Precious. She had to make sure Precious had left the flat. Had to get Precious and herself to Sophia's, where they'd be safe. She swallowed a frustrated sob, knowing she had no choice. Or no choice she could consider and live with. Without allowing doubt or regret to change her mind, Eva began running in the direction of Harley House. Her feet didn't feel the pavement, nor did the cold permeate her fear and desperation. She'd slow to a walk when she got too tired, then start running again, imagining someone behind her, chasing her. **Alex believes you have exhausted your usefulness.** David's words forced her to press on, to use the fear to run faster, harder.

The streets were damaged and dark, lit only by a half-moon, but she knew the way well, having been driven between her flat and the Savoy dozens of times. She barely had to look for the street names as she moved through Covent Garden and Fitzrovia toward Marylebone Road. It was nearly two miles, yet she made it in less than forty minutes. She stumbled up the front steps, panting, and stopped long enough to look in the drive to see if Alex or Jiri was waiting for her. She was glad when she didn't see them, having no idea what she would do if she did.

Lungs burning, she ran up the stairs, her gown tearing as she took the steps two at a time, fumbling in her bag to extract the key without touching the cold metal of the gun.

No lamps burned as she walked into the foyer. The blackout curtains hadn't been pulled. Eva closed them, noticing Precious's purse lying open on the foyer table. Realizing she might need to convince Precious that they had to leave, she removed the menu with the warning scribbled on it and stuck it in Precious's bag before latching it, leaving it ready to grab on their way out.

She straightened, the insistent tick of the mantel clock in the drawing room a reminder to hurry. Listening to her own rapid breathing, she walked through the flat, calling out Precious's name.

She was halfway down the long corridor when she heard a whimper from behind Precious's closed door. Eva threw it open, and facing the pitch-black room, the fear that had chased her all the way from the Savoy finally caught up to her.

"Precious?" A sickly-sweet smell coated the air, the taste of copper heavy in her mouth. It reminded Eva of discovering her mother after her father had left, the smell of blood and despair mingling so that it was impossible to distinguish which was which.

"Eva?" The voice was so weak Eva wondered if it had been her imagination. She stumbled toward the lamp that sat on the bedside table, almost knocking it over. The halo of yellow light illuminated a pale and sweating Precious, lying on the bed, nude, the bed devoid of sheets and blankets.

"It was so fast . . . ," Precious began, her breath coming in shallow, feverish gasps.

Eva's gaze slid down to the middle of the bed. What looked like a pile of bloody rags lay between Precious's legs. A thick grayish cord connected the rags to Precious. Eva stared for one long, horrified moment before she realized what it was.

With an unnatural calm she remembered from the times she'd had to put her mother back together, times that had forced away her fear of blood, she picked up the baby. A boy. Skin slippery with blood, slowly turning blue. She turned him over and smacked him on his little bottom, as she and her friends had seen the midwife do, again and again, as they'd huddled outside cottages while their mothers gave birth.

"Cry," she shouted at the still bundle. "Cry," she said again, unsure what she would do if the baby didn't. She spanked him harder, and this time a feeble sound like a trapped mouse came from the tiny body.

"What is it?" Precious asked.

"It's a boy." Eva looked around the room, remembering something else that needed to happen. She ran and fetched her sewing shears, remembering first to cut a ribbon from one of the sheets before she cut the cord. She tied each end with the ribbon, wrapped the rest of the sheet around the baby, and held him against her for a moment to make sure he was breathing, then placed him on Precious's chest.

Trying to keep the panic from her voice, she asked, "Can you move? We can't stay here."

"I can try." Precious's voice was no stronger than the baby's mewling as he rooted at her breast.

"I'm going to find a valise to put the baby in, to keep him warm, and get you dressed. David should be waiting outside. I'll go downstairs, and he can carry you, all right? Please, don't worry, Precious. We're going to take care of you." She had no idea if David was there, or what she might do if he wasn't, but she'd cross that bridge later.

Eva didn't wait for a response, but turned toward the armoire and pulled it open. She yanked a pair of trousers from a hanger and a folded jumper from the shelf and put them on the bedside table for Precious. Quickly, she changed her own clothes, completely unaware of what she slipped over her head.

The small valise Precious had used on her trip to nurse Graham sat at the bottom of the armoire, and Eva yanked it out, meaning to line it with towels and scarves and whatever else she could find to cushion and warm the baby.

"Don't . . ."

The feeble protest didn't reach Eva's ears until she'd already spread the top of the valise wide. She stopped moving, her body swaying as if she'd been speeding and had just hit a wall.

Five familiar envelopes, Graham's name on the front written in her own handwriting, lay scattered on the empty bottom. She picked them up, spots dancing in her eyes.

"Eva . . ." Precious's voice cracked. "I'm so sorry."

Eva looked from the letters toward Precious, then back again, trying to understand. Trying to pretend that "sorry" was enough.

"I didn't mean to hurt you. I didn't mean for any of it to happen."

Eva couldn't look at her, could only stare at the envelopes. They were still sealed. "You didn't mean to . . ." She met Precious's eyes.

"Forgive me, Eva. Please, forgive me."

"Forgive you . . . ?"

Precious was babbling something, words Eva was sure she should have been listening to, but the roaring in her ears made it difficult to make them out.

"I'm so sorry. I loved him, too. From the first time I met him. I tried not to. I really did. And when I saw you with Alex, and how he gave you all those things, I knew you couldn't love Graham as much as I did. Because how could you be with Alex if you did? But I couldn't say anything because you were my friend, and I loved you. You're like a sister to me, and I would never want to hurt you. But then, when Graham was wounded . . ."

Eva couldn't breathe. She wanted to throw open the blackout curtains and open the window and allow the freezing air to wake her from this nightmare.

A dim memory came to her, of Precious telling her after Graham had returned that it should have been Eva who'd gone to nurse him and not her. And it finally occurred to Eva why.

She closed her eyes, trying to block out the face of the woman saying such hateful things, but she could hear each word like the falling blade of a guillotine.

"I didn't mean for anything to happen. It wasn't me he wanted—it's always been you. But with you so far away, and occupied with Alex, I thought . . ." Precious shook her head. "It was only that one time, because he was so hurt and missing you. . . ."

"One time?" Eva repeated as if Precious were speaking in another language.

"He was so ashamed, he could barely look at me. He never stopped loving you—it was always you, and I was a cheap substitute." A fresh sob broke from Precious's throat, and she had to force out the words. "It was your name he called out. **Your**

name." She shouted the last two words, making the baby startle.

Forgive the unforgivable. Eva stumbled to the corner of the room and collapsed in a chair. The sense of urgency still thrummed in her veins, but she couldn't move. She thought her heart had stopped beating, yet somehow she continued to breathe, continued to hear the soft sounds of the newborn baby. Continued to hear Precious's confession.

She looked up, saw the baby's head. A new thought made her chest tighten. "Does Graham know?"

Precious shook her head. "No. I told no one. But I think Sophia suspects. I'm so sorry, Eva."

Precious began to cry quietly, her energy too depleted to make much noise. The baby stopped suckling and closed his eyes to rest. The fear returned, overriding the hurt and anger. Eva jumped up and began throwing things in the valise.

"We need to leave now, whether or not David is waiting for us." She reached for the baby, then froze as she heard the distinctive sound of a key in the front door. She tucked the baby inside the valise, then pulled up a blanket from the floor and flung it over Precious to cover her naked body before turning her gaze down the hallway to the foyer.

The approaching figure's hair was mussed, his dinner jacket rumpled, but he smiled as he neared them. "The night porter was kind enough to loan me a key." He held up a large brass ring. "I looked everywhere for you at the Savoy, Eva. I was worried."

Alex stopped next to the bed and leaned down to kiss Precious on the cheek, his face showing distaste as he spotted the top of the baby's head in the valise. "Congratulations. If I'd known, I would have brought a gift."

"Get out," Eva said. "Leave. You're not welcome here."

He smiled. "You know you don't mean that. I heard that you were to invite me to your bedroom tonight." He spread his arms. "Well, here I am."

She nearly choked on her own breath.

"My darling Eva. Walls have ears, remember? You and Mr. Danek should have been more careful."

Eva remembered the woman and her little girl at the table behind them at Horvath's. Just a woman and her daughter. But walls had ears.

"Where's Mr. Danek?"

"Dead. Feeding the fish in the Thames by now, I'd wager. It's why I'm a little late. My apologies."

Precious let out a moan behind them, but neither Eva nor Alex looked at her.

Eva kept herself from flinching as she forced herself to ask the next question. "And David and Graham?"

"Oh, what a tangled web we weave, Eva. You made it too easy for us. I suppose I should thank you. Although I'm most upset that you'd planned to run away to Bournemouth without telling me."

"Where are Graham and David?" she asked again.

"Your friend David is safe—we can't have too many dead bodies in one evening, can we? He's most likely still searching for Mr. Danek with the mistaken belief that he can be saved." Alex looked at his wristwatch. "As for St. John, at this moment he's on his way to the boating lake in Regent's Park, looking for you. We understand that the two of you have a particular fondness for that place." He smiled, as if they were sitting in a café, chatting about the weather. "He's been led to believe you're in danger. He thinks he has a chance to save you, but instead he'll be meeting Mr. Zeman and another one of my associates. We are everywhere, Eva. Everywhere. You should have realized that from the start."

She shook her head, trying to understand his words, but her brain refused to accept them. "Why would Graham believe such a thing?"

He looked at her as if she were a small, ignorant child. "My dear Eva, he was trying to get rid of me. I've simply turned the tables. Instead of me being dispatched this evening, it will be your St. John."

Adrenaline shot through her. She moved to walk past him, but he grabbed her arm. "You would save a man who deceived you with another woman?"

She didn't need to ask how he knew. He knew everything, his planted ears listening and reporting back. Eva kept her gaze focused on the hallway in front of her, but it was Graham she saw, his voice she heard. **We can only hope that when this is all over, we will find our way back to each other and learn how to forgive the unforgivable.**

She turned to Alex. "Yes."

Because Graham had once promised that he'd never let anything happen to her. Because he loved her. And because she loved him, and if she wasn't a forgiving person, she would become one. She was a master at reinvention, after all.

Eva looked past Alex to the bed, where Precious lay whimpering, the baby—Graham's baby—asleep in the valise. But she couldn't think about that now. She could think only about saving Graham. And praying she wasn't too late.

She grabbed her purse and managed to get past Alex just as the air raid sirens began wailing in the night sky.

She'd made it only a few steps when she heard a pistol cocking. "If you don't stop, I'm going to have to shoot you."

"Alex, no!" Precious's protest was barely strong enough to be heard over the sirens.

Eva put her hand in her purse, the blood rushing in her ears, and slowly turned. Alex lowered his gun and smiled at her. "I thought this would help you see reason."

I wouldn't let anything happen to you. Graham's words gave her the courage to put her hand around the small pistol as she moved forward to stand in front of Alex, so close that they could have kissed. "It does," she said. Her thumb flipped the safety as she lifted the pistol and pulled the trigger.

When he looked down at the growing spot of red in the middle of his white evening shirt, Alex seemed as surprised as she was. Precious screamed hoarsely as Alex slipped to the floor like a marionette with cut strings.

Eva backed up, toward the hallway, unable to look at the body on the floor or the hysterical woman on the bed or the sleeping baby in the valise. The pulsating wails of the sirens rang in her ears. Her gaze returned to the baby. With the sick realization that she was his and Precious's only hope for survival, she closed her eyes. There was time between the sirens and the planes. If she was fast, she could make it back in time. If she was fast. She looked at her friend on the bed, hesitated.

"Go," Precious said. "Graham needs you."

She looked at Precious, the bruise on her heart dulling, the pain replaced with pity. At least Eva knew what it was like to be loved by Graham. Eva pulled back, but Precious grabbed her hand. "Forgive me, Eva. Please."

Eva thought of who she'd been, who she was now. The woman she wanted to be. She could have only one answer. "I will. In time." She squeezed Precious's hand and dropped it. Without knowing why, she kissed Precious on the forehead. A show of forgiveness or a good-bye—she wasn't sure. She'd think about it later. "I'll come back. I promise to come back."

Precious reached up and grabbed Eva's hand again and squeezed, then released it. "I know. Now go."

With a reserve of energy she didn't know she possessed, Eva ran out of the flat and into the night, praying that she wasn't too late. Praying that the bombs would fall in another part of London tonight.

She'd made it only to the edge of the park when the first bomb dropped somewhere nearby, the percussion of the blast knocking her to her knees. The quick, bitter firing of guns and the grinding of the engines of the planes swarming above filled the night sky. Her whole body vibrated with the **boom boom boom** of more bombs tearing nearby structures apart. Fires lit the night, illuminating buildings, offering up targets like sacrifices. Eva could hear the yells of the firemen who were taming the flames just as another wave of planes flew over, the motors screeching in an unholy symphony.

She staggered, attempted to stand, looking back at the building she'd just left, where Precious and the baby were in the third-story bedroom. As she watched, an incendiary bomb dropped, landing with a terrific flash. Eva held her breath, trying to determine exactly where it had fallen, watching as the flash simmered to a pinpoint of dazzling white;

it disappeared, only to be replaced by a yellow flame leaping up from the white center, consuming everything in its path.

She took two more steps toward the interior of the park, where Graham was looking for her, not knowing he was in danger. Thinking she was in trouble. Because he had promised to keep her safe. But the sounds of buildings burning and people screaming came from behind her, forcing her to stop. She looked at the flames leaping up from the row of terraces behind Harley House. Looked toward the sky above; looked beyond it where pinkish white smoke ballooned upward in a great cloud and the flashing lights of the bursting antiaircraft shells glittered like tiny suns. As she watched, a hole in the pink shroud formed, and through it twinkled a star, the real kind that Eva had wished upon as a child.

She looked again into the darkness of the park. **You are much braver and stronger than you believe you are.** It was almost as if Graham were standing beside her, whispering in her ear. Only Eva could save Precious. And Graham's son, the child that should have been hers, whom she inexplicably loved already.

Her entire body shook with the aftershocks of the exploding bombs, her nose stinging with the acrid air. She wanted to run away. To hide. Fear filled her lungs like coal dust, choking her. **Being brave isn't**

the same as not being frightened. Being brave is feeling frightened and still doing what needs to be done.

Eva closed her eyes and whispered into the darkness, "Good-bye, my love." With a sob in her throat, she turned and ran back toward the burning building, nearly blinded by smoke and ash, and by the tears she refused to shed.

CHAPTER 39

LONDON
MAY 2019

“Then who is it?” James asked, his head turned slightly away as if he didn’t want to confront the photographic proof in front of him.

Without hesitation I said, “That’s the real Precious Dubose.”

Colin shoved his hands into his pockets. He’d gone very still, like a person who’d just been given a terminal diagnosis. Or had just learned that he’d been lied to his entire life.

Penelope moved closer to James, who wore the same expression as his son, and touched his arm. To Hyacinth, she said, “This is all so much to take in. I’m almost afraid to ask you what it is you’ve discovered.”

Hyacinth pulled out a manila folder from her bag.

"If you'd prefer to wait, I can leave this for you to look at later." She held the folder against her chest, waiting for Penelope to speak. But it was James who spoke first.

"No. We're all here now. And if there's anything we need to tell Precious, I'm afraid we haven't much time."

Hyacinth waited for Colin and Penelope to nod before speaking. "Well, then, let me begin by saying that your Graham St. John was a hard man to find, but I was up to the task."

"I never doubted it," Penelope said as Hyacinth removed a piece of paper from the folder and gave it to James, who held it out so we could all see. It was a copy of an official letter with a circular blue seal in the top-left corner, the word CONFIDENTIAL stamped in bold black ink along the top margin. The top-right corner, in blue ink, read HOME OFFICE, WHITEHALL and beneath that 29 JUNE 1941.

"The National Archives is releasing new information about the intelligence services during the war every six months or so, which is why I couldn't find him before. Then, just this week, I found this. Although I do want to prepare you. It's not good news."

With a quick glance at his wife and son, James took a deep breath and began to read the letter out loud.

Dear Mr. Eliot,

Thank you for your enquiry. We regret to inform you that Graham St. John has been confirmed dead. His remains were discovered in the burned ruins of a residence in York Terrace East. We have reason to believe he wasn't killed there, but that his body was brought there to appear as if he had been a victim of an air raid attack. Despite the grave damage to the body, we were able to ascertain that the cause of death was a bullet to the back of the head from a German Luger.

Please understand that the sensitivity and far-reaching implications surrounding St. John's last assignment require us to move forward as if he were still living and working in deep cover. His family will not be notified, nor will they be able to have an official burial. As of now, his remains are being interred in a city cemetery under a false name. They will be handled with honour and respect. You are not, under any circumstances, to share this information. To do so would be a treasonable offense, punishable by death. You are being made privy to the information solely because of your status with His Majesty's government,

and not because of your familial relationship to the deceased.

Please know that St. John died serving his king and country, and the debt owed to his family can never be fully repaid.

My gaze skipped over the name at the bottom, scrawled in officiously broad strokes. No one spoke as James returned the letter to Hyacinth and she replaced it in the folder on the table. "This is yours to keep," she said.

Penelope nodded, then smiled. "Thank you so much, Hyacinth. You've answered a lot of questions."

"I'm so glad. Please let me know if there's anything else I can do. If you like, I can begin searching the records for his burial location."

"Yes, please." James's voice cracked, and he paused to clear his throat. "Thank you for all your help."

Hyacinth gathered up her things and said her good-byes, passing a nurse entering the waiting room.

"Miss Dubose is awake, and she's asking for Maddie again." The nurse trained kind eyes on me as I stood. To Penelope and James, she said, "I'll be sure to alert you if there are any changes."

"Thank you." Penelope's phone dinged. "Arabella is on her way."

She gave us a worried smile that I tried to return

but failed to as I retrieved the ivory dolphin from my backpack, then followed the nurse out of the room.

Precious lay in a single bed in a tastefully appointed room decorated in pale blue and cream, a flat-screen TV across from the bed, a private bathroom attached. A large window spilled treacly yellow light across the white-and-gray linoleum floor, spotlighting a large arrangement of roses I imagined had come from Penelope's garden.

The slight scents of bleach and disinfectant drifted past my nose, and when I spotted Precious's pale face and dull hair against the pillowcase, I thought they might have accidentally bleached her, too, along with the sheets and floor.

She looked tiny under the sheets, her tall form diminished, as if the universe was already downsizing her, preparing her for her next move. An IV, held in place by tape, snaked into the top of her hand. Her thin arms and papery skin appeared as fragile as a kite, and for a moment, I was reminded of my mother and how she'd looked in the hospital bed my father had set up in the living room so she could be near the Christmas tree and her children. That was probably the reason why I hated Christmas but not hospitals. My hatred of hospitals had begun later.

I bent to kiss her cheek, smelling her familiar perfume. I then placed the ivory dolphin in her palm and closed her fist around it.

Precious didn't need to look at it to know what it

was. Her voice remained strong, although thready at the ends of sentences, and her mesmerizing eyes hadn't changed at all. "Thank you, Maddie." She frowned. "Where's your notebook? I have so much more I need to tell you, and it's all quite good."

I almost smiled but the thickness in my throat blocked it. "I didn't bring it, but I've got my phone to record you, if that's all right." I sat in a bedside chair and turned on my phone recorder, watching the lights of the equipment above her head dancing, as if measuring the amount of life remaining. If only such a machine existed.

"Good." Precious plucked at her sheets as if waiting for me to speak.

"We found Graham. And I think we found Eva, too." I looked at her for corroboration. "But you already knew where she was, didn't you?"

She smiled softly. "Yes."

I frowned, still trying to make the stray pieces fit. "So, what happened to the real Precious Dubose?"

Her chest rose and fell in shallow breaths as if she were a medium summoning the dead. "She died when our flat was hit during an air raid. The same night Graham died." She paused. "The same night their son was born."

"James?"

Precious nodded. "David arranged for Precious to be buried anonymously in a London cemetery. He thought of using Eva's name but wasn't convinced

I was ready to say good-bye forever. And Alex . . ." She paused. "David made sure that's one body that will never be found." A grim smile appeared, briefly illuminating her face.

I was missing Alex's part in her story, and hoped we'd have time for her to share it with me. But I had more immediate questions that needed answers. "And then you gave James to Sophia and David to raise as their son."

"Yes." She looked past me, and in her eyes, I imagined I saw the reflection of airplanes in a night sky, of flames bursting through windows. "Sophia nursed me, and then David helped me get to France. I needed to leave England. I needed people to believe I was dead, just in case they came looking for me."

"They?"

She gave me a lopsided smile that made her look like a much younger woman. "The bad guys. I worked with them, you see. Because I thought I had no choice. It's not an excuse. It's simply the truth of who I was: the woman I was before I learned how brave and strong I could be."

I turned away, unable to look at her, remembering why she hadn't wanted to tell anyone about her heroism in France. **Because no heroic deed is done for the simple act of heroism. There's always some payment due, some penance owed. Some wrong to right.**

"That's why you went to France? To atone for your sins?"

"Partly. And to die." Her lips wobbled. "But it's true, you know. Only the good die young."

Her Southern accent remained true, never straying from the persona she'd portrayed for almost eighty years. I sat back in my chair. "What did you do in France?"

"I'd found someone to sell my jewels and furs to, and I gave all the money to the Resistance, to build their trust in me. And then I did the only thing I knew how—I modeled for various designers and met Coco Chanel. She'd already sold her shops by then, but we became friends. I was invited to her parties, where I listened to her drunk Nazi friends who said things they shouldn't have. No one ever suspected I was Resistance." Her cheeks creased in a skeletal smile. "I even had a code name."

"A code name?"

"La Fleur. They called me La Fleur. I took the name from a very brave and heroic woman I'd only known for a short time. She was an inspiration to me, a reason I worked so hard. But I enjoyed my role, and I was quite good at it, probably because I wasn't afraid to die. I anticipated it, actually. But the work almost made up for who I'd been before."

"Because life is about reinvention. You said that to me."

"Because it's true. I decided that if I was still breathing, I needed to **live**."

"But when the war ended, why didn't you come back to England?"

"I wanted to. I'd planned to go live with my mother in Bournemouth. When I left, Sophia and David promised that they'd look after her and let her know that I was safe. That I would return when I could."

I sat up, seeing another piece of the puzzle fall into place. "K. Nash?"

"That wasn't her real name, you know. I made it up when she moved to the coast to escape my father." She smiled to herself, opening her hand to see the ivory dolphin. "Graham loved the architect John Nash—that's where I got the name. I had dreams that he'd join me there after the war. That he'd build us a house by the sea."

I didn't ask her what had happened, because I already knew. I'd seen the pictures, the obliterated row of homes. And Graham had died. "Why did it take you so long to come back?"

"London was full of Graham and my memories of him. My past had become the ghost that haunted me. I think you know what that's like, don't you, Maddie?"

Grief is like a ghost. I looked away, then answered with a question of my own. "Was it Sophia who asked you to come back to England?"

She nodded. "To be near Graham's son. She knew James would help heal me. And she was right."

I nodded, understanding. "That's why she took

the photos of Precious out of her wedding album, and cut you out of the pictures of the two of you together. That way, no one would ever suspect that you weren't the real Precious."

"We looked so much alike, Precious and I. Of course, I was the natural blond—she was born a brunette."

I almost laughed at this small nod to her vanity. "And Sophia didn't want anyone comparing the photos of you and Precious side by side."

"But she didn't throw them out. Sweet Sophia. Precious was her friend, too. She didn't want to get rid of her completely. She never expected that those photos would be found. Or that anyone would ever go looking for them."

"So you never thought to come back as Eva? Surely the people who were looking for you were gone after the war or no longer cared that you were alive."

She shook her head slowly. "Possibly. But Eva died with Graham. And for all those years in France, I'd reinvented myself as Precious Dubose. The new personality suited me."

I nodded, the words and pieces of the story loosening like an unfurling knot. "Why did you ask me to find Eva? Weren't you afraid we'd discover your secret?"

Her eyes brightened. "It was time. I owed it to Precious, to her son and grandson. They should know who she was. That, at the end, she was brave.

And I wanted you to be the one who discovered the truth."

"Why? Because I'm kin?"

"Partly. But partly because you, dear Maddie, needed to learn how to free your own ghosts."

I sat back, my chest heavy with the burden of secrets that still carried the power to wound. "So, whose story do you want me to tell? Yours or Precious's? My article—it needs to be about so much more than fashion in a time of crisis. I can't write the story of the clothes without sharing the lives of the remarkable women who wore them."

She squeezed my hand, the ivory dolphin digging into my palm. "It doesn't matter to me, Maddie. I won't be here. I'll leave it to you to write the ending." She let go, leaving my palm cupping the dolphin. "I want you to have that. To remind you that there is always beauty and love waiting for us, even during the darkest days of our lives." She focused her remarkable blue eyes on me. "Your story is still unwritten, Maddie. I've been given all those years your mother and grandmother were denied so I could have all of their wisdom to share with you before I die."

I wanted to tell her not to talk about dying, that she'd be going home soon, but I didn't want to lie. She had the waxy look I remembered my mother having, the skin pulled taut over sharp bones, turning a face into a skeletal mask.

I leaned forward, knowing I hadn't yet asked the

most important question. "Tell me, then. Who are you, really? Because I'm pretty sure that Eva Harlow never existed."

"Oh, she did, Maddie. She was a woman who made mistakes, who was brave and strong. Who loved fiercely. And she was a formidable woman. Like you."

I started to argue, but she held up a finger to stop me. "I was born Ethel Maltby in Muker in the county of Yorkshire in nineteen nineteen, the daughter of a drunk and a seamstress. Ethel died the day Eva Harlow was born. The day I decided to become more than what I was. And it's taken me nearly one hundred years to learn that we don't need a new name or identity to reinvent ourselves. We only need to believe ourselves worthy of love."

She settled back on her pillow and closed her eyes so that I thought she was going to sleep. But instead she began to talk, telling me the story of how a young, beautiful girl from Yorkshire became the fierce and brave Precious Dubose.

Arabella and Laura had arrived while I'd been with Precious, and everyone had a chance to spend time alone with her. We didn't say it aloud, but we knew we were making our good-byes. We were all together in the room with her when the alarms sounded. Doctors and nurses rushed in. Precious took her last breath two weeks shy of her one hundredth birthday, surrounded by people who loved her. Which, considering her age, was a testament to who she was, and to the person she'd been, regardless of which name she'd claimed.

Although her death hadn't been unanticipated, we still found ourselves stunned by it, walking stiffly like silent zombies as we left the hospital.

Despite Penelope's invitation to stay with her and James and Colin at their town house, I insisted on returning to Precious's flat, where I could touch the clothes that had illustrated her stories and imagine Eva and Precious, Graham and Alex, sitting around the wireless, listening to a declaration of war. Where good and evil weren't as clear-cut as I'd once thought.

And I needed a good cry. I hadn't cried yet, feeling that I shouldn't; I hadn't known Precious for long. Yet I felt as if I'd always known her, that what she'd said about her capturing the lost wisdom from my mother's and grandmother's shortened lives made her part of my own life in turn.

So I returned alone—Laura having to fetch Oscar—to the quiet flat, and walked into Precious's room, which smelled of Vol de Nuit. I looked out of the window toward Regent's Park, trying to picture the hellish night when she'd sacrificed one love for another. It was terrible and awful and wonderful all at the same time, the swirl of emotions draining me as I paced, listening to the creaking floors beneath my feet.

I cried then. Not just for Precious, but for Eva

and Graham and all those who'd died before their time. For my mother and grandmother, too. And I cried for the burden of Precious's story, of which I alone knew the full extent. I wasn't quite sure what I was supposed to do about it.

For a long time, I stood in the guest room, where the dresses and gowns of a bygone era hung on racks, each one with a story. I flipped on the light and spent two hours finishing the hangtags, remembering Precious with each story I noted. Laura returned and Oscar surprised me by licking my hand, as if sensing my sadness. As if knowing I needed to be alone, Laura disappeared into her room and closed the door.

I allowed my fingers to caress the fur collar of a once-white cashmere cape and the beaded chiffon of an evening gown that had danced at the Dorchester during an air raid, the bandleader conducting the music in time with the exploding bombs.

I paused in front of a fine navy wool siren suit, a version of a onesie designed to be pulled over nightclothes as the wearer scrambled to a shelter. It had been artfully tailored to cinch in the waist, the trousers skimming tactfully over the thighs. I straightened it on the hanger, documenting on the tag how Precious had told me it was made to look as if the wearer was attending a slightly chilly cocktail party, rather than about to spend the night in a communal shelter beneath the street.

As I continued with my pacing, I found myself

overcome with a horrible homesickness, thoughts of my family and the town in which I'd been raised like a rope around my heart, gently tugging. I felt like a survivor of some sort of internal catastrophe I could not name, and I wanted to curl up in the one place I knew I'd be sheltered. It had been too long since I'd been home, and I missed it now with all the longing of a wandering soul who'd finally discovered a soft place to lay her head.

I stopped pacing and began packing, washing sheets, and making up my bed. Throwing out old food in the refrigerator, including a jug of Laura's terrible sweet tea. I opened my airline app and checked for availabilities and booked a ridiculously expensive ticket on a flight from Heathrow to Atlanta.

Then I texted Arabella, telling her I was done with the hangtags and was now going home to work on the article and that I'd be in touch. I couldn't stay for the funeral—I hadn't been to one since my mother's, and I had no intention of ever going to another one before my own. I did tell her to say good-bye to Penelope and James. And to Colin.

It didn't really count as saying good-bye, but it was the best I could do. It was time to go before any more damage was done. But I was afraid I was already too late.

CHAPTER 40

WALTON, GEORGIA
DECEMBER 2019

Time marched slowly in Walton, and I sometimes wondered if it marched at all. It had been more than a decade since I'd lived here, yet it seemed everything had remained frozen in time, like a lightning bug stuck in amber. The welcome sign that greeted all visitors to our small town still stated proudly, **WELCOME TO WALTON. WHERE EVERYBODY IS SOMEBODY.** The unique Statue of Liberty sculpture with the driftwood head continued to give its come-hither look to the Confederate soldier on horseback on the opposite side of the town green. The Dixie Diner still did a brisk breakfast and lunchtime business, although they'd added a vegetable plate and gluten-free items to their menu. This last was served with a side of pork rinds, but the citizens of Walton didn't seem to mind.

Reverend Beasley still worked hard to come up with new slogans for his sign outside the First United Methodist church, and he had hired my fourteen-year-old brother, Harry, to help. This week's was **TWEET OTHERS AS YOU WOULD LIKE TO BE TWEETED**. The week before it had been **WALMART ISN'T THE ONLY PLACE THAT SAVES**.

It all made me feel as if I'd been away too long and at the same time like I'd never left. I'd sublet my New York apartment and had my mail forwarded; I spent my days keeping busy with Knoxie's wedding plans while accepting new freelance work and writing copy for my aunt Cassie's advertising firm, which I found I actually enjoyed.

I had finished and submitted Arabella's article. It wasn't the entire story I wanted to write, but the article simply didn't have the scope to include it all. But I'd kept my notes, my copies of the photographs and letters. I wanted to find a way to honor Precious and the lives of those who'd survived the turbulent war years, to capture all the wisdom she'd shared with me and taught me. I simply didn't know if I could give her story the dignity and justice it deserved.

My article had been published in the July issue of British **Vogue**, in conjunction with the new exhibition at the Design Museum. Arabella had sent me an invitation to a private black-tie event the night before the grand opening, but I'd declined, citing other obligations. It was only partly true, as I'm sure Arabella guessed.

I hadn't heard from Colin at all, aside from Arabella's communicating his disappointment that I hadn't said good-bye. I found myself wondering what she really meant by "disappointment"; the British understatement could have meant anything from a frown to the gnashing of teeth.

I told myself it was for the best, but in the wee hours, in my father's house, I'd sneak down to Suzanne's home studio, where she had her large-screen monitor, and stick in my memory stick to watch the videos I'd filmed in London. It hurt to see Precious, to remember that she was gone, but it almost hurt more to see Colin again.

Suzanne had walked in on me once when I'd frozen the frame on Colin's face. Immediately, she'd gone to the kitchen and brought back a half gallon of Blue Bell Buttered Pecan ice cream with two spoons. She sat next to me while I told her everything. About Precious and Eva. About Colin. She didn't ask me what I was going to do. Like Aunt Cassie, who'd also heard the whole story, she understood that I would eventually figure it out on my own. And if I needed a little advice, I knew where to turn.

After two months of carefully avoiding places

where I might run into him, I'd finally bumped into Rob Campbell with his pregnant wife and little girl at the playground named in my mother's honor. Contrary to what I'd imagined, I didn't burst into flames or tears, and the earth didn't open up and swallow me. Nor did Rob give any indication that he was haunted in the same way I was by the memory of what he'd said to me when I'd given him back his ring. It was very clear that he'd moved on and assumed that I had, too.

Seeing him hadn't brought me peace or closure or anger. Instead I felt an impatience with myself, a need to escape my past. Which, despite what Aunt Cassie said, would always be just one day away, dogging the heels of my present.

I stayed in Walton through the remainder of spring and the hot days of summer, and watched as the leaves turned and fell as autumn approached. I was no closer to making any sort of decision about my life than when I'd arrived on my daddy's doorstep with all my belongings in one backpack and one suitcase.

I made paper flowers and stuffed gift bags with Knoxie, met with the bakery and the Dixie Diner about the wedding reception, and discussed music with the organist Brunelle Thompkins at First United Methodist, but I couldn't make the first decision as to what I was going to do next either with my life or with Precious's story.

On the Saturday morning of the wedding day,

Suzanne drove me to Bitsy's House of Beauty, where we met with Aunt Cassie and the rest of the bridal party for the day of beauty required for any Southern wedding. My fifteen-year-old niece, Suzy, was the junior bridesmaid and had chosen the nail color. It wasn't that I didn't love lime green, but I wasn't sure if it matched the deep purple taffeta of our bridesmaids' dresses.

We all kept a watchful eye on the heavy gray clouds outside, which suspiciously resembled snow clouds. I was afraid to voice my fear, not wanting to create a panic, but I could guarantee that my sister would have snow on her wedding day. It had snowed only twice before in Georgia in my lifetime, and I wasn't eager to see a third.

I was sitting under the dryer with bits of foil stuck in my hair—Bitsy had insisted I get highlights—and cotton balls between my lime-colored toenails when my great-aunt Lucinda burst in, bringing with her an icy-cold blast of winter air. She was in her late seventies, but her recent marriage to the sheriff and her addiction to Zumba made her look and act about two decades younger.

She plastered herself against the front door, her eyes scanning the people in the salon until they rested on me. "Oh, my gosh, y'all." She closed her eyes and pressed the back of her wrist to her forehead. "There's a man just got out of an Uber car and walked into the Dixie Diner as I was leaving, asking for the nearest hotel. He's got a funny accent—sounds just like Prince William. I just about fainted when he looked at me. Oh, my word, y'all! Don't tell my husband, but that man is like a drink of ice-cold Co-Cola on a hot day."

I froze at the part about talking like Prince William and felt both Aunt Cassie and Suzanne looking at me.

Aunt Lucinda continued. "And just as the door shut behind me, I heard Hal Newcomb saying something about Bitsy's. What on earth would he be wanting over here?" She turned around to look out of the glass panes on the door, then quickly flipped around again and placed her hand on her heart. "He's headed right here!" She fumbled in her purse and pulled out three tubes of lipstick. "Anybody else need some color?"

Cassie and Suzanne were already yanking the cotton from between my toes and unraveling the foil in my hair when the door opened, letting in another burst of cold air. Colin's wide-eyed look of surprise matched my own; he paused in the open doorway, holding a small carry-on suitcase, his gaze passing over me twice before jerking back in recognition.

"Madison?"

Cassie helped me out from under the dryer, doing her best to block me as she and Suzanne continued to remove foil strips. I didn't need a mirror to know I looked like an alien from a 1950s science fiction movie. But I welcomed the embarrassment. It distracted from the collision of my head and heart.

"Hello, Colin," I said, grabbing Cassie's arms to get her to stop fussing with my hair.

"You must be Colin Eliot," Cassie said, extending a hand. "I'm Cassie Parker, Maddie's aunt. We've heard so much about you. We are just **tickled** you could make it to the wedding. And do not even **think** about finding a hotel room. Not only isn't there one within thirty miles, but I wouldn't hear of it. You're staying in our guest room, and that's settled."

"Yes, well, thank you. Not just for that, but also for the invitation. And the phone calls."

"You called him?" I asked, failing at not raising my voice.

"Somebody had to," Colin said softly, his cool gaze settling on my face before drifting upward to my hair.

Darlene Narpone, Bitsy's shampoo girl, handed Colin a **People** magazine. "Could you please open this up anywhere and read a page out loud? I just want to hear your accent."

I grabbed the magazine out of her hand and tossed it back on the stack. "He is not going to read out loud." I faced Colin. "What are you doing here?"

"I'm here for your sister's wedding. I hope that's all right."

About ten voices shouted some version of "Of course!"

Aunt Cassie stepped forward, her fingers flying on her phone. "My husband, Sam, is at the Dixie

Diner right now. I've just texted him, so he'll be expecting you. He'll bring you to our house and get you all settled."

I began leading Colin to the door. "I promise to come on over just as soon as I'm done here. So we can talk in private." I sent a warning glance to the ladies listening attentively behind me.

Colin settled those striking blue eyes on me but didn't smile. "I'll see you shortly, then. As soon as you're"—his gaze took in my half-foiled hair and the lime green paint on my toes—"done." He gave a polite nod to the other women in the salon, who were doing a terrible job of hiding the fact that they were taking pictures of him with their smartphones.

An hour and a half later—Bitsy had insisted not only on making my hair as big as she could get it, but also on doing my makeup—Aunt Cassie and I returned to the old house she'd lived in since inheriting it from my grandfather. It was where my mama and Cassie had been born and raised, and where my daddy had proposed to both of them. He'd married only Mama, of course, but he still liked to pull that story out every once in a while to get a reaction.

The wide white columns on the front of the house gleamed in the sun's valiant attempt to sneak between hovering clouds, the intermittent light masquerading as warmth as rays peered into the porch and reflected off the chains of the porch swing. Despite the chill in the air, Sam and Colin sat bundled up outside on the swing, drinking Budweiser out of bottles and laughing like they were old friends. They stood as Cassie and I approached, and Sam kissed Cassie on the lips in greeting while I pretended not to notice.

"That's some hair you got going there, Maddie," Uncle Sam said, indicating my new do with his bottle.

"The bigger the hair, the closer to God," Cassie said as she put her arm around his waist, nodding like she was serious.

"I approve of this young gentleman, Maddie. Colin's a pretty cool guy if you can get past that accent." Sam winked, and I suddenly felt sorry for his daughter, Suzy, and all the dating years she'd suffer through with Sam as her dad. "Hey, if y'all want to talk, I can go get a fire started in the living room," Sam offered.

"No, thanks. This won't take long. I've got to go get dressed so I can help Knoxie into Grandma's wedding gown."

"Okay, then. We'll leave you two out here for a little privacy." They moved inside, Aunt Cassie reappearing a short time later with a large plaid blanket. She handed it to me with only a wink before disappearing again.

I sat down on the swing and Colin joined me. After a moment of consideration, I pulled the blanket over both of us.

He looked up into the threatening sky. "I think it might—"

"Don't say it. Don't even think it. Nothing good has ever come out of a snow in Georgia. Except a spike in the birth rate."

A corner of his mouth turned up. "I think your aunt and uncle are smashing. I even like Walton, what little I've seen of it. Although I did wonder about that monument on the town green. I recognized the soldier on a horse but not the other."

I started to explain how our Statue of Liberty had been assembled from scrap all those years ago by well-meaning citizens of Walton, but stopped myself. "It's a Southern thing. Just go with it."

He took hold of one of the chains on the swing. "I like this, too. I'm going to get one for my parents, I think. I can't imagine a house in summer without one."

"It might be against the law for any Southern porch not to have a swing."

He raised his eyebrow, and I wanted to kiss him so badly I grabbed the beer from his hand and took a swig just so I'd have something else to do with my lips. "Why are you here, Colin?"

He pushed the swing with both feet, the chains creaking as it moved back and forth. "Because you didn't say good-bye."

"I told Arabella to tell you. That counts."

"No. It doesn't." I felt him looking at me, but I couldn't meet his eyes. "I brought something for you. From Precious."

That made me look at him, and I wished I hadn't.

I'd wanted to forget him, to pretend that he was an insignificant part of my past. That I didn't have any feelings for him. Lying to myself had always been one of my best talents.

"What is it?"

"A book of poetry. Wordsworth. She told me she wanted you to have it. I left it with your father at the diner."

I felt a little squeeze of my heart as I thought about Precious giving me the book that Graham had given her. "Thank you. Although it would have been cheaper to airmail it."

He gave me a half smile, the familiar expression that haunted my dreams more often than I cared to think about, and I had to avert my eyes. "She also said that I needed to remind you about something after she was gone. In case you forgot."

"In case I forgot what?"

He glanced down, studied the plaid pattern in the blanket. "Reinvention." He lifted his head, met my gaze. "How life is all about reinvention. If you don't like how your story's being written, rewrite the ending."

I nodded, hearing her voice in my head, her Southern accent fooling even me.

"And . . ." He stopped, laughed.

"And what?"

"And that you're a formidable woman. As was she."

I wanted to laugh and cry, remembering Precious

in all her incarnations. She was, indeed, a formidable woman. She could almost make me believe that she'd thought I was, too.

His face became serious again. "We found Graham's grave. The name on the marker was John Nash. Rather fitting, I thought."

"It is," I agreed, wondering if David had been behind that.

"We moved both Nana and Graham to the family plot at the local churchyard and buried them next to each other. We had the name Precious Dubose inscribed on her headstone, and buried Graham with the unopened letters. I thought you'd like to know."

I nodded, blinking back tears, comforted in the knowledge that they'd finally found their way back to each other. And that I'd played a part in it, albeit a very small one. "I love that. Was it your father's idea to bury them together?"

He shook his head. "No, it was mine. And now my mother and Arabella think I'm a true romantic."

I found myself studying his beer bottle intently so I wouldn't have to meet his eyes. "As if flying across an ocean to deliver a book of poetry wasn't enough to convince anyone."

He gave me that half smile again, and I wanted to tell him to stop, that every time he did it my heart stuttered and swelled and rose into my throat so that I couldn't breathe.

"I guess I'm going to have to tell our kin in

Memphis that Precious died in nineteen forty and is buried in England. I suppose this makes us cousins." The idea was so absurd it made me want to laugh. "So, why are you here?" I repeated.

"Because I wanted to give you another chance to say good-bye properly." He paused. "And because I love you."

My heart did that thing again where it got stuck in my throat and I couldn't speak. We swung in silence; I watched our breath rise up to the haint blue–painted porch ceiling. "I need to go help my sister." I slid off the swing.

Colin took my hand. "What are we going to do, Maddie?"

He'd said "Maddie" again. I wondered if he realized it. I didn't turn around. "There's nothing we can do, Colin. Nothing at all." I dropped the blanket, hurried down the steps, and ran most of the way back to my father's house while the sky hung heavy above me with the threat of inclement weather.

Knoxie made a beautiful bride. She wore the same wedding gown that our grandmother and Aunt Cassie had worn, but not our own mama—she'd eloped. Part of the family history, all stored in that one dress of ivory satin and Belgian lace, and as I looked at the glowing bride and groom, I took it as a harbinger of a long and fruitful marriage.

I stood next to my sister as she said her vows and

felt Colin's eyes on me in all of my purple taffeta and lime green nail polish splendor. I wondered if he could still love me with that image now permanently emblazoned on his brain.

For the reception, the wedding party drove to the old bowling alley in the funeral home limousine—the only one available for rent in Walton. Aunt Cassie declared it too much of a squeeze for everyone, including all the girls with their crinolines and heavy coats, and invited Colin and me to sit in the backseat of Sam's double-cab pickup truck.

It seemed as if Cassie and Sam were putting Colin through his paces, and when he managed to climb into the truck without grunting or asking where to put his feet, I imagined them giving each other a mental high five.

Aunt Cassie sat in the middle of the front bench seat so Sam could put his right arm around her shoulders while he drove with his left hand, and it seemed only natural that Colin would do the same in the backseat. I tried to remain unaware of his arm and his hand and the whole side of his body during the short ride, but by the time we reached the parking lot, my head had found its way onto his shoulder, and my nose might even have been pressed close to the side of his neck. On the radio, Hank Williams Junior crooned about a tear in his beer, and Colin was actually tapping his fingers in rhythm against my arm.

Without warning, Aunt Cassie turned her head to

look into the backseat. "Don't forget, you have your appointment with Dr. Grey next week. Although you've been home for months and you could have gone way before now."

I sat straight up. "Seriously? Do we need to talk about that now?"

"I just didn't want you to forget. I've also been meaning to tell you that my business partner and I have been talking about expanding the agency and taking it overseas. We already have clients in Ireland and England, and we're thinking of opening up an office in London. 'Atlanta, New York, London' looks good on business cards, don't you think?"

"I'm not . . ."

"That way, if you'd like a more permanent home base, you'd have a job that gives you the freedom to freelance when you want and more regular hours when you don't. It would be nice, don't you think? And then you and Colin . . ."

I hit the "down" button on my window so that cold air rushed in, drowning her words.

As Colin helped me out of the truck—not an easy thing to do with someone in voluminous taffeta and dyed-to-match heels—Sam looked up at the sky. "I think it might—"

"Don't say it," Cassie and I said in unison.

During the reception, Colin and I seemed to be circling each other like boxers in a ring, not sure when to engage. He appeared relaxed and happy, chatting with everyone, including the circle of admirers who followed him like he was some kind of a rock star. I even saw him sign autographs on cocktail napkins for some of the younger girls. I had to look away, afraid that if my heart kept doing that swelling thing, I'd have to be rushed to the hospital in the snow. Which wasn't going to fall, anyway, so I should stop worrying.

I busied myself with my maid-of-honor duties, which consisted mostly of making sure Knoxie didn't need anything and that she didn't put her chair leg on the skirt of the wedding dress each time she sat down. When she told me to stop fussing, I threatened to release some choice photographs from when she was a teenager if she so much as pulled a thread on Grandma's wedding gown.

It saddened me that some of the familiar faces from my childhood weren't there, including Principal Purdy, whose porch I'd painted pink all those years ago, and Senator Thompkins, who'd always delighted the children at community gatherings with his inside-out eyelid trick. And sweet Miss Lena, who'd love to read the juicy bits of her favorite romance novels out loud to anyone who cared to listen. Or didn't. Her house was now occupied by the new principal of Walton High School and her family, and I missed seeing Miss Lena waving from her front porch as I walked by.

The Sedgewick twins, Selma and Thelma, were

there in their outrageous hats, albeit now with walkers and a young, handsome caregiver who strongly resembled Ryan Reynolds. No coincidence, I was sure. Their backs might have been bent, but there was apparently nothing wrong with their eyesight.

The DJ was good, the music mostly danceable, and a rotating disco ball above the converted dance space added a festive flair, but I kept myself busy avoiding eye contact with Colin. He never seemed at a loss for dance partners, so I didn't have to feel guilty. After the cake cutting, while I was distributing hefty slices of the vanilla cream confection, Aunt Cassie took the plate I was holding, gave it to my old math teacher, Mrs. Crandall, then took my arm and pulled me aside. She kept walking until she'd pushed open a door and dragged me inside what had once been the bowling alley's shoe room. Rows of shelves stretched from floor to ceiling, shoe sizes still stamped beneath the empty spaces.

"What are you doing, Maddie?"

"I was trying to serve wedding cake until you stopped me."

Cassie looked up at the drop-tile ceiling as if asking for divine intervention. "I want to shake you and knock loose some of the good sense I know you were born with, but I know your kind of stubborn because I've got it, too. So I'm going to have to try to talk some sense into you."

I turned to leave but she was quicker, blocking

the exit. "No, missy. We need to have a little come-to-Jesus meeting, and I'm not letting you out of here until I've had my say."

I crossed my arms like a petulant teenager. "Since I don't have a choice, go ahead. I'm listening."

"My gosh, Maddie. We are so much alike I feel like I'm talking to myself. Do you not think I was in your same position after your mama died? I was near crazy with grief. I didn't know what I wanted anymore, and I almost made the worst mistake of my life by letting Sam go."

She took a deep breath as if preparing herself for a long speech. "If God gives you one more year or one hundred years on this earth, it's up to you to live every last minute of it. It's your responsibility, and you owe it to your mama to take it seriously. One year of happiness is worth so much more than a lifetime of just existing. There are no guarantees in life, and you have to accept that and love all the beautiful and ugly that life throws at you."

I tried to stop the tears, knowing what an ugly cry could do to my mascara. "Precious said the same thing."

"Well, from what you've told me, she was a very smart woman. I want you to picture her here right now, standing next to me, you hear? Did you know that Colin told Sam about his brother who died? Yet here he is with you, and he apparently has no intention of accepting your belief that you've got a preordained expiration date like a carton of milk. Because it doesn't matter to him. That fine young man out there would walk across burning coals for you. He flew from London to be with you at your sister's wedding in Walton, Georgia, Maddie. If that doesn't say love, then I don't know what does."

"You know that's not all of it." I sniffed loudly, and Cassie handed me a folded cocktail napkin to dab at my eyes. Mothers always seemed to have useful items at hand. My mother had, too.

"No, it's not. But I would bet my eyeteeth that when you tell that young man out there the rest of your story, it won't make a bit of difference to him."

"Are you done?"

"I sure hope so. The rest is up to you." She hugged me, squeezing me tightly, as if to make up for my long absence. "Don't ever forget that you are worthy of love."

I pulled back and looked into her eyes. "Precious said that, too."

"Well, then. And I know I could grab Suzanne to come in here, and she'd tell you the same thing. Maybe you should listen to some of the smartest women you've ever known and do something about it."

I left the room and found my way to the coatroom without being seen except by my brother Joey, whom I told to let my father and Colin know I was going home. The bride and groom had left directly after the cake cutting to try to make it to the airport ahead of the weather, so my official duties were done.

I let myself out of the building and into the frigid night air, which definitely smelled of snow. Huddling into my wool coat, I walked the short blocks to my daddy's house and let myself in.

When I flipped on the light in my bedroom, I saw a book had been left on my dresser. It was the worn leather-bound volume of Wordsworth's poetry that Graham had once given to Eva. I picked it up, thumbing through the pages with bleary eyes until something fell out of it.

I bent down and picked up Graham's photograph, the one where he looked so much like Colin. I looked at it for a long time, at the young hopeful eyes and grin, the face of a person who didn't know what was to come. Like the faces in every photograph, I supposed. I wondered if he would have done anything differently if he'd known how it would all end. I knew, somehow, that he would have still chosen to love. And to be brave.

I replaced the photograph and put the book down on my dresser, next to the white ivory dolphin that Precious had given me, the talisman of the love she and Graham had shared. I held it in my hand, solid and real, remembering what she'd told me about beauty and love.

After I got ready for bed and turned out the light, I lay in the darkness, holding the dolphin, listening to the stillness of the night, then the sounds of my family returning from the wedding. I listened as the water thrummed through the pipes and doors shut, as the house settled into sleep. And then finally, I listened to my own heart for the first time in years, and I knew what I had to do.

CHAPTER 41

WALTON, GEORGIA
DECEMBER 2019

I shivered in my coat while walking through a scattering of what looked alarmingly like snowflakes falling on the sleeping lawns and houses of Walton as I headed to my aunt's house. I passed the Harriet Madison Warner Memorial Park and the cemetery where my mother slept under pots of plastic poinsettias. Past blow-up snowmen and Santas with reindeer and sleighs that sprouted in yards like mutant trees, the brilliant displays of twinkling lights on every porch, roof, and railing a fitting backdrop to the festive statuary. A few creative people had even placed their Santa on top of the roof with the twinkling lights, adding something unique to the general festive air.

The lampposts all wore red velvet bows, and

several of the minivans parked in driveways sported red Rudolph noses and antlers, as did at least one mailbox. Although I was not a fan of Christmas, seeing it all in the quiet of the night made me nostalgic for the Christmases of my childhood.

As she promised, Cassie had put Colin in the guest room at the back of the house. A trellis conveniently led up to the window, as I'd discovered as a younger version of myself. I took off my gloves for a better grip, and after pulling to make sure the trellis could still support me, I began to climb. The windows were never locked, so I wasn't surprised when the window opened easily a few inches before I had to wrestle it the rest of the way up. I climbed through the window, then closed it behind me.

I faced the bed, taking off my coat and shoes to buy me a few moments of courage. The eerie light of an impending snowfall illuminated the four posts of the bed and the rise of the bedclothes where Colin slept. Except, as my eyes adjusted to the light, I realized that he wasn't lying down but sitting up. Probably awakened by the noise I'd made wrenching the window up. I imagined Aunt Cassie hadn't used the WD-40 on the sash for just that reason.

"Colin? Are you awake?"

"I am now."

"Good. Because I've come to a decision about Precious's story. I'm going to tell the whole story—starting with Ethel Maltby and using the clothes as the backdrop to an incredibly powerful life. I want to show how Precious lived every minute, all the good parts and the bad parts—it's still her wonderful life in all of its shades and colors, decorated with glorious clothes and accessories. That's how she'd want me to tell it. It might be an article, or I might want to make it bigger. Like a biography—I haven't decided. But I've come up with a title: **Reinvention: A Story of Friendship, Love, and Courage.**"

"I approve." He paused. "Is that why you climbed up to my window in the middle of the night?"

"No. I need to ask you something."

"All right."

"Remember before, in London, when we were looking at Precious's photos and you made me drink Scotch . . . ?"

"I didn't make you, Maddie. You drank of your own free will, as I recall."

"Yes, well, that night you told me something, and I just need to verify that I heard you correctly before I make any more decisions."

He was completely silent, and I was glad I couldn't see his expression. "Go on."

I swallowed, trying not to shiver. "Did you mean it when you said that I should allow those who love me to decide what they can and cannot endure?"

"Yes. I did."

"But how much can you endure?"

"All of it, Maddie. All of whatever life has in store. I'm not saying this blindly. I've been talking with a doctor friend of mine. I know that you have an eighty-seven percent risk of developing breast cancer in your lifetime. It took me five seconds to realize that it didn't matter to me. As long as we're together, we can face anything."

I took a deep breath, feeling overheated despite the chilly room. "Don't speak so quickly. There's more." I took a deep breath. "I had both breasts removed when I was eighteen. Aunt Cassie shares the gene, too, so we had our surgeries at the same time. None of my siblings have it—just me. I've had reconstructive surgery, but if you look closely, you can still see scars under my breasts. It's ironic, actually. The genetic testing is why Knoxie decided to do our ancestry chart. That's how we found Precious."

He sat up and moved nearer to the side of the bed, either to run or to get closer. Either way, it scared me. I hated uncertainty. That was why I always made a habit of ignoring it.

I felt his eyes on me in the dark as he spoke. "I also learned that removing the breasts decreases your chances but doesn't eliminate your risk entirely. That didn't change my mind, either."

I leaned toward him, his words damaging my resolve. I stepped back, took another deep breath, wanting to get this over with so I wouldn't have to wonder anymore what Colin would do. I already had a bad track record of coming clean. "Because of the genetic mutations, I'm also at high risk for ovarian cancer. My doctor makes me have blood tests regularly. My last test showed slightly elevated inflammatory markers. She wants to test me again. If those tests also show elevated markers, she'll order scans and look for signs of a tumor. My appointment is next week. If the test results aren't good, she'll recommend having my ovaries removed."

I swallowed, then pressed on. "I could never have children." I paused, letting my words sink in. "It's why my fiancé broke our engagement. Not just because he wanted children, but because he'd seen me go through my mother's illness and didn't think he was strong enough to see it happen to me. Because no matter what parts I get removed from my body, no surgery makes me cancer-proof."

I held my breath, waiting for him to speak.

"There are so many ways to bring children into a family, Maddie. Whether they're biological children or not, don't you think we'd love them just as much? And it's not your breasts I'm in love with. If you're trying to scare me off with any of that, it's not working."

"You're saying that now. But you might think differently in five years. Or less. You could change your mind about what you're willing to endure."

He calmly drew in a breath. Exhaled. "I could. But I won't. It's not who I am. I respect that your lifelong beliefs aren't going to change overnight, and that I can't win your trust with just a few words. But I love you, and I'm willing to be on this journey with you now whether you believe me or not. I will simply be content to have you in my life and to hope that in time you will accept that I have no intention of ever leaving you, no matter what happens."

I swallowed back the lump that had suddenly appeared in my throat. He was right. I wasn't ready. But I wanted to rewrite the end of my story, and Colin was offering to help me find the courage to try. I moved closer to the bed, feeling as if unseen hands were pushing me. "It could take a long time for me to believe you, you know."

"I expect it will."

"What if I get sick?"

"What if you don't? What if I do? We don't know what our future holds. The only thing I do know is that I would never leave your side. Nor would your family. Or mine. We would endure together. And whether we have a short time or a long time, I wouldn't waste a single minute."

He stood, pulled me against him. His chest was bare, and when I placed my hands on his skin, I felt the gooseflesh ripple under my fingers.

"Maddie?"

I looked up at him in the pale blue light. "Yes?"

"It's snowing."

I followed his gaze out the window. Fat white flakes tumbled past the glass, almost too thick to see the dark sky beyond. I sighed. "Snow in Walton. I guess miracles do happen."

Colin turned my face to his. "Yes, Maddie. I suppose they do." He kissed me, his lips warm and serious, as if sealing a promise. I kissed him back, propelling us toward the bed, managing to undo drawstring ties and unburden ourselves of clothing.

I tugged my sweatshirt over my head so that we were skin to skin as we fell together on the rumpled sheets, still warm from his body. His fingers rested on the gold heart charm that I hadn't removed since the day of my high school graduation.

He held it between his fingers. "What's this?"

"Suzanne gave it to me. It says, 'A life without rain is like the sun without shade.'"

He was silent for a moment, watching my face. "So very true," he said softly, and I wondered if he was thinking about his brother and all that had passed since, every good and bad thing that made up a life.

"It's taken me a while, but I think I'm beginning to understand what it really means. Precious taught me that."

He leaned down and kissed the spot between my breasts where the charm had lain, as if sealing yet another promise between us.

I looked up at him in the dim room, wishing he could see my eyes and all the silent truths they held. But it didn't matter. I'd have time to tell him. To show him. I put my arms around his neck, pulled him closer. "I love you, you know."

"I know."

I bit my lower lip. "But I really hate snow."

"Well, then, let's create new, happy memories so you'll learn to love it." And he lowered his lips to mine and we proceeded to do just that.

We must have fallen asleep at some point; the brightening light from the window woke me at dawn. Colin's body was melded against mine, our heads sharing a single pillow. I lay absolutely still, listening to his breathing, wishing I could jar this moment and preserve it forever. Yet I was fairly certain that Colin would ensure that there would be enough jars to fill an entire basement.

A sound of movement somewhere in the house brought me bolt upright, Colin sitting up along with me. "What's wrong?" he asked, his eyes as bleary as mine felt.

"My aunt and uncle can't find me in here." I looked outside the window at the tall pine tree, which I didn't remember being so tall when I'd last stayed in this room. Fat dollops of snow covered the branches, as if someone had emptied cans of whipping cream on them. I scrambled from the bed. "Suzy and Sam Junior will be up early and wanting to play in the snow. I've got to go—or at least walk around to the front of the house and use the front door."

I ran around, gathering clothes, attempting to put them on right side out.

Colin sat on the bed, looking at me with a satisfied grin on his face.

"What's so funny?" I asked, hopping on one foot as I attempted to put my sweatpants back on.

"From what I know of your aunt Cassie, she knows you're here and has already set a place for you at the table and started making your breakfast."

"It's not her I'm worried about—it's my uncle Sam."

He sobered quickly. "Does he own a shotgun?"

"Is a frog's butt watertight?"

He blinked. "I beg your pardon?"

"Sorry. I meant, of course he does, and so does my daddy," I said, hopping on the other foot. "They're from Georgia."

He slid out of the bed and joined me in a wild scramble for clothes, pausing long enough to kiss me. "They wouldn't really use a gun in a situation like this, would they? You are of age. And they both seemed rather civilized."

"Of course they wouldn't, but that's not the point. My mama raised me better, and we all choose to respect that."

"Understandable," he said, slipping on a pair of pants.

As I was buttoning my coat, I eyed the window.

"No, Maddie," Colin said, taking my hand and

bringing me to the bedroom door. "You're not climbing out of an upstairs window and down a snowy trellis. I'm not ready to go completely gray yet."

"Fine. But put your feet exactly where I put mine so you don't make the stairs creak."

"You sound like an expert at sneaking out of houses."

"That's because I am." I smiled to myself, remembering all the pranks and stunts I'd pulled as a teenager while supposedly tucked into bed.

We somehow made it out the front door without making too much noise, although I would have bet money that Cassie and Sam were standing behind their bedroom door, waiting for us to pass so they could go down and get breakfast started.

Outside, the world lay cold and white around us, the large magnolia in the front yard now wearing a glossy crown of snow. No footprints marred the pristine whiteness, like a blank page waiting to be written on. The borders between sidewalk and drive and lawn no longer existed, the snow offering paths waiting to be discovered.

"Come on," I said, grabbing his hand. "Let me show you the gazebo. And then we can come in the front door and pretend that you met me outside in the snow."

Despite not having the right snow wear, we barely seemed to feel the cold as we trudged to the backyard. The gazebo slept under a blanket of snow that had erased the steps, but only a dusting lay inside on the benches. Colin surprised me by scooping me up and carrying me over the steps, then joining me.

"Your nose is all red," he said, and kissed it.

"So is yours," I said, laughing. "I'm beginning to understand what you said about making happy memories of snow. I'm not hating it quite so much right now."

"Then I suppose we'll just need to practice more."

I turned around in his arms, looking past the snowcapped railing and the acres of white to the forest that bordered the rear of the property. "About ten years ago, someone wanted to tear down the woods and build a neighborhood there, but my daddy saved it. I'm glad. It's part of Walton and this house, and I can't imagine one without the other."

"I can see why. Do you remember what you told me once? Something your aunt said about home."

I smiled, surprised that he'd remembered. "Home is a place that lives in one's heart, waiting with open arms to be rediscovered." I shrugged. "I couldn't wait to leave, and I can't imagine myself living here again, but it's nice to know that it's here to come back to. You said that once, when we were at Hovenden Hall. You said it's where all your childhood memories lived, good and bad."

The sun struggled to peer through the clouds as the wind picked up, blowing tufts of snow off the roof of the gazebo. He kissed the back of my head. "Do you like the beach?"

"I love the beach. Before Mama got sick, we'd

take family vacations down to the Florida Panhandle every summer. It's my happy place."

"Good," he said, turning me around so that we faced each other. "Because I've bought a bit of property in Bournemouth. It's not far from London, so a nice place to escape the city from time to time. I'd like to build the house Eva and Graham dreamed about."

The heat of unshed tears brushed my eyes. "That would be . . . remarkable."

I could almost hear Precious agreeing that such a thing would be a fitting monument for a formidable woman. "She would love that. And so would Graham."

I thought of Precious, who'd taught me so much. **Grief is like a ghost.** She'd been right about that. But she'd learned to live with her ghosts, bringing them with her in each of her incarnations like trophies showing where she'd been. What she'd overcome. What she'd loved and lost. But also what she'd survived.

Colin's eyes held a strange light, and I wondered if it was simply the winter sky and the reflection of snow. "I thought Nana would like to have her story end there."

We kissed again as another gust of wind blew the powdery snow along the surface of the lawn, sparkling in the weak sun like lightning bugs. Then he took my hand and led me back to the house, where Suzy and Sam Junior were leaping off the front porch and shouting as only children playing in a rare snow could.

"We'll come back in summer so you can catch lightning bugs. I'll have Aunt Cassie make you your own jar with your name on it."

"I can't wait," he said, even sounding like he meant it.

The front door opened, and Cassie appeared with two mugs. "Hurry up and get out of your wet things, you two. Your breakfast is getting cold. I've made hot cocoa to warm your hands."

I shared a glance with Colin as we both smiled at our private joke. We left our wet shoes and dripping coats on the porch, then followed Cassie inside the house.

Home is a place that lives in one's heart, waiting with open arms to be rediscovered.

I hurried after my aunt, eager to share something I wanted to add.

And sometimes home is where one finds it, in the heart of another person who will always believe you are worthy of love.

I turned to see Colin, his eyes serious, as if he'd heard me say the words out loud. As if he, too, was remembering a formidable woman who'd shown us how bravery and reinvention could open up a life and enrich it with possibilities.

He smiled as he followed me into the foyer, closing the door of the old house behind him.

AUTHOR'S NOTE

I lived in London, England, in a beautiful Edwardian building near Regent's Park, for seven years while growing up. I remember being dumbfounded when our doorman told us that some of the windows in our building had been shattered during the Blitz. For the first time in my life, I felt the presence of the past, something immediate and present and not relegated to dusty history books. I never forgot it, and our flat transformed from a place to live to a piece of history I could touch and experience firsthand.

When I became a writer, I knew I would one day return to London, using it and my building as a setting for a future novel. This book is the culmination of nearly a decade of plotting, of using what I knew and adding research about the tumultuous years of the Second World War and the London Blitz.

Harley House is a real place, although vastly different from when I lived in it. I've used as many facts as I could to make it as accurate as possible but have had to resort to artistic license to make it fit into my story.

The historical facts of the time period are taken from eyewitness accounts, archival sources, and well-researched historical records. Any errors in recreating fact as fiction are completely mine.

ACKNOWLEDGMENTS

This book would never have been written without the constant e-mails from readers who'd read **Falling Home** and **After the Rain** and wanted to find out what happened to Maddie Warner, the eldest daughter of Joe and Harriet from those earlier books. This novel, in many ways, is Maddie's story. It takes place almost ten years after the end of **After the Rain**, and I hope it puts to rest the question of what happened to Maddie and the rest of the characters from Walton, Georgia.

Thanks to my editor, Cindy Hwang, and my agent, Amy Berkower, for their patience in listening to me talk about my ideas for this story for so long, and then waiting for this book to finally be written. I hope we can all agree that it was worth the trauma and the wait. Thank you both for your editorial insight, which saved the manuscript from being shoved under my bed and forgotten.

To terrific and talented author and friend Stephanie Scott, who graciously agreed to read the book for any errors in my Britishisms despite being in the throes of the hectic months before the publication of her first novel. I cannot thank you enough.

And thank you to Julie Zabrodska for generously agreeing to read through and correct the Czech phrases and references for accuracy and authenticity.

A huge thanks for the encouragement and extremely keen editorial eye of the amazing Genevieve Gagne-Hawes. She saw beauty and possibility in the first drafts that were invisible even to me, and helped me pull the good stuff from the wreckage. This book could not have survived without you—so thank you.

As always, thanks to my partners in crime, my critique partners Wendy Wax and Susan Crandall, who have been with me since the beginning twenty years ago, when my first book was published, and have read every word I've written. Thanks for always being there, and for pulling me back from the ledge when necessary.

KAREN WHITE is the **New York Times** bestselling author of more than twenty-five novels, including the Tradd Street series, **Dreams of Falling, The Night the Lights Went Out, Flight Patterns, The Sound of Glass, A Long Time Gone, and The Time Between.** She is the coauthor of **All the Ways We Said Goodbye, The Glass Ocean,** and **The Forgotten Room** with **New York Times** bestselling authors Beatriz Williams and Lauren Willig. She grew up in London but now lives with her husband and two dogs near Atlanta, Georgia.